C000303542

These two novellas were written by David Poole in the early 1980s. They were latterly scanned and edited from typescript by his son-in-law Nathan Percival, and published by his son William, in 2021.

This edition is published to celebrate the 80th birthday of David Poole's sister, Isobel Anne Poole, OBE.

© the family of D. E. Poole, 2021.
Designed and typeset by William Poole, 2021.
Typeset in Garamond and Minion Pro.
All images by Julie Poole or with permission. The coins are a tetra-drachm of Thasos of c. 400 BC, with Hercules as an archer; and a drachm of Smyrna of the late second century BC, depicting Homer with a scroll.

Available in printed and digital formats.

DORIC Publications, no. 1
ISBN 978-1-8382266-2-6 (print)
ISBN 978-1-8382266-3-3 (digital)

Two St Andrews Crime Novels

The Archer of Ceres

&

Death of a Dundee Teacher

D. E. Poole

DORIC

The Archer of Ceres

ᕭ Chapter 1

THE SCOTS HAVE ALWAYS BEEN their own worst enemies. It is not difficult to find instances of this lamentable fact. It is manifest both in the past and the present, and looks like continuing to be so in the future. For example, the whole world outside Scotland knows that the Scots are a mean race. Yet from Wick to Wigtown, and Betty-hill by way of Perth to Berwick, you will find very few people worthy of that description. To be fair, throughout the land, mean people do exist. They may be fewer than in Manchester or Maidstone, but they are there. How have they managed to infect a whole nation's reputation? The answer is simple. Unlike their counterparts in other parts of the world, they are publicly proud of their meanness. Hence, whether they stay at home or go abroad, they insist on advertising this somewhat antisocial aspect of their characters. The result is that everyone, everywhere, knows that all Scots are mean.

The Romans, it may be remembered, after putting down all organised military resistance in Scotland, withdrew to a line below the present border. It is to be assumed that they saw no future in holding nominal sway over scattered groups of people who would be permanently hostile to them. How then, it may well be asked, did the English ever take over Scotland? Again, the answer is simple. They were always aided by a large section of the population who considered clan feuds of far greater importance than any supposed national unity. When, for a change, in 1745 the population was almost united under the banner of Bonnie Prince Charlie, they marched victoriously into England. But when the whole of Britain was at their feet, and the London king was packing his bags for a hasty retreat to the continent, what did they do? They stopped at Derby. Ever since that time anything but an emotional belief in the greatness of the Scottish nation has deserted most capable Scots, and in their thousands they have chosen the path of emigration. They have led the armies of the Czar, they have opened up hitherto uncharted areas of the globe, and have established mighty businesses in the New World. Then what have they done for the country of their birth? Some, to assuage their feeling of guilt at leaving that land, have helped to perpetuate the false myths of their countrymen, to the detriment of all except the exporters of Scotch Whisky and tartans. Others have established huge educational funds, whose prime purpose seems to have been to train future generations in the skills necessary for following their migratory footsteps.

John Strachan was one of the beneficiaries of this last group. His parents were fine hard-working folk but were by no means endowed with supplies of wealth. However, in the days before the comprehensive school became endemic throughout the length and breadth of the land, they had no need to pay for an expensive education for their son. Over the years emigrants to Africa, India and America had contributed sufficient money to his local Senior Secondary School, to ensure that it provided as good an education as could be gained anywhere, as long as the recipients were prepared to take advantage of all they were offered. He continued from there to St. Andrews University, where his student grant was heavily augmented by an entrance scholarship he had won. Needless to say, the scholarship fund from which he benefited had been set up by a Scot who had taken his talents for making money elsewhere. John Strachan performed sufficiently well at the university, but perhaps not quite so well as his early promise had suggested; he gained a second-class honours degree, rather than the first which many had hoped for from him. Like the majority of his contemporaries, he had postponed a decision about his future career until he should know what level of degree he had obtained, but then found that he could put it off no longer. He was faced with the age-old decision of whether to settle for a middle-class respectability with no obvious future in the land of his birth, as a teacher or something similar, or apparent boundless opportunity elsewhere.

He was by nature a careful sort of man, and he had both saved money from his grant during his term-time and augmented this with income from employment during his long summer vacation. True to this careful character, he did not entirely cut himself off from either of the two possibilities which seemed to be open to him. He decided to train as an accountant in London. His father, to indicate his approval of this prudent course, had promised to provide him with sufficient funds to keep him alive during his proposed training period, provided that he would make every effort to support himself as well. He had relations in London, which was one of the reasons for choosing this destination in the first place, and modest terms were agreed upon for accommodation with them. He had always been led to believe that London was an immensely expensive place and was pleasantly surprised to find that this was not in fact so. As he had never been a person to spend money for the sake of spending it, he found things much less difficult than he had feared. The only expense he found irksome and unavoidable was the considerable outlay needed for travelling. Therefore, to eke out his meagre resources, he took a job as a barman for four nights a week in a pub near to where his relations lived. Thus it was that in the minimum time prescribed, at almost no cost to his family and with no debt to hamper him, he became a qualified accountant, and was ready to enter upon a career which, if not particularly exciting, was at least well rewarded from the financial point of view, and gave him the opportunity of working almost anywhere in the world he should wish to go. His first plan, however, was to gain some experience, and he found no great difficulty in obtaining a job in the city, in a small firm which rejoiced in the name of Sloane and Simpson. It seemed all the more promising to a young man setting out on his professional career, as the hint of a partnership was also thrown in.

The one new hobby that John Strachan had taken up during his sojourn in London was archery. While he was working in the pub, he had of course got to know some of the regulars quite well. Two of these happened to be staunch members of the West Ealing Archery club, and they had persuaded him to come along one Saturday afternoon and give the sport a try. Although he had been amazed by the difficulty at his first few attempts, he had insisted on perseverance, and after a few months of regular practice he had become an adequate shot and an ardent toxophilist. The club ran occasional social evenings, and at one of these he had first come across Susan Corston. By chance, a few days later he had met her again at Covent Garden Opera House. He himself went to the opera not infrequently as the price of the cheapest seats was only the equivalent of a couple of pints of beer. He soon discovered that she was a fairly regular visitor too. Her home originally had been in Lancashire, and she had attended Edinburgh University. In a similar way to John Strachan she had decided that the best place to start a career from was London. That was not to say that she was dedicated career woman, but she had understandably concluded that it would be wise to start a serious working life, in case she was condemned to remain single, or was forced to fall back on something later on. It is hardly unnatural, then, that these two became close and none of their friends was really surprised when they announced their intention of getting married. They accordingly went through the ceremony of matrimony shortly after John had obtained his first job. It was their plan that Susan should continue working for at least two years, to enable them to establish themselves in a house of their own and stock that house with all the things that they should consider necessary.

They found that John's salary on its own was quite sufficient to pay for their day-to-day expenses, as well as the mortgage they had undertaken on the house which they had bought shortly after their marriage. As a result they had begun to build up a handsome amount in savings, and so when, somewhat earlier than they had intended, Susan was found to be pregnant, they were not unduly worried on the financial front. There were, however, two considerations which did cause John concern. Primarily, he was becoming a little worried about his present job. He had seen no further sign of the partnership which had been produced as a carrot when he had first taken on the position, but this in itself would not have troubled him unduly at this stage. His concern arose more from the general running of the establishment. On more than one occasion he had been asked by his employers to falsify a few figures. The sums of money involved were indeed paltry, but he had refused to have any part in such practices. He was then informed, as he could see for himself, that such small sums were involved that he should really have no objection to the proposals. The intention was, after all, only to satisfy the whims of some old and valued customers. Yet in at least one case he was fully aware that the customer was not old, either in age or in respect of the firm's service to him, and so he still refused to do anything irregular. His employers had then laughed the matter off, saying that they probably wouldn't lose such long-standing customers for the sake of a few pounds. He had tried to treat the matter in the same sort of jovial manner, saying that it must be his penny-pinching Scottish upbringing which had moulded his attitude, and he hoped they understood. The matter rested there, but he couldn't help wondering how much of this was going on with the accounts to which he did not have access. He had by now noticed that, although his competence at the job could not be called into question, the affairs and even the names of some of the customers were deliberately kept secret from him. He understood that confidentiality was necessary, but this could be taken to extremes, especially when he was supposed to be a potential partner.

His second concern was far more personal, and he was no different from other men in it. As soon as a man has children, he is likely to alter his outlook on a number of topics. Was he to consider his own potential career first, or make the upbringing of his children the most important aspect of his life? Was it possible for him to combine the two? Did he really want his children brought up in the suburbs of London, or was he to move out into commuter country, with all the lengthy absence from home that that would entail, not to mention the personal inconvenience for himself? Alternatively, should he change his employment? He considered the various arguments for and against with his wife, and they at last came to the conclusion that they should move, saying that he could get a comparable job in a more pleasant area. After some further discussion they decided that North Yorkshire or East Scotland would be their priorities, and they would consider other places on their specific merits. John had not so far mentioned anything about the irregular practices of his employers to Susan, and therefore was very pleased that she had come to this decision without his having to bring his own professional worries into the discussion. Even the necessity of making a conscious decision about their new place of residence was taken from them when, a few weeks after they had come to their mutual conclusion, a suitable job was advertised in St. Andrews. The remuneration offered was to be a little less than they had been used to in London, but they saw no serious impediment on that issue. John applied for the job immediately, was interviewed a fortnight later, was offered the job on the spot and accepted it without hesitation.

His employers raised no difficulties about his departure, but asked him if he would oblige them by staying on for another three months to enable them to find a suitable successor to him. The St. Andrews firm had no objections to this arrangement, and so he readily fell in with their wishes. A couple of months later Sloane and Simpson had employed a replacement and John Strachan guided him gently into the job. The replacement was a man by the name of Ronald Blacklaw, who originally came from Lancashire. In fact both John and Susan already knew him, she because her family lived not far from his, and he through the archery club. Ronald Blacklaw was one of the best archers in the country, and for several years had been Lancashire champion. John Strachan had for a long time now been a great admirer of his skill at archery, even if he had certain reservation about him personally. Blacklaw had always made it quite clear that he had gone into the accountancy business to see how much money could be made from it, and also gave this as the reason for settling in London, for the time being. John had no objection to anyone who wished to make money, but was a little suspicious of anyone who gave this as their guiding principle in a professional occupation. In fact, the doubts he entertained about the firm were reinforced by this appointment. He felt quite sure that Ronald Blacklaw would have few qualms about satisfying the whims of old and valued customers.

Therefore, by the time they were ready to move up to Scotland, John Strachan was very pleased to be leaving. He even wondered if it was his duty to send a complaint to the Institute of Chartered Accountants about his strong suspicions, but in the end decided not to.

He and his wife intended, if possible, to live in the country outside St. Andrews, and not least among his personal reasons was the prospect of the cleanliness and purity he felt rural surroundings would instill into him, after his somewhat doubtful experiences with Sloane and Simpson. There were other more obviously practical reasons. As they had every intention of having several more children, they thought that such an environment would tend to be more advantageous. Also, John had no intention of giving up his favourite hobby, and hoped to be able to possess grounds large enough to pursue it on his own property. After a short search they found exactly the sort of house they wanted about six miles out of St. Andrews on the road to Cupar, just on the outskirts of the village of Ceres.

It was a good solid stone-built property, in need of a certain amount of necessary modernisation, and standing in about three acres. There was a short drive up to the house itself lined with magnificent beech trees of a great age. It had not taken them long to make the place reasonably habitable, and one of the first things John had done was to convert part of the grounds into an archery range. He had then founded an archery group named by way of a pun 'The Ceres Artemis Club', and a year after their move, there was quite a number of enthusiasts in the membership, even if their accuracy was somewhat variable.

The first annual competition of the newly-formed club had been arranged for Thursday, the twenty-ninth of June. The evening light stretched to beyond eleven o'clock at this time of year, and so an evening meeting had seemed not unreasonable, although the start had been arranged for five o'clock to take into account the possibility of the cold Eastern breeze making life a little uncomfortable later on. A certain amount of merriment was expected after the serious business of the competition was over, and so Susan, who had recently given birth to their second child, had decided to spend a few days with John's parents in Perthshire to keep out of the way. Her husband was taking his annual holiday at this time, and because of the recent addition had made no arrangements for a holiday any distance away from home. He accordingly took his family to his parents' house on the Wednesday morning. He had informed his wife that he felt it very important to make absolutely sure that all the arrangements for this, the first annual competition of the club, were watertight, and so intended to return to Ceres as soon as it was light on the Thursday. Despite her protestations about the necessary amount of time he was allowing himself for what were, after all, fairly simple preparations, he stuck to his plan, and found himself approaching Ceres shortly before half past four in the morning.

6❧ Chapter 2

DETECTIVE CONSTABLE JOHN WHITE was at the wheel of the car which was propelling himself and Inspector Malone of the Fife CID towards Ceres. They had both been woken up by the report of an emergency and White had immediately rung Malone to offer to pick him up. White himself was one of those people who are fully awake the moment they are aroused from sleep, but Malone was of the opposite sort, who need a certain amount of time before they can regain contact with the real world. For that reason, White had considered the arrangement the most sensible in the circumstances, and as a result, nothing but formal pleasantries had been exchanged between them so far. Malone now began to feel, unhappily, that he was back in normal waking life.

"You're a good man, White, but I think I'm just about all right now, and have accepted the daily inevitable. That means I am fully in command of my senses, I hope. Well, I was only given the bare outline of this business, but it appears pretty bizarre at first sight. There's definitely a corpse and I'm told it's attached to a tree by an arrow. The tree is situated in the drive of a house belonging to a Mr John Strachan, who is an accountant by profession. It was he who discovered the body. That is really the sum total of what I know at the moment. Do you happen to have come across this Strachan for any reason?"

"Aye, I believe I have, if the arrow is anything go by. He's something of an archery fanatic who moved into the area just over a year ago. He founded a club called 'The Ceres Artemis Club', one of your classical allusions I believe. I've only heard of him because a couple of people I know went along to have a go at the archery when it first started. I might add that when they found out how difficult it was they soon dropped it."

"Well, at any rate that begins to give some excuse for the presence of the arrow. If nothing else, there were almost certain to be some on the premises. Do you know exactly which house it is?"

"I think so. If I'm right, it's just round the next corner. Do you want me to drive right up to it or stop a little before we get there?"

"There's no point in taking the risk of destroying any possible traces just to save a thirty-yard walk, so stop a little bit before the house. With this drought we've been having, I don't suppose it'll make much difference, though."

White accordingly parked about thirty yards short of the entrance to the drive into John Strachan's property and they walked along the road towards it, observing the grass verge closely as they went. Just before they reached the drive, they could see clear signs of damage to the verge, where a car or similar vehicle had mounted it. Before they examined this, however, it seemed advisable to identify themselves to the constable who had come to the end of the drive and was watching their progress with obvious interest. Malone therefore produced his identification and introduced White. Constable Christie—it turned out that that was his name— then asked for instructions, but Malone asked him to wait until they had had a closer look at the verge.

"What would you say, White?" he asked, after they had both looked for a few minutes at the signs which had been left there.

"It hardly needs stating that there has been a vehicle parked here in the not-too-distant past. Even if you couldn't see that oil patch perfectly clearly, you could smell it a good way off on a fine morning like this. The obvious extension from that is that the vehicle involved had an oil-leak."

"Aye, you're quite right to leave your statement at that. It seems pretty likely that something heavy—presumably the body—was unloaded here, but I think we'd better be leaving such speculations to the experts."

There was a tall beech hedge fronting the grounds and this was broken by the drive. They turned into the drive, and suddenly stopped short. On the grass to their right at the foot of an aged tree, lay a bow, and a number of arrows were scattered haphazardly about it. That, however, had not been the reason for their sudden halt. Attached to the trunk of the tree, with its feet off the ground, was the dead body of a man. An arrow was driven right through his heart.

"I was wondering whether I should cover it with a bit of sacking or something, sir," said Constable Christie. "But as there was nothing of that sort lying around, I didn't want to go away and search in case someone came along, although to be fair, you don't usually get anybody coming along here at this time of the morning. It's a bit too early for the commuters and no-one working locally has any real reason for coming past here."

"Has there not even been any holiday traffic along?"

"No, there's been nothing till you came along yourselves."

"Where's Mr Strachan?"

"I told him to go inside the house and stay there until you folk should want to question him. The only thing I allowed him to do was move his car, as it was blocking the drive. It seems that he stopped as soon as he saw this in front of him and came running along to my house straightaway to fetch me. That's his car in front of the house. I did of course make quite sure that there were no traces in front of the car before I let him move it."

"You have probably done no harm, but it would have been better to leave it to the experts to decide if that were so."

"Mr Strachan himself still hasn't left the house?"

"Not from this side, at any rate."

"Fine, you can be getting back home now, if you like. We'll be along to see you later."

Constable Christie departed and Malone said to White: "I'm sure he was merely trying to be helpful, but I wish these people would realise that it would be easier for everybody if they simply followed standard instructions in this sort of matter. Did he expect we'd be arriving in the style of American cops, with sirens blaring and an amazing two-wheeled turn into the drive here? Never mind, it's very unlikely that any harm has been done with the bone-dry state of the drive. There should be two uniformed men arriving at any time, as well as the forensic team, and we can make sure that no further alterations to the status quo are made until they do. I only hope both parties have the good sense to park further down the road. Well, we might as well see what we can make of it before they arrive."

Malone walked up to the body on the tree and took a close look at it. It was immediately clear from an insufficiency of blood that death itself had not been caused by the arrow, but that the unfortunate man had died by some other means. In many ways, this appeared even more gruesome than the first impression: what sort of mind could imagine such a treatment of a dead body?

"Well, White, it looks as if we can be pretty certain of a number of things. This man was murdered somewhere else. The method used was poison, almost certainly cyanide, and he had no reason to expect an attack on his life. The body was then brought here in the hours of darkness and fixed in this rather horrible position. There are no other obvious marks on his body, and I don't suppose he would take cyanide merely to please those wanting to kill him, so I suppose he wasn't expecting to be given it. I, for one, wouldn't like to attempt this gruesome exercise during the hours of daylight, especially with the holiday season in full swing. The chances of someone coming past would be too great. If their attitude was the same, at least two of them came during the hours of darkness, parked their car outside, brought the body in here, tied it to the tree, and then drove an arrow through the heart to affix it to the tree. Whether they had premeditated this last action would be difficult to say. The evidence of the bow and arrows being scattered around in this way would suggest that it was an action on the spur of the moment. But you can see that the actual arrow which is driven through the body is nothing like the others here. That may well indicate that they brought it themselves. I think we'd better wait until the forensic men have done their stuff before we try to come to any other conclusions. Anything you think worthwhile adding?"

"Not really. Except perhaps that as they'd expect to find bows and arrows of different types accessible, I see no real reason why they should have brought their own along, even if this were premeditated. We may well find that there are other arrows of the same type. Apart from that, as these others seem rather a long time coming, do you think we should have a word with Mr Strachan immediately?"

"I think perhaps we might as well, if we cover this up first. Have you got anything in the car?"

White went off and returned a few minutes later with a rug, which he had taken out of the back of the car. They covered as much of the body as they could with this and then went up to the house. Malone was on the point of ringing the bell when the door was opened by a healthy-looking man of slightly more than average height.

"Hullo, I'm John Strachan. I have of course been watching you from the window, and when I saw you coming up to the house I presumed you wanted to see me. Constable Christie told me that on no account was I to leave the house and I thought I had better carry out his instruction to the letter. Do please come in. I've just made a pot of tea in anticipation of your arrival."

He ushered them into a sitting room of considerable dimension on the left of the entrance-hall. The windows commanded a view of the entrance to the drive and clearly were the ones from which John Strachan had been observing them.

"I don't suppose you'll mind if Constable White stands by the window, Mr Strachan? We need to keep an eye open for the arrival of more of our men, as well as watch out for any possible inquisitive passers-by. Not really the time of year for having a roaring fire, is it? Still, I suppose it's pleasant enough to see it."

"It would look a bit peculiar to you, I suppose. But I was feeling very cold earlier on—possibly something to do with the shock. Anyway, I felt I needed something to do. It's not easy to sit around doing nothing after an experience like that and the mechanical job of making a fire appealed to me."

"I'm sure it was very upsetting for you. I hope you won't mind if I put a few questions to you now."

"Not at all, I feel a lot better and I'd find it easier if I had to talk about it."

"Would you be good enough to begin by telling me exactly how you cane to find the body?"

"At the moment, if it doesn't seem a bit Irish, my family and I are staying in my parents' house in Perthshire. I had to come over here today to organise the first annual competition of the local archery club. I actually founded it myself, and the event was to take place here in my grounds this evening. As it was the first such occasion, I especially wanted to make a good job of it, and decided to get here early. It would have been just before five o'clock when I arrived, and as soon as I turned into the drive I stopped dead at what I saw. I'm sure you can imagine my reaction. I didn't even go up and have a close look to see if there was still anything I could do for him. I simply got out of the car and ran along to fetch Constable Christie, feeling as if Coleridge's frightful fiend was right behind me. I told him briefly what I had seen, he came along here in something of a spirit of unbelief, but as soon as he saw that it was indeed as I had said, he went straight off to put a call through to you people."

"He left you here while he went back?"

"Yes. He told me to go straight into the house and not to come out unless I saw anyone trying to interfere with the scene of the crime. I must say, after my reaction at the sight, I thought that would be rather unlikely, but anyway no-one came along until he returned about ten minutes later."

"This house was empty last night then?"

"Yes. We went to Perthshire yesterday morning, and it had been our intention to return on Sunday—apart of course from my trip here today."

"Did many people know that the house would be empty last night?"

"I've no idea. I made no secret of the fact that we were going away, but I didn't broadcast the fact from the rooftops. If anyone had really wanted to know, I'm sure they wouldn't have had too much difficulty in finding out."

"Have you noticed if the house was broken into?"

"Not as far as I can see. That's one of the things I've been checking on to fill in the time while I was waiting for you. All the doors and windows were locked when we went away, and they were all still locked when I went round. I haven't noticed anything missing, either."

"Are those arrows and the bow out there yours?"

"Yes. I kept them in the garage, and I'm afraid I hadn't remembered to lock the garage door."

"Who is likely to know that you kept them in the garage?"

"I suppose most people in the archery club, and anyone else who happened to have noticed them. But I think it's far more likely that they were found by accident. You see, the actual arrow that was sticking through him was not one of mine. I had a good look when I came back with Constable Christie. I'd lost my feeling of panic by then; it's amazing how much confidence the presence of a solid British policeman can inspire. It's not any type of arrow that I've seen before, and certainly not the sort you'd usually find used for sport. It's far too heavy and lethal."

"Have you any idea who the man over there is?"

"Oh yes. Didn't Constable Christie tell you?"

"I didn't ask him."

"Well, although his face is not a pretty sight at the moment, I had no difficulty in recognising him. His name's Ronald Blacklaw and he was an accountant by profession. I first came across him when we were fellow members of the West Ealing Archery Club in London. He was also the man who took over my job in a firm of City accountants when I left to come up here. It appears I moved at the right time, as the firm went into liquidation not long after I left. Ronald then managed to get a job in Edinburgh."

"When did you last see him?"

"Not since I was in London. That's more than a year ago now. But I did write to him in Edinburgh not many weeks ago, to ask him if he would grace this competition which is supposed to be taking place this evening. He was a very good archer, you see, and I thought he might add a little tone to the proceedings. I got a short note back from him almost by return saying he couldn't manage it."

"That was the only communication you have had with him since you left London?"

"Yes."

"May I ask then how you knew where he was employed?"

"My wife comes from the same part of Lancashire as his family. Her mother mentioned it in one of her letters, thinking we'd be interested, I suppose. The information was clearly correct too, as I wrote to him at the firm and received a reply."

"Can you suggest a reason why Mr Blacklaw should have been killed in the first place, or account for his body being left in your grounds in these somewhat strange circumstances?"

"I honestly don't know, but I have of course imagined a number of things—I thought it might be some sort of warning of what might happen to me."

"If you did what?"

"I've no idea, but once my imagination really gets going again I'm sure I'll think of plenty of possibilities. By the way, I can tell you that it would be virtually impossible for him to have been impaled in that way from a genuine bowshot. The arrow must have been knocked through him while he was held against the tree. It all seems pretty gruesome."

"I had already deduced from the damage to the end of the arrow that that was the most likely explanation. It also led to the conclusion that the person or persons involved were pretty cold-blooded in their attitudes, and that perhaps you were very fortunate to be away in Perthshire for the night. I presume that you are able to prove that you were in Perthshire last sight"

"I've been waiting for you to ask me that. I can certainly prove I was there until half-past three this morning, or thereabouts."

"You drove straight here?"

"Yes, but I was in no hurry. It was such a glorious morning. Being down in a place like London for a few years teaches you to appreciate such things, you know. The roads were quite empty and so I went at my own pace, and even stopped once or twice to admire the view. I also don't like knocking down the rabbits which are inclined to run across the road in front of you at that time of the morning."

"If you were driving fast on a clear road, how quickly could you make the journey?

"Assuming I was prepared to disregard speed limits, I ought to be able to do it in not much more than half an hour. Certainly less than three-quarters. But as I said, I was not in any hurry this morning."

"I see. There is one point which I feel I must pursue. It is now over an hour since you discovered the body, and you have been on your own almost all that time. It is unthinkable that you would not have had some concrete thoughts on exactly why this body was left on your doorstep. It is clearly inconceivable, given the fact that you knew the victim and have an interest in archery, that your house was chosen at random."

"You are of course quite right, and I suppose I might as well tell you what had occurred to me as the most likely explanation. There was a combination of reasons for my leaving London. One of them was that I suspected a certain amount of irregularity was going on in some of the accounts dealt with by the firm for which I worked. The firm, by the way, was called Sloane and Simpson. My suspicions were not without foundation, as I myself was asked on one or two occasions to falsify certain figures. No very large sums involved, you understand, but I got the impression that my employers were testing me out, before trying me with some even less creditable activities. I know that we're not supposed to speak evil of the dead, but I don't think Ronald would have had quite the same compunction as I had. I haven't a shred of evidence for saying that, but he never made much of a secret of the fact that he was mainly interested in the money to be made out of the job. I suppose I should have reported my suspicion to the correct body, but when it gets down to it, you never really feel like doing that sort of thing. Well, it occurred to me that he might be in possession of certain facts relating to some of the clients which it would be in their interests to keep hidden. He then could have tried to blackmail them. Their reply is to murder him and leave his body here to discourage me from trying a similar sort of game. If he was in possession of such facts, it would be reasonable for them to assume that I was as well."

"How do you fit the presence of the arrow into this theory?

"I don't know and quite frankly, I had no desire to think too deeply about it. You see, it would suggest that whoever had done this thing knew both Ronald and myself well enough to know that we both had an interest in archery.

There was no-one I knew of with accounts with the firm who was likely to have such information, but there were several accounts to which I was never allowed access. Anyway, the implication could be that somebody I knew quite well was prepared to kill me, and in a pretty nasty way. It's even more frightening when it looks as though poison was used. You'd start being frightened ever to eat or drink anything you hadn't prepared yourself again."

"What makes you suggest that they used poison?

"Well, I saw no other obvious marks on his body, and I've often read about the dreadful facial contortions you can get if you've been poisoned."

"Facial contortions can be present for a variety of reasons, but I can appreciate that you would see poison as a very frightening possibility. It gives you a general feeling of helplessness, whereas I suppose you feel that in the case of an assault you would have a reasonable chance of defending yourself."

"That's exactly how I see it. I hope you'll forgive the rather irritational way I may be talking, but I still don't feel myself. No other sensible explanation occurred to me, though I had thought of the possibility of some lunatic who had a particular hatred of archers and archery, and some even more unlikely theories."

"I think we can leave such suggestions as your last one until all other possible avenues are blocked. However, you would be as well to be on your guard. It would be your view then that the murderers came from London or that area?"

"I couldn't be sure of course, but if they have their financial affairs dealt with in London, it is more likely than not that they come from that area. There is nothing whatever to stop somebody from moving elsewhere and leaving their financial affairs in the hands of the company they've been dealing with for years, however. That would be especially likely if any irregular arrangements were in force. But as I don't know which accounts were doubtful in the first place, I can make no positive pronouncement."

"They've arrived at last," said White from the window. "I always wonder why it takes them so much longer than us."

"In this case, to be fair, White, they had much further to come. If you would excuse us for the moment, Mr Strachan, I'd like to speak to you again later. I don't think your presence out there would serve any useful purpose for the time being, so I hope you won't mind staying here until we're finished."

As they walked down the drive towards their newly arrived colleagues, Malone said: "Could you swiftly give me your impression of Mr Strachan?"

"I must say, despite his protests, he seemed remarkably cool for someone who had just come across a corpse, and a not very pretty one at that, in his front drive, especially when he realised that he could have been in a similar position himself. His explanation of the time taken to come from his father's house is clearly a little suspicious. I think it might well be worth looking into his wife's background to see exactly what relationship she had with this Mr Blacklaw before she met her husband—and afterwards possibly as well. It is also worth remembering that we only have his word for it that he did not go in for 'irregular practices', as he seems to like calling them. The whole business of the arrow could simply be a blind to cover up something much more simple."

"Aye. I think that's all very sound. I might add that it seems most peculiar to want to be here at such an early hour to make preparations for a championship due to be held this evening. There is even the simple practical fact that he would be unlikely to perform at his best if he had virtually missed out a night's sleep. If he was aware that circumstances would arise to make it unlikely that the event would actually take place, he would not have to concern himself on that account. The other point is that there almost certainly must have been at least two people involved, and so if Strachan is one of them, we must also look for his accomplice."

They approached the group which had gathered by the body. Dr Crenshaw, the police doctor, had removed the rug from the body and had begun to examine it. He asked Malone if it could be taken from its present position as soon as the photographer had done his work, and permission was readily granted. Malone and White set about the unpleasant task. The arrow was embedded far more deeply into the tree than they had imagined, and they had to call upon one of the uniformed men to help them, before they could complete the operation. The body of the late Mr Blacklaw was then laid on the gravel path with the arrow still protruding back and front, while Dr Crenshaw continued with his examination. The rest of the forensic team meanwhile went carefully over the ground round about, taking several measurements and a few photographs. After a few minutes, Dr Crenshaw stood up.

"Well, Inspector, there's little more of value I can do here. When I have taken the body away and looked into it thoroughly, I shall be able to tell you something exact about it.

Malone was used to this cagey approach from the doctor, and said: "Could you please give us some sort of outline now? You know I won't hold it against you if you happen to produce something which could later be misleading. You also know that I've never heard you do so yet."

"The man has undoubtedly been poisoned and that was almost certainly the cause of his death. The arrow was driven through him, not shot, a considerable time after death. Such unnecessary force was used, as you found out when you had to take down the body, that the sanity of the person or persons involved must be called into question. I don't mean that they have escaped from an asylum or anything like that, but such callous violence to a dead body is not what most of us would consider ordinary behaviour. The implication of that statement, of course, is that we are dealing with a man who could still be dangerous. The poison employed, as I'm sure you have noticed, is almost certainly potassium cyanide, but I cannot state that without reservation until I have carried out tests. The one other point of helpfulness to you, again as I'm sure you have noticed, is that he almost certainly took the poison without realising it, as there are no other signs of violence on his body."

"Thanks very much. I had indeed surmised most of that for myself but it's as well to have it confirmed. What about the time for the death?"

"Probably yesterday evening."

"All right, we'll leave it at that until you've made out the full report. A soon as the others have finished, you're at liberty to take the body away. Well, Sergeant, anything much from your end?"

Sergeant McBride had an uncanny ability to find traces of people where even his similarly trained colleagues could not, and seemed the ideal man for this situation. He also, as befitted the speciality of his job, had an immense knowledge of everyday things, such as types of shoe and measurement of the wheelbases of almost every known type of motor car. However he did not seem particularly optimistic on this occasion. "If you'll give me a little longer," he said, "I'll be able to tell you one or two things, but you'll understand that with the recent dry weather we've been having, careful men are not going to leave much for us."

After about another quarter of an hour's intensive search, he seemed satisfied with his efforts. He returned to Malone.

"You'll already have noticed some of this, and it's not all that much anyway. There was a car parked just outside on the grass verge and because of the state of the tyres, as well as the pronounced oil leak, I would say that it was not new. It was a blue Ford Cortina—they kindly scraped a bit of paint off in their hurry to leave. There were probably two men in the front, although it is theoretically possible that the second man was already waiting here, or arrived by some other method without leaving any traces. They removed a large heavy object from the back seat—presumably the body—and dumped it to the right of the gravel just inside the entrance and out of sight of the road. That may indicate that it was daylight, or it could have been a natural caution. They then walked up to the house. What they did there, I don't know. But as there are no signs of any attempt to force either door or windows, I presume they merely rang the bell and, finding that there was no answer, went to the garage to see if there was a car to indicate if there was anybody in. It appears that the garage had been left open, as there again there is no sign of forcing. They then went back to the body, picked it up, tied it to the tree and left it suspended there by the arrow, after removing the material they used for tying it up. There is by the way, no sign of any such material, but there would have been more obvious signs if someone had held the body in place. The arrow was knocked in, a large hammer being the most likely implement. The car then left at speed in the direction of St. Andrews, presumably taking both men with it, but again I cannot vouch for that."

"I must congratulate you for being able to see so much where we little. Would it be possible for the men to have possessed a key to the house and simply to have walked in, rather than ringing the bell?"

"That is certainly possible. It seems unlikely from the signs, but it could have been that one of the men was here all the time."

"Any chance of a description of these two men?"

"Only of a very general kind. They must have been reasonably fit to do what they did but that in no way means they were exceptionally strong. Neither their feet nor their strides were of abnormal size and so I would assume they were a little less than six feet. I realise that description covers about half the male population of the country but I'm afraid with the state of the ground I cannot be more exact."

"I quite understand. Any indications on the dead man himself?"

"Nothing that you and the doctor haven't noticed already. For whatever reason, the pockets have all been emptied and there wasn't so much as a handkerchief left. That could be an indication of robbery but there are also other interpretations which are equally likely. The type of clothes he was wearing do, of course, suggest that he was still dressed for work when he met his death."

"As you say, it's not all that much to go on, but it is considerably more than I could have gleaned for myself. I'll doubtless get your full report later. Well, White, I think another chat with Mr Strachan would not go amiss." They returned to the house and were again ushered into the sitting room.

"Well, Mr Strachan, I think it would be as well if you were aware that the people who brought Mr Blacklaw's body here actually came up to your front door. The natural deduction is that they were looking for you. If that is so, you may well still be in some personal danger. Are you sure that you can be no more specific about your suspicions?"

"I'm afraid I can't be. If what you say is true, though, it's rather frightening. What do you suggest that I do?"

"If I were you I'd go back to Perthshire for a couple of days. Better still, get right away for a bit. The only stipulation that I make is that the police are kept fully informed of your movements, both for your own protection and in case we need to interview you. Whatever you do, take great care."

Malone and White left. "You will have realised, White, that there is really no good reason, on the evidence we have, not to include Strachan as one of the two men involved. It would explain the lengthy time between leaving Perthshire and informing Constable Christie of the body, and also the footsteps up to the front door, accompanied by no signs of attempted or actual breaking and entering. However, the reason for going into the house is not immediately obvious."

"It occurs to me," said White, "that it could have been to light the fire. Also, the fact that they seemed to go straight to the garage to fetch the arrows might well indicate some sort of inside job, especially as they seemed to have no difficulty in knowing where they were going in the dark."

"Remember that the darkness was only a theory of mine, which I am inclined to abandon when faced with the facts as related to us by Sergeant McBride, and the remarks made by the doctor about the mental outlook of our man, or men. It was really those remarks which made me doubt the involvement of Strachan. I find it very hard to see him in either part played beneath that tree there. Still, you're undoubtedly right about the probability of the fire being used to burn possible evidence, or even simply the contents of Blacklaw's pockets. We had better send McBride back to see about it. Our other positive move will be to make certain that Strachan was indeed where he said he was last night."

🙳 Chapter 3

MALONE AND WHITE LEFT CERES and drove to Fife Police Headquarters in Kirkcaldy. When they were established in Malone's office with a cup of tea, the inspector said: "Well, White, it looks very much as if it's going to be our pigeon, even if Edinburgh looks just as good a bet for the place of the actual murder, and London seems a reasonable possibility for the origin of the whole affair. We'll have reports on Ronald Blacklaw from Edinburgh as soon as they can manage it and then I suppose we just take it from there. I must say it does seem rather an unpleasant business. It's not often that the solid Dr Crenshaw can be drawn to say so much about the character of the men we're looking for, and he's seen many much less pretty sights. It's easy to see his point. We can all understand and appreciate that a man wishes to get rid of another fellow human being. We've all felt like it from time to time. But then callously to maltreat a corpse after death does not occur to the average well-balanced man. One of the problems is whether such people are likely to do the same again. It could simply be an indication of the extreme hate felt towards Ronald Blacklaw, or it could be something much wider. Let's assume for the moment that John Strachan is speaking the absolute truth and that his explanation of the cause of Blacklaw's death is the correct one. If Blacklaw was trying to obtain money from some former client because of some information he had come across, is there anything unreasonable in supposing that the threatened individual took a trip up to Edinburgh, ostensibly to arrange payment, but instead of doing so, managed to poison Blacklaw? Would the further stage of dumping the body at Strachan's house, assuming he knew it was not too far away, seem too unlikely?"

"No, it's a perfectly tenable theory and would be especially sound if Strachan had tried a bit of blackmail himself. It could then easily be the case that the persons involved decided to have a clean sweep of those who possessed this information, whatever it may have been, but when they found that Strachan was out, left what they did as a terrible warning. That would at least give a rational explanation to their treatment of the body. But, if I may say so, it sounds such a reasonable theory that Strachan could easily have made it up for the occasion. Just as likely, I would have thought, is that Strachan found out something about a relationship, past or present, between his wife and Blacklaw, and took this revenge—the arrow through the heart could be a sick indication of the reason. If the supposed relationship had had its beginnings in the Archery Club down south, he might have thought this was a most suitable revenge. That would at least give some reason for the presence of the arrow, which your theory doesn't."

"That is certainly an explanation we shall have to consider, although it apparently takes no account of the second man. Still, I'm sure we could manufacture many other theories, but I think we'd be wiser not to until we have more information to go on. First we had better see exactly what Dr Crenshaw and Sergeant McBride have for us, then I think our best move would be to go to Edinburgh and try to establish Ronald Blacklaw's last movements."

The preliminary reports from both the doctor and Sergeant McBride did not take long in coming. McBride had nothing of importance to add to his verbal comments, and Malone noted that the evidence for his assertions was by no means conclusive. The doctor provided a little more information but there again there was nothing startling. He confirmed that potassium cyanide was the poison used, but

Malone was only too well aware how many reasons people would have for possession of that poison. The contents of the stomach were a possible help, as it was clear that Blacklaw had had a meal not long before he died, and the meal was of a type you would more often associate with a restaurant than a private house. That could prove decisive in establishing the dead man's whereabouts before his death.

"Well, White, it's a pity they wouldn't leave something a bit more obvious for us. Still, I suppose we've got the car and the arrow and the possibility of a restaurant—although exactly which eating places between Edinburgh and Ceres we should concentrate on is any one's guess. The trouble with the car is that a blue Cortina is hardly terribly rare and there are always so many vehicles passing through this area, sightseeing at this time of the year. It could also have been hired, stolen or borrowed with or without the owner's knowledge. Our best hope there seems to be the earliness of the hour, and the fact that it was driven off in the direction of St. Andrews— although that could easily be a blind or simply ignorance of the area. I think I'd better get on to Edinburgh straightaway and tell them that we're coming, and have enquiries started both on the arrow and the car from this end."

If the traffic is not too bad, Kirkcaldy to Edinburgh, by way of the Forth Road Bridge, is a drive of little more than half an hour. However, as it was the height of the holiday season, a multitude of cars drawing caravans of greater or lesser stability, slowed down their progress considerably. It was a glorious sunny day and the Forth shimmered far below them, while the railway bridge stood solidly with its majestic spans to their left. After a fairly tiresome last few miles into Edinburgh behind an apparently limitless supply of vehicles, they found themselves at Edinburgh Police Headquarters.

They were conducted to the office of Inspector McGregor of the Edinburgh branch. The Inspector, after welcoming them, offered them every assistance. All information which seemed to be relevant to their business had already been laid out on his desk. As was to be expected, there was nothing of any great surprise in these documents, but they did help to fill in one or two gaps in their knowledge. Ronald Blacklaw, it transpired, lived in a flat he owned himself at the bottom of the New Town, in St. Vincent Street to be precise. His employers, McColl and Duncan of Moray Place, were an old and respected Edinburgh firm, though of no great size. The senior partner was a Mr Reid. As far as was known at this stage, Blacklaw had left his place of work at his normal time of around half-past five on the Wednesday evening. It had been his habit after leaving work and before returning home, to drop into the Scott Bar. He had not been seen there on the Wednesday, but this had not occasioned great surprise, as it was by no means every evening that he came in. None of his neighbours had seen him return that evening, but with the arrangement of the building, it was rare for them to do so anyway. There was so far no-one else who had any information about his whereabouts from the time he left his work until his corpse was discovered nearly fifty miles away in Ceres.

Malone considered the information for a short while and then said: "I think our best plan of action would be to visit the offices of McColl and Duncan, as that is apparently the last place where he was seen. It is also possible that Mr Reid, or whoever is in charge at the moment, has other relevant information. Have you been there yourself?"

"No," said McGregor, "we have only got as far as the most routine enquiries. We contacted him by telephone as soon as he arrived at work and told him to expect someone along to see him later."

"I'd better let him know we're coming. Our next port of call, I think, should be the Scott Bar. I don't know it. What sort of establishment is it?"

"It's a straightforward sort of place. Being near Stockbridge, it attracts a very mixed sort of clientele. I would say that they would certainly know something about him there. It's not the sort of place where nobody talks to anybody else."

"That sounds a little hopeful. After that I suppose we try the neighbours. But it's surprising how little they can know about each other in some of these tenement blocks. We'll have to hope there's a busybody on the stair. By the time we get back, there may be some information from London."

After establishing with Mr Reid that he was willing to receive them immediately, Malone and White set off in the direction of Moray Place. Not many minutes later, they found themselves at the offices of the firm of McColl and Duncan, and were immediately shown into the office of the senior partner. The room was almost a caricature of how you might expect such an office to appear. There was almost no concession to modernity, and the general impression, from the books as well as the furniture, was one of brown and black leather, and stuffy respectability. Mr Reid rose from behind his solid dark-stained desk.

"Good morning, gentlemen. This is indeed a shocking business. I could hardly believe it when the police telephoned me this morning. It was very thoughtful of you not to interrupt me at home earlier, but I can assure you that in a matter so grave, I would certainly have had no objection. Now could you tell me in exactly what way you think that I can be of help?"

"You impute far too humane motives to our actions, Mr Reid. I'm afraid that the only reason you were not contacted at home was that you must already have left for work. I had better tell you first of all that we are detectives from Fife, as that is where Mr Blacklaw's body was found. May I ask you first of all if you know of any reason to take Mr Blacklaw to the St. Andrews-Cupar area?"

"Nothing that I know of. As you may or may not know, our Mr Blacklaw was a very keen toxophilist and very good as well, I believe. He used to practise at a club outside Dunfermline, but that is really the wrong end of Fife. I suppose it is always possible that some of the other members came from that part and he could have been visiting one of them."

"That could be so. We actually have certain evidence to suggest that his body was transported there from somewhere else. Do you happen to know if he was going in that direction yesterday evening?"

"I really have no idea. I have never considered it any part of my business to enquire into the private life of my employees. I have always insisted on the highest standards in our offices here—many would, I'm sure, call them old-fashioned, but that is what most of our customers like to see—and in return I have never made the slightest attempt to look into their private lives. I suppose that if some information was given to me about them which would seem to bring the firm into disrepute, I would have to look at it in a slightly different way. But that necessity has never so far presented itself."

"Do you happen to know of any special friends Mr Blacklaw had?"

"I'm afraid not. He was very uncommunicative about his interests out of work and, as that is an attitude of which I approve, I made no effort to change it. The only reason I had any knowledge of his archery was because he wanted time off work on one occasion to take part in some competition at this Dunfermline club. Fortunately, we had some fairly urgent business in the Dunfermline area and, as he was willing to combine the two, I was able to accommodate him. You should also remember that he had been with us rather less than six months."

"I understand perfectly. Could you be good enough to tell me exactly why you took on Mr Blacklaw?"

"I don't know how much you know about his past but, in the circumstances, I might as well tell you the whole story. First of all, of course, the firm needed an extra man. I had already, in principle, decided on a younger man who could, to some extent, be brought up in the ways of the firm. We have never really dealt with large companies, but have always specialized in giving individual service to a few private customers. It is true that as a result, we are perhaps not quite so prosperous a firm as many others, but professional men should not always be thinking merely of the size of the annual profits. My colleague, Mr Duncan, who is unfortunately in hospital at the moment, did of course hold similar views to my own, both on the correct position of the firm and the choice of a new man. Mr Blacklaw had some experience of this sort of firm in London but sadly for him the concern had been guilty of a degree of unprofessional conduct and had had to go into liquidation. When we met Mr Blacklaw, we felt that he was a very capable man who had been most unfortunate in his employers. We felt that it was almost our duty to give him a chance to make a reputation with a firm like ourselves. As a sort of insurance policy, we asked for a number of outside references but, as we found them impeccable, we decided to offer him the job. Although I must admit that we were originally partly influenced in our decision out of sympathy for the young man, I should also add that he never gave us any reason to regret our decision."

"I had already heard of the London firm; Sloane and Simpson I believe the name was. You were then quite convinced that Mr Blacklaw himself was in ignorance of the unprofessional conduct which took place?"

"We had his word for it and the assurance of his honesty from a number of respected referees. To be fair, we did make a few enquiries ourselves through contacts in London but they were of the same opinion. His whole attitude and bearing, coupled with the favourable response from our clients here, confirmed me in this belief after a very short time. As he had not been with Sloane and Simpson very long, it seemed unlikely that they would have entrusted him with their nefarious secrets."

"You can think of no reason yourself why anyone should want to see Mr Blacklaw dead? I had better make it absolutely clear that given the circumstances in which his body was found, there can be no possibility of an accident or suicide."

"I had rather gathered that fact from my conversation with your colleague earlier. No, as I say, I knew very little of his private life, but I can certainly say that I know of no-one connected with the firm, either employee or client, who is likely to have harboured such thoughts against him. I can of course provide you with a list of these people if you'd like."

"That would be very helpful, if you'd be so kind. Do you happen to know Ceres?"

Mr Reid looked totally mystified for a moment or two, and then produced a broad smile. "I'm very sorry, but at first I thought you were asking a question which presupposed a belief in the pagan deities. You are of course referring to Ceres in Fife. I know where it is, but I'm not actually acquainted with the place. Why do you ask?"

"Mr Blacklaw's body was found in Ceres. Is there anyone here at the moment who might know more about Mr Blacklaw's private life than yourself?"

"It's quite possible that my secretary, Miss Adamson, could help you out a little in that direction. I don't think she knew him particularly well but she's more his age-group than I am, if you know what I mean." He pressed a buzzer, one of the few things in the room which smacked of the twentieth century, and Misa Adamson, a small woman who looked to be in her early twenties, came into the room. Mr Reid addressed her in a serious but kindly voice: "I didn't like to tell you earlier, my dear, but I'm afraid we've had some rather bad news. Mr Blacklaw has been killed— murdered I'm led to believe. These gentlemen here are the detectives who are investigating the case. They want as much information as they can get about Mr Blacklaw's private life and I'm afraid that I have not been of much help. I was wondering if you might be of more assistance to them, as I think you probably knew him slightly better than I. I'm very sorry, my dear. I'm sure I should have broken the news more gently. It's bound to be a shock to you when you've been used to seeing him every day. Do sit down."

Miss Adamson had gone very pale and looked as if she might well collapse. "There, there," said Mr Reid, as he offered her a glass of water which he had just poured from a carafe on his desk. "I'm sure that'll make you feel better.

If you don't feel up to accommodating these gentlemen at the moment, I'm sure they'll understand and see you later."

"No, no, I'll be perfectly all right. It's just rather a shock. I'll be fine in a minute or two."

Malone then spoke to her. "I appreciate your reaction perfectly Miss Adamson and, as Mr Reid said, we'll be quite happy to see you later. But if you feel up to it now, it would certainly be more convenient for us." She raised no objection and so he continued: "As Mr Blacklaw apparently lived on his own and had only recently come to this area, it is difficult for us to know where to start, except with those he worked beside. But before I begin asking you any questions, would you like Mr Reid to stay or go?"

She hesitated for a while, and Mr Reid was not slow to take the hint. "I shall leave you alone with them, Miss Adamson. If you should want me for anything, just press the buzzer and I'll be straight back. And don't worry, I have no intention of taking offence."

After he had left the room, Misa Adamson addressed Malone.   "Thank you for getting him out. He's a very considerate man but he is immensely old-fashioned in so many ways, and it would be difficult to answer you if he was in the room. I don't know why he has this manner, as I shouldn't think he's fifty yet."

"Don't mention it. First of all, I'd like to establish Mr Blacklaw's movements yesterday evening as exactly as I can. We have been informed that he left here at his normal time of around half past five yesterday evening. Can you confirm whether this is correct or not?"

"There can be no doubt about that. He had to pass me on his way out. I was just getting ready to go myself and so I can be quite sure of the time."

"There was nothing abnormal about his behaviour? He didn't seem unduly worried or excited or anything like that?"

"Not as far as I noticed. He seemed to be his normal self."

"You did not by chance have any idea about his intended movements later in the evening?"

Miss Adamson, who now seemed to be totally recovered, blushed a little. This was especially noticeable after the former pallor of her face. "I think I had better tell you at this point that I know Mr Blacklaw quite well. That of course was the reason for my extreme reaction to the news of his death, and also the reason that I was pleased when you asked Mr Reid to leave the room. Although he hasn't slid into senility yet, I think he would have disapproved of any positive relationship between myself and Mr Blacklaw. He would have seen it as producing the wrong image for the firm."

"I shall not embarrass you at this stage by asking you how well you knew Mr Blacklaw, Miss Adamson. We have no desire to interfere with anyone's private lives unless the information has some bearing on the case. I take it then that you did know what his plans were for at least part of yesterday evening?"

"Aye, he had planned to take me out to dinner, as he had unexpectedly come into a small sum of money. But yesterday morning he apologised and said that something had come up which would not wait and we would have to put off the arrangement until Friday."

"I see. He gave no indication of what this important matter might be?"

"No. I immediately accused him of having another woman, but I don't think that was the reason—certainly not now."

"You have no idea where he may have obtained this unexpected sum of money?"

"No. I didn't give it much thought. If any explanation occurred to me, it was that he had been left it by a relative."

"As you admit to having known him quite well, can you give us particulars of any close friends he had in the area?"

"As far as I know, he didn't have any. For a start, he hadn't been here all that long, and then I don't think he was the sort to have many close friends. He was very self-sufficient. He did go to his local bar most evenings and must have known a number of people there, but I think it's unlikely that he would have been at all close to any of them. His great hobby was archery and he used to go to a club near Dunfermline most weekends. He may well have had friends there for all I know, but he certainly never mentioned them to me. He was always quite busy with his work, by the way, as his experience before had all been in England and there were a few differences in procedure and practice he had to come to grips with, before he could be absolutely sure of himself here."

"Did he go away much, apart from the archery club?"

"No. The only other trips I knew that he made were down to Lancashire to see his mother. She's a widow and he was the only son. She hadn't been very well recently and he did the decent thing by going to visit her. She got better with the warmer weather, however, and I don't think he's been down there for a month, or possibly longer."

"Do you know if he was acquainted with the St. Andrews area?"

"I know that he went to St. Andrews to play the Old Course about a couple of months ago. He wasn't much of a golfer but he told me that if he ever went back down to England to settle, he'd hate to admit that he'd never played at St. Andrews when he'd been so close. As far as I know, that was the only occasion he went there, but of course I did not know all about his movements, and hardly anything about them until three months ago."

"Did you ever hear of a place called Ceres?"

"It's funny you should ask me that, because he asked me the same thing only a couple of weeks or so ago. He had received a private letter addressed to him at the firm which had been sent from there, and he didn't know himself where it was. I was able to tell him, as it's the sort of name you remember. As far as I remember, the letter was from someone he had known through his archery in the south of England, who wanted him to attend some competition or other. It was on a weekday and he decided he couldn't go. I don't remember anything more about it."

"He replied to the letter then?"

"Yes, I remember that because he asked me to put it along with the firm's mail to save the postage. He was a bit mean in that sort of way."

"Did you have the impression that he knew his correspondent well?"

"From his attitude, I wouldn't have thought so but I have no way of telling. He was hardly likely to have told tales about 'Old Jimmy', or whatever his name was, in here. I suppose that if he had known him well, it's more likely that he would have received the letter at his private address."

"I think that would indeed be more likely, Miss Adamson, but men are not always quite as scrupulous at keeping in close contact as you women. Is there anyone you know of, or even have heard of, who could have wanted to see Mr Blacklaw dead?"

"How could I ever imagine anyone ever wanting that? I don't think you understand quite how I felt about him. But certainly I knew of no enemies he had in this part of the world. He was very ambitious, though, and people like that often suffer from jealousy in others. There may have been those in the south of England who felt like that. He said that he had come up here for more varied experience but there could have been other personal reasons, for all I know."

"May I thank you for your co-operation, Miss Adamson. I realise that this cannot have been very pleasant for you. I suppose we should have no difficulty in contacting you if we need to do so?"

"No, it should be quite easy. The office here is closed for next week but I don't think I'll be leaving Edinburgh for more than a day-trip. If I change my mind, should I inform the police?"

"If you'd be good enough. I did not realise that the office here was not in operation next week. Had Mr Blacklaw made any plans to go anywhere, do you know?"

"No, he hadn't. He talked about the possibility of a day out at the Open in St. Andrews but had no firm arrangements to the best of my knowledge."

"I see. Could you be good enough to ask Mr Reid if we could speak to him for a moment or two longer? Ah, Mr Reid, we're very grateful for your secretary's time. She has been of great assistance to us on one or two minor points. I would like to know now if there is by any chance any private mail for Mr Blacklaw which has arrived today. We know that he received nothing in his flat and it is just on the off-chance that I ask, as Miss Adamson informed us that on at least one occasion, he received private correspondence here."

"It does seem on the face of it a slightly irregular request. I am quite prepared to open any letter received here which, although addressed to Mr Blacklaw, is clearly to do with the firm's business but private correspondence is after all private correspondence. If I handed such a communication to you, I would undoubtedly be just as guilty as yourselves of opening it."

"I can assure you that if any such letter is nothing to do with our investigation, we shall have no further interest in it. We can of course obtain the necessary authorisation for such a course of action but that would waste both your time and ours on what might be a matter of no importance. I presume from your remarks that there is a letter which possibly falls into the category of my request?"

"Yes, there is. I suppose that the circumstances are sufficiently serious to warrant such an intrusion on a man's privacy, but I still do not like being party to it. However, as you say, if I refuse you will merely come back tomorrow and demand it, so I might as well surrender gracefully. It should be on his desk in his office. As I hadn't informed Miss Adamson of the tragedy until your arrival, she will have carried on as if we were still expecting him to come in."

"Thank you. I assure you that if we find the contents are of no relevance to the case in hand, as we shall probably find, we have no desire to keep it."

They went through to Mr Blacklaw's office and Malone picked up a letter which was lying on the desk. "Mr Reid," he said, "why did you open this letter? Your attempts at covering up the fact are, I may say, rather clumsy."

"I didn't think they were very good, and that was the main reason for trying to put you off. You'll have to forgive me, but you see the letter, or the envelope I should say, is addressed to him in his own handwriting. I was wondering if the poor man had been in some peculiar mental state and had taken his own life. From what you say this is impossible, but it seems very strange to address an envelope to yourself, except if you are entering some commercial competition or such like. I felt he was far more likely to have given his home address if that were the case. Quite frankly, I would have destroyed it if it had been an admission of suicide, as such a revelation could do the dead no good, and would undoubtedly have damaged the good name of the firm."

"I'm glad you did not take any such drastic action, Mr Reid. Would you be good enough to leave us to look over this office on our own? We shouldn't be too long."

Malone and White proceeded to carry out a careful search of the late Ronald Blacklaw's office. They were unable to find anything which was not of a strictly professional nature, with the sole exception of two paperback novels of doubtful literary merit.

"Well, White, it doesn't look as if there's anything about to help us here. We'd better send in some men to give the place a thorough going-over, but I doubt they'll have any more luck. Now tell me what you make of the contents of Mr Blacklaw's last letter."

White took the letter and the envelope. The postmark was central London and it had been sent by first class mail. The letter consisted of one small piece of paper on which were printed the words FAWLEY BAR 4, and nothing else. "Apart from the obvious deductions about the place of posting, I can only suggest that it is some appointment in a pub, which for his own reasons the sender did not want anyone to trace to him. The obvious thought is some sort of blackmail. But how that fits in with the self-addressed envelope, I don't know."

"Aye, that does seem very strange indeed. However, I can in fact enlighten you as to the probable place suggested by the message. Rabid golfers like yourself may be unaware of the fact, but the Open Championship is not the only event in the sporting calendar. Down by the banks of the Thames in the town of Henley they celebrate the aquatic sports, and Henley Royal Regatta starts today. One of the bars in the Stewards' Enclosure goes by the name of the Fawley Bar. I can't imagine that the coincidence is an accident. The existence of this communication makes Strachan's theory of London-based blackmail a lot stronger, anyway. Still, let's leave the speculation for a bit and try the Scott Bar and the deceased's neighbours." Mr Reid was waiting for them outside the door of Blacklaw's office. "I hope I have not put you to any inconvenience as a result of my activity, Inspector. I trust that you will appreciate that my motives were of the highest. Is there anything else I can do for you before you leave?"

"No, I don't think so. It seems that little harm was done by your action. Goodbye, and thank you for your time."

"Perhaps before you go I should inform you that I am going down South tomorrow—pleasure, thank goodness, rather than business. We were going to shut down for a week from tomorrow, but in view of the circumstances, I think that a day sooner could not be inappropriate. I intend to be back next week in time for the Open in St. Andrews but I can easily inform you of my whereabouts in the meantime."

"That would be a great help. Goodbye again."

"Some are luckier than others, White," said Malone as they regained the street. "Unless we can get this matter dealt with fairly easily, I can't see much chance of us enjoying some time off at the Open. What was your impression of Miss Adamson?"

"As always, I am bound to take a more suspicious view of a woman than you are. She certainly put on a good act of a damsel in distress, but I wasn't totally convinced myself. One thing it does do is open up the possibility of a relationship between Blacklaw and Mrs Strachan. If the only real friend he bothered to make in Edinburgh was a female, it suggests that he was that way inclined. But it is to be remembered that we only have her word for everything she said, and it could be that she was making up the whole connection."

"You're quite right that my impression of her was somewhat more favourable than yours appears to have been but I have not lost sight of the fact that she has no corroboration for her statements. We shall hope to find some such confirmation from the neighbours and, if not, have enquiries made. Exactly why she should want to make it up is, however, not at all clear. What did you think of Mr Reid?"

"If it hadn't been for his opening the letter, I would have taken him for exactly what he was pretending to be—that is, a very respectable man who was very concerned about his professional image and the well-being of those employed by him. The re-sealing of the letter was very strange. We don't know if he had taken anything out, or had himself put that piece of paper in. It's surprising, but then again if his story is true it would at least be to character. He would attempt to restore the letter to as near its original state as he could. I think the only thing we can be sure of at this juncture, is that none of the statements we have heard so far are necessarily untrue; a fact which does not take us very far."

They had been walking in the direction of St. Vincent Street on the grounds that it was hardly worth taking the car such a short distance, and also that on such a fine day, there could hardly be many finer urban scenes in Europe than the New Town of Edinburgh. The simple elegance of the crescents and streets, with the common central gardens for the residents, is surely unparalleled in the centre of a capital city. Commerce is not of course absent from them, but they still contain a thriving population of genuine residents, who could no more move to the suburbs than to Leeds or London. They came across the Scott Bar before reaching the late Ronald Blacklaw's flat, and so dropped in and ordered a half-pint each. After they had taken a few mouthfuls, Malone made it known to the barman who they were and asked about Blacklaw. The barman had certainly known well enough who he was but was unable to give any additional information. He had certainly come in most nights at around quarter to six, and drunk one or, at the most, two pints. He had partaken in general conversations but never seemed to be the sort of person who would instigate them. One of the regular customers was called over and he confirmed this general impression. He knew that he came originally from the north of England, worked as an accountant, lived nearby and was keen on archery, but that was all. They were reasonably sure that no other customer knew any more about him. Malone and White left the bar.

Next they tried Ronald Blacklaw's neighbours. Most of these were out, but the two whom they did see could tell them nothing fresh and doubted if any of the other neighbours could be more helpful. They had not particularly noticed whether he had any visitors or not, but, inclined to the opinion that he did not. They then tried the interior of his flat. As the police had, of course, already been over the place, they did not really expect to find any worthwhile clues which might have been missed. All his private papers had already been removed and had revealed nothing of immediate interest. Not surprisingly, they drew a further blank themselves.

"We might as well get back to Headquarters, White. I don't think in our present state of knowledge we're going to find anything more of interest here."

They returned to Moray Place and picked up the car. "I suppose the one thing of value we have picked up is the note about the Fawley Bar. It is always a possibility that it's some sort of blind planted by Mr Reid, but I doubt it. I think it's far more likely that he would have been mystified about it himself. But we had better enquire as to whether he was ever a rowing man. The next thing to consider is whether it is an appointment that we should consider keeping. If we assume that the murderer was being blackmailed, it would hardly be worth it, but it's by no means impossible that the two facts are unconnected, or that there was more than one person who was having the screw put on them. The murder certainly doesn't look unpremeditated and it would be difficult to fit in the note with the actual murderer for that reason. Still, it is at least something which could lead us to find a reason why an apparently respectable Edinburgh accountant should be murdered."

"Aye, but the blackmail was only a theory at the outset. It does not seem likely, but that could just as well be a communication from a married woman."

"I think it most unlikely for a variety of reasons, but we must bear in mind a variety of explanations for the note. It could be part of a totally harmless game for all we know."

Inspector McGregor was waiting for them when they returned to Edinburgh Headquarters. He had a certain amount of additional information about Ronald Blacklaw, but none that seemed to be leading them anywhere. They had found out that he was a fairly frequent visitor to the Edinburgh Public Library, and the staff there remembered that he usually asked for books to do with Scottish law. This confirmed Miss Adamson's statement about the use of part of his spare time, but nothing else. Some reports had also come in from London which seemed a little more promising. One concerned the now defunct firm of Sloane and Simpson. The firm had gone into voluntary liquidation before certain evidence was made public, which would have forced the closure. In the case of the business of three clients, it was clear after investigation that substantial altering of figures had taken place to the detriment of the Inland Revenue. It seemed impossible that this could have been managed without the collusion of the firm and it had been the Institute of Chartered Accountants who had made the investigation and forced the closure. There may well have been more than these three involved but there could at least be no doubt about them. The customers consisted of two private individuals and one family firm. Apart from the fact that they employed the same financial advisers, no connection between the three parties was known and they had no connection except the business one with Sloane and Simpson. Further enquiries were being pursued in the matter.

"Well," said Malone, "Don't think there's any way we can avoid going down to London ourselves. I suppose we should be grateful that there are only three lots involved, but whether we can find any reason why any of them should want to rub out Ronald Blacklaw is another matter, unless we adopt some sort of blackmail theory. What lever he would have for extracting money from them is not immediately obvious. I'd have thought the associates of anyone with a lot of money, who had avoided giving large slices of it to the taxman, would be more inclined to ask them for tips than to cut them dead. The average man in the street, providing that he has some money, completely loses his sense of legality when dealing with the Inland Revenue. I'm afraid, White, our chances of being around in the right place for the Open seem to be moving rapidly over the horizon, but perhaps we'll be able to take in Henley Regatta as a consolation prize. I think we had better go down to London tomorrow and see if we can get any further with interviewing people there, unless by chance something turns up in the meantime to obviate the necessity. We'll have to leave the Dunfermline archery club and Strachan's wife to others, as well as trying to get somewhere with the blue Cortina. If they come up with anything, they can let us know down there almost as quickly as up here. We'd better go home now and give our families a bit of warning before departing for the south. Have you got any other openings to suggest, Inspector McGregor?"

"No, I think that's probably your best plan. I'll have Blacklaw's financial affairs looked into as soon as I can manage it, but as far as I understand it, they're pretty complex and may take some time. Apart from that, we'll work on trying to find anyone who might have seen Blacklaw after he left the office. We'll also look into Mr Reid and Miss Adamson to see if there's anything which they might be holding back from us. Apart from that good luck." Leaving these projects in progress, Malone and White left Edinburgh.

🙲 Chapter 4

INSPECTOR MALONE AND CONSTABLE WHITE took the morning train to London. Nothing of any material assistance to their case had turned up on the rest of the Thursday. Enquiries about blue Ford Cortinas in North-East Fife seemed to be getting absolutely nowhere and there was no news from Edinburgh of anyone seeing Ronald Blacklaw after the time he had left the offices of McColl and Duncan. Restaurants in the centre of Edinburgh had been checked to see if anyone of his description was remembered but, as there was no help from that direction, Malone was forced to assume that he had dined on private premises that night. It was always possible that a restaurant further afield was the one in question, and these were being investigated. However, once an assumption was made of an eating place outside the capital, the task was monumental. Blacklaw's mother had been contacted but she had nothing but praise for her only son, and it was clear that he had been very good to her ever since the death of her husband. She could not supply any motive for his murder, or indeed throw any other light on the matter.

They were met at King's Cross by one Inspector Peagram, who had been detailed to look after them in the metropolis and was in charge of the case at that end. Their first need was accommodation, as it was reasonably certain they would not finish their business that evening. In fact, assuming that they followed up the clue at Henley, it was most unlikely they would be leaving before the Sunday night. Both Malone and White, when they had considered the Henley clue on the journey down, had been in grave doubts as to whether it was worth pursuing. First of all, they did not even know which day was referred to, assuming they had understood the message correctly in the first place. Malone had insisted that either the Saturday or Sunday was intended, because Blacklaw had apparently given no hint that he might need to absent himself from work on the Friday, whereas thereafter he would have been on holiday. They agreed that this was the best basis to work on. Whether it was worth keeping the appointment or not was another question. If it had been arranged for the collection of blackmail, and the man who was being forced to pay had murdered his persecutor, it was hardly likely that he would keep the arrangement now; but on the other hand, it was possible that the two were not connected. If they could find the man who had sent the note, therefore, they might come across some valuable clue as to Blacklaw's other activities. They were both in agreement that it was by no means certain that the person in question would have heard of the murder. Their conclusion had been that if nothing transpired to make such a journey superfluous, they would make the trip to Henley.

They found themselves in a comfortable, if unpretentious, hotel less than a mile from King's Cross. It was Malone's plan to get down to work immediately. He hoped first to deal with the firm whose irregular accounts had contributed to the fall of Sloane and Simpson, before the weekend shutdown, during which traditionally it is impossible to find anyone in a position of responsibility. He asked Peagram for any information he could give about the firm.

"The company is called Cartwright and Sons, and, for a change, means exactly what it says. The original Cartwright is called Joshua and he started in a small way about forty years ago. He doesn't have too much to do with the place nowadays but still goes in occasionally to see how things are getting on. His wife died about five years ago. His elder son, Albert, did well at school and actually went to Oxford University, where he didn't do too well with his books but came out a bit better on the sporting side. Nothing brilliant, you understand, but he rowed for his college eight and that sort of thing. He now runs the outside part of the business—advertising, selling, finance, that sort of thing. The younger son, John, was always much keener on practical activities and left school as soon as he could to learn the business of the firm from the shop floor. They basically deal in wood. You can actually go along and buy planks off them, but their main line is high-class carpentry and cabinet making. They're said to be one of the last few places in the country where you can still buy first-rate hand-made furniture. You pay for it, mind, but it doesn't fall apart. They also do a small amount of metal work but that's mainly an adjunct to the furniture making."

"They sound like a very interesting firm. I wonder why they should want to cheat the income-tax. Och well, I suppose they don't like to see their profits disappearing any more than anyone else."

Malone rang up the firm and was told that Mr Cartwright would be quite happy to see him, if he wouldn't mind coming round to the premises. Malone confirmed that he would be there as soon as possible. Peagram left them with a car and driver and they were taken towards Stepney where Cartwright and Sons had their home.

When they entered the workshop, the first impression they had was of immense activity. They found themselves in a large barn of a building with piles of different woods of all shapes and sizes stacked at haphazard intervals. The level of noise from saws and lathes was almost deafening and there seemed to be people everywhere. It made Malone wonder what the wages bill of such a concern must be. It was by no means clear where they should go to find Mr Cartwright, and so they asked the first person they came across. He was a young black apprentice who was carrying a large pile of wood, and simply indicated that they should follow him. This they did, carefully avoiding all the hazards which appeared on the floor at irregular intervals. The youngster stopped in front of one of the lathes and shouted: "Here's the wood, Mr Cartwright, and there's two gentlemen here looking for you. They look like the police to me."

The man working the machine, who was clearly Mr John Cartwright, turned it off and came over to greet them.

"You must be the detectives who rang a short while ago. Please come to the office."

He led the way over another obstacle course towards the office. It was little more than a glass-panelled cubicle, stuck in the bottom right- hand corner, as if it was an intrusion on the real purpose of the workshop. There was already a secretary in this 'office', busily typing at a very small desk, and it seemed doubtful that all four of them would be able to fit into the confined space. Mr Cartwright solved this difficulty by telling the secretary that, as it was almost time to finish, she might as well go now. She thanked him, packed up with alacrity and left.

"Well, gentlemen, I hope you'll forgive the confined space, but it was always my father's view, and remains mine, that administration or whatever fancy word you want to use for it, was there to make the job easier, not the other way round, as it seems to be in most establishments nowadays. We therefore give as much space to that side of things as seems to be appropriate to its importance. Now what can I do for you?"

"We're investigating the death of a Mr Ronald Blacklaw, an accountant who was recently working in Edinburgh but, before that, in London. First of all, did you know him?"

"Ronald Blacklaw? No, can't say I remember the name. What makes you think I might have known him?

"Does the firm of Sloane and Simpson mean anything to you?"

"Oh, you're not dragging them up again, are you? I thought we'd finished with all that."

"Mr Blacklaw was an employee of Sloane and Simpson."

"Oh, I see. You know, that business just about finished my father. Until all that happened he was in here most days, taking over jobs for anyone who might be off sick and generally helping about the place; I mean helping too; he didn't just get in the way. Now we're lucky if he comes in once a week. Knowing how long they always take to look into finances, I'm always a bit worried in case there's some charge hanging over our heads. It's actually my brother Albert who looks after the financial side of the business and he insists that it was all the accountants' fault and we did nothing irregular. But as the faults were all to our benefit, I don't suppose the authorities will be inclined to believe that. In fact, when you rang, I was a little worried that it might be for something like that, especially when I heard your Scottish accent. Anyway, all I know about the matter is that we've got to find a considerable sum of money to satisfy the Inland Revenue. This has always been a very steady business, but our profit margins are small and, quite frankly, I don't know whether we'll be able to find it. Apart from any personal sentiment, I think that would be a great shame. As you may have noticed, we employ a lot of people and they all end up as first-rate craftsmen. My brother's solution to the problem is to sack half the workforce, but the result would be a big sacrifice in quality and I'm not at all sure I'd want to carry on in those circumstances. Still, it appears you're not really here to talk about that."

"Not specifically, but it was your connection with Sloane and Simpson which first put us on to you. Did you know another accountant called John Strachan?"

"No. As I said, my brother was the man who dealt with the firm's finances. Not that I think he would have spent any time seeing our accountants. My father, I know, never did. He just had the relevant figures sent to them. He always saw them as some sort of parasite on real working men and wanted as little to do with them as possible."

"Tell me, is it normal for you to be working the machines?"

"Certainly. I know it's not modern practice, and my brother wouldn't be seen dead doing it. But it's the way my father always acted and I followed his example. I don't normally have permanent projects on myself; but as I learned the business from the bottom, I can do every job in the place and, quite frankly, I think the men are more inclined to do a good job if they see that the so-called boss can do it as well as they can. At the moment, I'm filling in for a man called Fred Baldwin. He's stroke for Thames Tradesmen and, as you doubtless know, Henley Regatta's on at the moment. That's another thing I copied off my father; he always reckoned that it was his duty as an employer to encourage amateur sport, which really meant allowing men time off work when they needed it. His view, and mine, is that otherwise only the rich and those who go to universities have any chance of doing well in that sort of thing."

Malone certainly thought that the attitude of the Cartwrights was most commendable but he was very surprised at the mention of Henley Regatta. He decided to press the point. "Do you take much interest in rowing yourself, Mr Cartwright?"

"Not a great deal, but I usually try to get to Henley Regatta for the last day. My brother's far keener than I am; he used to do quite a bit of rowing when he was at university."

"Where do you usually watch the Regatta from?"

"Stewards' Enclosure. My brother usually supplies me with a badge."

Malone did not know how to pursue the point. If, by chance, the man making the appointment with Blacklaw had been John Cartwright, he would now know, if he had been unaware beforehand, that Blacklaw was dead, and there was no point in keeping the arrangement. He did not, however, dismiss the possibility that John Cartwright could have been involved in the murder. He therefore continued his questioning.

"I'm afraid we seem to be getting a little off the point. I would now like to ask you a very personal question and I realise that your answer may be a little unhelpful; I ask you, however, to remember that we are engaged in an investigation into a murder and a particularly unpleasant one at that. Can you think of anyone connected with this firm who might wish to take revenge on the firm of Sloane and Simpson for bringing you to the verge of financial collapse?"

"I hope you're being too dramatic about our position but it's certainly not good. I'm sure none of the employees has enough knowledge of our bank balance to realise quite how serious things could be. We had of course to tell them something about it but it won't help our quality or output if they think they're about to join the dole-queue. That leaves my father, my brother and myself. You'll have to take my word for it that we wouldn't dream of doing such a thing. My father, although a very fit man for his age, is hardly likely to be able. My brother wouldn't because, quite honestly, he wouldn't be that concerned if we did go to the wall. It might be a bit annoying to him to have to get another job but none of us have done too badly out of the firm over the years. In his case, too, his wife's rolling in the stuff and so he wouldn't have to bother about money anyway."

"Do you think your brother may have had any knowledge of what was going on at the accountants?"

"He said he hadn't and I've no reason to believe that's untrue. But I must admit that that would mean that he wasn't very well up with the real financial position of the firm, which, after all, is largely what he's paid for. You could probably blame him for lack of enthusiasm, but that's all. He's always been a bit of a believer in the theory that if you can get someone else to do the job, so much the better. He probably saw the accountants in that light and left it all up to them."

"You are, perhaps, being generous towards him, Mr Cartwright, but we'll let that pass for the moment. Could you give me the addresses of your father and brother?"

"Certainly. I'll write them down immediately. My brother's won't help you much at the moment, though. He normally stays with friends near Henley over the Regatta and I don't know the address offhand. My father might, I suppose."

"Thank you very much. I shall now have to ask you what you were doing on Wednesday evening."

"This last Wednesday? Well, my father always likes to celebrate the birthday of the firm and that was last Wednesday. We took the day off and I drove him into the country. We went down to Hampshire and stopped off to do a bit of coarse fishing. I suppose we got back some time after midnight."

"Can you prove this?"

"Prove it? My father will tell you the same but I suppose that wouldn't be good enough for you. The trouble is, we weren't looking for company, just for quiet. We did stop off in a pub in Basingstoke for a couple of pints on the way back, but as it was rather full, I'm not at all sure if they'd remember us."

"What was the name of the pub?"

"I honestly can't remember. My father might, but I doubt it. I think it was one of those common names like 'The White Hart' or 'The Red Lion'."

"Could you tell me exactly where you were fishing?"

"I suppose I could find it roughly on a map. We were just looking for somewhere quiet, where nobody would come up and tell us it was private."

"I shall have to ask your father if he can furnish more details. Could you tell me what sort of car you drive?"

"My own car's an Allegro but I've been having trouble with it recently and so I hired a car on Wednesday. As it was supposed to be a celebration, I decided to do things properly and hired an E-type. I can give you the name of the garage."

There was a knock on the glass of the office and a workman came in. "Oh yes," said Cartwright to his question, "just sign for it here." After he had signed, he was handed a tin of chemical of some kind. "Sorry for the interruption," said Cartwright, "but that contains potassium cyanide. I'm sure I don't need to tell you people how dangerous it is. It's used in the small amount of electroplating we do and we always try to make sure every bit is accounted for."

"Very dangerous, as you say. Who has access to it?"

"Nobody is allowed to use it without the express permission of my father, my brother or myself."

"You've never had any go missing?"

"Not to the best of my knowledge. I suppose it would be theoretically possible for somebody to claim they've used more than they really have, but I don't think it's likely."

"I see. You yourself were back here at work on Thursday morning, I presume?"

"Actually, no. I suffer badly from hay-fever and the trip into the country didn't help it at all. In fact, I could hardly see on Thursday morning. I have some pills to take and, after a good dose of them, I felt able to come in in the afternoon."

"I think that will be all for the moment, Mr Cartwright. Thank you for your time."

Malone and White threaded their way out of the workshop and returned to Scotland Yard to converse with Inspector Peagram. On the way, Malone said: "On the face of it, he seemed a pleasant, straightforward sort of chap but some of the coincidences were amazing. Blacklaw died of cyanide poisoning; the first person we interview down here has a ready supply of cyanide. We have a possible clue which leads us to Henley Regatta. The same man has a connection, and is even intending to be there. Blacklaw was murdered, presumably somewhere in Scotland, on the night of last Wednesday; the same man is at the time in possession of a very fast car, which could theoretically have taken him up there to do the deed. Furthermore, he admits to being absent from work on the Thursday morning, with the entirely possible reason of hay-fever; however, the red eyes caused by that affiliation could just as well have been the result of overtiredness from travelling. In fact, unless his father can prove some alibi for both of them, there's no earthly reason why John Cartwright should not have committed the murder."

"Aye, I'm sure it would be theoretically possible for such a journey to have taken place, but with all the traffic on the roads at this time of year, I shouldn't think it would be easy. You'd certainly need to see a total disregard of speed limits and that could be awkward if you don't want anyone to know where you've been. I suppose two reasons could be given for the murder in that case; first of all, John Cartwright was being blackmailed for some reason, and secondly the firm was heading towards possible bankruptcy. The birthday of the firm would then be a very appropriate time for carrying out the deed, but foolish if you wanted to avoid suspicion."

"Exactly so. That all holds together fairly well, except for the note. Why send that if you intended to put the man out of the way in the meantime? It could be so as not to arouse his suspicions but then surely arrival in person could be liable to a much more sinister interpretation. We must also remember that the car involved in the actual dumping of the body was not the same as the one hired, though of course another could have been hired or stolen for the final scene. We'd better find out if Edinburgh have any knowledge of stray E-types around on Wednesday night; at least it's the sort of car which someone might have noticed. Also we'd better find out if any such car was booked for speeding on the way up or down—whichever route they might have taken."

When they reached Inspector Peagram's office, he was amazed by the apparent luck that they had had at the first place they had visited. The main thing that bothered him in the case against John Cartwright was the travelling. He admitted to the belief shared by the majority of the Southern English that Scotland was not far short of the North Pole and, although he was willing to admit that such a journey was eminently possible, he had a strong feeling that it was unlikely. He pointed out that most people from his part of the world would feel the same way and would, therefore, be unlikely to try such a thing. Malone then asked him for some more information about the firm of Sloane and Simpson, especially the principals involved. He was informed that there had been two partners, by name Mr Braithwaite and Mr Cousins. Mr Braithwaite had retired to South Africa, he was informed, while Mr Cousins had suffered from a serious stroke after the demise of their firm and was still totally paralyzed down the right-hand side. A telephone call to Pretoria had soon established that Mr Braithwaite could not possibly have been in Scotland at the time in question. The only way these two could have been involved was through agents. No whisper had come through that any attempt had been made to hire men for such a murder. As Peagram pointed out, they did not hear about all such contracts but they did hear of a surprisingly large number. Add to this the fact that the circumstances the corpse was found in hardly looked like a professional job, and it looked as if Braithwaite and Cousins could be scrubbed from the reckoning. On the irregular accounts he was able to supply the information that one of the three parties, an elderly lady called Miss Euphemia Parkwood, had died just over a week ago. The only possible way I can connect her with the business, continued Peagram, "would be if she had some disappointed heirs, who found that the tax demands did not leave them with the legacy they were relying on. It's unlikely, but marginally possible, that they should want to take it out on an employee of the firm who frustrated their expectations. But again the peculiar circumstances surrounding the body seem to make that almost impossible."

"I agree. The only factor which seems to throw any suspicion that way is her recent death. I presume you are having the matter investigated, but unless we get a strong surprise from that direction, we can probably forget about it. There's one further thing I'd like you to do for me. Could you send some men to get any information they can about both Blacklaw and Strachan from the West Ealing Archery Club? It's some time now since they were both members there, but something might turn up. Now what about the third account?"

"Ah yes, Mr Connolly of Ealing. We have his address and a small amount of information about him here. It appears that he was an engineer abroad for about twenty-five years. He was from a perfectly well-to-do family but left home early to try his luck in Brazil. He became an engineer there. He prospered and afterwards was employed on pretty lucrative long-term contracts in Australia and Singapore. After that he was working in several different countries in Africa. He retired while still fairly young a few years ago, bringing back with him a small fortune. It's not at all clear how he managed to get his money out of some of the countries he was in latterly, as their currency restrictions should have made it impossible. It doesn't seem too surprising then if he was not too keen on paying it out to the government here. He lives on his own in a small house standing in its own grounds. He's known locally for being a bit batty but generally harmless. He's a fanatical model-maker and small-time inventor, and when he's deep in one of his projects, he's been known not to leave his house for days on end. When he's been on one of these work-periods, he tends to have a big blow-out in the local pub as soon as he's finished. He insists on telling everyone exactly how he's done the job, with details they can't of course understand, and does it even more exactly when things have gone wrong. They find him quite bearable there, as he's obviously aware of their general lukewarmness towards his experiences, and as a result, always provides plenty of drink for those willing to listen to him. There is nothing against him either in the local police station or on our records, except for the financial business at Sloane and Simpson's. And on paper, that was nothing really to do with him."

"I think perhaps White and myself should try to see him tonight. I'll give him a ring and see if he's available. From what you've been saying, it might be tactless to break in on him in the middle of some complex structuring of nuts and bolts, or whatever he makes things out of."

A few minutes later, Malone had arranged to visit Mr Connolly at his house in an hour's time. He had been subjected to a stereotyped routine, being informed that the country was becoming more of a police state every day, and that no longer was anyone allowed to spend their evenings without interruption from some official or other. It was a great pity that he, Malone, had nothing better to do with his life than carry out such policies. However, Mr Connolly had continued, as he was a good honest citizen, he had no desire to fall under suspicion in such a system and he was prepared to give them any assistance he could, as long as they didn't take up too much of his time. He was, after all, a busy man. He was at present designing a new golf club and could not be taken away from it for too long.

The Archer of Ceres

Mr Connolly's house stood in a quiet side-street and was itself of no great architectural interest, a property it held in common with the other buildings round about. The garden was laid out in an exact geometrical pattern and was kept in an immaculately tidy fashion to suit the lay-out. They rang the front doorbell several times but failed to get any response. They began to wonder what the next line of approach should be, when a first-floor window was thrust open with some force and a fair-haired, balding head wearing spectacles appeared. Mr Connolly—he was clearly the owner of the head—addressed them in a grudging voice.

"I suppose I'd better let you come in. You'll be the policemen who rang not long ago, I presume. It is a most inconvenient time to call and you certainly can't expect any hospitality when you call at this time without any proper advance warning. If you walk around the back, you'll find the door there open. Just walk straight in and up the stairs and you'll find me in the workshop. I don't really want to leave what I'm doing at the moment but I suppose I'll have to."

They followed his instructions and found themselves in Mr Connolly's workshop. It was extremely untidy, which was perhaps not surprising for a room which was, by all accounts, in so much use, but it provided a strange contrast with the garden outside. Wood and tools lay all around and there were a number of shelves which supported bottles of various liquids. There were also two lathes and a long workbench with vices attached to it at various intervals. Several gadgets which had been constructed from Meccano were in evidence, most noticeably a clock which hung from the wall above the bench. Mr Connolly now sat down at this bench and continued coating some pieces of wood with a particularly foul-smelling varnish.

"Well, what do you want to know from me?"

"Does the name Ronald Blacklaw mean anything to you?"

"Never heard the name to the best of my knowledge. Should I have?"

"He used to work for a firm of accountants called Sloane and Simpson."

"Oh, I see, you're wanting to bring that stuff up again, are you? Well, I'm saying absolutely nothing about it. The enquiry showed that the firm was totally to blame. Not that it did them much harm; they just retired on all their fat fees. We were the people who suffered, the ones who'd made the money. It's always the same. I got a hefty demand for non-payment of income-tax. But don't you worry, I'm fighting it and that's why I'm saying nothing. It makes me wonder why I bothered to work all my life. You know, I've been all over the globe and everywhere I used to maintain that this was the finest country in the World to live in. I worked in some of the most god-awful conditions and places you can imagine, just so that I could come back here and live in reasonable comfort. And what happens? The so-called government wants to take it all off me, telling me I don't deserve it. And what do they want to do with it? Give half of it to themselves and the rest to some riff-raff who wouldn't recognise a spade if you showed it to them. I might as well have sat on my backside in some warm office all my life, doing nothing except justify my pension by churning out mountains of wastepaper every day. You mark my words, I had a devil of a job getting most of my money back here, with the restrictions they have in some of the countries I've been in, and I assure you they won't find it that easy to steal it off me now. I don't blame the natives out in Africa for wanting to keep it there, they need it. But when I see what they do with it here, it makes me sick."

"I'm glad you're prepared to make your position on the matter so clear, Mr Connolly, but I'm not interested in that case as such at present. May I ask now if you knew the other clients of Sloane and Simpson who found themselves in the same position as yourself?"

"By chance, I used to buy wood from Cartwright and Sons, and still do, for that matter. They're a good honest firm who don't throw away their money on a lot of wastepaper. But I had no idea they had the same accountants until I heard some of the results of the enquiry. I can't even remember the old woman's name. Before you ask me, I've never had anything to do with Cartwright and Sons, except for buying wood off them and I don't suppose for a moment anyone in the firm knows me."

"How then can you make such a remark about the efficient administration of the firm?"

"Look, I'm not some weekend do-it-yourself type. I want to know what I'm dealing with when it comes to an important thing like quality of wood. I went to see what they dealt in before I bought any. When I found the standard was good, I continued ordering from them and I've no reason for being sorry. When I went there, I immediately got to speak to someone who knew what he was about and I wasn't palmed off with any smooth talk."

"Have you been to Scotland recently?"

"Scotland? No, whatever for?"

"You are quite sure you were not in Edinburgh on Wednesday evening?"

"I most certainly was not. Would you tell me why you are asking such absurd questions?"

"Ronald Blacklaw, whom I mentioned earlier, was murdered on Wednesday evening, probably in Edinburgh. Can you prove you were not there?"

"Good God, are you now trying to accuse me of murder?"

"Not at the moment, and if you can give me some simple proof that you could not have been anywhere near Edinburgh on the evening in question, the idea will not have to enter my head."

"Now you see why I tell you we're living in a police state? I stay here minding my own business and all that happens is that I'm accused of murdering someone in Edinburgh. Well, if it will keep you quiet and get you away from me, I'll tell you what I was doing, though I've no idea why I should. The average black in South Africa has to put up with less interference in his private life. You people, you know, are the agents of those traitors who want to drag the last vestiges of freedom and independence from the back of this land. It was those two things you know that made this tin-pot country the boss of half the world. Take those away, and you've got—what we're left with, a tin-pot country. Anyway, you see that mattress over there? That's where I sleep when I've got a job on. You see that cooker over there? I cook on that. In that way I don't have to interrupt my work for any longer than is strictly necessary. Well, I came in here on Tuesday morning and I didn't leave this room, except to go to the lavatory, until this afternoon, when I was satisfied that I had the job under control. And if I was in here all Wednesday, I couldn't have been in Edinburgh, could I?"

"Indeed not, if you really were here. Have you anyone who can substantiate your statement that you were here?"

"How the hell could I have, if I was here on my own? But no-one saw me anywhere else, you can be sure of that and there's plenty of people around who'll tell you that's how I operate when I've got anything important to do."

"Have you ever heard of a man called John Strachan?"

"No. Who's he supposed to be?"

"He used to work for Sloane and Simpson too."

"Look, I didn't know anyone who worked for that firm. I always did my business by post and, for the reason I gave you before, I'm saying nothing about that business. If you've got nothing else to talk about, perhaps you'll leave me in peace."

"As I said, I'm not interested in your accountants as such. Ronald Blacklaw's body was found in the grounds of the house belonging to John Strachan."

"Yes, in Edinburgh, but that's got nothing to do with me, if I was down here, has it?"

"Not in Edinburgh, in Ceres, near St. Andrews."

"You said he was murdered in Edinburgh before but as I wasn't in St. Andrews either, it makes no difference to me. Have you got any more contradictory statements to make?"

"There was nothing contradictory in what I said, Mr Connolly, but we'll let that pass. I must thank you for your information then."

Malone made towards the door and White joined him. Just as they were about to leave, Mr Connolly said: "Just a moment, did you say you were from St. Andrews?"

"No, I did not, but it happens that Constable White lives there."

"I wonder if you're trustworthy people? Tell me Mr White, do you play golf?"

"Aye, a bit."

"In that case, I'll take the risk and tell you what I'm working on. I've been designing a new driver. It's based on a rather complicated theory about the grain of certain woods. I wouldn't tell you about it, even if I thought you'd understand. There's far too many idlers around who want to take advantage of other people's inventions without me adding to them. Anyway, I made the first driver of this type this week and, if you know anything of golf, I'd like you to try it out. You'll be the first person except myself to do so."

White did not know how to refuse and, therefore, he followed Mr Connolly to the other side of the room. He was halted in front of a complicated structure of iron and wood which had a golf ball fixed in front of it.

"I designed this machine myself. It's much stronger than it looks, so there's no reason to be frightened of it. The dial there gives you a perfect idea of how far you'd drive the ball, and in what direction. I'd like you to try first with an ordinary club, and then with my new one. I shall hand it to you when you've finished with the normal one."

The 'normal' club which White had been handed was certainly not one which he would have used himself. It occurred to him that any reasonable club should produce a better result than this one. However, he carried out Mr Connolly's instructions and was not totally surprised to find that the result from his new club appeared better on the machine than his first effort.

"Well then, what do you think of that? I reckon it might revolutionise club making."

"Aye, it seems a pretty good club but it's difficult to have a proper idea until you've used it alongside your normal driver. I don't think I could give a proper opinion until I'd tried that."

"I like your Scottish reserve. You're quite right to be so cagey. Every week someone is bringing out some product or other which claims to be faster, cleaner, slower, dirtier or whatever suits them than the one they brought out last week. But in fact it's only the advertising that's cleaner or dirtier. D'you think I could get them interested in it in a place like St. Andrews?"

"I honestly wouldn't like to give an opinion. There's only one way to find out about that, and that's to try."

"Perhaps I shall; and anyway, I don't think you've seen enough of it to try to copy it yourself, even if you know how to. I still think policemen in this country are by and large an honest lot, despite your allegations, at least so far as stealing another man's invention goes. The great thing is that they can always be reported if they do a thing like that, and the newspapers always like stories on dishonest policemen, don't they? Yes, I'm sure I can trust you. You know, it may not be long before all the top golfers in the world are literally beating a path to my door to order one of these clubs. You know what I'll do then? I'll sell the secret to some big firm and come to some agreement with them that'll keep the taxman off my back. I don't mind telling you, because I'm sure I'll find some fool-proof method of doing it."

Malone was then asked if he would like the honour of trying the club and he thought it best to satisfy their host's whim. He again found it superior to the other club offered but was reminded of claims for the standards of modern educational achievement: it purely depended what you made comparisons with. He therefore made a similar non-committal remark to White's and thanked Mr Connolly for giving him this rare opportunity. Apart from anything else, he hoped to have gained some of the inventor's confidence by this approach. His aim seemed to be successful for Mr

Connolly said: "I must thank you for your opinions. They're clearly worthwhile, as you've made no attempt to flatter me and I know as well as you do that there are clubs on the market superior to the one I gave you first. It's much better at accentuating the advantages of my new design, and that's why I make comparisons with it. As you have been honest with me, I'm prepared to tell you anything else you might want to know."

"As you offer, Mr Connolly, there are two things I would like to know about you. Firstly, do you go to Henley Regatta?"

"Never have and I've no real intention of going, unless I hear of a new design in boats which seems worth a look. I'm more interested in the boats themselves than the people rowing them, you see. Not that I mind for a minute anyone enjoying themselves in whatever way they want, as long as they don't interfere with me. The only sport I ever took part in was golf, and then not much of that."

"Thank you. Secondly, do you have any dangerous poisons about your workshop here?"

"I've got some potassium cyanide somewhere. I use it in a certain photographic process. There's nothing unusual in it. And I signed for it at the chemist's. If you don't want to believe that, you don't have to but I'm not giving you the name of the chemist. Ah, I see, your Blacklaw, or whatever his name was, was poisoned and you're trying to find some of the stuff on me. You're not the only people who are allowed to make deductions, you know. But as I was nowhere near St. Andrews, you can't try to pin it on me."

Malone realised that he would get no further with Mr Connolly once he had returned to this frame of mind and so he took his leave, while White thanked him again for the opportunity to test out the new driver.

"Well, White," said Malone as they were driven away from the residence of Mr Connolly, "I think we've seen enough people for today and in many ways we've been very lucky. We have been able to dismiss the two partners of Sloane and Simpson from our reckoning, except on the most unlikely ground that they may have hired assassins for the job. Miss Parkwood similarly has probably been disposed of. On the other hand, we seem to have some positive indications that we're on the right track. Neither John Cartwright nor his father, unless they can produce some more evidence, have any proof that they were not in Scotland on Wednesday evening. We have also established a link between them and Henley Regatta and have discovered that they have access to a ready supply of cyanide. Mr Connolly similarly does not appear to be able to account for his movements satisfactorily on Wednesday evening and he too admits to having cyanide in his possession. It's very difficult to know what to make of his supposed deduction, that cyanide was the cause of Blacklaw's death. I had made sure not to mention it by name myself. On the other hand, his apparent inability to distinguish between the place of death and that of finding the body seemed perfectly genuine. What would you say to a combination of John Cartwright and Mr Connolly as the murderers, with old Cartwright there as an alibi for his son?"

"I'm afraid I don't really see that we've got any more on them than we have on Strachan, except perhaps for the availability of cyanide; but you know as well as I do how easily somebody could get hold of it if he really wanted to."

"True, but Strachan certainly can't have done it on his own. We should remember that two is a minimum number for the murderers as well; it could easily be a joint effort by more. At least by the circumstances of the killing, it seems that we're not dealing with a homicidal maniac and the only other person in any possible danger would be Strachan. With the forewarning he's had, I think he ought to be able to cope with any such attempt and so we shouldn't need to be in a desperate hurry. As usual, it might be easier to keep harassing all those we have any suspicions against, in the hope that they'll make a false move. They usually do. It is always a possibility that the second man had no actual connection with Blacklaw but was used for the occasion by someone who did. It would seem a rather peculiar thing to do if blackmail is at the bottom of it, as it would lay the person open to another area for being squeezed. The trouble is that, when otherwise reasonable people get out on this sort of caper, they don't always act rationally."

"None of the people we've come across so far seem to be the type to know people who would come on such a jaunt as this with them and, as you say, they'd be leaving themselves open for trouble afterwards, so I think our former assumption—if we ever actually made it—that they both knew him, is more likely."

"I agree. I'm just trying to float possibilities. I think we should give it up for today; I at any rate am beginning to feel pretty weary. Tomorrow first thing we'll go and see Cartwright senior. I realise that'll give his son plenty of time to prime him on his story, but the willingness with which he divulged the address suggests that has been done already or, of course, young John was telling the truth in the first place. After that we could get in a sporting mood for Henley Regatta. We might as well follow up that clue while we're down here. Well, we'd better see what Peagram has for us before we retire."

Peagram did not have anything, as he put it, calculated to set the Thames on fire, but there was one piece of information which was being pursued.

"You'll never guess, he said, "what Albert's wife's maiden name was. Don't try. I'll tell you. Parkwood."

Armed with this additional information, Malone and White, in a spirit of research and education, sampled one or two of the local London brews before returning to their hotel.

ꝗ Chapter 5

AS USUAL, WHEN HE WAS ON A DEMANDING CASE, Malone got up early. He by no means liked doing so but, in the event, never found it any worse than if he rose later. As White always found it difficult to sleep long after dawn, he had long since been up and dressed and had even taken a walk by the time Malone surfaced. They had a long leisurely breakfast over the newspapers and then made preparations to visit the founder of Cartwright and Sons. Malone was well aware that lying in bed late in the morning was usually a habit of younger people and, therefore, did not expect Joshua Cartwright to rise late. He was not on the telephone and so they did not warn him of their impending arrival.

He lived in a very modest flat about a quarter of a mile from the premises of Cartwright and Sons. The environment and the external condition of the building he inhabited were a bit of a surprise to them both. As they were well aware of some facts about the financial position of the firm he had founded, it was clear to them that he could, in the past at least, have afforded something distinctly more grandiose and salubrious. They mounted some rather dirty stairs and knocked on the door which bore his name. It was opened almost immediately by a middle-sized, fit-looking man, whom they would certainly not have placed in his sixties, had they not been aware of his true age. He did not appear to be greatly surprised by his visitors' arrival.

"Good morning, Mr Cartwright. I'm Inspector Malone of the Fife CID and this is Constable White. I'm sorry to call on you in this unexpected manner but, as your name did not appear in the telephone book, I had little option. I wonder if you could give us a little of your time?"

"Certainly. Actually, I've been half expecting you anyway. My younger boy came round after you'd been seeing him and told me you'd asked for my address. I don't suppose you'd done it for fun. Please come in."

They were conducted into a shabby sitting-room, which was dominated by a large television set. From the few things that John Cartwright had said about his father, Malone knew that the older man was a widower and this was clearly to be seen. At any rate, there was no evidence of the tidiness generally associated with a female presence.

"Yes, I never liked telephones. I found I was always being interrupted in the middle of some job which needed my whole attention. It got so bad sometimes that I couldn't even start some jobs for fear of being stopped at the wrong point. Of course, that was in the days before I could afford a secretary to deal with that sort of thing. But even when I did employ one, I always connected that ringing with some problem I'd have to sort out afterwards. That's why, even if I had to put up with one at work, I never had a telephone in the house. A lot of people told me I was sure to be losing orders over it but at least I didn't go bonkers."

"If you've been talking with your son, I presume you'll have a pretty good idea of what brought us down here. We're investigating the death of one Ronald Blacklaw who was murdered in the East of Scotland on Wednesday night. Mr Blacklaw used to be an employee of Sloane and Simpson and that is the reason for our interest in your firm."

"Yes, so I gathered. If you don't mind me saying so, I never understood why anyone would want to go up there in the first place. All cold and mountains and heather and, I suppose, football hooligans as well. Give me the heart of London—although they seem to be trying their best to knock that heart out of it. Most people I used to know round here either got pushed out or, if they could afford it, left before they were given the shove. I hope they'll let me stay here until the day I die. It may suit some of the younger people to go and live in big towers or natty suburbs but not me and my kind. And I couldn't stand living in the country either. It's a wonderful place to go on trips to but it always seems a very lonely place to live."

"Had you ever heard of Mr Blacklaw?"

"No. Not until my son mentioned him."

"Or John Strachan, who recently worked for the same firm?"

"No."

"Could you tell me why you had your accounts dealt with by Sloane and Simpson?"

"It was quite a long time ago now. I was really always a man to get on with the job and I was always annoyed about all the money I seemed to have to pay out for this, that and the next thing. I was never all that much good with figures and so when an old friend of mine told me how much money they'd managed to save him, by claiming on lots of different things, you know, I thought I'd let them have a shot at my money too. It seemed a very good arrangement, as they were very surprised I wasn't claiming on a lot of things. When they let me know what could be done, I felt a bit of a fool, to tell you the truth. But I never could understand these forms you get sent out to you. Between you and me, I don't think we're supposed to be able to. That way the government makes a lot more off us. After that, I just left my money matters up to the accountants."

"What was your reaction when you found out that they had been presenting false figures to the Inland Revenue?"

"It was a great shock to me, to tell you the honest truth, and I don't know what I'd have done without my son,

Albert. You see, I've always believed in honest trading and, to have this happen right at the end, makes it look as if there might have been something fishy all along. I know it's only the taxman and they'll take anything they can off you, but it's still dishonest. You see, I was always known for not overcharging people, and that was one of the reasons I always got orders when some others were finding things difficult. I always had a lot of business overseas, especially in America, and that was before Albert went out of his way to expand the foreign side. He said you have to nowadays and I expect he's right. There's hardly anyone left over here who can afford quality nowadays and we always dealt with quality. Anyway, Albert tried to make me see things in a less depressed way. It is, after all, very easy to make mistakes with all these new tax-laws they keep bringing out, especially if you're doing what you can to save your clients' money."

"Did you ever suspect that your elder son might have known what Sloane and Simpson were doing on your behalf before the matter came to light?"

"I hope no son of mine would connive at that sort of thing: I always tried to bring them up to be honest. To tell you the truth, I did wonder a bit at first. It's easy to see how anyone could get sick and tired of all the money we had earned being taken off us to be poured down some drain. It's not natural and it's not fair either. It reminds me of the tale they used to tell us at school about Procrustes and his bed. You know, if anyone's too big for the bed you cut them down to fit it, and if anyone's too small, you stretch them out until they fit. It always seemed a bit stupid and unlikely but, as far as I can see, that's exactly what they're trying to do to us at the moment. So, as I was saying, I did wonder about Albert at first but, when I asked him straight out, he said he hadn't known anything about it. And I'm not going to call any son of mine a liar unless I have to."

"Perhaps you're right, Mr Cartwright. But you know, I find it hard to believe that an old respectable firm like Sloane and Simpson should risk—and in the event lose—their reputation and livelihood, just to benefit the financial position of your business. It would seem on the face of it far more likely that one of you would either provide them with false information in the first place, or could offer them a considerable financial inducement to bring about the state of affairs which actually existed. Is it possible that your younger son would have been involved in any such plan?"

"I'm unlikely to start accusing my own sons of any dishonesty, you know. But, anyway, there's not really a chance. I could almost see him doing that sort of thing if he thought it had to be done to save the firm. He's even more fond of it than I am, if that's possible. But he wouldn't have had the chance if he had wanted to. John's always made sure the job was done and, like me, he was never that keen on figures. That's why Albert dealt with all that side of the business. I'm quite lucky they were both so different, you know. Ever since we got large enough to need someone full-time on sales and publicity, Albert's been dealing with it all. There's a lot of people, and Albert's one of them, who think that's a far better job than being in the workshop all day. But John wouldn't change positions with him for anything. Albert would hate to be in the workshop all day, but with his connections, he's very good at the other side. So you see, as Albert would be dealing with the accountants and not John, John couldn't have done anything wrong even if he'd wanted to."

"Perhaps you are right, Mr Cartwright. Tell me, when you talk about Albert's connections, what exactly do you mean?"

"You're a bit personal, aren't you? Still, the quicker I convince you that there's nothing wrong with my sons, the quicker you'll leave us alone. I'll give you an example. A few years ago we needed rather a big sum of money for replacing old equipment. I'd been very lucky when I was young and got a good lot of second-hand machinery cheap; I built up most of the rest of our equipment in the same way. Good as it all was, and much better quality than you usually have to put up with these days, it wasn't going to last forever. Also the designs of a number of things—though not half as many as the advertisers would try to make you believe—have improved a lot since I first bought. The trouble is then, if you decide to replace some things, you find you have to replace a lot more others. With this decimal stuff or metric or whatever it's called, coming in, we thought we'd better renew almost everything. Well, with interest rates what they were, we didn't know exactly how we should raise the money, but Albert decided to look into it. It turned out that one of his sporting pals was high up in just the right sort of business, so he managed to get the stuff with plenty of time to pay. we bought direct from the maker, you see, with a pretty hefty order at that."

"You're quite sure that it was only the firm that benefited financially from the deal?"

"I suppose you're trying to suggest now that Albert could try to cheat the rest of his family? I can tell you he wouldn't. If you're not convinced, I don't mind telling you that his wife's got so much money they don't need to go around getting more in any sly way like that."

Both Malone and White were well aware that possession of money by a wife was the last thing to guarantee such behaviour by her husband and many relevant cases sprang to their minds. However, in the circumstances, Malone thought that it would be neither polite not advantageous to mention this fact to Mr Cartwright senior.

"I understand that we're unlikely to catch Mr Albert Cartwright at home at the moment?"

"No chance of it. He's gone with his wife to stay with some cousin of hers near Henley. They always go and stay somewhere near there when the Regatta's on. I can't tell you the address straight off but I could find it out if you really want to know it."

"Thank you very much but I think we can obtain such information if we find it necessary. I believe you were with your son John in Hampshire on Wednesday evening?"

"Yes. He told me you were asking about that. And before you ask there's no way I can think of we can prove it. I don't think anyone saw me until after lunch time on Thursday, either. You see, it was a bit of a nostalgic time, celebrating the birth of the firm and it's not the sort of thing you tend to bring outsiders into. And I suppose that's especially true after our recent troubles."

"I believe you yourself still go along sometimes to give a hand in the workshop?

"Not so much now. Just like my boy John still does, I used to be in every day, unless there was something really important to stop me. But I haven't had the same heart for it ever since that business with the accountants. I think I'm just as fit and capable as I was but I haven't got the urge any more. It may simply be old age catching up with me, if I was willing to admit it. I certainly was too old-fashioned for this modern way of business they have nowadays. If Albert hadn't taken over the finances, I think there's probably a good chance we'd be in a decline now. It's mainly all the wages we have to pay to keep the same quality in the products. As Albert kept pointing out to me, quality on its own is no good for people in this day and age. You have to persuade them that you really are offering what you claim. It was sad to me to think that crafty advertising and what they call aggressive selling was better than making something good, but we've done more business ever since we started that line. I think it was that as much as anything which made me think of packing up but it was this trouble with the accountants that really decided me."

"I can understand that it must have been very hard for you. Do you still have access to whatever stores you should want there?"

"I'd normally mention it to John if I wanted anything so that he wouldn't think it had gone missing but, as I said, I'm not often there now."

"The same could be said of your elder son, I suppose?"

"Of course. We own the ruddy place don't we?"

"Yes indeed. Thank you very much for your co-operation, Mr   Cartwright. We can see ourselves out. Goodbye."

They left the elder Mr Cartwright's residence and began the journey back to Scotland Yard. They took a fairly long time over this, as is bound to happen in London, especially on a Saturday morning, when so many motorists seem to play a vehicular version of the game of seeing how many people can be stuffed into a telephone kiosk.

"Well, White, you haven't had much to say for yourself. What do you make of Mr Joshua Cartwright?"

"I haven't said much because there hasn't really been anything to say. He seemed to be a fairly straightforward man who has worked hard all his life but is not particularly interested in coming to terms with some of the changes that would be forced on him if he stayed in the front line of business. I suspect that the way he kept going off at a tangent was not so much the wandering of an old man, but a method of indicating that he was not too keen on being interrogated either about the finances of the firm or the part his sons may have played in them. I'd say that there was certainly more to the Cartwrights than meets the eye but that doesn't necessarily mean they've got anything to do with our business or any other illegal matter at all."

"Very much the impression I got but I'll go a little further. I'm almost certain that old Mr Cartwright suspects that his son Albert was well aware of what was going on at Sloane and Simpsons. You don't build up a successful business from scratch if you're quite so ignorant of the financial side as he pretends to be. But, as you say, that doesn't mean we're any nearer finding out if they had any reason to get rid of Blacklaw, unless we fall back on the blackmail theory. I think it's important to remember that that's only a theory which was first put into our heads by a man who must be considered as under suspicion. The only shred of evidence we've had to support that explanation is the cryptic note sent to Blacklaw in Edinburgh. If we hadn't had any such idea in our minds at the time, we might well have interpreted it in a totally different way. The only field I can see where blackmail could have been used with effect is if Albert was fiddling his father and brother to a pretty hefty extent and Blacklaw had proof of this. But from the old man's indulgent attitude towards him, I can't see why Albert should be driven to murder over it."

"Should we be making more of the presence of the arrow? Even if, as seems reasonably likely, the way the body was left was a theatrical stunt to put us on the wrong foot, it does at least indicate that the murderers knew of Blacklaw's connection with archery and, almost certainly, Strachan's too. It's still very possible that the Sloane and

Simpson connection between the two men is a red herring, and the real link is in their common interest in archery. For all we know, the murderers are a couple of irate husbands from Dunfermline who found out that Blacklaw and Strachan were messing about with their wives. After all, we only have Strachan's word that he had not seen Blacklaw since London."

"That, or something like it, has always been a strong possibility and, if it is so, I'm sure McGregor and his men will ferret out something to point in that direction. If it could be shown that the planting of the body on the same day as Strachan's proposed toxophilists' jamboree was not purely fortuitous, that would strengthen the archery angle greatly. My view, I must say, is that it was fortuitous, except in so far as it might have given Strachan the chance of operating in the absence of his family. But why is it that everyone we see down here appears to be so suspicious? We have visited three people and, lo and behold, we find that they all have easy access to cyanide and none of them has a satisfactory alibi for Wednesday night. I suppose that is not unlikely enough in itself for people living on their own; but then we find that they can't account for Thursday morning either. I know there must be hundreds of other people in London in the same position but why do we pick on three in a row?"

"What about the car the Cartwrights hired? Can we find out if anyone saw it down here when we might assume it was in Scotland?"

"Peagram will be checking on that and also the exact time it was returned to the garage. Hopefully, we might find out how far the Cartwrights travelled in it as well. That will not necessarily tell us anything, as they could of course have changed cars at some point. But it would certainly be a strong indication one way or the other."

"Are we still planning to visit Henley Regatta this afternoon?"

"I see no reason not to. Unless some surprising information is in Peagram's hands at this moment, it would be the most constructive thing to do. We'll have managed to arrange badges for the Stewards' Enclosure by now. We also need a car with a driver. If by chance anything does turn up and we need to leave in a hurry, we'd look pretty foolish if we didn't have transport ready. The driver is necessary because, if we fall in with the spirit of things, we might find ourselves above the legal limit. I must say, if by chance any startling news is in from either Peagram or McGregor, I wouldn't be too disturbed about giving Henley a miss. I can't see that we can really hope to gain much from being in the vicinity of the Fawley Bar at four, even if this is the day referred to and we have the correct interpretation of the message. On the other hand, it's some time since I've been to the Regatta and I rather enjoy it. We'll see what happens when we get back to Scotland Yard."

"I suppose it's always possible that the writer of the note will keep the appointment, even if he's heard of Blacklaw's death. There's a chance that he would send an agent, who might possess the same hypothetical information as Blacklaw himself. The fact that he was poisoned suggests that he was not questioned on such a possibility, or I'm sure he'd have been on his guard against the administration of cyanide. If that is so, our man may have the same idea for the agent as he had about Blacklaw and could even be carrying the poison for the purpose on him."

"That's within the bounds of possibility, White, but it assumes a great number of things, none of which are more than the merest conjecture. But you could say that about most of what we appear to have to go on. Let's see what, if anything, Peagram has to offer us."

They had arrived back at Scotland Yard and made their way to Peagram's office. Inspector Peagram was himself there and from his manner of greeting, they held out no great hope of any new discoveries. The facts confirmed his manner.

"I hope you two have made more progress than I have. I've sent men to cover the West Ealing archery club but the only report they've managed is to the effect that they don't expect to get much information immediately. For the start the number of members who were around at the same time as both Blacklaw and Strachan is not too great. Of these, over half are away on holiday and some of the others are by no means regulars any longer, and may take some time to trace. People are well known in such clubs as elsewhere, for not providing information of changes of address. Still, they're doing what they can. One point that can be made at this stage is that none of the people you've been interviewing so far is, or ever has been, a member; furthermore, no one my men have so far contacted has heard of any of them.

Malone agreed that there was nothing of great moment in this information and pointed out that he himself was faring no better. He then turned his attention to some reports from Edinburgh. There was, to begin with, a little more on the arrow. The experts there considered that it was highly unlikely that it was ever made to be fired from a bow, and tended to the view that its purpose was ornamental. As there was no indication of a maker or provenance on it, it seemed a plausible theory that it had either been made abroad or privately. Peagram suggested that the Cartwrights or Connelly could have manufactured it privately. White pointed out that it might be the sort of souvenir a retiring colonial might bring back with him; they were all agreed that it was most surprising that the cyanide, the Wednesday night and now the arrow could all be connected with their London suspects. Malone continued: "Of course, for all we know the arrow belonged to Blacklaw and the murderers removed it from his flat. It could always be some trophy, or part of one, which he won in some competition. That might even explain the lack of a maker's mark. We shall have to check that possibility. It could be that Miss Adamson knows of such an article. She may never have been in his flat, but, as yet, we know of no-one else who was on visiting terms with him."

There was also information about the Dunfermline Archery Club. Nobody had been found there who was close to Blacklaw; he was known as a first-rate practitioner at the sport, but was considered a trifle standoffish. Kinder spirits put this down to shyness, others to arrogance. All the other leads, such as the blue Cortina and the possibility of stray fast cars from London, were getting no further forward.

When he had finished with these reports, Malone asked Peagram about Miss Parkwood's relatives.

"I'd better deal with Albert's wife first. Like the other heirs she was a great-niece, and like them she's supposed to be pretty comfortable in her own right. None of them expected any great legacy. They had no reason to believe their great aunt was poor, but had assumed that inflation over the last few years would have reduced her means to a very modest level."

"If Albert was in cahoots with Blacklaw," said Malone, "he could have had a better idea of her real financial position."

"That's possible, but they all appear to have cast-iron alibis for Wednesday night, though to be fair Mrs Cartwright's is only supported by her husband. There are one or two other things I might mention. We checked airports and no-one answering the descriptions of either the Cartwrights or Connolly flow to Scotland on Wednesday. Theoretically disguises could have been used but, unless we know what sort of disguises, we can't go much further on that line. There are no reports of speeding offences which seem to have any relevance to our case from the police on the way up to Scotland—or down for that matter. The garage from which John Cartwright hired the car is again no help. He returned the car on the Thursday, around lunchtime. They have no record of how far he went in it. It seems a bit surprising, but people are so often much more slip-shod than you would normally think. They probably also keep as few records as possible, for the obvious tax reason. We're trying other car-hirers on the off-chance that the first hire was a blind but there are so many of them, it's a pretty hopeless task. If they're big hirers, it's unlikely that they'll remember any individual customer anyway. There are so many people hiring cars for holidays at this time of year it makes it all that much more difficult. That's the reason we haven't really bothered with trains—I can't see much chance of our men being recognised at this time of year."

"Could you try trains anyway? There may have been some unlikely circumstance which could have made them recognisable. They'd have to be very foolish for that to happen but always there's the possibility of something outside their control taking place. I say 'their' but of course there's no reason why there should be more than one of them for this end—if anybody at all. Well, if we consider our position at the moment, it doesn't look very advanced, does it? We have a body, which was undoubtedly murdered. We know it belongs to one Ronald Blacklaw. It was found in the grounds of a man who knew him in London. The victim was murdered elsewhere—we don't know exactly where but Edinburgh is probably a good guess. We know that at least two men deposited it where we found it in Ceres. They were reasonably fit men of average, or slightly above average, physique. They knew of Ronald Blacklaw's connection with archery. They were almost certainly not professional killers but had a very cold view towards what they were doing with the deceased's body. We have so far come across four men who look as though they could have been involved. If Strachan is one of the guilty men, he couldn't possibly have been acting on his own and I think we can assume that he was not one of the poisoners—we should have heard by now if his Perthshire alibi would not stand up for the time of the actual murder. Any, or indeed all, of the other three, the two Cartwrights and Connolly, could have acted with him. They also had easy access to potassium cyanide and could with no difficulty have manufactured the arrow found in the body. Although any combination of the three could be involved, if one Cartwright is in it, the other must be an accessory. The trouble is that we have absolutely no evidence that any of our three men were out of the South of England at the time in question and no positive evidence to connect them with Ronald Blacklaw."

"I think," said White, that we should not totally forget Mr Reid. There was one thing I found rather suspicious about him: the police did not manage to contact him at his house. I'm sure he had a satisfactory explanation for this, but I still find it surprising. I must admit, though, that it's not easy to think of any reason why he should want to get rid of Blacklaw."

"We're paid to be suspicious so we won't lose sight of him—and Miss Adamson too, if you want to include her. It strikes me that there's one useful piece of information I haven't got yet and that's whether Mr Connolly has a car and, if so, what sort. Can that be found out swiftly, Inspector Peagram?"

"It already has been. Perhaps I should have mentioned it but it didn't seem worthwhile. Neither Connolly nor the elder Cartwright have cars and, as you probably know, John Cartwright has only the one, an Allegro, and a pretty aged one at that. In the case of the Cartwrights it's an irrelevancy, as we know that they were in possession of a car which could easily have taken them to Scotland and back in the time available. I can also tell you that neighbours of the Cartwrights can neither confirm nor deny their version of their movements on Wednesday night. You have noticed that your Edinburgh Mr Reid hasn't got a car either?"

"No, I hadn't; I must have missed that. Thanks for pointing it out. It certainly makes any simple link between him and Strachan appear unlikely. Still, we must remember that he could have hired, borrowed or stolen one for the occasion. He could have done the last two even if he didn't possess a license. Do we know if he did?"

"That information hasn't been given us. But as you say, the possession or lack of possession of a license wouldn't necessarily cut him out, just make him less likely if he didn't have one."

"As I remember from the report, we're no nearer blue Cortinas which are likely to have been involved. Two stolen in Glasgow on the Wednesday, one of which was found in Largs and the other in Edinburgh. The last, though a theoretical possibility, showed no signs to the experts which might indicate it was used. As yet, hiring firms in the Edinburgh area have nothing to offer. They've probably covered them all, too. No, I can't see what more we can do except wait for something to turn up from the enquiries already in progress. I think White and myself might as well go to Henley Regatta on the slight hope that something might transpire from the clue there. We'll be in close contact with the police in Henley, so don't hesitate to let us know if anything of importance turns up. Quite frankly, I don't expect we'll be doing much there except enjoying the racing and generally amusing ourselves; there's no reason to have any compunction about bringing us back here."

6❧ Chapter 6

"WELL, WHITE," SAID MALONE, as they were being driven in the direction of Henley, "even if nothing turns up, we should at least have a pleasant afternoon—at least I will and I don't see why you shouldn't as well. It's a good number of years since I was at the Regatta and I'm looking forward to it. Although we shall be fairly obviously non-rowing men from our clothing, we should be able to mingle fairly well with others of that ilk on the Saturday afternoon. The genuine article usually wear their old rowing blazers to prove it, and there are doubtless others who wear similar gear to try to look as if they are the genuine article. I should point out that some of them might strike you as a bit like Tenniel's drawings of Tweedledum and Tweedledee, if you know them, but somehow that fits in very well when you're there. And as I say, being the Saturday, a large proportion of those present will be social visitors anyway."

"Henley Regatta is a marvellous occasion for several reasons. Apart from the obvious fact that the standard of living is as high as you'll find anywhere else in the world, I've often had the impression that it's one of the last genuine sporting gathering left. The basis of this is probably the fact of the amateur nature of the entry but it's also something more than that. If you're a dyed-in-the wool cynic, or social leveller, you'll probably think that the Stewards' Enclosure is some hangover from Edwardian days, but if you simply look at it the way it is, you're more likely to decide that it's one of the last resting places of British civilization. Then look at it from the professional view of us policemen. As well as the vast crowd in the more expensive enclosures, there are people lining the river bank right up to the start. I've no idea how many people there are there on the

Saturday but they'd certainly make a good size football crowd. Again, both in the Enclosures and along the bank, a lot of alcohol is shoved down various throats and there is a fair amount of partisanship about certain crews. Yet for all that, there is almost never the slightest sign of antisocial behaviour and most people go home at the end of the day in a better frame of mind than when they arrived. Compare that with Ibrox, or even Murrayfield nowadays for that matter."

"As you know, I don't know much about it but I've always had the impression that it's rather posh—a bit like Ascot, if you know what I mean, though I don't know what that's like either. It makes me wonder if I might be conspicuous for other reasons than my clothes."

"I'm sure you'll find the general carry-on in the Stewards' Enclosure rather strange to begin with and, if you make a judgement purely on the way people speak, you'll certainly feel a bit out of it. But I shouldn't be too concerned; you have the great advantage of being a Scotsman and a fairly well-spoken one too. Generally, in social gatherings, the Scotsman has a great advantage over his English counterpart. Unless he's verging on the illiterate, there's no way of assigning him to a handy social slot on the way he speaks alone, something which can be done with a fair degree of accuracy among Englishmen. Also, probably as a result of the history of Scottish education, the average Englishman, for some unaccountable reason, considers seriously every statement which drops from the mouth of the Scot. You could easily manufacture a general rule: if you want to talk drivel, always talk in a Scottish accent and you will be listened to. If you still insist on feeling inferior, may I point out that in any sporting gathering you have a great advantage over myself. I know you've lost your scratch handicap and are down to one, but I'm sure you're well aware that there aren't many people walking the streets or the Stewards Enclosure who can match that. A St. Andrews handicap makes it even more impressive. You may have to be careful that you don't agree to play rounds on half the courses in the South of England before the day is out. Anyway, you'll need to remember that we're down here on a job. Just keep in mind that most people are there purely to enjoy themselves and a first-rate occasion of amateur sport, and, as an excellent practitioner in that field yourself, you have no reason to be disturbed. The only difficulty I can foresee, is if something does turn up in the Fawley Bar and we find it necessary to cause a scene there; as I was suggesting, it's not the sort of place where scenes usually occur. But I am fairly confident that if any such thing did happen, we'd be guaranteed immediate assistance from every quarter, as long as we made it clear what side we were on."

They passed the rest of the journey admiring the different shades of green of the countryside they were passing through, all the more impressive after the acres of man-made colours which make up the vast area of London. Here and there an autumn hedge held a rigid line, or a cup of barren trees broke the gentle leafy contours to indicate starkly where the epidemic of Dutch elm disease had left its mark. Despite that, the general impression was one of peace and calm after the hectic life of the metropolis. It was not difficult to appreciate why John Cartwright should bring his father out in this sort of direction for a birthday treat, and easy to imagine them going somewhere quiet to dangle a hook in a quiet stream for a few hours before returning to the large conurbation they considered their natural home. The number of people with the same idea on Wednesday night must indeed have been vast, and the likelihood of the Cartwrights being remembered in a busy pub in Basingstoke seemed sufficiently remote.

When they arrived in Henley, their first port of call was Henley Police Station. Prior warning of their impending presence had of course been sent, but it seemed to Malone not only polite but also sensible to make themselves known to some of the local men before going about their business. He also had no intention of spending too long at the station, as clearly at this time it would be a very busy place indeed. After a brief stop, therefore, during which time they were offered every assistance, with the proviso that it might not be as immediate and efficient as they would normally like because of the enormous upheaval caused by the Regatta, Malone and White made their way towards the Stewards' Enclosure. Their driver had been instructed to park in the Enclosure car park, in a position which would allow a speedy departure if it should prove necessary.

The streets of Henley were bright with decorations and the elegance of women of all ages. The sun shone brightly down upon them and the men who accompanied them, dressed in the sporting manner thought fit for the occasion. White was immediately reminded of Malone's reference to the Edwardian era but found after a short while that the whole style and appearance of the people seemed to blend with the weather and the atmosphere of the town and the river which rippled and glistened under the sun's rays. Malone thought that White should have a look at some boats before entering the enclosure, and so they turned sharp left along the side of the river after ambling across the crowded bridge. On their right, the Leander Club exhibited a substantial number of jolly-looking people, many bearing pint mugs in their hands. He pointed out the pink colour of the ties and socks of the members of the club and White, falling in with the spirit of the occasion, observed that in many cases, they were a good match for their owners' faces, which, he was sure, had not all gained their rosy complexion from the brilliance of the sun. They passed by the boat tents and, after being held up for a while to allow a couple of crews to carry their craft down to the river, proceeded along a dusty track towards the Stewards Enclosure.

Before they had time to gain their objective, a policeman in shirt-sleeve order, but still wearing the helmet which Scotsmen always find so strange to behold, approached them and said: "I presume you'll be the detectives from Scotland. I won't hang around you any longer than is strictly necessary, as I'm sure you don't want everyone to suspect you for what you are, but please remember that if you're in any need of assistance there's always one of us at least around here, and more within easy call."

"Good heavens, are we that obvious? True, we've made no effort to imitate intrepid oarsmen but I thought that we could at least pass for members of the general public."

"Well, I couldn't swear that I'd have noticed you among this crowd if I hadn't been told you were on your way. I was looking out for you, after all. But you do have the air of policemen about you. I suppose we all do and there's no sense in denying it. I don't know exactly what it is; perhaps it's a suspicious way of looking around. Anyway, I shouldn't worry; schoolmasters often have the same look about them and there'll be several around here. But again, I suppose most of them have rather long hair nowadays—at least in comparison with a lot of the people you get here."

They were somewhat relieved by these words, although the last thing they would normally have wished to be mistaken for was a schoolmaster; however, they were forced to admit that, in the circumstances, that was preferable to being taken for what they in fact were. As they were about to pass through the entrance to the enclosure, White fingered the unfamiliar badge he had attached to his jacket and almost expected to be challenged on its validity. His concern was totally unfounded, and Malone immediately led him to the bank of the river beside the floating stand. "I think it would be a good idea to watch the end of a couple of races before we start moving around," said Malone. "The afternoon diet is just beginning and I'm sure it will make you feel a bit more in the swing of things if you watch a bit of it. Let's see who's performing. The programme should be attached to the tree there." Malone let out a hearty laugh as he looked at it. "You may think the supplies of cyanide in the possession of both the firm of Cartwright and Mr Connolly were a bit of a coincidence, but that's not a patch on the competitors in the next race. It's the Cairo Police against the Garda Siochana—Irish police from Dublin, if you didn't know."

White, from his experience with his golf, was well aware that the police in Britain were generally keen on physical fitness and as an extension of this, would support their members if they showed excellence in sport, as long as it did not interfere with the performance of their duties. He himself had always been accommodated as far as was possible when he wanted time off to play in various golfing competitions. He was therefore not surprised that other police forces entertained the same notions. However, to find this combination immediately on his arrival at a Regatta which he had expected to find totally alien, was indeed a surprise.

"Time at Fawley—three minutes, twenty seconds." This announcement over the loudspeaker system was a mystery to White, although he had heard the name Fawley two days before. Malone explained that Fawley is fractionally less than half-way over the course and that the time was a fast one for a heat.

"Cairo Police lead Garda Siochana by half a length."

"You never know, White, but we might get a close finish for your first race here. If I remember rightly from my paper this morning, the Irishmen were expected to win. Although a well-rowed eight is a fine thing to see at any time, all too often the race as such is over by the time they reach this point. Let's hope this is different."

"At the mile-post, Cairo Police lead Garda Siochana by a quarter of a length. Cairo Police striking thirty six, Garda Siochana thirty five."

"That's the Irishmen catching up. It's always difficult for a well-drilled eight not to come up to its true rise even after a bad start, unless something happens to go wrong with one of the oarsmen or their boat suffers damage. I think we'll find they've caught up soon, especially as they're striking at a lower rate."

"As they pass the Stewards Enclosure the crews have drawn level."

Shouts for the two boats began to rise in the Enclosure but as they passed Malone and White, it was clear that form had indeed correctly predicted the winner. Garda Siochana finished half a length up.

"Fine eight, eh, White? And I must say you're very fortunate to have seen such a close finish in your first race here. You might have had to wait all day for that. As they're often so far apart by the finish, in many ways you're as well to watch them by the island near the start, but I'm afraid we won't have time to go down there today any rate. Still, let's go along to the open stand to get a different view of things."

They passed along the side of the river. The covered stand stood on their right, while on their left, between themselves and the river, there were several rows of deckchairs. Most, but by no means all of these were occupied and more noticeably by the female of the species. It could be deduced with a fair degree of accuracy that their male companions were lingering over a post-prandial drink or two in one of the bars. At the end of the covered stand they crossed a narrow strip of grass and mounted the Open Stand. In front of it, and continuing right up to the edge of the enclosure, the rows of deck-chairs still covered the space nearest the river.

From their vantage point in the stand, they strained their eyes up-river to catch sight of the competitors in the next race. It was between an eight from Oxford and another from Cambridge. Even if they had not heard the announcement that the Cambridge college was leading by two lengths at the Barrier, it was clear from what they could see that one of the crews was trailing badly. But suddenly a very strange thing happened. To the left of the crews, there was a large number of pleasure boats of different shapes and sizes, but fortunately at the moment they were doing nothing to interfere with the course. And so it came as even more of a surprise to see the leading boat begin to veer sharply towards the bank. There were a few gasps from the knowing and the suggestion was put about that the boat had lost its rudder. However, almost immediately it went back to its proper course, apparently having lost little, if any ground. From then on, the race was a mere formality with the Cambridge college winning by the verdict easily. "You've now seen the two extremes of eight racing. Well, I'll bet there were a number of faces behind the binoculars in the floating stand of a colour to match their owners' socks when that extraordinary thing happened by Remenham. It was most peculiar, but I suppose there may have been some hazard we're not aware of to cause that swerve. It might have been an antisocial bather or a swimming dog. If it had been the horses, it's the sort of thing which would lead to an immediate enquiry—but then again, if it had been, I don't suppose the apparent offender would have gone on to win easily. Always seems a nasty verdict, that, I must say. Well, what do you say to a glass of Pimms'? You can hardly come here and not have at least one, and I'm sure it won't affect us too much for any business we may have to see to later; it's mostly lemonade anyway. We have a certain amount of expenses granted for the trip and I don't think one drink would be too excessive."

They made their way to the top of the stand and began to walk slowly down the stairs at the back. Malone shook his head and said: "I'm afraid change and decay seem to have struck here of all places. The elusive Fawley Bar used to be in front of us and slightly to the left, but it appears to have changed into the Ladies Lavatory. I hope a number of confused gentlemen are not going to wander in there by mistake. Ah, I see where it's moved. That's it over there, at the end of the enclosure. I don't think we should make ourselves conspicuous there yet. It'll fill up as the afternoon wears on, and anyway we've got nearly an hour before Blacklaw's appointment—if that is indeed what the note meant, and this is the correct afternoon. We'll try the Champagne enclosure over there."

They descended the rest of the steps at the back of the Open Stand and walked diagonally to their right for a few yards towards the Champagne enclosure. The strains of the military band in the bandstand to the right of it could be heard ever more distinctly as they approached the tent which acted as the dispensary of drinks. Suddenly, to their surprise, they were hailed in an oblique manner from a table under a tree to their right.

"Good Heavens, the St. Andrews plods are upon us!" A large portly figure of a man in his late thirties or early forties rose and approached them. "Mr White, let me get you a refreshment. We're getting an order at the front of the queue. Two? Fine, I'll get them added on." He went off to arrange this.

"Pal of yours, White? Everyone within fifty yards must by now be well aware of our profession. Too bad. That's the trouble with having too many friends, I suppose."

The portly gentlemen was approaching them again. White was at a loss to know how he should effect introductions. He had eliminated his former habit of ending most of the remarks he made to Malone with the over-formal 'sir'—they had been working together too long by now to make this sound anything but ridiculous. But he had never called Malone, 'Alexander', let alone 'Sandy', and he couldn't see himself starting to do so now. Fortunately for him, he was released from this problem by the affability of the portly gentleman. "Jolly Balsdon, I'm usually called," he said, holding out his hand to the Inspector. "Sandy Malone," he replied. As he surveyed Jolly Balsdon, White was indeed reminded of Tenniel's illustrations or Tweedledum and Tweedledee and he had to make a great effort to hide his amusement. Malone was speaking. "I'm sure I saw you some years ago now, performing here. I forget which eight you were in, but I think it was from Oxford."

Jolly Balsdon laughed. "I was clearly right in placing you as a plod. You were obviously born for the job if you can remember that far back. You must have been quite young then. I am well aware that I was by far the heaviest man in the boat, if not in the whole Regatta, and I take no offense at all if that's why you remember me. In fact, I'm quite proud of it. As you'll probably remember, we did rather well. Are you a rowing man yourself?"

"Unfortunately, no. I spent too much time playing golf and, then when I went to St. Andrews University, there wasn't really any opportunity."

"Another golfer, eh? Not better than John White here, I presume?"

"I'm afraid not, although he's been improving my game somewhat over the last few months. Should I make the obvious deduction that you have played against him on some occasion?"

"The incisive mind of the enforcer of the law again. Yes, we were playing in the annual game of the Kilrymont club against the properly local clubs. As he'll say it if I don't, I was not far off breaking my clubs into little pieces afterwards, as I'm sure you'll understand. It's a good job that he's in full-time employment or I probably would have. There's always the chance that next time I meet him, he'll have been too busy to practise. Any chance of that, John?"

"I hope not but you never know. It's sometimes pretty hard to keep in practice even now, so don't despair."

"I'll try not to. But talking of easy victories, what did you make of that peculiar piece of steering in that last race? I couldn't believe my eyes at first. Still, it made no difference to the result. Ah, here are the drinks."

"Thank you very much," said Malone, as he accepted the glass offered. "D'you think I could have a quiet word with you before you rejoin your company? I don't want to sound mysterious but, much as I would like it otherwise, we're here on business. I must say it's very pleasant to be greeted here in the friendly manner with which you regaled us, but I had rather hoped that we could keep our line of business quiet for some time. I presume that we can trust your discretion, so I'll tell you something about it. We're engaged in a murder investigation. If you've been down South here for some days, you may not have heard about it. It hasn't been widely publicised at our request. The body of a man who had undoubtedly been murdered, was found in Ceres. I'm in charge of the investigation and John White here is assisting me. As a result, the less said about out line of business the better."

"I'm terribly sorry about that but, you know, it doesn't strike one immediately that chaps poling in here for a drink are really seeking out murderers. In fact, it's about the last thing anyone would expect here. Still, I shouldn't be too worried about my greeting. There are dozens of people round about hailing each other in loud voice in a variety of strange ways so that, unless anyone within earshot had a special reason for listening, I'm sure it will have passed unnoticed. Come and join the rest of us anyway; it'll look even more strange if you don't. Actually, the main reason I noticed John White in the first place was that I'm expecting some friends from St. Andrews at any moment. They were off to have lunch with some other crony and expected to be back about now."

Neither Malone nor White could see any advantage in not complying with this suggestion; they would be far less conspicuous or suspicious if they were already with an established company when anyone else who might recognise them appeared. They therefore went over with Jolly Balsdon to join his friends. As he introduced them, Jolly made much of his golfing connection with White. To accentuate this facet of White's character, he dwelt on his extraordinary skill at approach shots, a skill which had frequently stood him in good stead on those rare occasions—though not quite rare enough for the good of his game—when he sliced his drive. Someone else then spoke of his own extraordinary ability to pull almost every drive he made, and soon the knowledge that the newcomers were policemen had completely disappeared from the consciousness of the members of the company. Soon someone got up to go and fetch another tray of Pimms', without the formality of asking if anyone really had a desire for more. Malone began to wonder if they would be in proper command of their faculties, if by chance there should be a need to expand them to the full in the Fawley Bar at four o'clock. Nevertheless, the drinks appeared and there seemed to be little option but to begin to consume them.

They were quietly getting round this new refreshment when Jolly Balsdon suddenly hailed some new arrivals. Malone and White, following a natural reaction, turned their heads to see who they were, and were fully taken aback by what they saw. Jolly Balsdon's friends were three in number. There was one man neither of them had ever set eyes on before, a man who appeared to be in his late forties or early fifties. However, they had little difficulty in recognising the other two. They were none other than Mr Reid of Edinburgh and Mr Strachan of Ceres.

6♦ Chapter 7

MALONE HAD BEEN WELL AWARE of the possibility that he might run into one or two people he knew at the Regatta, but they would have been old friends or acquaintances who would naturally assume that he, like them, was there for the occasion. That White might be hailed from afar by a member of the Stewards' Enclosure had never for a minute entered his head. He had also been prepared to meet John Cartwright and possibly his father as well, but the present circumstances were completely beyond his calculations. Any hope of anything approaching anonymity had now probably disappeared, as had therefore the likelihood of learning anything positive in the Fawley Bar at four o'clock. He even considered telling the new arrivals why he and White were there, to avoid any embarrassing questions but dismissed the idea. What was clear was that there was no way they could avoid passing some words with Mr Strachan and Mr Reid, even if they only consisted of superficial politeness. He also wondered in the circumstances if they should give the Fawley Bar a miss, as, unless Albert Cartwright had been the sender of the note, it was unlikely that anyone would materialise there. He decided to stick to his original plan on the off-chance and to find out a way of having Albert Cartwright pointed out to him. He was not forgetting the fact that the envelope to Blacklaw had borne a London post-mark. He then turned his mind to the identity of Jolly Balsdon's friends. True, Mr Reid had informed them that he was coming South for pleasure, and he himself had recommended to John Strachan that he should get away for a bit, but of all the possible places they could have ended up, why should it be here? Had either, or both of them, made the arrangements to fit in with the Fawley Bar appointment? Mr Reid at least, given the timing of his office holiday, must have decided on the trip well in advance and there was nothing to have prevented him from sending the letter via an agent in London. It seemed unlikely enough, but could Mr Reid be a fit subject for blackmail? His thoughts were interrupted by Jolly Balsdon effecting introductions.

"May I introduce you to Gordon Reid, John Strachan, James Connolly . . ." At the mention of the name Connolly, Malone lost interest in the further formalities and he noticed that White was reacting in the same way. Was it only his imagination after hearing the name Connolly or was there in fact a facial resemblance between this Mr Connolly and the man they had recently visited in Ealing? There were undoubtedly some similarities but he could not be sure whether he was exaggerating them. However, from White's reaction, it was clear that the same thoughts were passing through his head. He wondered how they could establish whether there was a connection between the two without arousing too much suspicion as to the motive for the question. He decided that a private word with Jolly Balsdon was the most discreet method he could adopt. He thought of the possible danger involved in taking him even more into their confidence. Was there any way that Jolly Balsdon could be tied up with the murder or the communication with Blacklaw? On the first point, he decided that it was inconceivable that Sergeant McBride could have failed to have noted the size of one of the men who had delivered Blacklaw's body, if their companion had indeed been one of them. In the matter of the letter he decided that there was no way at all of being sure; he therefore would discuss the matter with White briefly before making a move. He waited long enough so as not to appear rude and then said: "John

White and myself sadly haven't got too long here and, as this is his first visit here, I think I'd better show him some of the main reason for the gathering. Anyone else coming to see a race or two?"

He had especially chosen a point when another round of drinks was being offered, though he and White and, he noticed, James Connolly had declined a further refreshment. His suggestion was accepted as a perfectly normal thing— he really had no reason to doubt that it would be—and there were murmurings from several quarters about coming to join them in a few moments. Fortunately, no-one wished to accompany them immediately. The two policemen therefore went off together and mounted the stairs at the back of the Open Stand. They were by no means isolated when they found themselves a position to stand in, but everyone around seemed to be wrapped up in a loud discussion of the merits and demerits of certain rowing clubs and Malone thought it unlikely that they would be overheard, even if there was anyone within earshot who had any interest in their business.

"Well, White, what do you make of it?"

"It's very difficult to say. Here we come to an event I had hardly heard of and what do we find? Almost everyone we've been speaking to in the last few days is here, or may be at any moment. The only one who denied he had any intention of coning here was Mr Connolly of Ealing and then what happens? We're reintroduced to Mr Reid and Mr Strachan and with them is a Mr Connolly—not the one we'd already met, granted, but I'd be surprised if they weren't related. If we'd hoped to get a line on one of our men here, it begins to look as it we've been totally wasting our time. In fact the whole thing starts to look like a vast conspiracy."

"Yes, and don't forget that that is exactly what it could be. You know that at least two men were involved in the murder and we have absolutely no proof that either of them was responsible for the letter to Blacklaw. Note also that all the people we've seen with the possible exception of father Cartwright—and I stress the word possible—could fit in with the description, vague as it was, given by Sergeant McBride. It is possible that they knew that the Fawley Bar note would fall into our hands and so came here en masse to confuse the issue."

"That theory would exclude Mr Reid, wouldn't it? He would simply have destroyed the note rather than let it fall into our hands. I suppose he could have been unaware of the significance of the communication, although still mixed up in a plot, but it would seem rather unlikely. May I also point out that Jolly Balsdon does not fit into the description of the two men in Ceres and it was evidently he who invited these people along?"

"Aye, I wasn't including him. That's really what I wanted to ask you. How well do you know him?"

"Personally, not well at all. As he said, he was playing me in the match against the Kilrymont Club—foursome as you know—and we all had a couple of drinks afterwards. We have also met in the golf club once or twice since and passed the time of day. I'm sorry, but there's one thing I should have mentioned about him immediately. He's an accountant by profession. In the circumstances that would seem to be almost too much to be a coincidence. However, from what I know of Mr Balsdon, anything which was not strictly above board would be completely out of character for him. He's one of those affable people who never seem to have an unpleasant word for anybody. That, I presume, is why he's called Jolly."

"Is it then your opinion that we would be perfectly justified in taking him into our confidence?"

"If it weren't for the fact that he was an accountant, I could be absolutely certain. But if you're going to have to approach one of them, I'm sure he's your best bet. The difficulty is that I begin to wonder if we can trust any of them."

"Well, I think it'll either be that or a wasted afternoon—as far as the job goes at any rate. If they all come and join us, as the general opinion made likely, I have to try to detach Mr Balsdon from his pals. If I manage to, try to come along too as discreetly as possible."

As it turned out, this was not necessary. They had just witnessed the end of another race when a voice behind them said: "It always seems most unkind when you hear that verdict. It was a pretty fast time and I don't suppose that the chaps in the winning boat are feeling that it was all that easy. By a long way, yes; easily, in that time, I doubt it." It was Jolly Balsdon who had detached himself from his friends and was on his own.

"Hello," said Malone, "Are your friends finding it difficult to abandon the Pimms'?"

"They're still finishing. I disposed of mine with a certain amount of alacrity, as I especially wanted to see this next race. As I'm sure you're aware, it's a heat of the Diamond Sculls and could be pretty close."

As it would be a minute or two until the scullers came into their clear view, Malone decided to seize this opportunity of sounding out Jolly Balsdon. "Mr Balsdon, or Jolly, if I may be familiar, John White and I are not here solely for pleasure, as I told you before. I didn't then give you the specific reason for our presence here, and I appreciated your discretion in not asking me. I think it might be wise to tell you a little more about it now, before your friends rejoin us. In fact I'd like to ask you for a little assistance. I don't know whether you noticed but we were totally taken aback by the identity of your guests. From their surprising lack of reaction, I expect the same was true of them. If you're with them much longer, I'm sure they'd tell you why, as it must be uppermost in their minds at the moment. However, I intend to give you that information first. I mentioned that a man had been murdered. His name was Ronald Blacklaw. Does that mean anything to you?"

"No, I certainly can't remember having heard of anyone of that name."

"I ask because he was in the same line of business as yourself. Now to the reasons for our surprise. He was found in the grounds of John Strachan's house in Ceres and he was employed in the firm of McColl and Duncan of Moray Place, Edinburgh. I probably don't need to tell you that Mr Reid is the senior partner of that firm. We have therefore come across them in the course of our investigations in Scotland during the last couple of days. Our enquiries then led us to London where, among others, we interviewed a Mr Connolly of Ealing. Both of us were struck by certain facial similarities between him and your friend James Connolly. On top of that, we know of at least one, and possibly three other people who may be connected with the case who will be here today. Do you by chance know a man called Albert Cartwright?"

"Good heavens, yes! I presume there can be only one of them. I hope so at any rate. Dreadful snob. He was actually in the Champagne enclosure when you arrived unless he had just left."

"That's all we needed. If he was there when you hailed us, he'll know who we are too. That means that pretty well everyone we might have wished not to, will know we're here. We might as well have displayed Police badges instead of the regulation ones."

"I'm terribly sorry. I suppose it's really my fault. But to be fair, I had no way of knowing that you were trying to be clandestine cops. Still, as it seems I've been instrumental in putting you in your present predicament, if you want me to do something to help you to get out of it, just fire away. I'll probably be willing."

"Don't feel you have to. I don't consider it in any way your fault that we're in this position. However, I would at least be grateful for some information. First of all, could you tell me what you know of Mr James Connolly?"

"To tell you the truth, I don't know all that much about him. The reason I came across him is that he's a fellow-member of the Kilrymont Golf Club in St. Andrews. He used to be a high-powered accountant out East, Ceylon as far as I remember. Because I'm in the same general line, I was an obvious person for him to be introduced to when he joined the club about a year ago. Apart from his work out there, as I understand it, he was a great bible-thumper. I don't know why he left at such a comparatively early age to come back to this country—it might have been his health, though I've never heard him or anyone else suggest that as a cause. He's a very straight man and in some ways a surprising member of the club. For instance, while the rest of us tend to take our golf mainly as a social pastime, he takes his extremely seriously and has never been seen to take more than a couple of gins after a game. For that reason I was rather surprised when he asked me if I could get him a badge for the Regatta here. I know there's no reason why anyone should partake of much alcoholic refreshment here but if he expected to be in my company, he must have known that I at any rate would be shifting a glass or two. Anyway, I was pleased to be able to supply him with a badge."

"Did you also provide badges for Mr Reid and Mr Strachan?"

"I notice you have fallen into the formal address of police questioning. Yes, I did and quite independently of James Connolly. Gordon Reid is also a member of the club and when he was over for a game one Saturday—I think it was about three weeks ago—he asked me about the Regatta. John Strachan, whom I knew from playing golf and also from being in the same line of business, approached me only last Monday, not long before I was leaving for coming down here. He was rather tentative at the time about being able to get away and he rang me up on Thursday to finalise the arrangements. Surprisingly enough, he didn't appear to know the other two, although they had met each other in the club. By the way, I'm not suggesting that it was a sudden desire on their part to come here. I remember talking about it to James and Gordon sometime in the middle of winter. You know how it is when the icy Eastern winds have been battering you as you walk up to the eighteenth green; talk about summer days such as this and in these surroundings always is rather attractive. They both expressed the wish to come here then but it was only recently they appeared to have come to a firm decision on the matter."

"We'd better see the end of your race before we carry on." The result seemed in little doubt as the two scullers approached the Stewards' Enclosure. One of them was trailing by about six lengths. But the loser, as he seemed doomed to be, suddenly put on a tremendous effort and could be seen to be closing the gap. His effort though was surely too late. Then to the surprise of the spectators, as the leader was approaching the covered stand, he caved in completely. The second man came through, sculling beautifully and won the race, verdict easily.

"Another example of the peculiarity of the verdict easily," observed Malone. "Now, if you'll allow me to return to what I was saying before the others retire discomfited from the Pimms', I must tell you what specifically brought us here to the Regatta. A letter which would have reached Mr Blacklaw the day after he was murdered came into our possession. It contained nothing except a piece of paper with the words 'Fawley Bar 4' printed on it. For reasons which will be obvious to you, we came to the conclusion that this was the place and occasion referred to and that the '4' referred to an arranged time of meeting. For other good reasons we decided that the day was either today or tomorrow. If anyone involved in the sending of the note has been keeping his ears open in certain quarters, I don't suppose there's too much point in seeing if anyone tries to keep that date, for us at any rate."

"What you're about to suggest is that, as I was the reason for the disappearance of your incognitos, perhaps I wouldn't mind hanging around the Fawley Bar myself, just in case anything obvious should happen. I'll certainly go, as I don't think my presence would be thought untoward there. The only trouble is, I'd have no idea what I might be looking for. Also, may I make a local point? If I wanted to conduct a clandestine meeting in the Fawley Bar at four o'clock, I would undoubtedly choose tomorrow rather than today. That would be not too long after the final of the Grand, but just long enough for the chaps to shove down a few glasses of the stuff and therefore be not too interested in any serious conversation being conducted beside them. I'll pole along there now and come back and report to you if I see anything which seems suspicious or catch sight of anyone on his own who appears to be waiting for someone else. I must say, though, that it seems a pretty long shot. It's sure to be fairly crowded."

"Before you go," said White, "I think we ought to impress on you that it is a murder we're investigating. Don't for goodness sake do anything unnecessary. I'd hate to think that any harm came to you through trying to help us out."

"Don't worry yourself about that. No-one would be mad enough to try anything violent in a gathering of this sort. He'd have absolutely no chance of getting away with it."

"I think he's right," said Malone, as Jolly Balsdon departed in the direction of the Fawley Bar. "I'm sure it was an unnecessary warning, though to be fair he should be left in no doubt as to the seriousness of the matter. It's very easy to take it too lightly in an atmosphere such as this. Such unpleasantnesses don't seem terribly likely in these surroundings. I must say that for my part the lingering doubts are more for his trustworthiness rather than his safety. Still, I'm sure we have nothing to lose."

"Time at Fawley—three minutes, forty-seven seconds." They turned around to watch some of the best performers in the world at their chosen sport, until Jolly Balsdon should return. This he did after about twenty minutes, with his grants for the day in attendance. He was speaking to them in loud tones, apparently to compete with those around them.

"You've no idea what a peculiar feeling it is, now they've shoved the Fawley Bar from where it used to be. For years and years you're used to seeing it in the same place and all of a sudden you find that it isn't there anymore. The Ladies' lavatory seems rather an unexpected substitute. Well, as you found your own way there, I presume without a mistaken detour through the Ladies, there's only the Bridge Bar left to sample, if you feel like going there later."

They joined White and Malone, who realised that the number of decibels used for these statements was not only dictated by the volume of the speech round about. Clearly Jolly Balsdon was letting them know that Reid, Connolly and Strachan had all been at the Valley Bar at the time they were interested in. It was, of course, impossible to decide from this information whether it had been the result of a prior arrangement or not. It also occurred to them that if any of these gentlemen were connected with the note, it would also be pretty obvious to them that Jolly had made these audible remarks for the benefit of the policemen. They hoped for Jolly's sake that this was not the case. That gentleman seemed totally unperturbed by the thought of any such possibility and was speaking again.

"It's quite amazing how you keep coming across people in the Regatta. Here's John Strachan feeling a bit out of things and of the opinion that there's nobody here but ourselves that he knows, and in the Fawley Bar he runs into someone he knew while he was working in London. Know the chap slightly myself, as a matter of fact. Fellow called Albert Cartwright."

After this last statement, he steered the conversation into somewhat less personal topics, mainly to do with rowing. Again Malone and White hoped that what was so obvious to them had not also been so to anyone else. Yet the facts that he had produced were very confusing, unless they were to fall back on coincidence, or a theory of conspiracy.

Malone began to consider the curious fact of the presence of these people at the Regatta, but the more he considered it, the more natural it seemed. Both Albert Cartwright and Jolly Balsdon were members of the Enclosure and both habitual regular attendees at the Regatta. What could be more natural than that two cronies of Balsdon from his Golf Club should want to come and see what this occasion had to offer? Perhaps Strachan was a little harder to explain but if he alone had to be accounted for, it was not so difficult. Even the appearance of them all at the Fawley Bar at the significant time of four o'clock was not as surprising as it had seemed at first if looked at in this light.

After another couple of races John Strachan suggested that they should try the Bridge Bar and so complete the round of the drinks areas. Malone said that he and White would love to join them, but they would need to get back to London. He tried to give the impression that they had spent more time in this diversion than they could strictly afford, although he was well aware that at least Gordon Reid, if not all of them, was well aware of the true reason for their visit. As they passed the bandstand, a few couples were executing some sort of dance to the military music. This caused a necessary break-up of their group and Jolly Balsdon managed to find himself alone with White. Malone stayed with the others to make the separation appear fortuitous. They all waited by the entrance until the other two should catch up. They arrived a few moments later and Malone and White said their goodbyes, amid hopeful remarks that they would find the time to come again the next day. The policemen then left the enclosure.

"Did he have anything of importance to tell you, White?"

"I'm afraid it was that obvious again, wasn't it? I warned him strongly again to be careful, but I don't think he took me very seriously. Anyway, as you'll remember, it was almost four o'clock when he reached the Fawley Bar. He mingled with the crowd, as much as his bulk would allow him to, and kept his ears open. Then to his surprise, he saw

Reid, Connolly and Strachan walking up to the bar. Soon Strachan began to look around a bit, caught sight of Albert Cartwright and hailed him. He then went to join him, leaving Reid and Connolly at the bar. Balsdon then tried to get nearer to Cartwright and Strachan, as he wondered if there could be a prearranged meeting. At this juncture, he was loudly called by name by an old friend. Cartwright and Strachan had clearly heard too, so Balsdon could do nothing except walk straight up to them as if he'd just noticed them. He told Strachan some tale about having looked for them in the Champagne Enclosure and, as he hadn't found them, he had decided to try the Fawley Bar on the off-chance of finding them there."

"What were Connolly and Reid doing while he was trying to get nearer to Cartwright and Strachan?"

"He doesn't know, as they were behind him. I did of course point out to him the obvious possibility that they were watching his movements all the time; that was when I warned him to be careful. However that might be, the upshot was that he heard nothing of what passed between Cartwright and Strachan, not even so that he could give an opinion as to whether it really was a chance meeting. He still rather felt from the way that Strachan had been looking around at the start that it was arranged but he admitted that it was nothing more than a feeling. After joining them, he talked of nothing except rowing and golf for the rest of their time there. He was convinced that none of them had noticed anything suspicious about his actions, and I pointed out again that he could not be certain of this, and that it had appeared pretty obvious to us why he had been speaking the way he was when they rejoined us."

"It's all rather inconclusive, isn't it? If Jolly was right in suggesting that Strachan was feeling a bit out of it because he knew no-one, it would be perfectly natural to make much of seeing a familiar face. I note that there was no mention of the other two Cartwrights, who might reasonably have been supposed to be with Albert if they had been there. But then again, they could have been keeping a low profile for reasons of their own. You could see from where we were that the bar was pretty crowded at the time. Och well, we didn't really expect anything concrete to come from the message. Still, I suppose we'd better try tomorrow as well and even have a couple of plainclothes men planted there just in case. It can do no harm, seeing that so many people connected with Blacklaw are here, for whatever reasons. We'd best get back to London now and see if anything has turned up there. There might be some news from Edinburgh as well. We've got tomorrow morning to deal with things if needed and I think that if nothing transpires to keep us, we might as well return to Edinburgh tomorrow night."

❧ Chapter 8

MALONE AND WHITE RETURNED AS SWIFTLY as they could to Scotland Yard and went at once to Inspector Peagram's office. He immediately gave them some information which had surprised him but was no longer news to them. It was to the effect that Strachan had travelled south the night before to attend Henley Regatta. He had asked his wife to inform the police, but she had been so long in doing so that the news had only reached Peagram an hour before. She had confirmed, for what it was worth, that this was a recent decision of her husband and that he was to be a guest of Jolly Balsdon. Malone told Peagram that they had already seen Strachan but was pleased to note that Mrs Strachan had kept the police informed as to her husband's movements. The only thing that disturbed him was the timing of the information. Was it possible that he had intended the police to know of his whereabouts only after the four o'clock meeting had passed? He told Peagram of the extraordinary presence of Mr Reid of Edinburgh and also of Mr James Connolly, who bore an unmistakable likeness to the gentleman of the same surname they had seen in Ealing the night before. Next he rang the Fife CID to institute enquiries about James Connolly and especially to establish if he had any connection with Mr Richard Connolly or Ealing. His colleagues in Fife promised to give it their immediate attention.

As he had promised, Peagram had investigated the possibility of a second car-hire firm being used by the Cartwrights. There was as yet no news from this front, and Peagram repeated his doubts as to any favourable outcome. Enquiries at King's Cross and Euston had, as they had foreseen, failed to add anything to their knowledge.

"By the way," said Malone, "how did you manage to get hold of photographs for identification purposes?"

"Nothing terribly mysterious about that. As it seemed likely that we would need them, we just had men stationed outside their houses with cameras this morning. I suppose I should have mentioned it to you but it hardly seemed worthwhile. There are so many people taking pictures of all manner of things nowadays, I don't suppose they noticed."

"I see. Well, we don't seem to be any further forward in establishing whether the two Cartwrights are telling the truth or not. I suppose there was nothing from the pub in Basingstoke they mentioned?"

"No. We don't know which one it was, of course, but there's nothing so far. There are so many strangers dropping in for one or two in the evening at this time of year that it's unlikely they would have been noticed, even if they are telling the truth. Similarly we've found no-one there who can remember the car, but that's no indication one way or the other. I might add that there is no evidence of Mr Richard Connolly hiring a car on the Wednesday or thereabouts either, but a false name and a slight disguise would be quite sufficient to account for that—or of course incomplete records and a bad memory for faces."

"What about stolen cars of the power necessary to make the trip to Scotland and back in the time we envisage?"

"All those which have been recovered have been searched for any possible traces of the men who were in Ceres, but none have shown anything of the kind. We weren't too sure what to look for anyway, except in the case of blue Cortinas."

"I'm afraid all that seems like so much wasted effort. Still, I suppose most of our job is. Anything on Albert Cartwright's movements?"

"He at least possesses a possible car. As your idea was to keep away from him for the moment, we haven't questioned him personally; but we do know that he was at the Regatta looking fit and healthy before one o'clock on the Thursday. That seems almost to put him out of the reckoning for Edinburgh and Ceres. So you still want us to leave him alone?"

"I think you might as well until after four tomorrow. He's almost certain to have heard about Blacklaw by then, if he hasn't already, but we might as well stick to the outside chance of something happening tomorrow afternoon. After that, the more you can find out about him, the better. You've got nothing more on the arrow, I suppose?"

"We're fairly certain that it was not made in Cartwrights'. The local police have asked some of the employees they know they can trust, and it would have been difficult to do it without the knowledge of any of them. That is unless we allow for secret midnight working, which seems a little far-fetched, especially as it might well have been noticed by normal patrols if it had gone on."

"Well, I think we'll hang on for a bit to see whether my colleagues in Fife have come up with anything immediately on James Connolly and, if not, pack in for the day. It's been a pretty long one for all of us."

There was nothing forthcoming within the hour and so Malone and White spent the rest of the evening in a similar manner to the one before. After a leisurely breakfast, taken early, they went straight to Scotland Yard to see what news there might be from Fife or Edinburgh. Clearly there could be nothing of obvious and outstanding importance as they would have been contacted already if this were the case. However, it was always possible that something which might seem trivial to others would assume different proportions in their eyes, in view of their extra knowledge. They were conducted to Peagram's office again, and although the Inspector was not yet there himself, they were told that he had insisted on having some reports taken to him at home to see if they justified interrupting the Scottish detectives. He decided that they were not that immediate and had therefore returned them to his office. Malone was pleased to see that the first one of these was information on Mr James Connolly. The facts that were assembled were as follows. Firstly, he was the elder brother of Mr Richard Connolly of Ealing. Both of them had gone abroad in their youth and both had made a considerable amount of money in different ways. James had qualified as an accountant in Australia, where he had also been a lay preacher in a strongly Methodist sect. He had later moved to Ceylon, where he had been the chief accountant in a large tea firm. He had retired from this lucrative position early, partly because he strongly disapproved of the government and partly because he found with advancing age that the climate did not agree with his health. There were also rumours that he had found it convenient to leave because, in a fit of "righteous anger" he had beaten one of his servants savagely for dishonesty. On this last point it was stressed that there was no independent corroboration for the charge and such accusations were frequently made about ex-colonials without any evidence. There was no other information about him, except that he was a bachelor, a member of the Kilrymont Club, and lived alone in a modest house in the outskirts of St. Andrews. He was not known to be in close communication with his brother.

"Well, White, it's as we thought. They're brothers. So that's another connection established between London and Fife. But whether it's purely fortuitous or the sort of association we're looking for is anybody's guess. I don't know whether you know the curious fact that Bach, Handel, Scarlatti and Gay were all born in the same year? Yet it would be excessively foolish to suggest that therefore their parents all got together the year before and decided that something should be done about the future of culture. Inspector Peagram and his merry men will have to be put onto ferreting out any more relevant information about Mr Richard Connolly, especially as regards any contact with his brother. It is after all a perfectly tenable theory that Richard, for some financial reason, decided to get rid of Blacklaw and enlisted the help of his brother who was not far away from Blacklaw's new place of residence and very handy for leaving a warning to Strachan. The excesses with the dead body might have been a bit easier for someone who had lived a pretty hard life abroad, as Richard seems to have. And don't forget McBride's statement that the blue Cortina left in the direction of St. Andrews. That's something else we must have established, by the way. Exactly what cars James Connolly and Strachan had available to them. We might as well add Jolly Balsdon to the list to be on the safe side. Well, it's not far off the time to be taking a leisurely run out to Henley. I presume the car and driver are still available to us. We might even stop on the way and sample the delights of an English pub on a Sunday lunchtime. At least we're certain to find one which serves lunches."

They reached the Stewards' Enclosure shortly before half-past two, a little later than they had intended. The weather was again ideal for spectators and the roads to Henley had been extremely crowded. Malone had suggested that they keep up the act of merely being dedicated Regatta visitors, as to suggest otherwise would clearly be of no advantage to them, even if those they were interested in were well aware of the true reason for their presence. There was always the strong possibility that the appointment at the Fawley Bar had been made by someone who was as yet unknown to them.

"I can't help feeling this Fawley Bar thing is a total waste of time, White."

"I'm not at all certain. I was very much inclined to that point of view before our trip here yesterday but I'm not sure now. It seems as if a solid collection of people interested in Blacklaw had arranged to meet here, and Blacklaw himself had been told to attend. It may be totally fanciful but is it possible that all these people had, as it were, met to try Blacklaw on some extra-legal charge and had decided to issue their judgement here? If he were blackmailing not only one of them, but the whole lot, such a theory could make sense. But then I grant you it's a pretty weird place to choose. It's not as if they could do anything to him here."

"What could be a better way to guarantee his presence? He'd be sure of not walking into some sort of trap—at any rate, it would seem like that to him. But since his death, any such proposed meeting is purely an academic question."

"Certainly. But if we hadn't come here, we might never have realised, or at least at only a much later stage, that they had all intended to congregate here. And anyway, I can't think of any other place where we'd obviously be of any more use."

"That's true at any rate. But remember, we don't as yet have an ounce of proof that Blacklaw was blackmailing anybody, let alone a whole collection of people. As you say, though, we're no better anywhere else as far as we know, and at least some people who can reasonably be termed suspects are here with us. By continuing to pressure them by our presence, there is always a chance that one of them may do something foolish. Guilty men under strain can do the most stupid things."

"Ah-ha; it's the plods." Jolly Balsdon had come up behind them and clearly saw no reason to obscure their way of life from any other would-be listeners. "I've just managed to detach myself from my guests for a while and I was hoping to run into you. Fact is, I'd like to have a few words with you, and fairly privately too. You see, when I left you yesterday I didn't take John White's warnings at all seriously. But now I'm not at all sure that he wasn't right. In the light of what you were saying, one or two of the remarks passed by my friends seem mighty queer, especially as I don't think I was intended to hear them. It was when they were speaking about archery. May ask you if archery had any connection with the demise of Ronald Blacklaw?

"Yes," said Malone, "very much so. And as that aspect of the matter hasn't been made public, the sooner you tell us exactly what this is all about the better. Strachan, by the way, would have known about it and might have communicated the fact to the others. But any discussion on those lines is bound to make me suspicious. Oh dear, here are your friends. Perhaps they want to prevent you from speaking to us alone. Never mind, there'll be plenty of opportunity later. Now remember, although I'm sure you'll be absolutely safe in here, be on your guard. And whether you like it or not, I'll have a man put onto you for your protection as soon as you leave here this evening.

Messrs. Reid, Connolly and Strachan came up and greeted them in a jovial manner—especially John Strachan who, despite the earliness of the afternoon, had clearly already taken more than his fair share of refreshment. He insisted that they should proceed forthwith to the Champagne Enclosure, where he would be pleased to provide the next round. James Connolly made a number of disapproving remarks about the state that Strachan was likely to reduce himself to, but the general feeling was of agreement with his proposed line of action. The rest of the company therefore commandeered a table under the shade of a tree—the sun was rather hot—while Strachan saw to his side of the bargain.

It soon became clear that some of the company—two or three other friends of Balsdon's had also come to join them—had no intention of calling a halt at the one refreshment. Malone and White therefore declared their intention of observing some more of the rowing. Malone was well aware that they might have to partake of more to drink later and neither he nor White could afford to be in any way befuddled at this stage. It also occurred to him that it was more likely that defences could be dropped in the absence of policemen and the presence of substantial quantities of alcohol. Then, if Jolly Balsdon was to be trusted, he might pick up something of value to them. As the final of the Grand had been postponed until later, because of damage caused to one of the boats on the way up to the start through the antisocial activities of one of the pleasure craft, it seemed unlikely that any of their acquaintances would be in a hurry to leave. Therefore it was to be expected that sometime during the afternoon Jolly Balsdon would be able to report to them if anything strange had taken place, and also complete his unfinished confidence of their earlier conversation.

"If Balsdon doesn't manage to contact us in the near future, said Malone, "we'll keep the Fawley Bar at four appointment ourselves. Apart from other considerations, he'll know that he should be able to contact us there."

Jolly Balsdon had been unable to leave his company, so it seemed, and therefore shortly before four o'clock Malone and White made their way to the Fawley Bar. It was fairly well patronised but not so heavily as Jolly had anticipated if the final of the Grand has actually taken place at its advertised time of three o'clock. They went up to the bar, ordered two small Pimms' and then tried to make themselves as inconspicuous as they could. None of the company they had left with Balsdon had turned up, but they had noticed Albert Cartwright sitting down at a table with his brother and father. The father was looking a little strange in an attempt at sporting-style clothes but they all seemed to be enjoying themselves. Anything looking less like a party of people about to be squeezed by a blackmailer was hard to imagine. Malone reflected that it was possible that their contentment with life was caused by the knowledge that that potential danger no longer existed. At about quarter past four, two elegantly dressed women—one of them presumably Albert's wife, the former Miss Parkwood—approached the Cartwrights. They all appeared to be pleased to see each other. The Cartwrights rose, finished their drinks and left with the two women in the direction of the river.

Malone took a swift look round. "Well, White, I can't see any future in staying here. It was to be expected that this supposed appointment would bring us no concrete return. Still, I think our trips here have had their value, especially if Jolly Balsdon has something of importance to tell us. As he's not been in contact, it's a fair bet that his cronies, or at least some of them have been trying to keep a close hold on him. We shall undoubtedly have to make sure he's well protected from the moment he leaves here until this whole business is cleared up. I must say I didn't expect things to get to that state."

"You don't think he's in any danger while he's in the Enclosure?"

"I can't see what danger. For a start we're here and the others know we are. Secondly, as I've said before, this is not the sort of assembly in which I would like to try any strong-arm thuggery—there'd be too much immediate opposition. Thirdly, if they want to do anything unpleasant to Jolly, they're bound to fancy their chances better if they do it later on."

They made themselves as available to Jolly Balsdon as they could for the next hour or so by strolling slowly round the enclosure, but they did not see him and assumed that he was being closely watched by his supposed guests. White expressed some concern at his continued absence, but Malone repeated the undeniable fact that they really had no evidence at all to connect any of the people there with the death of Blacklaw, except a number of coincidences, which were explicable, and the suspicions of Balsdon himself, which might have little foundation for all they knew. They decided they might as well get a good view of the final of the Grand Challenge Cup and so mounted the open stand in good time.

They had little difficulty in finding a crew to support, as the contest was between the Irish Police, the Garda Siochana, and an American University which rejoiced under the name of Butler College. The crowd by now had become very thick and it was as much as they could do to keep their view.

"At the island, both crews are level." The voice came over the loudspeaker system as clearly as ever. There were hopeful murmurs all round of a close race. A few minutes later: "At Fawley, both crews are still level. Butler striking thirty seven, Garda Siochana, thirty six." There were more murmurs from the knowing about the significance of the rate of strike.

"At Fawley, the time three minutes twenty-two seconds." By now the crews were in sight of the open stand and necks were being craned in the hope of a better view. The learned passed more knowing remarks, commenting on the fact that the Americans had half a stone advantage per man. It was therefore a pleasant surprise to Malone and White that when they passed the Open Stand, the Irish Police were half a length up. Despite a late challenge from the Americans, they retained this lead and won by half a length.

They had been so absorbed in the race, they had momentarily forgotten their prime reason for being there, and immediately it was over, Malone suggested that they should try and find Jolly Balsdon as soon as possible and, on some excuse however flimsy, speak to him on his own. Apart from his information, they needed to find out his probable movements later, so as to be able to provide the protection that they sincerely hoped would not be necessary. They could not immediately find Balsdon himself, but they soon caught sight of Strachan, Reid and Connolly. They approached them and Malone asked where he was, as they would have to be taking their leave. Connolly answered him: "I'm afraid we haven't seen him for a while and were hanging round here ourselves waiting for him to come back. We'd have to be going anyway but it seems that our departure may have to be more precipitate than we had intended." He looked scornfully at John Strachan, who was clearly having difficulty in supporting himself. "As a matter of fact, he complained of feeling a little ill just before the final of the Grand and said he needed to have a short walk. Not, I might hasten to add, for the same reason as some people around here might need to. We were wondering if he might have wandered off to look for you two, as he seemed to have rather taken to your company."

Malone and White were suddenly alarmed. Blacklaw had been poisoned. It was not at all clear how anything similar could have been carried out here, but it was possible with particularly ruthless people. Before they could consider a course of action, a sudden commotion arose among the deckchairs to the right of the Open Stand. As is to be expected when anything happens in a crowded place, a large number of responsible persons was converging on the centre of interest, ready to give superfluous advice and assistance. Malone and White joined them. As they approached the scene, their worst fears began to be realised. Someone was saying: "Jolly Balsdon asleep in a deck chair after the final of the Grand? Quite impossible. He hasn't missed it in about twenty years. There must be some mistake." At this Malone and White produced their identification and forced their way forwards. There was Jolly Balsdon, sprawled in a deck chair, a grotesque expression on his face, which contrasted unhappily with the name by which he was known. His lips had an unnatural bluish colour about them. White rushed up to him, but it was soon clear that he was too late. Jolly Balsdon was dead.

Several of the Stewards had arrived by now and Malone asked them if they would clear away the crowd as quickly as possible and alert the local police. This last precaution proved unnecessary, as one of the plain-clothes men Malone had had posted in the Fawley Bar had immediately reported the matter. He had assumed, quite correctly, that their presence had been required for good reasons although they had not been warned that anything like this might occur— and had acted accordingly. Two uniformed men could be seen making their way through the thinning crowd and two doctors had already offered their services. Other officials had departed as swiftly as they could to ensure that no further people were allowed to enter or leave the enclosure. Shortly afterwards an announcement came over the loudspeakers to the effect that there had been an accident and the police had requested that no-one should for the moment leave the enclosure. A few rumours spread among the crowds away from the scene of the tragedy, but the general feeling was that nothing of any disastrous import could have happened in such a place. It was certainly not worth spoiling an enjoyable afternoon bothering about it.

The doctors soon confirmed what the policeman had already realised must be the case. There could be little doubt about the cause of death. The appearance of the dead man's face and the smell on his lips precluded any other conclusion than cyanide poisoning. To Malone and White the reason for the murder was also manifest. A person or persons probably known but just possibly not, had noted Jolly's communication with the police and decided that he knew too much. Short of some unexpected revelation, that knowledge must be to do with the murder of Blacklaw. Did that narrow it down to Reid, Connolly and Strachan? Malone tried to recall the exact words used by Jolly Balsdon when he admitted to them that something seemed to be wrong. Had he referred to his guests or was it 'friends' in general? He asked White if he could remember. White was sure that the word friends had been used, as he had noticed the change from 'guests' to 'friends'. They would clearly have to find out first in whose company Jolly had been just before feeling unwell. It struck him that Connolly had seemed totally unconcerned, although, if he were a cyanide poisoner, he must be well aware of the immediate effects of a good dose. Reid had appeared similarly unruffled and apart from the obvious fact of his drunkenness, Strachan had not seemed at all put out—he certainly did not give the impression of a man fearing imminent arrest for two murders. Self-recrimination began to replace rational thought. Why had he assumed that another murder, unless it were that of Strachan—was nigh on an impossibility? It was rare for Dr Crenshaw to say more than was strictly necessary, and he had spoken heatedly of the mental state of the murderer of Blacklaw. Why had he assumed that no harm could possibly come to Jolly Balsdon in the Stewards Enclosure? That may have been a fair assumption about murderers in their right minds, but he had no excuse to have considered his man as such. Why had he not himself kept a close watch on Jolly Balsdon?

He was interrupted from these depressing thoughts by the arrival of the ambulance man with a stretcher, who requested permission to move the body. He looked down again at Jolly and concluded that little advantage could be gained from leaving him in his present position. It was almost certain that the poison had been administered before he started feeling unwell. He would of course have to establish who was sitting next to him at the time of his death but any attempt at forcing him to take anything with which the poison could have been administered must surely have been noticed. After all, it was a rule that no picnics were to be brought into the enclosure and drinks were not allowed beyond the vicinity of the bars. Furthermore, he did not wish to leave Jolly to the gaze of any inquisitive person who might be attracted by such sights. He therefore told the ambulancemen to carry on. With the quiet efficiency that is their hallmark, they removed the body.

One of the Stewards then came up to ask if there were any other instructions. Malone watched the ambulancemen departing and decided that he would gain no thanks from the dead as well as the living if he interfered with their enjoyment of the Regatta any more than was strictly necessary. He merely requested therefore that everyone should leave their name and address on the way out and preferably produce some sort of identification to prove it. A minute later an announcement to this effect was heard over the loudspeaker. Malone began to hear the distant strains of the band again and wondered if they had been performing all the time the tragedy was being enacted. The joyful tune they were playing seemed to him grotesquely out of place, but he reflected that perhaps it was better so. A further announcement was then heard, to the effect that the prize-giving was about to begin. It further stated that Mr Clifford 'Jolly' Balsdon had been taken ill during the final of the Grand and asked that anyone who had been sitting near him should report to the Secretary's tent. Malone wondered if this had been thought of by the Stewards, or if it was the work of the local force. At any rate it was clearly a good idea, although he doubted very much if any worthwhile information would result from interviewing these people. The announcement seemed to satisfy most of the curious and the business of the Regatta carried on.

A few people objected to giving the personal information asked for on their way out but, when they found that the alternative was to be held back for an unspecified length of time, they complied. Malone had had to insist on some precautions to ensure that correct particulars were given and so the departure of the very large crowd took some considerable time. It had been necessary to point out that even members of the Stewards Enclosure and their guests were capable of using such pseudonyms as Joe Kilroy or

Horatio Stalin, especially if they were a little confused at the end of a hard day.

Malone and White then repaired to Henley Police Station. Statements had been taken in the Secretary's office from eleven people who admitted to being near Jolly Balsdon when he had been sitting down. All these had agreed to make themselves available later in the evening if necessary. Reid, Connolly and Strachan had also offered themselves as witnesses, as had the two younger Cartwrights and two others who had been drinking with Balsdon just before his illness. Malone could not help but wonder why they were so keen on doing so if they really thought that he had merely been taken ill.

They began to look through the statements of those who had been in Jolly's vicinity when he had met his death. As he expected, there was nothing of any surprise there. Most of them had seen him come and sit down, 'looking pretty ghastly' as one of them put it. They had not really taken much notice of him, as they had assumed that he was the worse for drink. Another admitted to being somewhat surprised at the fact, as he had known Jolly slightly and thought that at that stage of the proceedings it was a bit out of character. He had however assumed that the reason had been the postponement of the race. It appeared that the dead man had tried to speak to the woman immediately on his left but as she had assumed he was strongly affected by drink, she had firmly taken no notice.

"Well, White, I can't see any reason for keeping these people from their dinner any longer, can you? If any of them had been up to anything fishy, I think it very likely that one of the others would have noticed."

"I can't see any point in doing so. When we've got almost all our possible suspects in his company just before he felt ill, it seems pretty clear that that is where we look for his killer. But if it's some sort of conspiracy, we'll have the greatest difficulty in proving anything."

"You're probably right. The sad thing is that Jolly himself probably put his feeling of illness down to the same cause as his neighbours in the deckchairs, until it was too late. Potassium cyanide works quickly. It must have been administered just before he wandered off, or he probably wouldn't have managed to make a seat. He must have been totally unaware that he had taken anything untoward. It looks to me that it must have been in his last drink. There will of course be no way of checking that now, but I suspect we can take it as a near certainty. Our next move must be to establish who bought or distributed the last drink Jolly Balsdon took on this earth."

The seven people who had admitted being in Balsdon's company just before he had gone to sit down had kept their word and were easily brought along to the Police Station. First of all, they saw the two who had not come into their reckoning before. They were both old friends of Jolly's, and the policemen did not expect that they really had anything to do with the murder. However, their statements would then be all the more valuable if any or all of the rest intended to produce false information. They were also asked to account for their movements on the Wednesday before, but their explanations were to all appearances quite satisfactory. Malone put through a telephone call to have their alibis checked and then thanked them for their co-operation and told them they were free to go.

"Well, White, assuming they're perfectly innocent, we might be fortunate with some of our other people. If they try to mislead us, we'd have a pretty good reason for suspecting them."

They were not in luck. Although he questioned all of them in something less than a polite manner, they all came out with the same version of the circumstances leading up to the departure of Balsdon. All of them remembered the facts of the last round. It had begun with a rather drunken Strachan suggesting that their pints of Pimms' contained no more actual alcohol than a half-pint. They had no reason to suspect that this was in any way true, and all except Connolly had found this aspect of his inebriation rather amusing. Connolly himself had suggested that it was about time Strachan at least, and probably some of the rest of the company, transferred to some non-alcoholic beverage. This had also been greeted with a certain amount of amusement but, to keep the peace with everybody, a compromise had been decided on. Connolly would drink lemonade if they could obtain it for him and the rest would have two half-pints instead of their normal pint. Connolly pointed out that this would at least guarantee a good supply of 'fruit and vegetable on the top'. This arrangement—peculiar as it might seem inside the cold walls of a police station—required a fair number of carriers; Reid, Connolly, Strachan and John Cartwright all helped to transport it from the bar. It was shortly after they had begun their drinks that Jolly Balsdon had left them. They had not been told at the start that their friend was dead, and none showed anything but surprise and shock when informed of the fact. As a matter of routine they were also thoroughly searched but none of them showed any signs of possessing any cyanide or indeed anything in which they could have carried it. They had all been in each other's company since the tragedy and none of them admitted to noticing any of the others trying to get rid of anything. They were all asked to wait in the police station.

"Have you got any indication as to who might be guilty, assuming it must be at least one of them, White?"

"None of them have given anything away at all and I can't even think of any way to try to break them down, except by irregular methods. The only other thing that occurs to me is that the cyanide could have been intended for someone else. Strachan for instance."

"You certainly have a point there. With fourteen half-pints of Pimms' floating around, there must be some margin for error. But for all that I think it unlikely. Someone as well on as Strachan appeared to be, and a Scotsman to boot, is likely to be rather protective towards his own drink, even if he wouldn't mind too much helping out others who were a little slower in consumption than himself."

"Do you think that we could make anything of Connolly's desire to drink no more alcohol? That would at least mean that he was immune himself."

"I don't think so. It seems too much in character from what we've heard. The same could be said of his attitude towards Strachan. No, what's disturbing me at the moment is that, although we're as certain as we can be that at least one of the five is a double murderer, we don't seem to have the slightest bit of evidence on which to charge any of them. I think we had better see them again but if we get nothing more out of them, I'm afraid we shall have to let them go. If we could only show that no more than two of them could have been both here and in Scotland on Wednesday night, we'd have enough circumstantial evidence to detain them. But we can't show that."

They were duly questioned again but nothing more was gained. They all gave the strong impression that they quite understood the reasons why they were being detained and in no way blamed the police for it. They were only sorry that they could be of no more help and, try as they might, could think of no explanation for Jolly Balsdon's death themselves. Exasperated and with a hollow feeling of frustration, Malone let them go.

It was now too late for them to catch the night train back to Edinburgh—it seemed to them that this was still their best course of action—and they had no desire to travel by road or air with the resultant lack of sleep. They therefore gratefully accepted hospitality offered by one of the local men in Henley. Their reasons for travelling back northwards immediately were twofold. Firstly, they could not see how they could deal with matters in London and Henley any better than their colleagues who were already on the job, and secondly Reid, Connolly and Strachan had announced their intention of returning as soon as they could to Scotland. In addition to this, all five seemed to have been drawn closely together by the common experience they had just gone through and Strachan had invited the two younger Cartwrights up to Ceres to attend the Open Championship which began in St. Andrews on Wednesday. The Cartwrights had volunteered this information when being questioned about their probable whereabouts over the next few days. From Malone's point of view, it seemed an excellent arrangement, as he would have all his suspects in the same area again and he made no effort to try to interfere. He reflected that they would all feel under suspicion and out of self-interest the innocent parties—assuming some of them were innocent—might do some of his work for him. He also felt that after their recent experiences they would be sufficiently on their guard. They would also be closely watched, with more care than the unfortunate Jolly Balsdon.

They left the police station in the company of the sergeant who had offered to put them both up. He was full of apologies for the makeshift nature of the hospitality but said that an attempt to find commercial premises at this time of year would have been pointless. Malone assured him that they would far prefer private accommodation anyway. If the sergeant and his family did not object, it would also be more convenient, as they would have to make an early start from London in the morning. The sergeant led them to his car and began to relate a tale of an amusing nature about the activities of one of the younger rowing supporters who had partaken of an excessive amount of champagne. Malone was again struck by the difference in type of behaviour of the drunken rowing supporter and his football counterpart. They had just set off when Malone was jerked back from such speculations into the business at hand.

"Could you stop please. You see that man walking towards us? That makes a genuine full house."

The car headlamps added to the street lighting left him in no doubt as to the identity of the nocturnal walker. It was Mr Richard Connolly of Ealing and he was wearing a Stewards' Enclosure Members' badge.

🙶 Chapter 9

MALONE AND WHITE GOT OUT OF THE CAR, just in front of the approaching figure.

"Good evening, Mr Connolly," said Malone.

"Good God, not you damn policemen again? Can't I walk down a street anywhere without being accosted by you people?"

They had parted in Ealing on what seemed reasonably friendly terms. What, Malone wondered, was the reason for this change of attitude? Or was it simply a deep-rooted mistrust of officialdom?

"Could you tell me why you did not leave your name when you left the Stewards' Enclosure this afternoon?" Malone was unaware whether he had or not but it was a plausible reason for questioning him.

"I don't see why I should have my night wrecked by your damn fool questions. Goodbye." He made as if to walk straight past them but White blocked his way. Malone continued:

"I'm afraid I can't let you go as easily as that, Mr Connolly. I require an answer to my question and to one or two others as well."

"And if I don't give you any answers, I suppose you'll arrest me for walking the wrong way down a one-way street or being out and about after midnight without a pass, is that it?"

"I hope it won't come to anything like that, Mr Connolly. I assure you that if you give me satisfactory answers, there will be no need to detain you for more than a couple of minutes."

"I suppose that doesn't give me much option, does it? Well, to answer your first question. I have no idea why I should want to leave my name in the Stewards Enclosure and secondly I couldn't have, as I've been nowhere near the place."

"Can you therefore explain why you're wearing a member's badge?"

"I don't see what business it is of yours, but I suppose I had better tell you. I was in a pub earlier and a drunken fellow came in with all his rowing man's kit on, blethering about how his crew had won some cup or other. He was making a lot of noise and ended up challenging anyone in the bar to a game of bar billiards for a fiver. Eventually some fellow got fed up with his noise, so took him on. But then, to everyone's surprise, the drunken man won. He became even more unbearable then and offered to take anyone on for a tenner. I played him and beat him. He paid up his tenner decently enough and insisted on giving me this badge. Then he left. Everyone in the bar wanted me to put it on, so I did just to humour them. I'd forgotten to take it off. That's all. If you don't believe me you can ask in the pub. It was called the Plough."

"That sounds almost unlikely enough to be true. Did you know that your brother was at the Regatta today?"

"How did you know I had a brother?"

"Never mind about that. Did you know he was at the Regatta?"

"I had no idea. I presumed he was in St. Andrews, where he lives. If you didn't know that, you can have the information for nothing. Now, if you've no further objection, I'd like to continue my walk."

"Just one or two more thing before you go, Mr Connolly, if you'd be good enough. Have you ever heard of a man called Clifford Balsdon, more often known as Jolly Balsdon?"

"No, I haven't, any more than I'd heard of that other fellow you were asking me about the other day. I suppose he's been murdered too?"

"Yes, Mr Connolly, he has and in the same way as the other fellow I was asking you about. Are you absolutely sure you were not in the Stewards' Enclosure this afternoon?"

"I've told you before, I wasn't. If you want to know what I was doing this afternoon, I was travelling here. I was on my own and I don't suppose anyone would remember me. Like a good citizen, I handed in my railway ticket at the station, so I haven't got one of them either."

"Wouldn't it have been more normal to take a cheap return?"

"If I knew where I was going when I left here and when, I suppose it would, but I don't. Anyway, I remember telling you before, I'm not very keen on watching rowing races."

"How close are you to your brother?"

"That's none of your business and I can't see what excuse you can make up to suggest that it is."

"One last question, Mr Connolly. Will you tell me what you're doing in Henley at this time of year, if it's nothing to do with the Regatta?"

"Not everyone goes to Kenya to shoot elephants, any more than everyone goes to Munich to drink beer."

"You have not answered my question, Mr Connolly. I strongly advise you to do so."

White suddenly burst out laughing. Malone considered this somewhat inappropriate and told him in no uncertain terms to keep quiet.

"I'm terribly sorry," he said, "but I couldn't help remembering the Meccano clock on Mr Connolly's wall. Tell me, Mr Connolly, do they still hold the annual Meccano exhibition in Henley?"

"Yes, they do. And I must say I'm glad to see at least one of you has the sort of knowledge you ought to possess. As a matter of fact, they're showing some of my efforts and I thought the least I could do was to appear here in person."

Malone was a little taken aback by this revelation and made no attempt to stop Connolly as he walked past him. When he had recovered himself, he too felt like laughing but instead turned to the sergeant and said: "I suppose you heard all that? That is so about the Meccano exhibition?"

"Certainly, but I'm not sure why you let him go. The pub story seemed a bit thin, if you don't mind me saying so."

"We've met Mr Connolly before and I suspect it's true. But I think we'd better go back into the station and have someone follow him, if for no other reason than to check when he arrived at his lodgings, wherever they may be. We can also have his pub tale verified at the same time."

A man was immediately despatched to follow Connolly, and, at the second attempt, they found the correct 'Plough'. The landlord, although a little grumpy about being woken up just after he had gone to sleep at the end of a hectic day, had no hesitation in confirming Connolly's story down to the detail of the badge. He didn't think he would recognise the rowing type again, saying that after all, when they were dressed that way they did look pretty much the same, didn't they? He doubted whether any of the customers would be much more help in that direction either, though he'd give them a few names if they wished. Yes, all in all they'd been pretty proud of Mr Connolly, if that was his name. He seemed a good straightforward sort of person.

The constable who had been sent after Connolly soon returned. He had not had far to go. Connolly had entered a house which was run as a small bed and breakfast establishment by a woman whom the constable knew quite well. He had therefore spoken to her with no difficulty and had received the following information. Richard Connolly was a regular visitor to the Meccano exhibition and had put up for several years now at the same establishment. Apart from the fact that he liked to take a late walk every night, thereby preventing early locking-up, he was a model guest. He had, as far as she knew, arrived by train that afternoon. At any rate, he had appeared at about half-past four, which was the time she would expect him at if he had taken the train. He had gone out shortly afterwards and returned punctually for the meal at seven. She couldn't for the life of her imagine what interest the police could have in him.

On receipt of this, Malone and White decided to continue their plan of getting some rest. Before they went to sleep, Malone said:

"Well, White, I'm glad your knowledge of toyland is so exact. But doesn't it look a bit like the perfect alibi? He's been coming here for years and so his presence will occasion no surprise. The four o'clock appointment would suit him perfectly, assuming his business was of no great duration. All the other suspects are assembled here, and even his brother. I don't know what it all means."

"I can't say I can see much sense in it either. If it hadn't been for the death of Blacklaw, and now that of Jolly Balsdon, it could all seem perfectly natural. As you say, it looks as if it were meant to look like that. Maybe we'll have some bright ideas in the morning."

"I hope so. We might have something more to go on from the blackmail angle soon. The Edinburgh men should have got some idea about Blacklaw's finances by tomorrow, even taking into account the weekend and the holiday season. But then again perhaps these accountants have their money kept in complicated ways, to avoid the sort of taxes

others don't know how to. Och well, let's consider the
matter tomorrow. I'm too tired and annoyed by the death
of Jolly Balsdon to consider much in a rational way at the
moment. I had great difficulty in remaining reasonable with
our men this evening. I wasn't too short of trying to beat
the truth out of them."

They rose early and were driven to Kings Cross for the
morning train to Edinburgh. They were met at the station
by Inspector Peagram who had seen to their baggage. He
also brought them up to date on the routine matters he had
been investigating. They were getting absolutely nowhere
with enquiries about the hiring of cars by the Cartwrights.
As he pointed out, this was probably because their version
of their movements was probably true; but anyway, he was
sure that if they had really wanted to cover up their tracks
in such a transaction, they would surely have managed to do
so. The enquiries at the West Ealing Archery Club were still
continuing but one fact had come to light which could
possibly have some bearing on the case. Although John
Strachan might have known his wife from elsewhere, the
first his fellow-members of the club had known of this
attachment was at one of the club's social gatherings. The
occasion had been recalled, as she had come with Blacklaw
but had left with Strachan. There had been no hint of
unpleasantness about the evening but it had struck one or
two people there as rather strange. The overt explanation
was that Blacklaw had known Susan when they were
children together in Lancashire and had merely brought her
along to give her the chance of meeting some people.
However, in the circumstances it had seemed a fact worth
recording. Added to this, at least one member had insisted
that he had good reason for believing that Blacklaw had
been closer to the woman than that suggested. Even when

he was warned that such information, if true, could be very suggestive, he did not withdraw his statement. He refused to expand but further enquiries on those lines were being pursued. Peagram promised to let Malone know immediately if any further information, however slight, came to light, in addition to any routine reports. Malone and White then said their goodbyes and thanked him for all his co-operation.

The journey to Edinburgh was uneventful and they passed it with sporadic conversation and a certain amount of sleep. When they reached Waverley Station, a car was waiting to drive them to Headquarters. They were informed that Inspector McGregor had just received some news which he wished them to share straightaway. He was waiting for them when they arrived.

"It's good to see you. I'm sorry about that business in Henley. It looks rather as if we're dealing with some pretty dangerous men. I'm afraid that so far we haven't been of much help at this end. But suddenly at lunchtime something turned up. A man came in who'd been persuaded by his pals in the Scott Bar to come along and see us. We don't know as yet how valuable his information is, but it was this. He stressed that he wasn't absolutely sure—he said that that was why he hadn't visited us before—but he was fairly certain that he had seen Blacklaw walking along Frederick Street in the direction of Princes Street at about quarter to six last Wednesday. And he wasn't alone. He was accompanied by a man and a woman. He didn't notice what they were like and he said the only reason he noticed at all was that he would have expected Blacklaw to be walking in the other direction, towards the Scott Bar. He said he could be fairly positive about having seen Blacklaw but couldn't swear to the rest. As he couldn't remember anything about the other two, he assumed they must have been the sort of respectable people he would have expected Blacklaw to be with. He stressed that he hadn't taken any particular notice and even if he was right about the man and the woman, they could have been anyone."

"Well, that's something at any rate. Assuming it was Blacklaw he saw, it's a fair assumption that he didn't go home that evening. Any further developments on that score?"

"None at all. We are attempting to establish who they might have been, but we haven't had that long and it's difficult to know where to start. I was actually wondering if you might have any ideas. But before we get onto that, I'll bring you up to date with our knowledge of Blacklaw's financial position. We've now got a pretty good idea of it, though we're still lacking some details. To begin with, he was a fairly rich man. Next, there's nothing positive to make him look like a blackmailer, but there is one peculiar fact which may point that way. He received regular monthly payments from other sources than his employers. He had told the bank that these were the fruits of some freelance work he was doing. It is always possible that either this work was of an extra-legal nature or that it was straight blackmail payment. None of this money, by the way, was paid by any of the people we've come across in the case. Apart from that, he had drawn out a number of sums over the last six months and we don't know of any woman. He already gave his mother a regular monthly payment. The possibility of gambling is being explored but there is no evidence or it yet."

"Thank you. That's at least something positive to work on. Firstly, I'm no wiser than you on the identity of Blacklaw's companions—the only candidates which spring to mind are Mr Reid and Miss Adamson, unless we allow the possibility of Albert Cartwright and his wife. By the way, when you say we don't know of any woman, what about Miss Adamson?"

"We immediately had her bank account checked and enquiries made about clothes and jewellery. We drew a complete blank."

"Well, I think we'd better ask for anyone who was in the vicinity of Frederick Street on Wednesday evening at about quarter to six to come forward and then get on to Mr Reid and Miss Adamson. I think we might try the young lady first."

He rang Miss Adamson's private address, as the firm of McColl and Duncan were on holiday. He had strong hopes of finding her there, as she had not indicated to the police that she had gone away. His hopes were realised, and she agreed to come to see him immediately, adding that she wanted very much to be of any assistance she could. Less than half an hour later, she was seated opposite Malone in McGregor's office. White was also present.

"I'm sorry to trouble you Miss Adamson," he began, "but as I expected at our last meeting, I require some more information from you."

"I don't know exactly how I can help any more but please do ask me anything you care to."

"Thank you, Miss Adamson. First of all, will you please tell me when you last saw Mr Blacklaw?"

"I thought we had been through that before. I last saw him when he left the office at about half-past five last Wednesday. I did tell you that before, didn't I?"

"You did indeed. But both you and I know that you told me a lie."

"How can you say that? It's true, I tell you."

"I see. Then would you be good enough to tell me exactly what you did when you left the office?"

"Well, I usually catch a bus at about quarter to six but I decided not to that night. I caught a later one."

"At what time?"

"I don't know exactly."

"I see. At what time did you return home?"

"I can't remember. Let me see now. My mother was going out about half-past seven. She had left when I got back. Yes, it must have been just after half-past seven."

"Can you produce anyone to confirm that?"

"No, of course not, I was alone in the house at the time."

"When did your mother return?"

"About half-past ten, I think."

"Then you cannot satisfactorily account for your movements between the time you left the office at, you say, half-past five, or shortly thereafterwards, until half-past ten."

"Of course I can. When I left the office I walked along Princes Street doing some window-shopping, and after that walked up the Mound towards the castle. No particular reason, you know, just taking a stroll. The weather was very pleasant, if you remember. I then sat in the Gardens for a bit and then went home, getting there at about half-past seven or just after."

"Is there anyone who can substantiate any of these supposed movements?"

"I don't think so. Why should there be?"

"It would be a sight more convenient for you if there was. You see, I happen to know that you are not telling the truth. I know that you were with Mr Blacklaw for at least part of the evening."

"There must be some mistake. I wasn't, as I told you. Oh, do you realise how horribly painful all this is to me?" Miss Adamson had clearly decided to take refuge in the time-honoured feminine method of getting out of an unpleasant situation. "If I can't tell you anything useful to help you get at Ronald's murderers, I'd prefer to go home." She began to get up.

"Sit down, Miss Adamson. Why did you say murderers in the plural?"

"I don't really know. I think you must have said there were two of them when you spoke to me last time. Or perhaps Mr Reid told me. Anyway, I can't imagine any one person getting the better of Ronald. He was a very fit and strong man."

"I see. I suppose you would be in a good position to judge his physical condition."

"You're absolutely horrible. I want to go. You've no right to keep me here and you know it. I want to see my lawyer."

"I think that might be a very sound idea, Miss Adamson, unless you are going to give me a satisfactory explanation of what you were doing with Mr Blacklaw on Wednesday night and why you lied to me earlier."

She had begun to sob uncontrollably now, and Malone could see little future in prolonging the interview. He therefore told her she could leave. She got up, gave him a nasty look and left without another word.

"Well, White, I hope I did the right thing there. I'm afraid things are far too serious to bother about the feelings of one young lady. Did you think she was telling the truth?"

"I really don't know. Remember she had originally planned to go out with Blacklaw that evening and said that he had put her off. If that's true, she might have acted in the way she claims, but not for the innocent reasons she suggests. I mean, she may have been hoping some other man would pick her up. You know how women act sometimes."

"That could be so; but wouldn't she then have admitted it to give more colour to her story?"

"I don't know. I don't pretend to understand the way women's minds—if I may use that term—work. It wouldn't have fitted in very well with the character she was trying to put over when we saw her last, would it?"

"That's very true. Well, I can't see what we've got to lose by assuming that Mr Reid was the other person seen by our man from the Scott. Let's see if we can get him along."

Reid's number was engaged when he tried it at first. The strong possibility that Miss Adamson was the cause did, of course, occur to Malone. When the line was finally clear, he found that Reid was quite as willing as Miss Adamson had been to help. Malone offered to send him transport but he declined saying that he would prefer it if his neighbours did not see him picked up in a police car.

He arrived in about half an hour and Malone wondered if he should immediately ask if he had been in contact with Miss Adamson. He found this was an unnecessary question.

After being greeted, Mr Reid volunteered: "I think you ought to know that Miss Adamson rang me up just before you did. The poor girl was in a terrible state. I understand that after that unpleasant business in Henley on top of everything else you will be feeling the strain but I feel I must put a word in on her behalf. I'm sure she will have told you the absolute truth, and even if you can't see your way to apologising to her, you should at least leave her alone in the future. I appear to be one of the few responsible people she can appeal to for protection and so I might at least demand that I should be informed if you intend to put her through such an experience again."

Malone disregarded this statement. "Mr Reid, I have not until now thought it necessary to establish your movements on Wednesday evening with any exactness. Will you be good enough to tell me what you were doing between, shall we say five o'clock and the next morning?"

"That is very simple, Inspector. I left the office at about six o'clock and went home. I took a taxi. I have no idea whether the driver would remember me or not, if you were going to ask, and I remember nothing special about him or the taxi. Just a normal Hackney Carriage. I took a fair amount of work with me, as there was quite a lot to catch up on before the holiday. I made myself a snack and then worked until around eleven o'clock. By that time I was very tired and went to bed. As I live on my own, there is of course no way I can prove that those were my movements. I am not often called upon to account for them and can see no reason for taking special care in establishing proof of alibi."

"We shall of course attempt to find the taxi-driver, if he existed. But I don't believe he did, Mr Reid. You were seen in Frederick Street with Miss Adamson and Mr Blacklaw at about quarter to six."

"That is the same preposterous accusation you made against Miss Adamson—I can use no other terms for it. And if you are going to continue in this vein, you will not get another word out of me. Furthermore, I shall make a formal complaint about your behaviour, both on my own account and Miss Adamson's."

"Before you add that you will consult your lawyer, may I suggest that such a course might be prudent? Good evening, Mr Reid."

After he had left, Malone turned to White with a weary expression on his face. "We had better have it properly checked but what's the betting that James Connolly was also on his own that night? Again, not being used to accounting for his movements and having no guilty conscience, he will have seen no reason for establishing an alibi."

Immediately a request was put through to establish what could be learned of James Connolly's movements. Malone asked for this information by the morning at the latest. He said to White: "We might be in luck and find ourselves able to drop him from our list but somehow I don't think so. That would be too much like a lucky break and we don't appear to be getting any of those on this job. Look at the mess we're in. First of all we've got Strachan. He arranges for his house to be empty and then appears there at a wholly unnecessary time in the morning to make final arrangements for an archery beano. He claims to have discovered the body of Blacklaw on his arrival there. He has no explanation of a convincing type to explain why his house should be chosen at a time when it is conveniently empty. He had to admit his professional connection with the dead man and even volunteered an old family relationship between his wife and Blacklaw. We now have reason to believe that this relationship might well have been deeper than that. He has motive therefore and even seems to have set up part of the opportunity. But then we know he can't have done it on his own. It was through his suggestion that we went off to look at the London end, perhaps aided by the self-addressed note to Blacklaw."

"That brings us to Reid. Admittedly we have no obvious motive to connect him with anything like a murder but there could easily be something private we know nothing of. He certainly had the opportunity—at least he can't prove otherwise—and we could easily imagine a motive in connection with Miss Adamson. Which takes us to that young lady. She cannot, I suppose, have been anything more than an accessory but, if for some reason Reid wanted to make Blacklaw feel safe, she was an obvious tool. Also she would clearly have been invaluable for leading us up the wrong road. I might add against Mr Reid that his explanation for opening Blacklaw's mail was rather weak and there was nothing to prevent his putting that note in the letter merely to confuse us. It certainly did that and if it had not been for the unfortunate Jolly Balsdon, whose death can really put us in no doubt as to our suspects, we might have been looking anywhere by now."

"And then we come to our London men. Firstly there's the Cartwright family. Albert admittedly looks a long shot but John and the father had the opportunity, the poison and some sort of motive. Add to this the fact that the murder took place on the anniversary of the firm. If only one of them was involved, the other must still be an accomplice. Richard Connolly's reasons would appear to be a bit more obscure but he is certainly a strange man and used to living in parts of the world where perhaps the value of human life is not rated quite as highly as here. He had both the opportunity and the poison and a family connection in the area. Which takes us to James Connolly. Not too likely on the surface but easily could have been involved with his brother—or for some reason we haven't fathomed yet, with one of the others. Any or all of them could be double murderers and we don't know who. I would add, that if only two of them are involved, they're trying to make it pretty difficult for us, by keeping all the others in the foreground."

"Aye," said White, "but wouldn't that tend to put Richard Connolly out of the reckoning? After all, he claimed not to know the others were at Henley and to be there for a totally different reason himself."

"It would, if he were telling the truth. But we've got at least two liars and I for one can't see how to distinguish who they are. Well, with Peagram and McGregor still going at it hammer and tongs, I'm sure something is bound to turn up soon. There seems to be nothing more for us to do at the moment, so I think we might as well go and see our neglected wives again."

6♦ Chapter 10

AT NINE O'CLOCK ON THE TUESDAY MORNING, Malone
and White were back in the Inspector's office in Kirkcaldy.
Although they both were a little tired after their trip to the
South, they felt a pleasant sense of security in the familiar
surroundings. The first piece of news they received that
morning surprised neither of them. Mr James Connolly
maintained that he had been in his own house reading all
the last Wednesday evening. He had seen no-one until about
ten o'clock on the Thursday morning. Neighbours had been
asked if they remembered lights on in his house that evening
but none of them could remember. As Malone pointed out,
even if they had, it would be inconclusive. Leaving lights on
is the most obvious precaution to take if you wish people to
believe that you are at home when you are not. White then
volunteered some thoughts.

"I've been feeling rather guilty about Jolly Balsdon's
death, especially since we got back here. As a result, I spent
a bit of time looking up my poison book this morning to see
about cyanide and its effects. As you probably know, it
breaks down into something quite harmless in the presence
of carbon dioxide and water. Well, even if you're drinking a
strong Pimm's, there's a lot of lemonade in the mixture.
That I would have thought makes the last drink the only
possibility—as we had assumed already. But I wonder if we
might go further and add that it was more likely to have
been introduced at the table, rather than during the buying
of the drinks."

"That's a good point. But our only problem is that we
don't know how much was introduced into the drink in the
first place. Obviously there would be less risk of the drinker
noticing if there was as little as possible; but as yet we don't

know how much risk our men were prepared to take. But it certainly precludes the possibility that anyone apart from our principals were involved in that murder and therefore in Blacklaw's too. But on the other hand, it also means that we can't separate carriers of the drinks from the others. That means we'll have to have the two friends Jolly had with him looked into a bit more carefully. Yet I don't think we'll find anything amiss with them."

"Do you think we could cut them down by considering who had access to the poison?"

"We could try to but I don't think it would be very helpful. In the first place, only one of our men need have had the stuff and secondly the others may have been able to get hold of it in some way we don't know of. No, I think it would be unwise to make an assumption on those grounds. I'm afraid we'll just have to see if our colleagues can come up with something soon. Ah, perhaps we'll have something here."

A few reports had just been brought in and Malone looked at them eagerly. The first was from Peagram with news on the movements of the suspect men. Malone could not help smiling a little as he read it. "I'm afraid it's not really that amusing, White, and if anything begins to point more towards an element of conspiracy. It's just the way that the good Mr Connolly of Ealing does it that makes me smile. It seems that he walked into Henley Police Station to tell them that, to save them carrying out their persecution, he'd tell them where he was going. His destination is, of course, St. Andrews and he gave his brother's address. When they asked him why he was going, he told them it was none of their business and he wouldn't have been asked such a fatuous question by the 'Scotch policemen, at any rate the younger one'. The difficulty is, of course, he's quite right. If you happen to know that he's got a new driver to show off and a brother living in the town to boot, where more natural to go than the Open in St. Andrews? It's the same with the others. They're all definitely coming here—the London ones, that is. And like good citizens, they've indicated their intention to the police. They're all staying with Strachan, the old man included. Gordon Reid and James Connolly, as members of the Kilrymont, will surely be there as well. What does it all mean?"

"They've managed to make it all seem very natural but common sense cries out against it," said White. "They must all, or nearly all, be in it together. Your composer thing was all very well but they didn't all die in the same year."

"No, White, they didn't. But the year Gay died, Haydn was born."

"In that case, I only hope that there's not another Jolly Balsdon."

"We shall certainly have to watch. But let's face it, we don't know for certain that he was a totally innocent bystander. He did after all invite some of our suspects to the Regatta."

"Yes, but for goodness sake, he was murdered for his pains."

"Perhaps he had not realised what level of conspiracy he was entering and had given the principals the impression that he would give them away. I know it seems unlikely but we don't know why they decided to get rid of him—if indeed he was the intended victim. They must have felt pushed in some way. It was a pretty desperate risk on the face of it. I liked him instinctively as much as you clearly did. But we mustn't let emotion cloud our judgement."

"I don't think that's quite fair. It's not purely emotion. We know from his size that he couldn't possibly have been involved in the dumping of the body. Also he's just the sort of popular person our men would like to have to cover their actions."

"I agree that he's a most unlikely candidate for such a plot but all I'm saying is that we can't drop him absolutely from our calculations just because he was a popular man. The more pressing question is what we are going to do now?"

"Do you think it's about time we dragged some of them in and gave them a good going over?"

"If you mean verbally, I think you're right. It may come to more later but I don't think we should consider that now. I think we'd best start with Strachan."

Malone obtained Strachan's telephone number and rang him. John Strachan was very insistent about his desire to help as best he could, especially after the appalling business at Henley. He was quite happy to come to Kirkcaldy immediately if they wished. As they probably knew, he had some guests, but he was sure that they would think it quite as important as he himself did.

"I think, White," said Malone, "that unless we get something positive from our interview with Strachan, we might as well go to St. Andrews ourselves and take in some of the practice rounds. I suspect our men will be doing the same thing, if only to keep up their outward appearance of being in this area for the golf. As for Strachan, I don't see any reason why we need to be too pleasant to him. If he's innocent, he should have no real objection—at least after we've finished with the case."

Strachan was soon in their presence, and clearly had meant it when he said he would appear immediately. After rather cold formalities, Malone spoke.

"Well, Mr Strachan, I suppose I should thank you for appearing so promptly. However, in the circumstances, if you still desire to uphold your innocence, I don't think you had much option. After all, as I'm sure must have occurred to you, it is bound to strike us as an odd coincidence that you discovered—or so you claim—the body of Blacklaw, and were also present when Balsdon was murdered in a similar manner. You will therefore answer some questions and answer them truthfully. If we find subsequently that you have been lying, it could count heavily against you. Firstly, tell me how well you knew the Cartwright family before the Regatta?"

"Don't worry, Inspector, I quite understand your suspicions and I want to take any opportunity I can to prove to you that this business has nothing whatsoever to do with me. About the Cartwrights, then. I knew Albert Cartwright slightly through business with Sloane and Simpson but I didn't know him at all well. I hadn't met the other two until the Regatta but I believe I knew of their existence. I ought to point out that when I was with that firm, I never dealt directly with the financial affairs of their business."

"I see. You hardly knew Albert Cartwright then. And yet you hailed him as a long-lost friend when you saw him in the Fawley Bar?"

"Yes. I know it may seem a bit weird but when you're in a gathering and you see a familiar face, you're inclined to act that way, especially when you don't really know many other people. A lot of folk carry on like that abroad when they come across a compatriot, whether they know him or not."

"That may well be true, but I would have thought in the presence of Jolly Balsdon you wouldn't be stuck for company. Still, we'll let that pass for the moment. Why then on such a slender acquaintance, did you invite all three of the Cartwrights up here for the Open?"

"Again that may seem a bit strange when we're sitting here. But it seemed the most natural thing in the world there, especially after we had undergone the same unpleasant experience."

"Did it not strike you that you were perhaps inviting a murderer to your house?"

"Not at the time. It didn't seem possible. But I must admit that the thought has occurred to me since and quite honestly has been bothering me. That's one of the reasons I'm very keen to help you."

"Has anything since their arrival caused you to suspect any or all of them?"

"Nothing at all. Poor old Mr Cartwright hasn't been too well since Jolly Balsdon's death, but I assumed that was a mixture of shock and age; that's why I added him to the invitation later. His sons both appear to be very solicitous about his health, and, in their different ways, very pleasant. Of course, they haven't been here long."

"How well do you know James Connolly's brother Richard?"

"James Connolly's brother? I didn't even know he had one."

"Even when I tell you he lives in Ealing?"

"Oh, I'm sorry, you must mean the man who was a client of Sloane and Simpson. But I assure you, I didn't know he was James Connolly's brother until you mentioned it just now and I never met him while I was employed by that firm."

"Do you not find it strange that two of the parties who had irregular accounts—or in one case their immediate family—were in the same company at the Regatta?"

"It certainly does seem an amazing coincidence. But you see, I didn't know at the time."

"I would put it to you, Mr Strachan, that when we add that you were a former employee of the firm, it stretches belief if you maintain that there was no connection."

"I know it seems unbelievable but there was certainly no prearrangement as far as I was concerned. I can't of course speak for the others."

"You have some reason for thinking that one of them may have arranged it?"

"I didn't say that and, as it was Jolly Balsdon who invited most of us, I can't see how it could have been that way."

"Can you tell me whose idea it was that you should all come up here for the Open?"

"I'm not too sure. Jolly had certainly been suggesting it on the Saturday and it was on the Sunday afternoon that it was really put forward as a concrete suggestion. But it was only after his death that we finally decided that it might take our minds off that tragedy. We were also aware that the police might well be questioning us, and it seemed more pleasant to be together when that was happening. But as I say, it hadn't really entered my head that one of them could have killed Jolly at the time."

"It didn't strike you as peculiar that the Cartwrights could rush up here at a moment's notice?"

"No, but I suppose it might have done if I'd thought about it."

"Tell me, Mr Strachan, do you possess any potassium cyanide or have easy access to it?"

"I suppose there's no point in denying it. Thousands of people must have some lying about their garages and garden sheds. I've got some in my garage. When we moved into the house, certain parts needed fumigating. I was recommended to use potassium cyanide. I know I should have got rid of any excess. But it's like medicines and weedkillers, you always tend to keep them in case you should need them again."

"You haven't used it since the fumigation?"

"No, and to tell you the truth, I couldn't swear that it's still there. I thought of looking yesterday but somehow I didn't like to. It was a sort of mixture of being frightened to find it had gone, and leaving my own traces if it was still there. It seems a bit silly now."

"Yes, Mr Strachan, it does, doesn't it? Like several other of your actions of late, at least the way you explain them. Now tell me how well your wife knew Ronald Blacklaw before you met her."

"What sort of question is that? I don't mind answering personal and even unpleasant enquiries about myself but I can't see what my wife's private life a number of years ago has to do with you, and I see no reason to reply to you."

"You don't, Mr Strachan? First of all, it is for me to decide what is germane to my investigation. Secondly, I had better remind you of the position you're in. Two men dumped the body of Blacklaw in your grounds. We don't as yet have a very good description of them but you could easily fit what we have. To an outside observer your reason for being in Ceres at that time of the morning would seem rather thin. Blacklaw was poisoned with cyanide: you, on your own admission possess some. Then there was the unpleasantness of the arrow: you are an archer. We didn't find one or two things we might have hoped to on his body: you had lit a fire on a warm summer's morning. You were connected with Blacklaw in some way both through your occupation and your wife. It is easy to divine some reason through either of these why you might want to get rid of him. In somewhat peculiar circumstances you went to Henley: Jolly Balsdon was about to give me some information which he thought was valuable and he was murdered. The same method was used as with Blacklaw. You had ample opportunity to do the deed. I might easily have asked you straightaway who your accomplice was. I'm sure men have been convicted on less evidence. Instead, I'm still inclined to give you the benefit of the doubt, provided you will answer what I ask you. So I say again: how well did your wife know Blacklaw before you met her?"

"All right, I suppose I'd better answer you. But I may tell you that I don't believe for a minute you could arrest me on such flimsy evidence, even if there was the slightest chance that I was guilty. Like everyone else, I suppose, I was told not long before I got married by self-styled friends that I would be wise to look into my future wife's past, especially with reference to Ronald Blacklaw. Quite frankly, I cared about it as much as most other people in love—that is, almost not at all. I had no more desire to examine her past love-life than she had to search out mine. Neither of us wanted to know. But if you want my opinion, any suggestion of an affair with Ronald Blacklaw is a spiteful fabrication."

"You never gave him any thought as being a potential rival?"

"I never gave him much thought except as an archer and, very occasionally as an accountant. Before you ask me, I had of course considered the possibility of being asked about him and my wife. If I must answer, I say I don't know, I don't care and I don't want to know."

"You exhibit a fine broad-minded attitude, I'm sure, Mr Strachan. However, you would not be the first to react to such a relationship, if it existed, in a different manner. Have you ever thought that some liaison between your wife and Blacklaw could have taken place after you were married?"

"If I wasn't in my present position, I would answer you in a more primitive manner. As it is, all I shall say is no and I'm quite sure that it would have been impossible. Perhaps you spend your time wondering who's in bed with your wife whenever you're called to the south of England or wherever for a case?"

"I think you might as well go now, Mr Strachan. But before you do, two words of warning. Firstly, the police will be watching every movement of yours very carefully. Secondly, if you are telling the truth, and you had nothing to do with either of these murders, watch yourself very carefully. Remember what happened to Jolly Balsdon and bear in mind it could easily be you next."

After John Strachan had gone, Malone turned to White. "You haven't been saying anything. What did you think? Was he telling the truth?"

"It's difficult to say. I wouldn't have thought the circumstantial evidence against him was any better than what we've got on the others. And remember, as we haven't heard to the contrary, his alibi for Wednesday night must stand up. In that case, he can't himself have been involved in the actual murder of Blacklaw. If he had been, he would almost certainly have made much of the fact that he couldn't have been. He also doesn't strike me as the sort of chap who'd go in for the mutilation after death bit. For all his talk, he's probably as capable as anyone else of reacting to a strong feeling of jealousy but I don't see him desecrating dead bodies. If there were more than two in it, of course, that could have been done against his will. Once you're in a murder conspiracy, you have to go as low as the lowest man or give yourself away."

"I'm not at all sure, White. I can't get over the feeling that there's something wrong with him. The thing that troubles me most is his behaviour on Sunday. He was supposedly very drunk in the afternoon. When we saw him in the evening, he seemed to show no signs of it. You might suggest that the shock sobered him up. Well, he travelled up here yesterday, after a lot of drink and a shock strong enough to make him sober, made arrangements for putting up unexpected guests and then can appear here now looking bright as a button. If you'll forgive me for mentioning it, you don't look in such fine fettle as he does and I'm quite sure I don't. Even if we take that as a sign of a clear conscience on his part, we must be dealing with a pretty cool man."

"Well, if he's got nothing to hide, he should be worried now. You made it pretty clear to him that as far as we're concerned one of his companions at the Regatta must have been guilty and probably at least two. If he still shows no sign of alarm, it certainly will look rather incriminating. From what we know, we can probably put Albert Cartwright out of the reckoning for direct complicity in the death of Blacklaw. Do you think it might be worth leaning on him a little?"

"A rather unpleasant American expression, White, but I think a certain amount of pressure in that direction might possibly produce dividends. When someone is under the impression that the police are breathing down his neck, he can become remarkably keen on finding a substitute for the attention. I hope that's the sort of effect we'll have had on Strachan. I'd like to wait a few hours to see if he can come up with anything to help us and then I think we might try the good Albert."

There were one or two further reports to be looked at. The only two of immediate interest were concerned with the financial affairs of Albert Cartwright and Ronald Blacklaw. The former had apparently been in regular receipt of certain unexplained sums of money and the latter had seemingly been paying out a not dissimilar sum.

"That may be coincidence," said Malone, "or more likely leads to the intriguing possibility that we had it the wrong way round and for some reason Blacklaw was paying out money to Albert. That would certainly explain the peculiarity of the self-addressed envelope. Such a scheme would be a great assistance in preserving the anonymity of the sender.

"Aye," said White, but I can't really see why a blackmailer should want to get rid of the person who was paying him money. You would normally expect it to be the other way round."

"Exactly so. For all we know, Albert's secretly cursing whoever did it. I wonder if we can draw any conclusions about Mr Reid's actions from this supposition, if it's correct. The way he opened that letter and then replaced the contents has seemed very strange all along. It could be that he was wanting to start a false scent by leaving it for our attention. It might have appealed to him, if he knew that a number of possible suspects would be assembled at the Regatta at the same time. He's certainly as strong a candidate as anyone else for our guilty party."

"That's the trouble," said White. "They all seem to be as possible as each other."

"I don't think it's quite as bad as that but it's very much still a question of probabilities. Well, I think our best plan now is to change into something a bit more suitable for the occasion and try our luck at pretending to be harmless spectators at the practice round in St. Andrews. At least we should keep in fairly close touch with our men there and we were hoping to see some of the golf. You never know, Peagram may come up with someone or other who's been totally out of the reckoning and we'll need to go south again."

They arranged to meet in the bar of the Lochnagar Hotel, which commanded a view of the eighteenth green of the Old Course. They reasoned that it would therefore be full and so useful as a place to meet. Malone was the first to arrive and ordered two half pints of heavy. He had actually expected White to arrive first but he did not have many minutes to wait.

"I'm sorry to have been detained," said White, "but my wife has got the wind up a bit over the murder of Jolly Balsdon. She's quite sure that I'm the next on the list. I tried to point out that the death of a policeman always caused far too much disturbance for anyone who hoped to get away with other killings, but she took quite a lot of convincing."

"Let's hope that she has no grounds for her concern. Like you, I think it most unlikely that whoever our men are they'll try anything on us, but I never thought they'd try it on Balsdon either. Without getting jittery about it, we might as well watch our step."

"Such as refusing to drink any Pimms' if we're offered it?"

"Not quite. But joking apart, we'd be as well to make it clear that we're on duty if we do find ourselves in such a position. I want to make them feel they're being watched. As they drank their beer, they fell to discussing its comparative merits with the brews that they had partaken of in the South and Malone was quite adamant that he would prefer to risk a doubtful pint of properly kept beer untainted by CO_2 gas than drink the rather tasteless liquid they had before them. He would prefer to have something positive to say; this stuff was just uniformly uninteresting. White decided that he could not agree and maintained that, although he had preferred one or two of the brews they had sampled in London, at least they could be sure that this stuff was drinkable. It was clear that they were unlikely to reach agreement on this complex point. Malone had just offered the helpful tag 'de gustibus nil disputandum', when White interrupted him.

"It looks like we've just about been dealt a full house again."

Malone turned to discover the reason for this remark and was surprised, if no more, to see that the two younger Cartwrights, the two Connollys and Gordon Reid had entered the bar. They had already reached the bar, when John Cartwright looked round and recognised the policemen.

"Well, well. It looks as if we can't go anywhere without seeing our two favourite coppers. Still, I suppose this must be almost your local manor. For all that, I'm surprised to see that they give you time off when you're deep in the investigating of murder. Anywhere nearer your man yet?"

Malone answered. "It depends on how I interpret that last remark of yours, Mr Cartwright. In one sense I think it very likely that I am near to at least one of our men. But I must confess that I'm still a little short on proof. Are your father and Mr Strachan not with you?"

"No. My father wasn't feeling very well. He's really a bit old for all this gallivanting around but he wanted to get right away after the shock. I'm sure you'll understand. John Strachan kindly offered to stay with him. They hope to come and join us soon if he feels better. John wasn't looking too good after he came back from seeing you. Still, I suppose we're all a bit jittery in one way or another. It's the thought of Jolly Balsdon dying just after he'd been with us. The sooner you find whoever was responsible, the more relieved we'll all feel. You seem to have some spare seats around you. Have you any objection to our joining you?"

"None at all. As soon as you've got your drinks, just park yourselves. We'll have to be going fairly soon anyway."

The party came to join them. They were all drinking beer in half pints except for James Connolly who was sporting a glass of orange juice. He was the first to speak.

"It's a good job we know you. All the other seats are occupied. It must be some aura you policemen carry about with you." When no-one smiled, he added: "I'm sorry, I hope you haven't taken offence; it was meant to be a joke."

"No offence taken at all, Mr Connolly," answered Malone. "But I would point out that the clientele might be even more averse to sitting with a company who were the last drinking companions of Jolly Balsdon. It might look a bit too much like an unlucky gathering."

None of them knew exactly how to reply to this and they began to discuss the circumstances of the death of Jolly Balsdon. They were all by now perfectly aware of how he had met his death and were all quite adamant that they were mystified by the whole business. They couldn't see how anyone could possibly have administered the poison for the start. Richard Connolly, the only one of them who had not been there, declared that it was a clear case of suicide, adding that he was tired of hearing that Balsdon was not that sort of chap. Genuine suicides, he maintained, as opposed to attempted cases, were carried out by all manner of different people. You could never tell what was going on behind people's facades.

"What then," said White, "do you make of the fact that Mr Blacklaw was killed in the same way?"

"Simple coincidence—except he probably got the idea of how to do it from hearing about this person Blacklaw. I

177

suppose you still want to maintain that it wasn't coincidence that brought me to Henley at the same time as my brother and these fellows?"

"We might yet."

Gordon Reid had clearly decided that the conversation was becoming a little embarrassing and began to launch into a criticism of modern British golfers. As usual, he said, one or two home players would start off with a remarkably good first round and the papers would be full of the possibility of the first British victory for umpteen years. Then, just as predictably, they would blow up half-way through the second round and the favoured Americans would take the lead and hold onto it until the end. He declared that unless people over here grasped the fact that being a professional meant just that—being prepared to dedicate your whole life to the business in hand—this would continue to be the situation in the foreseeable future. No-one could find any way of disagreeing with this obviously correct summing up of the state of affairs. James Connolly added that as far as he was concerned, it didn't matter too much where the player came from, as long as he played some good, inspired golf. The conversation continued for a few minutes on these lines, until Albert Cartwright, noticing that most of the glasses were empty, suggested another round. James Connolly then said that the most he could manage in the alcohol line at this time of day was a weak Pimms'.

Malone was waiting for a reaction at this, but to his surprise they all decided that Pimms' was indeed the thing at this juncture. He suddenly realised that some of them at least had as yet not connected the fact of the Pimms' at Henley with the death of Balsdon. He was forced to discard any possible idea of a conspiracy containing them all or admit that they were all consummate actors. He wondered vaguely if this was a pointer yet again to the guilt of Strachan. He had admitted to a fear that one of his guests might be responsible, and this surely indicated that he understood how the deed was done. Before he could continue with these thoughts, he was interrupted by the voice of Albert Cartwright.

"I'm sure you good bobbies could do with one too. It won't knock you off your feet. And that was supposed to be a joke too."

Malone granted him a forced smile. "I'm afraid we'll have to refuse your kind offer, Mr Cartwright, as we're distinctly on duty at the moment. Some other time perhaps."

"Nonsense," said Albert and went up to the bar to join his brother who was seeing to the drinks.

"You must stay and have one with us before you go," said James Connolly, "I don't know exactly what your business is here but it can't be that pressing or you wouldn't have come in here in the first place."

Both Malone and White insisted that they had only been there for the purpose of meeting and indeed must go. However, they would expect to see some or all of the company in the not-too-distant future. Before this last remark had to be amplified, they all heard the voice of Albert Cartwright welcoming some newcomers. The policemen turned round and there at the bar had appeared John Strachan and old Cartwright, looking on the face of it none the worse for all his experiences and travelling. Malone toyed with the idea of staying but came to the conclusion that a departure would suit his purposes better. He and White rose but immediately John Strachan put two half-pints of Pimms' in front of them.

"Albert insists that you have these before you go. James is just bringing the others over on a tray. I must say, I'm a little surprised at the choice of drink after what happened at Henley, but it seems to have been agreed on before we reached here."

Albert and James Connolly returned at this point and Malone thanked them very much for their generosity. However, he was quite adamant that they had to be going and White agreed with him.

"It was a very kind thought," said Malone, "but we did refuse. From what I remember of Henley, Mr Strachan here should have no difficulty in drinking them for us. If any of you should want to contact us we'll be based in the Police Station here."

With that Malone and White left the bar.

6❧ Chapter 11

THEIR DESTINATION was St. Andrews Police Station. Malone had asked for any urgent messages to be sent there and he judged it wise to pay a visit before they proceeded with anything else. For a start, the place would be extremely busy because of the Open, and he saw no point in making things more difficult by neglecting a small politeness. It was always possible that they would need unexpected assistance. Neither he nor White had managed to find a parking space very near to the Lochnagar and so they decided to walk the few hundred yards to the station.

"Well, White," said Malone, as they left the area of the golf courses, "do you wish you were playing?"

"Yes and no. I always feel sure that I could do just as well as a lot of fancied people who are bound to lose their nerve. I can of course get a bit worked up myself but when it's over a familiar course you know, there's no reason to get put out by one or two unlucky shots. That's especially true on the Old Course, as you know. But on the other hand, when there's absolutely no chance of finishing in the first dozen however well you play, it hardly seems worth it. Another point is that there's not so much fun in it with the length of the rounds nowadays. With a quick player off-season I can still easily get round in less than two and a half hours; the thought of four and a half is off-putting."

"Aye, you're right about the length of time. Many was the time when we were students that we'd start a round at half-past two closing time and be back at the pub hammering at the door at five o'clock opening. Still, I suppose so much money is at stake in these tournaments that you can't blame the professionals for wanting to leave nothing to chance. It's their livelihood after all. Well, unless we get some light on this case pretty quickly we'll not be seeing much play, however slow they make it."

When they reached the police station, they were greeted by Sergeant Johnson, who had been the mainstay of the local force when White had been a constable in St. Andrews before he had transferred to the CID. Despite all the bustle caused by an influx of an estimated twenty-five thousand people a day for the golf, he was still his normal unruffled self.

"I'm very pleased to see you," he said. "I'm afraid I can't offer you the greatest of facilities at the moment, as I'm sure you'll understand, but I've made a corner of the room at the back available for you and you can certainly take it over in its entirety for short periods."

"That's very kind of you, Sergeant. I suppose I had better promise not to entice any more likely young constables away from you in return. You'll of course know something about our case but I'd better fill you in with what we know for certain.

Malone informed the Sergeant briefly of the state of the case.

"I hope there's no possibility of them trying it again."

"That would be most unlikely, I think, but they're all being watched discreetly just in case."

"Have you tried pulling them all in and giving them a good going over?"

"Not yet. I'm trying to hold off doing so but I'm afraid we'll be left with little option soon. The trouble is that none of them would let it lie if they were innocent. We'd have all hell to pay if we picked the wrong ones. Most of them are the sort to take the line that they don't mind that sort of thing happening to criminals but no-one's going to get away with it where fine upstanding members of society are concerned."

"Och well, never mind. Make yourselves at home with a cup of tea for the moment. We've of course been asked to make enquiries especially as regards Mr James Connolly and your elusive blue Cortina but I'm afraid we're not getting anywhere at the moment.

The telephone vas ringing. The constable who answered it called across to Sergeant Johnson. "Sergeant, I've got a man here who says he won't speak to anyone except yourself, or not a mere constable at any rate. Sounds like an American."

The Sergeant turned to the two detectives. "We get a lot who insist on talking to the man in charge nowadays. I always feel I've got to do my bit for the tourist trade, so I suppose I'd better answer."

Malone and White took little notice of the call, assuming like the Sergeant that it was some request for special treatment. They were therefore very surprised at his words when he replaced the receiver.

"Well gentlemen, after what you said, that's some surprise. A caddie named Iain McDaid has just been taken to the hospital with cyanide poisoning. They're just in time to save his life, but he was in a pretty bad way."

"What? How did it happen?"

"He was seen to be in a bad way in the bar of the Lochnagar Hotel. Anyone who knew him would assume it was just drink, even at this time of day. Luckily for him, there was an American visitor in the bar at the time who wouldn't believe it and insisted on commandeering a car and taking him straight down to the hospital. The American, a Mr Alfred Weidhammer, will call on us as soon as he can get here. He wants to make an official complaint; why he should choose to make it to us, I don't know." The telephone rang again. "I expect that will be the hospital giving us the same facts."

The hospital did confirm the fact that their patient was suffering from potassium cyanide poisoning. They would of course help the police in any way they could, as in the circumstances it did not look as if it were an accident.

"It looks like I've been wrong all along," said Malone. "I didn't think Jolly Balsdon could have been in any danger and now this. Do you realise, Sergeant, that when we left the Lochnagar not half an hour ago, our suspects were gathered there to a man? But why a caddy?"

"I can't help wondering," said White, "whether the half pints of Pimms' we refused have anything to do with it."

"You may well be right. If Mr Weidhammer is about to appear we'd better hear what he has to say and then get down to the Lochnagar as quickly as possible. Sergeant, could you get on to them immediately and tell them to wash no more glasses until we get there? We may well be too late already but there's no harm in trying."

Mr Weidhammer was not long in coming. It was obvious from the expression on his face and the manner he was assuming that he intended to give a good piece of his mind to whomever he thought it might concern. However, his position of moral superiority was a little shaken by Malone anticipating him by speaking first.

"Mr Weidhammer, I presume? I'm Inspector Malone of the CID I must begin by thanking you very much for your prompt action just now. There can be no doubt that you saved a man's life. He's a good deal luckier than the last one we came across in similar circumstances. From that you can deduce, I'm sure, that we're very interested in everything surrounding your actions. We would be very grateful, therefore, if you could tell us all about it."

"Well," said Weidhammer, "I had intended to tell you what I thought of the attitude of the local inhabitants and the bartenders in the Lochnagar especially, to the sight of a man who was clearly ill. But the way you put it, it sounds like you need information as quickly as you can get it, so I'd better come over with that first. I'd just walked into the bar after watching a few people holing out at the eighteenth. There were a couple of pretty ropey looking characters sitting down— caddies I guessed. I noticed them immediately because one of then suddenly started acting queer. It's not a thing I'm used to in your bars over here. I mentioned it to the bartender who just shrugged and said he'd clearly had too much. Well, it seemed a bit early in the day and, as I said, I'm not used to seeing that sort of thing over here, so I asked the bartender again what he was going to do about it. He just ignored me. That made me pretty angry, so I went over to see what I could do for the poor fellow. No-one seemed interested, not even the fellow he was with. I got him on his feet and took him outside. I then hailed the first car with enough room in it and told them to take us to the hospital. The driver refused at first and I had to offer him money before he would. To be fair, when we got to the hospital, he wouldn't take anything. The people in the hospital were pretty prompt, I must say, and they told me what was wrong with him."

"Thank you for being so clear, Mr Weidhammer. You didn't by any chance notice what McDaid had been drinking, did you?"

"I'm afraid not. I was only in the bar a minute or two and I was more interested in the fellow than his drink. There's really nothing more I can tell you."

"Don't worry about that, Mr Weidhammer, at least you saved his life. Now if you want to make a statement of any sort, could you please give it to Sergeant Johnson? Constable White here and myself had better get down to the Lochnagar as quickly as we can."

Malone and White left the olice Station and made their way as quickly as they could back towards the Old Course and the Lochnagar Hotel.

"I suppose as a matter of routine," said Malone, "I should have requested that no-one be allowed to leave the bar. But as McDaid clearly took the poison a good bit before we heard of it, and I feel we can be pretty sure of the source, it didn't really seem worthwhile. Anyway, it shouldn't be difficult to find out who was near the caddies just before McDaid took ill. As to the glasses, I shouldn't expect we'll have any luck there. All the bars near the courses have extensions all afternoon for the Open; that means that they'll probably have employed someone full-time just to pick up glasses and wash them. Unless he's been extraordinarily idle, he'd have disposed of the relevant ones long before our telephone call."

They went straight into the bar and identified themselves to the manager who had already begun to conduct his own investigation. He told them straightaway that the glasses had indeed been washed, as he would have expected from the efficiency normally required of the staff. Malone pointed out that he was not too perturbed, as he had guessed that this might well be the case. The manager seemed keen on producing a number of explanations and excuses for such unpleasant scenes as had been enacted but Malone cut him short.

"If you'd be so kind, I think the quickest way to get the information we require would be to interview your staff who were here at the time. You were not here yourself?"

"No, but I can assure you that I've already asked them all the relevant questions and could easily give you a résumé of what happened."

"I'm sure you could. But I hope you don't think it rude if we go over the ground again with them. Just possibly there's some fact which would be significant to us which might have escaped you."

"As you wish. I suppose you know your job better than I do."

Malone turned to the barman. "You were here when Mr McDaid took ill?"

"Aye. He came in with Jock Henderson shortly after you and your friend left. They were sitting at the table next to yours. When your other friends got up and left, they moved into the position you had all been in. It wasn't long after that when some American suggested to me that Iain McDaid was ill. I've seen him the worse for drink so often that I reckoned that was his trouble as usual. You can't blame me for that. Jock Henderson clearly thought the same."

"You didn't notice what he was drinking?"

"Aye. He normally ordered a nip and a half pint, but this time it was just a pint."

"Was he the sort of person to drink up a stranger's drink if it had been left?"

"He'd do that quick enough. So would Jock."

"You didn't notice if he actually did that?"

"No. Nor would anyone else, unless they were especially looking out for it. And we've been too busy for that today."

"I see. Where would I find Jock Henderson now?"

"He's out on the course. Iain McDaid had been lucky enough to be signed on by one of the more fancied Americans, Abe Carson. When he was taken ill, Jock decided to go in his place. My theory is that he slipped McDaid something so that he couldn't take the job. If Carson does well, there'll be a lot of money in it for his caddy as like as not. It's been known for players to give their caddy all their prize money, relying on the publicity for their share. Someone like Henderson might have thought it well worth his while to put McDaid out of action and be on the spot himself."

"Thank you for your information and indeed for your theory. There could be some truth in it. Well, they can't have gone many holes, so I think we'll go straight out and find Jock Henderson."

They ascertained from the starter that their men were on the Old Course and set off in pursuit. They came up with Abe Carson and his caddy just as the American was preparing to drive off at the third. Malone went up to the golfer and said:

"I hope you'll forgive me for interrupting your practice, Mr Carson. We're police officers and we'd like to interview your caddy in connection with the non-appearance of your original employee. I explained the matter to the starter and he promised to send out a replacement immediately."

"Dammit," said the American in a cheerful voice, "here I am just trying to get in a bit of practice and I have to change caddies three times in as many holes. What'll it be like when the real competition gets started? You don't suppose someone's trying to get at me, do you? Some guy from the ranks of the anti-American Imperialism Front or some damn thing?"

"No," said Malone, "nothing so harmless, I'm afraid. We're engaged in a murder investigation and if one of your compatriots hadn't acted promptly we'd be dealing with a third corpse—that of your original caddy. I'm very grateful for the light-hearted way you're taking it. I do appreciate that you must be under a considerable strain at times like this."

"Don't worry; it causes a bit of a diversion. Ah, this must be the replacement caddy coming. Jock, could you please hand my clubs to our friend here and go and answer a few questions for these gentlemen?"

Jock Henderson was far from being happy at the suggestion. He was very pleased with himself for having managed to poach McDaid's man and was by no means keen on giving up so easily.

"I don't see why I should do what the polis say. They've got nothing on me," he said to Carson. "I'll just carry on with you, if you don't mind."

"I'm afraid I do mind," answered the American. He fished around in his pocket and drew out a ten-pound note. "Here you are. That's not bad for three holes you never expected in the first place."

Henderson was temporarily mollified and surrendered the clubs to his replacement. Carson immediately took his drive and went off down the third fairway, leaving Henderson with the two policemen.

"Well, Jock," said Malone, "you'd better come with us to the Police Station and answer a few questions. It was pretty convenient for you when your pal took ill, wasn't it?"

"What are you trying to suggest? I had nothing to do with it. If the fool can't keep sober enough to turn out on the course in the afternoon, that's his look-out. And I don't see why the hell I should help you out when you've done me out of one of the best jobs in the championship."

"There might be those who'd suspect that you did your pal out of the job in the first place, as I was suggesting. If you don't want that said, you'd better come along with us and let us prove that you had nothing to do with it. Look, you know John White here and you should remember me. We're not the sort to interrupt either Mr Carson or yourself without good reason. If you didn't hear me telling him, we're conducting a murder investigation and if you do anything to hinder us you might find yourself in serious trouble. D'you understand?"

"All right, all right. But it's pretty hard on me. Just a measly tenner."

"You fellows are never satisfied. If you'll answer our questions on the way back, we can cut down the time at the police station. First of all, tell me exactly what happened between you and McDaid in the pub."

"I suppose I'd better tell you. We were both hanging around the starter's box looking for a job and hadn't been lucky enough to get anyone to carry for. Suddenly along came Abe Carson and engaged Iain. He said he wouldn't be needing him for an hour, so Iain offered to get me a drink before he started. Between you and me, it was quite clear that Iain had had a few already. I told him he'd better watch it or he'd lose his job as quickly as he had got it, but he said he only meant to have one pint and no nips. Anyway, we went to the Lochnagar and, just as he said, he only ordered a pint for himself and one for me. We sat quite a long time over it and after a bit he said he'd have to go to the lavatory. When he came back he was in a pretty bad state, so I thought he must have had a half-bottle in his pocket and had taken a good swig. It didn't bother me because I reckoned that if he couldn't make the tee, I'd go along and get his job. Anyway, some American come up and thought

Iain was ill. Everyone, including the barman told him it was just a question of drink, but he wouldn't have it and said he was taking Iain off to the hospital. Well, obviously I didn't object and that was the last I heard of it until you came up and took my job away from me, and now you're talking some nonsense about a murder case. I tell you, Iain was just the worse for whisky."

"You haven't told us about the drinks that were lying on the table. Did he drink them?"

"How do you know about them?"

"Never mind. Just tell us all about them."

"Well, if you know about them, I don't suppose it'll do any harm to tell you. There were two half pints lying on the table with a lot of lemon and stuff on them. I reckoned we should drink them rather than let them go to waste. He said he wouldn't, as he had to carry for Abe Carson and had had enough already. So I drank one of them. It tasted like lemonade and I told Iain that is all it was as far as I could see. He still refused to drink the other one, so I put it down instead."

"What? You drank both of them and he didn't touch either?"

"That's what I said. I can't understand why he went off and drank that half-bottle straight afterwards. If there was anything in those half-pints, it wasn't much."

"Think clearly, Jock. Are you quite sure you drank both of them and Iain didn't touch a drop?"

"I've told you twice already. I'm not simple you know. All he did was eat some of the fruit stuff on top."

"Good God, White, that explains your point about the decomposition of potassium cyanide in the presence of CO_2 gas. Look Jock, I had good reason all along for not thinking you were trying to poison Iain. I had to get all the information I needed as quickly as possible. Two people have been murdered already and Iain's very lucky he wasn't the third. The poison, by the way, was meant for one or both of us. Those were our drinks you had. Now unless you want to get involved in this business, you'd better go along to the police station and tell Sergeant Johnson exactly what you've just told us. And say that we've gone to Ceres."

Jock Henderson muttered a few obscenities about being done out of an honest pound or two and went off in the direction of the Police Station. "I think my car's nearer, so let's make for it and get to Ceres," said Malone.

"What do you hope to do in Ceres?" asked White.

"Do my best to narrow down suspects. This is getting far beyond anything I've dealt with before. You realise that by leaving those drinks there, whoever is responsible was prepared to take the risk of anyone being killed, as almost happened to McDaid, rather than let any suspicion fall on themselves by disposing of them? It was mad enough to try to poison us, but the callousness indicated by leaving the glasses there is monstrous. I suppose they thought that as they seemed to get away with it in Henley, they could do it again here. The good doctor told us at the start that we were dealing with a lunatic. I wish to God I'd taken him more seriously."

"I suppose we can assume the fact that they left the glasses and made no attempt to get rid of the liquid is a pretty sure indication that they're not all in it?"

"Exactly so. If they had no fear of discovery, I'm sure they would have removed the evidence. But as it stands, it's well worth their while to make sure that the whole group of them is equally under suspicion. That, by the way, is why I'm saying they: they know that there are two of them and they know that we know that; therefore they also know that we can't exclude those who were not actively engaged in buying or carrying the drinks but have to keep everyone under suspicion. That'll make them feel safer. But how do they know that all of them have a rather doubtful alibi for the night of last Wednesday?"

"They must have asked. I wonder if that's what Jolly Balsdon was puzzled about and was unable to tell us?"

"You may well be right. As the rest of them knew that we were interested in their movements that night, they might not have even noticed subtle questioning along those lines. But Jolly, assuming he was an outsider to the whole business, would have found it peculiar. Well, we're nearly at Strachan's now. The first thing I want to do is check his potassium cyanide. If it hasn't been touched, I'm going to have to make the decision that he's innocent and carry on from there. You might point out that no-one in their right senses would use poison from a supply they admitted to just this morning, but I'd merely say that we're not dealing with someone in their right senses. The other reason I'm inclined to discount Strachan is that he told us that Balsdon had eaten the fruit from the top of his drink just before he began to feel ill. The murderers would probably have been inclined to keep that subtlety quiet, especially as there was an outside chance that we could have analysed dregs in the bottom of the glass involved. I don't know whether any could have seeped into the drink or not—on the whole I would imagine so—but it's quite possible that this would not have occurred to our men. They would then hope that we would have to look elsewhere for the vehicle for the poison. Well, we're just about there now. Let's hope we haven't miscalculated again and find another death on our hands."

Malone, who was at the wheel, swung into the drive at speed, but immediately slowed down at the sight that met his eyes. At the front of the house was a group of four people, two adults and two infants. One was still in its mother's arms and the other was making a few doubtful steps. It was however the fourth figure that had caused Malone's action, which was now accompanied by a hearty laugh, in which White joined. Far from being in any apparent danger, John Strachan was engaged in convolutions and gestures which to any outside party would seem the result of brain damage but is considered normal by any father showing affection for his young offspring. He arose from his somewhat undignified position as the policemen approached and greeted them somewhat apologetically.

"I'm sorry to appear in this rather demented capacity but I'm afraid you don't always expect visitors such as yourselves when playing with the children. Come into the house and let my wife get you a cup of tea or something."

"Thank you very much but I don't think we will. Did you return here alone?"

"No. Old Mr Cartwright wasn't feeling up to any more and asked if I'd be good enough to bring him back for a rest. I must say I was glad of the excuse. It was really those Pimms' that put me off. Albert must be a pretty insensitive so-and-so to order them for our company."

"Insensitive, possibly. Where is Mr Cartwright now?"

"I think he's in the dining-room. He promised to have a look at an old chest of drawers which is a little damaged. He seemed to be quite taken with it. He even admitted that he couldn't have made it any better himself. Come through and we'll have a word with him."

As they entered the room, old Cartwright got up stiffly from the floor from where he had been examining the feet of a large oak chest of drawers. One of them had been broken and had been repaired in a rather rough and ready manner. "No taste or sense of balance, some people," said old Cartwright. "I don't mean you, of course," he added hastily looking at Strachan. "You have here what is one of the finest pieces of work I've seen in a long while and what's happened to it? Some damn fool has taken the proper legs off and put these things on. What's worse, they've used third rate wood. You're lucky only one of them is broken. Still, if you've got a decent craftsman round here who'd let me use his facilities and supply me with the right sort of wood, I can have it back as it should be in no time."

"Thanks very much. But I suspect at the moment that these two gentlemen would like a word with you."

"Don't worry, Mr Cartwright," said Malone, "we have no desire to interrogate you. We really wanted to make sure that you were not unwell."

"Frightened I might have been poisoned or something?"

"As a matter of fact, yes. Mr Strachan, could you please show us your supply of cyanide?"

"Certainly, if I can find it. I rather think it's in the garage. I'd be grateful if you'd take it away with you when you leave as well. They left the house again and made their way to the garage. Strachan, in fact, had no difficulty in locating the tin of cyanide. It was in a prominent position on a shelf running along the back of the garage at about eye level.

"That's strange, he said, as he moved to pick it up. "I'm sure I never left it there."

"Don't touch it," and White. He quickly moved over to the tin and looked at it. "I thought so," he said to Malone. "There's no dust at all on the top. It's quite clear that this has been opened a good deal more recently than your fumigation, Mr Strachan."

Strachan went red in the face. "I assure you I haven't touched it and I know my wife won't have after what happened here. I can't understand it."

"It's a great pity," and White to Malone, "that we didn't have anything positive on the state of this tin from the search after the body of Blacklaw was found. Still, I suppose no mention probably indicates the likelihood that at this time it hadn't been disturbed. Have you had any other visitors recently Mr Strachan?"

"No, there has been nobody here that I know of except the Cartwrights."

"Well, I shall certainly take you on your kind offer and remove this tin. At least it won't take us long to find out if you've been touching it recently. White, could you pick it up carefully by the base and lock it in the car? Well, Mr Strachan, I had just about decided to eliminate you from my suspects. Your actions at our arrival did not seem to be those of someone who had tried to murder us earlier in the day."

"Murder you? What do you mean?"

"Just that the Pimms' we fortunately did not drink contained some potassium cyanide. An innocent caddy is in hospital at the moment. Luckily for him he was treated in time. I wish we could say the same for Jolly Balsdon."

Malone was about to take his leave of Strachan, when another car came up the drive. The occupant swiftly pulled up and got out, and looked with some amazement at the policemen. "Good heavens, I hope my father's all right," said Albert Cartwright after a few seconds. Strachan immediately assured him that there was nothing wrong with the old man but before he could say anything else, Malone asked: "Why exactly should you be so concerned about your father, Mr Cartwright? You weren't by any chance worried that he might have been poisoned?"

"Yes . . . No . . . That is, as he wasn't well and you were here, I couldn't help wondering after what happened to Jolly Balsdon . . ."

"You had no more specific reason for wondering? You weren't, I hope, expecting something of that sort to have happened?"

"No, of course not. I don't know what you're talking about."

"We shall see, Mr Cartwright. I shall have to ask you to accompany me to St. Andrews police station, where I shall be very grateful if you would answer a few questions. I do not advise you to refuse."

Albert Cartwright looked at Strachan but saw no sign of encouragement. The two policemen merely stood looking at him. He shrugged his shoulders. "From your tone, you seem to be about to charge me with something. I assure you that I have a perfectly clear conscience and to show it, I suppose I had better come along with you and disabuse you of whatever strange conclusions you have come to."

The journey to St. Andrews was completed in silence and Albert Cartwright was led into the room at the back of the station. There was no-one else there. Malone indicated by a gesture that he was free to sit down and then, with White looking at him from the side, stared at him for a few minutes, again in silence. Cartwright was the first to give in. "I've heard of this sort of treatment, you know, still you've got nothing against me, and you know as well as I do that I can walk out of here whenever I want. In fact, I've a mind to do so this very minute."

White immediately moved to a position behind him, between him and the door. Albert Cartwright, who had risen as if to leave, immediately sat down again. Eventually Malone spoke.

"Albert Cartwright, why did you conspire with your brother and father to bring about the death of Ronald Blacklaw?"

"That's a lie. I had nothing to do with it."

"Oh yes? Then who did?"

"I tell you, I've no idea. I know no more about it than you appear to."

"You would then also deny any implication in the murder of Mr Balsdon and the attempted murder of myself and Constable White, and a St. Andrews caddy by the name of McDaid?" Malone's tone of voice had become threatening, especially when he mentioned White and himself. This did not escape Albert Cartwright.

"Look, if I could tell you anything about those things, I would. But I can't. I wish it were otherwise; it's been bothering me enough, wondering whether I might be the next on the list."

"We have experts in our profession, Mr Cartwright. Your attempts to cover up your traces were amateurish to a degree. We shall have no difficulty at all in proving that you sent the note to Blacklaw to arrange a meeting in Henley. That was what brought us there and why we are watching you."

"But doesn't that prove I couldn't have had anything to do with his death? Yes, I know I'm admitting I sent it. It was only to get a few pounds out of him. He never did anything with his money anyway. He could easily afford it. But can't you see, I would never have dreamt of sending him that if I hadn't been expecting to see him at the Regatta?"

"How did you know about the attempt on White and myself?"

"I didn't. I thought you made that up to frighten me."
Malone was silent for a moment. "Mr Cartwright, we're glad
to have had your help in clearing up the business of the
letter. Now, for your protection as much as anything else,
you will be conducted to the cells. I have more to concern
me than petty blackmail at present."

Albert Cartwright seemed to have nothing to say, and was
led away by White. When White returned, Malone said:
"Damn it. We need more information from somewhere."

"Aye, but from where?"

A few minutes later there was a knock on the door and a
constable entered. "Sorry to interrupt your sir," he said,
"We've just heard something that I'm told is likely to
interest you. We've had a complaint from a local farmer who
has just returned from holiday. His car has been used in his
absence and he had given no-one permission to borrow it.
He's certain from the mileage that he's right. You know how
careful these Fife farmers are. Anyway, the car's a blue
Cortina."

๖♦ Chapter 12

"THANK YOU, CONSTABLE. We'll certainly look into it immediately. This farmer would, I suppose, have no objection if we went to see him straight away?"

"The opposite I should think. Understandably, he had assumed that it was one of his employees taking advantage of his absence. He's already accused each of them in turn, but they all deny any knowledge of it. As he says, it's not just using some of his petrol and risking his car, but the fact that it might have been anything else. He's demanded immediate action from us. The sergeant says he would be very grateful if you would go, as we're totally committed with all the visitors. There'd be chaos, or at any rate complaints if we had to withdraw a couple of men. The farmer's name is David McLean. He's a fairly typical Fife farmer— hardworking, never admits to having two coins to rub together but never appears to be short for a new car or an expensive holiday. The farm's called Balsmithie, about three miles out of town on the Largo Road. You can't miss it; there's a sign with the name up."

Malone and White went straight out and took the direction indicated. There was, as they had been told, no difficulty in locating the farm. The farmhouse itself was a sprawling two storey building with a large number of outhouses spread around it. The door was answered by the farmer himself.

"Ah, the police. I didn't really expect you quite so quickly. I fully appreciate that you have your hands full with the Open at the moment, so I must thank you for being so prompt. I don't really like knowing I'm in the position of having a thief about the place and having to suspect everybody. And that when the really busy time's just coming up. You'll appreciate that we rely a lot on the goodwill of our workers at harvest time and going around accusing them all of thievery isn't likely to promote it. I was hoping the culprit would admit it. All I would have done is dock his wages an appropriate amount and let him know in no uncertain manner what I thought of his actions. All my men are far too good to lose over a couple of gallons of petrol. But if they don't admit it, I don't know what it might be next. We have a lot of very costly stuff about nowadays, you know."

"Before you show us the car and where it was kept, can you be absolutely certain that it was stolen?"

"I thought you might suggest that. No, I was not drunk or anything else like that just before I went away. I'm a very careful man. We farmers have to be nowadays, you know, when we're expected to keep all the useless people of this country in cheap food and get taxed out of sight for our pains. Now, I didn't actually write down the mileage when I went away—I'm not that suspicious—but I did notice what it was because it was easily memorable. It read 66666.5. The last time I was using it I wondered if it would finish up all the sixes. When I saw it after my return, it read 66791.7 and still does for that matter. There's no real possibility of a mistake on my part. That's enough to get to Edinburgh and back and do a bit of larking around as well."

"Exactly what I was thinking, Mr McLean. The sooner we look at your car the better."

Mr McLean led them to a ramshackle garage of wood and corrugated iron which was secured by a large padlock. He handed the key to Malone who unlocked it. The blue Cortina was inside and White immediately got down to his hands and knees. He stood up again quickly and said:

"Well, the oil leaks in about the right place. You can see for yourself that the tyres are barely inside the law."

"Mr McLean," said Malone, "unless there has been some extraordinary coincidence, you can stop having any doubts about your employees. We shall have to get the experts to check but it is very likely that this car is an important clue in a murder case we're investigating. It is therefore very important that you co-operate with us. First of all, would you tell me if you know any of the following people. A father and two sons named Cartwright who own a cabinet makers firm in London?"

"Never heard of them."

"Gordon Reid, an Edinburgh accountant and John Strachan, another accountant who lives at Ceres?"

"Ah, I heard about the body that turned up at Strachan's place. I've never heard of your Reid but I know Strachan slightly. My fourteen-year-old son goes to his archery club."

"Mr Richard Connolly of Ealing and his brother James Connolly, now residing in St. Andrews?"

"I attend the same church as James Connolly but I didn't know he had a brother."

"Would either Strachan or James Connolly have known you were going away on holiday?"

"I see no reason why they shouldn't, but I had no reason to tell them. It would be a fairly natural conclusion to draw from my absence in church or my son's absence from the archery."

"Have you ever had any close dealings of any sort with either of these two gentlemen?"

"Mr Connolly once gave me some very useful advice on how to cut down the rabbit menace on my land. He'd been out in Australia earlier and had a fair bit of personal experience in the matter."

"What," said White, "did he advise you to do?"

"Well, the whole process was fairly complicated but basically it was to poison them."

"And what poison did he recommend?"

"Cyanide."

"Have you any of it left?" said Malone.

"As far as I know. It was only month or so ago that we used it and I made sure I had plenty. I expect to be using it again."

"Please don't touch it until our man comes round to examine your car. If I can use your telephone he should be here shortly."

They returned to St. Andrews police station in silence. Malone was told that an Inspector McGregor was wanting to speak to him urgently. He immediately telephoned his Edinburgh colleague. After a brief conversation he replaced the receiver and turned to White.

"This looks like it, White. A barman in Edinburgh remembers a company of people which probably included Blacklaw on Wednesday night. He wasn't at all sure he could identify him positively from photographs but was sure there was some sort of likeness. He remembers the company and that they were drinking Pimms', as that isn't an order he usually has to deal with. One of them, the older man, had specially asked for a good supply of fruit. The third member of the company was a young woman. He has a further reason for recalling them, as the younger had taken ill shortly after they had started drinking. The barman had offered assistance but it was politely refused. He hadn't given the matter much thought, as he had assumed that the sick man had either had too much to drink or had eaten something which disagreed with him. As he said, those are the two most common reasons for anyone taking ill like that. Oh, there's one more thing. Although he couldn't again positively identify the woman and the older man—it would obviously be somewhat difficult with casual customers in the sort of lighting common in bars nowadays—he sent one of his regulars out to make sure they got off alright. This man saw them get into a blue car and drive away. When he was questioned closely he could be sure only about the colour. When pressed, however, he said that they had all got in from the pavement."

"A pretty clear indication that there was already a driver in the car."

"Exactly so. Anyway, I asked McGregor to bring the barman and Miss Adamson here separately—as quickly as possible."

"How are you going to deal with them when they do come?"

"That will have to be carefully orchestrated. I also want Strachan, Reid and James Connolly here at the same time."

"None of the others?"

"Not for my specific experiment I want to try out in about an hour's time."

Malone then proceeded to give exact instructions to White and a constable he had commandeered for the purpose. Then he and White sat down and waited in silence.

They had only been waiting for about half an hour when the constable announced that Mr Connolly was insisting on seeing them now. He was told to hold him up for another couple of minutes and then send him in.

"I don't know what he's doing here this early but we'll have to see what can be done about detaining him," he said to White. "I hope this doesn't shove my whole plan out of gear."

Presently the door was opened and to their surprise—and Malone's considerable relief—it was Mr Richard Connolly, not his brother, who appeared.

"What can we do for you, Mr Connolly?" asked Malone pleasantly.

"Nothing amiss, I hope?"

"Yes, there is," replied their visitor in a belligerent tone. Would you deny that you've had one of your damned flat feet follow me around wherever I go?"

"No, I wouldn't deny it for a moment. I may add that he's partly there for your protection. Nor do I wish to deny that we want to know of any suspicious movements you may make."

"Suspicious movements! What's suspicious about trying to interest people in a club which could revolutionise the science of driving?"

"Nothing at all, if that's all you're doing."

"Has it occurred to you that it's a little difficult to appear like the honest craftsman I am, when there are policemen breathing down my neck? I tell you, it's a public scandal, as well as a personal affront."

"It is our normal experience, Mr Connolly, to find that innocent and honest people are delighted to have the forces of law around them, even to the extent of breathing down their necks on occasions."

"What sort of accusation is that? Do you think I've been crawling around trying to poison your local councillors or other eminent individuals?"

"Let us hope not. As for the man who is detailed to keep an eye on you, he will be withdrawn as soon as we decide there is no longer any danger to you or the public. If you would excuse us now, we're rather busy."

"Busy are you? Don't worry, I was in my brother's house when he was asked to come here. I suppose you'll want to be busy throwing baseless accusations at him. Well, I'll tell you, I'll be waiting outside to make sure you don't get up to any of your tricks with him."

"I cannot prevent you from waiting outside, Mr Connolly, and if you think it would be more comfortable, I'm sure you will be provided with a seat in the front of the station."

"I don't need any of your favours, thank you."

Malone said nothing and Richard Connolly left.

"I can't help wondering," said White, "whether he was sent by his brother to see what we were planning for him."

"You may well be right. He should know by now our approach to Albert Cartwright—or I hope so. He may well have felt he needed an ally."

"It also occurs to me that Albert's relations have not taken much interest in his fate."

"I don't see any reason why it should have occurred to them—that is until we told them a short while ago. We would have had to anyway—he's been making all the correct noises about solicitors—but by doing it now, I hope to have all, or almost all our original suspects here at the same time. If, as I hope, we get to the bottom of this in the near future, it'll save lengthy explanations to them all individually."

They lapsed into silence again. The next man to arrive was John Strachan. As Malone had expected, he did not come on his own. He was shown in in the company of John Cartwright, who was the first to speak.

"Inspector Malone, unhappily my father was too ill to come here —or perhaps fortunately, for all I know. We've always been a family who had proper respect for the law and so it comes as a shock to us to hear that Albert has been locked up in this place. Even if you have anything against him—which we both doubt—as you knew we were easily available, you should have let us know."

"I have indeed good reasons for holding him where he is, Mr Cartwright. Perhaps it would be advisable for both you and your brother if you went along to the cells to speak to him. I can only allow you half an hour at this stage, but I think that should be sufficient."

"I suppose I should thank you for your belated consideration. Am I to have supervision, in case one of us drops some incriminating evidence by mistake?"

"I don't think that will be necessary and anyway our local men are rather overworked at the moment. Just ask the Constable at the desk to show you to your brother."

There seemed nothing left to say and so John Cartwright left the room. Before Strachan could say anything, Malone spoke to him.

"Mr Strachan, earlier today for the sake of economy, I decided to treat you as innocent in this affair. I would therefore ask you now if you would be kind enough to act in the manner I require of you. Now I hope to have this whole matter cleared up before very long and I have good reason for hoping so. A couple of bits of information have come into my hands which might well make the whole case clear. If you want to get rid of the lingering suspicion which must still hang over you, I advise you to co-operate. Are you able to act the part of a worried and guilty man?"

"I don't know about the guilty, but I won't have to act much to give the impression of being worried."

"Fine. Some people will be coming here in a moment, some of whom you know, and I merely wish you to give that impression. I would rather not tell you any more. And please don't overdo it."

"I'm prepared to do anything you suggest if you really think that it'll clear up this matter once and for all. I can hardly look anyone in the face any more for wondering if they think I'm a murderer."

"Well, if you'll just sit down over there, we shouldn't have long to wait."

Whether John Strachan was beginning to put on his act or not, over the next few minutes he managed to give just the expression which Malone had asked for. He fidgeted in all manner of ways, ran his fingers through his hair in a despairing manner and occasionally tried nervous conversation. When this met with absolutely no response from the policemen, he giggled nervously and returned to his fidgeting. This was eventually interrupted by the arrival of Mr James Connolly. Malone beamed at him.

"Please come in, Mr Connolly. Do sit down."

James Connolly looked rather suspiciously around him at the disturbed figure of John Strachan and then at White, who was positioned a little behind to the right of the chair he was offered. However he did as he was asked.

"Inspector Malone," he said, "I trust that you have a good reason for taking up my time in this way. We have all of us been very co-operative with you and I hope that you will have the decency to reciprocate. I must say, however, that I find my reception here rather hostile."

"Mr Connolly, why did you decide to murder Ronald Blacklaw?"

Connolly, without glancing in the direction of Strachan, said:

"That rather absurd approach may work with some of the riff-raff you deal with, especially if they have the mark of guilt written on their souls, but I would advise you to adopt different tactics with an innocent man without a stain on his character and hopefully very few on his soul."

"We've examined the car, Mr Connolly. You were clever enough to leave no obvious traces elsewhere—even on Mr Strachan's cyanide tin—but a car is often a different matter. Especially when a man of your age tries to drag a body out of it. You don't know what car I'm talking about, I suppose? Mr McLean's as you well know. Tell me, did he leave the padlock undone or did you manage to pick it? The former, I would suggest, as you don't give the impression of a man with the skill to pick locks. No, don't bother to interrupt. I can go further than that. When your accomplice, whom you may think to be as solid as yourself, hears another piece of evidence we have from Edinburgh, I think it very likely that he will be prepared to compromise you as the instigator. He is probably already feeling very guilty about the death of Jolly Balsdon. Ah, we appear to have some more visitors."

Mr Reid and Miss Adamson were shown in. Both of them seemed a little startled at the assembled company in the small room.   Malone beamed at them in the same manner as he had used to greet James Connolly. There were however no seats available for them. "I'm so pleased to see you," said Malone. "I have just reached the final stages of my enquiry and was sure that you would be interested in the conclusions. I'm   sorry—ah,   what's   this?   More interruptions?"

A young man of well-dressed appearance was admitted. He immediately turned round and pointed:

"There's absolutely no doubt about it. It was him."

It was Edward McCaig, the barman from Edinburgh and he had immediately pointed at Mr Reid. Malone spoke:

"And was this the young lady?"

"There can be no doubt about that either. Anyone will tell you I never forget a face. Geoff who went out of the bar after them recognised the photographs too, as you know well."

"Do you recognise anyone else here?"

"Can't be sure that I do. But I wouldn't be at all surprised if that youngish man over there was driving the car. Yes, it looks a bit like him, but I wouldn't like to swear to it."

If John Strachan's worry had been feigned beforehand, it certainly was not now.

"What the dickens are you talking about? I've never seen you before in my life."

"I think, Mr Strachan, that should probably be a matter for the courts to decide. Gordon Reid, Rosemary Adamson and John Strachan, I arrest you for the murder of Ronald Blacklaw of Edinburgh on the night of last Wednesday and it is my duty . . ."

"What nonsense is this?" It was John Strachan who had interrupted. "I thought I had come here to help you. Where does this man claim to have seen me?"

James Connolly rose with a grave face. "If you will excuse me, Inspector, I now quite understand the reasons why you acted as you did earlier, and I think it would now be better if I took my leave."

Before he had taken two steps towards the door, Miss Adamson, her face the picture of fury, rushed up to him and began to tear at his face.

"Oh no you don't. You don't think you'll get away with it this easily, do you? I could kill you with my bare hands." She was restrained by White and turned to Malone. "It was he who put us up to it. It was all his idea. A lot of stuff about not allowing these clever criminals to get away with their gross corruption. Well, I'm not going to let him get away with it now. Listen to me, Inspector, I was never that close a friend of Ronald Blacklaw. If you really want to know, I've been Gordon Reid's girlfriend or mistress—call it what you like—for the past four years. I only made up to Ronald on his suggestion, to see if he was honest. Well, it didn't take me too long to find out that he wasn't. But when we looked into it, he'd been amazingly clever at it. It seemed unlikely that we could expose him in a court of law. Then this man Connolly, who was dining with us one night, suggested that there was only one way to deal with such people. He managed to persuade us with his talk, and we agreed to get rid of him. That would have been all right, if he hadn't then insisted on getting rid of John Strachan here, because he was sure he knew something. That plan misfired and a totally innocent man died. If he thinks he's going to walk out of here now without a suspicion against his own version of high-minded morals, he's got another think coming."

"Well, Mr Connolly," said Malone, "what do you say to that?"

"It's the sort of outburst to be expected from a hysterical woman in the circumstances. It convinces me even more that I should leave you to your necessary, if unpleasant job."

Gordon Reid looked up. "No, James, it won't be so easy. I have just had a solid reputation built up over many years reduced to nothing in the last few minutes. You'll not get away with yours unscathed. Inspector, everything that Miss Adamson said is absolutely true. Mr Strachan is entirely innocent of the charge you laid against him. I had better tell you what happened. First of all, Miss Adamson had no real connection with the matter. She was just there because I was. I admit that I conspired with James Connolly to bring about the death of Ronald Blacklaw—there doesn't seem much point in denying it now. Anyway I'm sick of the whole business. If it had stopped with him, you wouldn't have heard me saying this. I believe that he was a genuinely evil man and, when you know more about him, you might agree with me. But there's another genuinely evil man involved, and I wish to God I had realised it earlier. It's one thing to give someone a very swift poison to rid the world of him but what happened thereafter—it's been a solid nightmare to me. But after I had administered the poison myself, I had to fall in with that devil's wishes. As you have heard, the car was waiting for us outside the bar. The driver was James Connolly. After Blacklaw was dead, he gloated like a cat which has just killed a bird. We dropped Miss Adamson almost immediately and drove off to dispose of the body. I thought we would just go to some quiet place and dump it. But no, my accomplice had other ideas. He pointed out that John Strachan was probably as guilty as Blacklaw, as he had preceded him in his job and perhaps it would be a good idea to do the same thing to him. I was horrified and said that we had absolutely no reason to believe in any such guilt. When all his arguments failed to convince me, he threatened me with exposure over the death of Blacklaw. I had done the deed and he would deny any connection. And so at last I agreed to go with him to Ceres. Luckily Strachan was not in. We waited around for a time and still he did not appear. Then to my horror, James Connolly produced a strong steel arrow from the boot, which he said he had had made for the purpose, and forced me to help him in that gruesome task, about which you will know some of the facts, but not all. I almost confessed to you at Henley after the awful business of Jolly Balsdon. That was a mistake: the intended victim had been John Strachan. Although it was uncharacteristic, John was very drunk at the time. James was convinced that any abnormal behaviour would be put down to excessive alcohol, and as a result there was no danger of the plan failing through prompt medical treatment. He again threatened to deny any involvement, and so I held my peace.

At every turn the fortuitous convention of all the people you could have reason to suspect aided his evil schemes. To me, the worst was when he decided to frame John Strachan. He even went out to his house again last night to disturb the cyanide, whose existence we had learnt of at Henley. He magnanimously suggested that life imprisonment rather than death was his appropriate penalty."

Mr Reid seemed to have nothing more to add. Malone said: "I assume then that you had no knowledge of the attempt to poison Constable White and myself?"

"What? Has he gone that far?"

They all looked at James Connolly. He had gone red in the face and began to suffer from a fit of choking. He drew a large white handkerchief from his pocket and blew into it loudly. The handkerchief was still in position when he fell back with a ghastly look. Malone sprang up.

"Quickly, White." They were too late. The dose of cyanide was not sufficiently small to allow a portly rowing enthusiast to wander off to a deckchair, or a circumspect caddy to be taken to a nearby hospital.

James Connelly was dead.

After Mr Reid and Miss Adamson had been removed, Malone turned to Strachan.

"I'm sorry for the trouble we've caused you. The only consolation I can offer is that without that charade we'd not have had enough evidence against anyone, and you'd still be under suspicion. You can go away now and do your best to forget about it all."

"I don't think that'll be easy. I can't see the archery club meeting again." He got up and left.

"Well, White," and Malone, "that turned out very satisfactorily in the end, although I still had plenty of doubts right up until Miss Adamson's outburst."

"Another example of 'Verdict – Easily'?" said White.

Death of a Dundee Teacher

Death of a Dundee Teacher

5♥ Chapter 1

JIM HOLDROYD MARKED THE LAST EXERCISE, put the books back in his battered briefcase and heaved a sigh of relief. He sat down with an air of satisfaction in his spacious old leather armchair, sank back deeply into it, lit a cigarette, and stared into the fire. With a certain amount of pride, he reflected how glad he was to see flames in a fire, not the monotonous stalagmites of gas, but the leaping life of coal. He was not so selfless as to put it down to luck; he congratulated himself on having the good sense not to live in a smokeless zone or a chimneyless house. He could never understand how those who were not prevented by circumstances from this pleasant luxury could be so idle as to complain about the limited amount of labour involved in carting coal and ash. However, he himself was not particularly good at sitting down and basking in this pleasure, and so he got up and checked that the coal-bucket had sufficient contents for the morrow, and that there were enough sticks on the hearth for kindling. He then began to wander aimlessly about the room, until he stood in front of the bookcase. It was the only thing in the room which was not tidy. He wondered for the hundredth time if he should get down to work and put the books in some reasonable order, but for the hundredth time he decided that as he knew where to find them all it would be but wasted labour. He then looked at his violin case, wavered, but then decided against that too. He looked at his watch for a few seconds and came to a decision. He put the guard in front of the fire, checked that there was nothing which could spit out into the room—he had never suffered from a fire personally, but was always cautious about such things—then went out.

217

Death of a Dundee Teacher

His inside front door led immediately onto a narrow steep staircase, which had another door at the end of it. This opened out onto a narrow close, at the end of which to the right lay South Street. To the left it led into a garden area which he and the other inhabitants on the other side of the close held in common. His neighbour considered gardens a liability, and so he was able to treat it as his own. As he left his flat, he reprimanded himself yet again for not getting either his own stair light or the close light, both of which had been out of commission for some time, repaired. However, as it was not yet dark, the inconvenience for the present was slight. He went into South Street and turned left. It was his habit to go out to the pub for two or three pints, and occasionally more, most nights of his existence, and he usually started at the White Horse Bar in South Street. He was feeling a bit depressed tonight and so decided to give the White Horse a miss for a change. He began making his way straight towards the St David's Hotel, hoping as it was a Tuesday that it would not be too full of rowdy students. As he walked slowly down South Street, the thought as usual came to him that he could hardly hope to live in a finer town than St Andrews. The street was almost silent, and he could smell the fresh sea air, so different from the smell of Glasgow or Dundee where he worked. On his right stood the ruin of the Blackfriars chapel, a reminder of a more religious and relaxed age; behind it rose the frontage of Madras College, a school which looked as if serious learning could still take place within its walls. On both sides of the street were houses built in solid grey stone, a symbol of hope in the future; and in front of them the pollarded limes, a legacy of Victorian elegance. He turned left by the Church of the Holy Trinity, guardian of the tomb of the murdered Archbishop Sharp, a reminder of the violent passions, as well as the peace, that can spring in man from the wells of religion. He had soon passed into Market Street and walked straight into the welcoming bar of the St David's Hotel.

He was feeling a good bit more cheerful than he had been when he had left his flat, but was still pleased to see, as he entered the door, that the clientele had a reasonably civilised look about it. There was indeed a sprinkling of students, but they were not of the boisterous type, and most of them were regular drinkers there during their term time. He was on Christian name terms with many of them, as was a small group of regulars who were leaning comfortably against a substantial bar. These men, like Jim Holdroyd, were in for a pint or two most nights in the year and were not too taken with some of the students who could make their drinking fairly intolerable on some occasions. They themselves, however, had established themselves over a period of years, and had no intention of being shifted by such passing trade.

"What-ho, Jim," said several of these people. For some reason best known to themselves this was their normal form of greeting. "What ho, Jim, Jim, Jim, and Bill," was the reply: by chance an unnecessarily large sample of them seemed to have been named after the same Apostle. "Just in time to stand your round," said one of the Jims, who possessed the surname Cormack, a man of middle age, middle height and middle income. He always managed to produce the same remark when any of them arrived. None of them had really fathomed out whether he said it from hope or habit, but as they never took any notice it hardly mattered. "That'll be right," said Jim Holdroyd, and gratefully accepted the pint offered by Bill Watson, who was also a schoolmaster like himself, but unlike him was married with three children. Jim McCabe, a young, rising academic, was holding forth on one of his latest theories. It was connected with establishing a causal relationship between the decline of language and great civilisations. The rest of them half listened to this for the duration of a pint, but after the next had been ordered, Jim Coulson, who worked for a Building society in Leven, deftly switched the subject to something less taxing. "Are you going to tell us what's been wrong with you lately?" he said, after the talk had drifted for a bit. "Anyone might surmise that sex had reared its beautiful head. You have to watch these things as you get older, you know. They can become dangerously serious."

"Nothing so exciting," laughed Jim Holdroyd, "it must just be old age setting in." To indicate his dislike of this line of interrogation he changed the subject, and it was not pursued.

After another pint Jim Holdroyd had to visit the gentleman's lavatory. He was followed in by Paul McLeod, one of the students who was in the bar, and had been clearly making a good evening of it. "I hate you, you sod," he said belligerently and somewhat drunkenly.

"Oh yes? Why now?" was the urbane reply.

"Don't try to come the smoothie with me. I know you were with her last night. Don't try to deny it."

"If by 'her' you mean Miss Shaw, as I've told you on countless occasions before, I go to see her merely for a drink and a chat. If you don't want to believe me, that's your problem, not mine. Let me give you some advice. If you want to get to know Miss Shaw better yourself, if I may put your designs so politely, you should try doing something about it. I assure you I have no objection. And you'd certainly stand a better chance if you spent your time chatting up Miss Shaw rather than calling me names."

Almost suiting the action to the word Paul McLeod said: "You middle-aged smoothies make me want to puke. Miss Shaw. How correct can you get?"

Jim Holdroyd, at the age of thirty-one, objected slightly to being called middle-aged, and slightly more so to the appellation 'smoothie'. But it was many years since he had bothered to waste time trying to pursue a conversation of a rational nature with someone clearly drunk, so he held his peace.

"That's typical. Bloody smirking again," said Paul McLeod in a loud voice as he followed his chosen antagonist out of the lavatory. "I tell you, one of these days somebody'll kill you, and I'm damn sure I for one won't blame them." He walked in a somewhat unsteady fashion out of the pub.

"What's with him?" said Jim McCabe, when Jim Holdroyd joined the group at the bar again.

"The same fantasy about what I supposedly do to his girl-friend—Miss Shaw, you know. Although I've never seen him making any positive effort which would make the title 'girl-friend' suitable. The trouble with these young chaps is that they can't conceive of any relationship between a male and a female which doesn't contain immense amounts of animalian sex. Still, I suppose we were a bit like that once, weren't we?"

"You are somewhat patronising you, know, Jim," said Jim Cormack, "and I must say I'm not surprised that people like him get a bit annoyed. You ought to watch yourself a bit, you know." The conversation drifted off again.

The dulcet tones of the barmaid roared around the room, asking the same rhetorical questions as can be heard in any bar at closing time. She apparently wished to know whether they were of fixed address, whether they were in full-time employment, and if they thought she herself had nothing better to do and no better company to keep. As all dedicated pub men will in these circumstances, they lingered longer than was strictly necessary over their last few mouthfuls. As she seemed even more insistent than she was normally, they encouraged Jim McCabe to expand another theory of his— this time on the reasons for the wretched state of scholarship in all universities other than St. Andrews—for as long as he cared. Thus, it was fully half-past eleven before they launched themselves out upon the night.

It was a fine bright night, with clear stars and a full moon, such as those cooped up in conurbations where the sodium lamp rules have forgotten exists, unless by chance the wayward behaviour of those responsible for providing the nation's electricity has inadvertently thrust the memory upon them. However, as most people do with things familiar, they noted it, took it for granted and moved on. Jim Holdroyd, as he had drunk a little more than was his custom, joined by Bill Watson, went off in the direction of the chip shop. After they had both consumed a statutory poke of chips, they went their different directions home.

It is usually at this time of night that the unattached male wishes he were in the blessed state of some of his acquaintances and had something more exciting to look forward to than a cold bed in a cold room. Jim Holdroyd had that consideration far from his thoughts as he strolled slowly along South Street towards his flat. He had a lot to think about, and still would have to get up early in the morning, for his daily drive to work in Dundee. He hoped that the five pints he had consumed would be sufficient to land him firmly in the arms of the god of sleep, but if not, he was not unduly worried. On many occasions recently he had lost a good portion of a night's sleep, and still managed to obey the alarm clock.

He turned into his close. Damn, he thought. Why ever had he not got that close light fixed? Yes, he'd see about it tomorrow when he came home from work. It could hardly cost very much. He felt for the first door and fumbled for his keys. To his surprise he found that the door was not locked. He supposed that forgetting to lock it was a good indication of the state of his mind. It didn't actually bother him that much, though; if ever he left his key upstairs, he did not normally take the trouble to go upstairs again to fetch it. He considered the likelihood of theft remote enough to begin with, and anyway he didn't really possess anything worth stealing. He stumbled up the steep stairs, and opened the flat door, which was, as often, also unlocked. The door to the sitting room on the left was also open too, and enough light came from the streetlamps in South Street for him to see the sitting room light switch. He turned it on.

"Hullo," he said in a surprised tone, "Whatever are you doing here?"

"Are you trying to pretend you don't know why I've come?"

"I pride myself in having many qualities, both by birth and education, but my mother was not Gipsy Rose Lee."

"How dare you."

So taken aback was he, and possibly the effect of the alcohol added to his consternation, that he did not raise his hand quickly enough to defend himself. The last he knew was a tremendous blow to the side of the head.

🐝 Chapter 2

"HE'S DEAD. HE'S DEAD."

A distraught youth was shouting through the hatch in St Andrews Police Station. The constable on duty had not seen him come in, as he was totally engrossed in the interminable forms which had to be filled in, and which appeared as if by magic from nowhere, to go, as far as Constable White knew, back to nowhere. That part of his mind which fought to entice him away from the business on hand, occasionally took him to a pleasant realm of fancy where he was a successful professional golfer, playing in the Open, with vast crowds in the flesh and on the television screen avidly following his every shot. In that position he would have no objection to people changing the subject whenever he walked into the club or the pub. Therefore, his immediate reaction to this interruption of his work and his dreams fell somewhat short of disinterested charity. He felt that these students should be given more work to do; that might prevent them from interfering with ordinary people who had an honest living to earn. Accordingly, he got up from the desk in his own good time, and pen and notebook in hand, progressed slowly towards the hatch.

"Can I help you, sir?" he said in a dull official tone.

The youth broke down into tears, and tried to repeat his message, but the words would not come.

"Calm yourself down, laddie, and tell me what you've come here to say." Constable White had begun to speak in a kinder, milder voice, as he saw that, for whatever reason, his visitor was in a dreadful state. This approach seemed to have at least some of the desired effect, for the youth, with an obvious effort, managed to relax his hysteria long enough to say: "He's dead, I tell you!" before he relapsed into his

224

former state, and leant on the counter with his head buried in his hands, sobbing.

Constable White, in common with most people, was at heart a kindly man, and began to wonder what dreadful imaginings were driving the poor youth to this awful state. There was no doubt in his mind, that some sort of illicit drug was responsible. He reflected on the fact that he had been about the same age not many years before, and wondered how he would have reacted if someone had tried to influence him to take whatever substance was responsible for this. He made further friendly efforts to communicate, but these met with total failure. He then had to consider what he should do. He could not leave the Police Station himself, as he was at the moment the only person there. Sergeant Johnson and Constable Smith, who were the other men on duty, were at present doing the rounds in the car. They should be back any minute, but clearly what this young chap needed was immediate medical help. They had always been told not to take too much notice of casual takers of drugs, unless there was clear evidence of trafficking for profit, or it was forced upon their attention. The reason given was that they had far more important things to deal with. He now wondered if this was the right thing to do, when you could see pathetic cases like this. He came to the conclusion that he had better ring the University doctor, who would be sure to know what to do. There seemed no other useful course he could follow until his colleagues returned. He went back to the desk, looked up the number, and rang it.

"Doctor Cathcart? This is St Andrews Police Station. I'm very sorry to interrupt you at this time of the night, doctor, but we've got one of your young students here. He looks and sounds very much as if he's been taking too much of one of those drugs they go in for. I can't get any sense out of him myself. Yes, I know it's late. In fact, it's almost exactly one o'clock. You'll come as quickly as possible? Thank you very much, doctor."

He looked at his customer and decided to do nothing more until either his colleagues or the doctor arrived. The poor lad was still sobbing on the counter, apparently oblivious to what Constable White had been doing. Almost immediately, however, a car drew up outside and Sergeant Johnson and Constable Smith came in.

"What have we got here?" said the sergeant, as he saw the huddled figure at the hatch. "Another of these students who hasn't learnt how to hold his drink yet?"

"I couldn't smell any drink, sergeant, and he was behaving in such a funny way, that I decided it was drugs. I called the University doctor. He should be here any minute."

The figure at the hatch roused itself and turned round to face the newcomers.

"Sergeant Johnson," the youth shouted in a near hysterical manner, "will you listen to me? He's dead I tell you!"

"Here," said the sergeant, "that's not a student. It's young Eric, Davie Athlone's son. I'd like to get my hands on whoever has been supplying him with drugs. He's still at school; he'll only be sixteen or seventeen. John," he said to Constable White, "pour the lad a cup of tea. It'll certainly do him no harm and maybe settle him down a bit. Then he might be able to tell us where he's been.

"He's a local lad then? I'm sorry sergeant, but I haven't really been round long enough to know that many folk. I just assumed he was a student, seeing the state he was in."

Eric Athlone was shaking his head in despair. The sergeant felt genuinely sorry for him and held the cup of tea which he was handed to the unfortunate's lips.

"Come on, lad, drink some of this, and when you feel better you can tell us all about it?"

Eric Athlone took a few gulps of the tea, and then burst out: "For Christ's sake, don't you understand? He's dead. I tell you. Why won't you do something about it?"

In the middle of this statement Doctor Cathcart had entered. He went straight up to his prospective patient and looked at him closely.

"Do you know this lad, sergeant?"

"Aye, his name's Eric Athlone; his family live in the town. I suppose he's not strictly part of your list, but Constable White here understandably assumed he was a student, seeing the state he was in. Anyway, if you wouldn't mind looking at him, now you're here, you probably know more about drugs than any other doctor in town."

"Doctor, will you listen to me? He's dead, dead, dead!" The doctor took no notice of this interruption from his patient, but immediately proceeded to examine him. "Don't worry," he said soothingly, "you're among friends here."

The lad gave up at this juncture and allowed the doctor to complete his swift examination. When he had finished, he said: "Well, you've had a nasty shock. Perhaps you'd better tell us about it."

"I've been telling you for the last ten minutes only you won't listen. Can't you understand? He's dead." He leant against the wall and returned to his convulsive sobs.

"Sergeant," said the doctor, "this lad is not noticeably under the influence of drink or drugs. But he is totally exhausted. He looks as if he hasn't slept for a couple of days, and he's certainly in a state of shock. I suggest you listen to what he as to say."

The sergeant took the doctor's advice—he never could see the point in experts unless you took their advice—and rather doubtfully, but in a kindly tone, said: "The doctor says you've had a nasty shock. Do I understand that you think somebody has died? Is it a friend of yours? Come on, Eric lad, tell us."

"Think I saw him dead!" he spluttered. "I tried to get him to answer me but he couldn't move. It was horrible." He began sobbing again.

"If you'll forgive me sergeant," broke in Constable White, "if there's really nothing wrong with him in the way the doctor says, the sooner we look into it the better."

"Yes, John, that's exactly what I'm trying to do." He turned back to young Athlone. "Yes, lad, you were about to tell me who you thought you saw dead. Not anyone at home, I hope?" he added soothingly.

"Mr Holdroyd. I've been trying to tell you that for ages. Oh, why won't you listen to me?"

"Well laddie, perhaps you'd be good enough to show us where Mr Holdroyd lives. Would you do that for us?"

At this juncture the doctor broke in: "Look, I didn't ask to be called out at this time of night, but now I'm here I intend to do my professional duty. This lad is in no fit state to go back to a house in which he thinks he saw a corpse. Whether there is a corpse there or not is irrelevant to his state of mind. He's in an advanced state of exhaustion and shock, and I intend to take him down to the hospital. I'll make it my personal responsibility to see that he's still there in the morning if you want to see him then. You can see that he wouldn't be much help to you now anyway. The only Mr Holdroyd I know of in town, by the way, is a teacher who lives in South Street"—it was clear from the movements from Eric Athlone that this was the correct one—"And I'm sure the lad can at least give us the number."

"235," said the dejected youth, with a certain relieved resignation.

"Aye, of course," said the sergeant, "I know who you mean now. He used to be a student here about ten years ago, and he's now a teacher in Dundee. I know the flat he lives in. It used to belong to old Mrs McKay, who died about five years ago. And you're sure you can look after the lad properly for the moment, doctor?"

"Certainly. As soon as I've got him into hospital, I'll give him something to put him to sleep. He should be in reasonable shape by the morning if you want to speak to him then."

The sergeant was a little doubtful about his duty in this matter, but decided that the doctor should have his way. Although Eric Athlone was a tall lad, he could not really see him overpowering the doctor. Once he was put under in hospital there would be no more problem. Perhaps his main reason for conceding the doctor's request, however, was the strong suspicion, that, whatever young Athlone might believe, there was nothing seriously wrong with Mr Holdroyd. He said as much to Constable White after the doctor had departed with his patient.

"John, will you come with me to see if anything's wrong with this man Holdroyd? We'll walk there. It'll be just about as quick as taking the car, and the exercise will do you no damage after all that pen-pushing." They left the Police Station in the hands of Constable Smith and made their way towards South Street.

"Mind you," he continued, "I don't really expect much to come of this. You haven't been here as long as I have. I haven't seen much of our Mr Holdroyd in a number of years, but I remember him when he was a student. He often used to hang around with a bunch of people who could really put it back. So, I think all we'll find is that he's passed out on the floor. I suppose with all the strain these teachers have to put up with nowadays it must be quite a relief for them to get plastered from time to time."

His companion said nothing, although he was not averse to something a little more exciting than another drunk. In his saner moments, as he thought them, he was quite content with the relatively quiet life a policeman led in St Andrews, but he was by no means disturbed by the prospect of something a bit more out of the ordinary than an individual rendered horizontal by alcohol; the only outstanding feature would be the fact that it was Tuesday night, not Friday or Saturday. He was therefore eager to see what their journey would reveal and was glad when they reached the close which formed the entrance to No. 235. There was a light above on the left apparently from a room in Mr Holdroyd's flat. The sergeant shone his torch down the close: the outside door of No. 235 was open. They walked slowly in and ascended the stairs. The inside door of the flat was open too, and as they came up to it they could see a light coming from another open door on the inside to the left. They went straight into the lighted room. James Holdroyd lay on the floor in front of them. There was no noticeable smell of drink in the room, despite the sergeant's prognostications. Constable White walked carefully up to the body, knelt down and felt the pulse. To his surprise, though it must be admitted not totally to his dismay, he felt nothing. He looked at the limp hand which still grasped the front door key, and with the clarity reserved for such occasions he saw the broken watch and its implications. The hands stood at ten minutes to one.

"My god, sergeant," he said, "the laddie killed him."

Sergeant Johnson was not surprised by the presumption of death, as he had already noticed the unpleasant wound in the side of the head. Not too serious at first sight, but in a very dangerous place. He did not, however, understand the reasons for the accusation.

"Which laddie, John?" he said patiently.

"Young Eric Athlone, of course." He pointed to the watch. "Clearly, he killed Mr Holdroyd, and when he realised what he had done, came round to the Station to confess, but broke down on the way."

"It could well be as you say. But look, I'd better get back to the station and see that the CID are informed immediately. I'll leave you here. I'm sure in the circumstances I don't need to tell you not to touch anything. As things are, I'll have to send Michael Smith down to the hospital to keep an eye on young Athlone. That'll mean I'm stuck in the station until we can get another man in. Never mind, I hope you won't be kept on your own too long. Although after all this reorganisation things can be very slow to move, I think when there's something as important as this they can still get their skates on. But again, I suppose there's not much they can do which couldn't keep for an hour or two, and they'll know it. There's no doubt he's dead, so I won't bother with a local doctor unless they tell me to. Their people know what's best done when this sort of thing happens, and thank goodness our local men haven't had much experience."

Constable White was left with the corpse. As soon as he reached the Police Station, the sergeant despatched his remaining constable down to the hospital as a precaution, and then rang Headquarters. Yes, he was told, he had done all that was necessary. Yes, as he knew it was far better if nothing was disturbed until they got there. No, he needn't bother with a local doctor; they would be there almost as quickly. He had been quite correct in leaving Constable White at the scene. Yes, they appreciated that he himself could not now leave the station until reinforcements should arrive. They were pleased to hear that the only suspect was already under surveillance. They would be there as soon as possible.

Next, he rang Doctor Cathcart. He tried the hospital first, and fortunately found that the doctor had not yet left. "I hope you'll forgive me, doctor, but I'm afraid I've had to send an officer down to keep an eye on your patient. Yes, I know it's probably not necessary, but if you hear the reasons, I'm sure you'll understand. You see, Mr Holdroyd is dead, and he did not die a natural death. The first indications are that he was assaulted, and that the assault took place less than ten minutes before your young lad appeared at the Police Station. So he's at least going to be an important witness, if not actually a suspect. It could be that he'll need somebody there for his own protection. Aye, doctor, thank you very much."

As there appeared to be nothing of any use he could do until the arrival of the CID men, Sergeant Johnson did not attempt to do anything. In less than half an hour, both to his surprise and his relief, they appeared, bringing with them an extra constable in case he was needed for temporary local duties. There were only three in all who entered the Police Station: Constable McPhee, the replacement who had also driven the car, Dr Crenshaw the police doctor, and Inspector Malone of the Fife CID. As they entered, the inspector said: "Don't be surprised at the numbers, sergeant, we're short staffed too. Now, to get down to business. Is there anything we need to do here before going to the scene of the crime, if crime it be?"

"I don't think so, Inspector, and I might as well tell you of the circumstances leading up to the discovery of the body on the way round—that is if we can leave someone in charge of the station here." Constable McPhee, the replacement, was left to look after things, and the other three walked briskly in the direction of James Holdroyd's flat. Sergeant Johnson continued: "It's just about as quick to walk, and there's less chance of unwelcome busybodies if there's no police car in sight. As I was going to say, a young man came into the Police Station shortly before one o' clock, in such a state that Constable White, who was in charge at the time, assumed that he was under the influence of drugs. We get students in like that from time to time. Constable White took no notice of what he said and rang for a doctor. I returned from a routine patrol before the doctor got there and recognised the lad. His name's Eric Athlone and he's not a student. In fact, he's still at school. He kept going on about someone being dead, but we took no action until the doctor assured us that it was not the effect of drugs. Constable White and myself then went to Mr Holdroyd's flat, and I suppose you've heard the rest."

"You had good reasons for believing that death had occurred not long before you arrived?"

"Yes, Inspector. You see, Mr Holdroyd's watch was broken. It must have happened when he fell. It had stopped at ten minutes to one."

"At exactly what time did you discover the body?"

"Twenty minutes past one."

"You weren't able to have the streets searched to see if there was anyone around, who could at least tell you if they'd seen somebody else?"

Sergeant Johnson looked a little offended. "I'm afraid there were only the three of us on duty. One had to stay with the body, one had to keep an eye on the only person we already knew was in the vicinity at the time, and one had to man the Station. I'm afraid we don't have any lee-way when this sort of thing happens."

"I know, I know," said the inspector in a mollifying tone. "There was clearly nothing else you could do. And I'm sure people in St Andrews will be perfectly willing to volunteer any information of that sort."

They had reached the dead man's flat. As they entered, Malone shone his torch on both of the doors and looked at them for a few seconds. He then led the way into the sitting room, politely asking the sergeant to stay at the door, while Dr Crenshaw, a man of few words, knelt by the body of the late James Holdroyd. The inspector spoke.

"Constable White, I presume? I'm Inspector Malone. I presume I can take it that you've touched nothing?"

"Not since we established he was dead, sir, and I don't think we touched anything before that, except with our feet."

"You haven't even sat down?"

"No, sir, though to be honest I had half a mind to if you'd been much longer. That's to say, I thought I'd have a longer wait."

The Inspector contrived half a smile. "We're not quite as slow as most of you people seem to think. The main problem is when people expect us to be in more than one place at the same time."

Without moving more than necessary, he then took a careful look round the room. The late owner had clearly been a man of some taste but just as clearly had not had enough money to indulge it. The furniture had all been originally of very good quality but was mostly rather shabby. It had obviously been bought cheaply at auction sales or from the previous owner. That was not to say that the place was untidy; far from it; it was clearly cleaned meticulously and often. For this reason, the bookcase, a large Victorian piece, provided a rather strange contrast. Books of all shapes, sizes and colours decorated its shelves. Russian classics rubbed against bright new paperbacks of dubious literary content, and the *Iliad* of Homer leant against William Burrough's *Naked Lunch*. A man of strange tastes, thought Malone.

Dr Crenshaw stood up. "Died not long ago from a sharp blow to the side of the head. I would normally suggest about twelve o' clock but it's difficult to tell. I'll have more exact information for you when you've allowed me to take the body away for proper tests."

Malone was used to the doctor's cagey approach and was glad of it. It meant that he never started with false information.

"Could you hazard a guess as to a possible weapon?"

"I never mentioned a weapon, Inspector. For all I know he could have fallen against one of these pieces of furniture. If he fell heavily enough it's quite possible that he could have met his death that way. The blow is in a very vulnerable place."

"In that case no great violence would have been needed?"

"If you mean have you got to look for a six-foot-six heavyweight, the answer is definitely no."

Malone walked carefully across the room, and without touching it examined a heavy metal candelabrum which stood on a chest. He collected such items himself and had partly gone over to look at it from the point of view of an amateur collector. However, the possibilities of the sharp-pointed corners of the base could not escape him. "Doctor," he said, "I know it sounds straight out of a party game, but could this have been the weapon used?"

"Undoubtedly, but so could a dozen other things of that weight and manoeuvrability."

There was not one, let alone a dozen other similar objects in the room. Assuming that the doctor's theory about a fall would be proved wrong, Malone was forced to the conclusion that this was indeed what was used. The only other possibility was that the instrument had been removed. As the candelabrum could not have got up and walked across the room, there was clearly a good chance that whoever had wielded the instrument had left a good number of traces on it. At any rate, he thought, they would soon find out, as the forensic men should arrive at any moment. He selfishly wondered why they could not have appeared as quickly as he had done.

He did not have long to wait. A car drew up outside, and at a word from Malone, Sergeant Johnson went downstairs to show them in. When they arrived, after a minimum of ceremony, they set about their professional task in a brisk, efficient manner. The Inspector suggested to Sergeant Johnson that he should return to the station, but asked if he might retain Constable White, as he had been concerned with the case from the start and could give him any further information he needed. The sergeant pointed out that White had only recently come from the West and was not very well versed in the local population. Malone replied that he didn't think that would matter very much at the moment; he would, however, pick the sergeant's brains for local information later.

Death of a Dundee Teacher

As soon as the forensic men had finished and the body bad been removed, Malone began to go through the flat himself. This presented no great labour, as it was not very large. Apart from the spacious living room they were in, there were only two other rooms off the hallway, a kitchen and a bathroom/lavatory combined. Off the living room was a small bedroom, the whole presenting a most peculiar shape, such as is sometimes found in flats in the centre of old towns. To White it appeared he had found little of interest, for the only things he took away with him were the contents of the man's pockets, which he had emptied before the removal of the body.

"Well White, I think we might as well go. There doesn't seem to be anything of obvious interest around, but as I don't know what I should be looking for yet, that may not be surprising. I must say from a short look that it appears that Mr Holdroyd was either a man with nothing to hide, or so much to hide that he kept it pretty well concealed. If we don't try to be devious the former is the most likely. That would make our job easier, wouldn't you think?"

"I'm not very experienced in this sort of thing, sir, but I would have thought that it looked fairly straightforward already. All we need is some positive proof, which your forensic experts should be able to provide shortly, and we have the guilty man."

"You mean this young lad Eric Athlone? Let's hope you're right. It'll save a lot of work." He led White out of the building, still taking great care not to touch anything. "I'm afraid you'll have to come to Headquarters. The voracious paper machine will require not only my efforts, but yours as well."

6❧ Chapter 3

"CONSTABLE WHITE, IF I CAN HAVE YOU SECONDED, would you agree to join me in this investigation?" It was shortly after four o' clock and certain formalities had been concluded. "We're a bit short staffed here as everywhere else. It's not an exciting prospect, as I'm sure you know well. It means that you'll have to go wherever I want you to, and keep the hours I want to for the next few days—or a good deal less if your view of the case is correct. I've been impressed over the last few hours with your general attitude to the job. The majority of people of your age—if you'll forgive the patronising approach—would have attempted to force themselves on the assembled company to indicate how keen they were. But it seems to have occurred to you that others may have more experience of the circumstances than yourself. By the way, have you come across any murders before?"

"Several, sir, when I was in Glasgow. But they were more often than not one bunch of criminals attacking another, or the standard family stuff. The one thing I did learn from them, sir, was that the most obvious explanation was usually the correct one. In reply to your offer, I'd be very pleased to accept, but I think you've probably got the wrong person. I've only been in St. Andrews a couple of months, and if you think this business is more complex than it appears at first sight, you'd be better with someone who knows the town better. I'm only just getting over the belief that St. Andrews is a historical monument surrounded by golf courses, a university and old retired colonels."

"You also have a fine turn of phrase, White, and even if that aphorism is not original it's none the worse for having been used before. I don't need someone with a vast knowledge of St. Andrews—in fact I know the place pretty well myself, as I was a student there for four years. I even knew James Holdroyd by sight. I was in my final year when he started, and what with plenty of work to do and sufficient friends already, I wouldn't normally have known him. But he was a very noticeable sort of person. From the way you've seen him that may seem a surprising statement. He didn't look much to most people, but he had the most extraordinary eyes. It always seemed as if he knew things which he couldn't possibly have. You'll need to remember that if we have to go deeply into this matter. I'm probably a bit too emotionally involved in St. Andrews myself, and your lack of involvement could in fact be a positive advantage. If you'll agree, then, I'll see if I can fix it immediately. Don't worry, I have no intention of starting in earnest until I've had some sleep. If we haven't got our man already, no purpose will be served by looking for him when we can't think. Besides, my wife, like most people's, finds it difficult to believe that I'm actually working when I don't make the regular visits home."

"I know the problem, sir," said White, with a shy smile at his own presumption.

"And they get no better as they get older," said Malone, gently putting him back in his place.

Not long after midday Malone was driving along the Guardbridge road towards St. Andrews, carrying with him the necessary authorisation for taking over Constable White for as long as he should need him. White himself had agreed to report for duty at St. Andrews Police Station at one o' clock. Malone reflected on the first time he had come to St. Andrews at the age of eighteen to go to the university. He could not recall the state of his mind at the time, but did remember, that the approach to the town had made a strong impression on him. He had come on the train then, when the Beeching Axe was nothing but a shadow in a far-off wood. The railway had passed a few hundred yards nearer to the sea than the road, but the view from both was substantially the same. The Auld Grey Toun stood out as strongly as ever, guarding the bay with its gaunt presence, one of the few unchanged landmarks in a grossly over-changed world. The acres of golf course prickling with whins formed the stately drive up to its great edifices; but all too soon the soulless reminder of international tourism interrupted the view. By the old railway line where the coal-sheds had stood, there reared a building masquerading as a luxury hotel, but giving the impression more of some floating new-town office block, helplessly moored hundreds of miles from its own wharf. In comparison with this, the concrete and glass structures of the new science departments, which commemorated the enthusiastic if misguided University expansion of the Sixties, looked coyly decent as they crouched to hide their lack of inspiration beneath the great raised beach of the North Haugh. Still, Malone reflected, such blots were as nothing compared with the destruction entire and total of so many urban areas of Scotland.

When he reached the Police Station, he found that White had already arrived. "A fine show of enthusiasm," he observed. "I hope that the absence of a uniform doesn't make you feel naked?"

"Not at all, sir. If anything, it's the other way round. People stare at you if you're naked, and they stare at you if you're in uniform. If you're dressed normally, they're more likely just to pass you by."

A room at the back of the Police Station had been reserved for Malone's use for as long as he should need it.

White showed him through and indicated a pile of papers on the desk.

"These came for you earlier, sir."

"Aye, thank you. They'll be the various reports I asked for earlier today. I told them to send everything on here. There'll be more to come; for instance, they won't have had time yet to get any information about Holdroyd's relatives. You know yourself how often that can lead to discovery of reasons for someone's death. Let's see. What have we here? Ah, good, Dr Crenshaw's report. They're always a pleasure to read, as he never writes anything more than is absolutely necessary, and always sticks closely to his side of the business; not that he won't offer very helpful suggestions if you ask for his personal opinion. However, he always keeps it in the right place. I don't think there'll be anything of great significance in the report—it seems to be quite clear how Holdroyd died—but there might be a few useful indications."

He perused the report for a few minutes then handed it to White. When he had glanced through it, Malone continued: "Not much there, you see. The blow was from in front which is suggestive; he had about enough alcohol in his blood to lose his driving license, but not much more. He seems fairly certain that death occurred shortly before midnight, which seems rather strange in view of the watch. They're usually accurate, but individual bodies can act in different ways. For all I know the alcohol could have had some effect. The only other point, which he made in the flat, is that the blow was not an immensely hard one, and there are no other signs of injury."

He glanced at some more papers and extracted the forensic report. "You see the value of reports, White? They may be annoying to fill in, but at least we don't have to go gallivanting halfway round Fife to get this information. Let me see. It seems immensely melodramatic, but it was the candelabrum that was used. Mm. That's very strange. No fingerprints belonging to anyone but the deceased anywhere except on the candelabrum. You'd think that if someone was careful enough not to touch anything but the weapon, he'd have enough sense to leave no traces on it. It's also strange that there are no other prints at all. You could easily see that Holdroyd liked to keep everything clean and tidy, but that is rather extreme. Perhaps he was not a man to entertain on his premises. Ah. There are signs to suggest either that someone wearing gloves was there of late, or a deliberate attempt had been made to clean surfaces. We'd better find out if Holdroyd wore gloves himself. Any views, White?" he asked as he put down the report.

"Well, sir, if you'll excuse me, I rather like the idea of having something complicated to deal with, but aren't we possibly wasting time? All we need to do is to match up the fingerprints on the candelabrum with Eric Athlone's, and we've got our man. I can easily see how the doctor can be right about the time. In the state the young lad was in, he could easily have killed Mr Holdroyd at twelve o' clock, and then gone round the flat clearing up his traces. Given the way he was, he could have forgotten about the candelabrum, then lost his head completely, and for some reason best known to himself, smashed the watch before coming round to see us."

"You may well be right, White. But what has been bothering me so far is the type of person Holdroyd appears to have been, and the absence of any obvious reason for his death. If he had been a person of doubtful character in any way, I'm sure Sergeant Johnson would have known. But from his silence on the matter, he clearly had no cause to think ill of Holdroyd. It is of course possible to manufacture a dozen reasons for his death, but they're not reasons which usually apply in a place like St. Andrews. I can't remember when they last had a murder here. People get beaten up, robberies occur, and there are plenty of drunken brawls. Any of these can by chance lead to someone's death, but we have no evidence of any of them happening in this case. As far as we know there was no robbery, no drunken brawl, and only one blow was struck."

"Well, sir, I see no reason why such a thing shouldn't happen here. They're only people after all. May I add that I don't remember any attempt by young Athlone to deny that he was responsible."

"Perhaps you're right. I'm always in danger of romanticising about St. Andrews. Well, we should be able to check on the fingerprints fairly easily. There ought to be a statement here from Eric Athlone. Ah, here it is. It'll have his fingerprints attached. I assume he hasn't confessed, or I'd have been told about it immediately. He says that Holdroyd was dead when he entered the flat. He doesn't know exactly what time he went along, or how long he was there for, but thinks he arrived sometime after half-past twelve. He admits he put the candelabrum where we found it, saying that it looked untidy lying on the ground. A very strange reaction. We'll clearly have to question him again, but the doctor has left instructions that he should not be disturbed again this morning unless absolutely necessary. You'll note that no reason is offered for his presence in Holdroyd's flat." Malone then took out the forensic report again, and there was no doubt that the fingerprints on the candelabrum and these of Eric Athlone were identical. But as he admitted to touching the object Malone realised that this took him no further.

"That seems just about to establish his guilt," said White.

Death of a Dundee Teacher

"I hope so for our peace of mind. But I'm afraid I'm by no means as convinced as you are. You see, I can think of a number of reasons, all perfectly valid, why the young chap should be visiting at that time of the night. I know that the majority of people go to bed at eleven or so, just as they do anywhere else, but there is a substantial number who don't. Take the University to begin with. I'm not suggesting for a minute that either students or staff are any less hard working than other people, but there is a big difference in the way they have to work. They have very few fixed hours and as a result many keep hours which the average man would find impossible. Then take the hotel trade. If you're a barman, you don't finish work until about midnight. Therefore, the most natural thing in the world is to do your visiting about that time. When you've got a number of people regularly keeping late hours, it's hardly surprising if others follow suit from time to time. By the same token I can think of a large number of reasons why a seventeen-year-old could be visiting a man in his early thirties—perfectly respectable reasons too. We can't of course discount such possibilities as robbery, homosexuality or drugs, but I'm trying to point out that these should not be the first explanations to leap to the mind. We may well get some light on the last two suggestions from Sergeant Johnson; it's clear that he's very well up in local knowledge. Amazing man too. As soon as this business turned up, he volunteered to stay on for the whole day, although he had already been working all night."

Constable White did not bother to comment on this praise of his immediate superior. The energy and dedication of the sergeant were doubtless highly commendable, but when he expected every other officer to imitate his excellent example whenever he thought fit, the policemen involved could feel a little put upon.

Death of a Dundee Teacher

There was a knock on the door, and the sergeant appeared, clearly satisfied with the results of his researches. "It's been fairly easy to establish the movements of Mr Holdroyd before he went home last night, Inspector. I thought it would save time if I looked into the matter. By asking one or two people, I found out that he usually goes to the White Horse bar shortly after nine o' clock most evenings. I happen to know the manager of the White Horse fairly well, and went along to have a chat to him. He confirmed that this was indeed Mr Holdroyd's habit, but for some reason he didn't go there last night. The manager assumed that he must have gone straight to the St. David's, if he was out at all. Apparently, he would go along there later most nights, as it didn't close until eleven o' clock, whereas the White Horse shuts at ten-thirty usually. So, I went to the St. David's and was told that he had indeed been there, and he had arrived a little earlier than usual. He was drinking with the same people who he used to see there most nights, all respectable people by the way. I went to see one of them, a Mr Cormack who's in charge of the Social Security Office. I thought he'd be the easiest to find. Mr Cormack had already heard of the death of his friend and realising that he might well have been one of the last people to see him alive, he had already prepared a statement, which I have here. Anyway, he told me that both he and the others in the St. David's had noticed for some weeks that Mr Holdroyd had been worried about something, but whenever they asked him about it, he would always change the subject. He didn't know if he had done anything special earlier in the evening, but he certainly hadn't mentioned it if he had. Apparently, he used to do some private tuition on Tuesday and Thursday evenings, but for some reason, which he hadn't given his friends, that had stopped last Thursday. The person he used to teach was Eric Athlone."

"That's very interesting. What did he teach him?"

"Russian."

"Russian? I didn't realise that was his subject. With R.A.F. Leuchers only a few miles away, certain suspicions have to present themselves. I'm not trying to overdramatise and have you search behind every tree for men called Boris with fur hats and black coats, but do you by chance know of any connection between Leuchers and either James Holdroyd or Eric Athlone?"

"Strangely enough, Inspector, Davie Athlone, Eric's father, has been working at Leuchars for a number of years now. But Davie's an ex-serviceman himself and as straight as they come, and I can't see how we can bring his son into it. It's not as if Davie's working on anything which would bring him into direct contact with classified information."

"I'm sure you're right, but it's best to have any information which may be relevant as soon as possible. Have you got anything more of immediate importance? If not, would you arrange for statements from the other people Holdroyd was drinking with last night, and find out names and addresses of any other particular friends of his, or indeed anyone he's known for a long time?"

"All the people he was with last night have deposited statements already, Inspector, and as far as I can make out, he didn't have all that many of what you call friends. He knew a lot of people, but he didn't seem to be very close to them. The only information which seems to be of interest in their statements comes from Mr Watson, who's a local teacher. Apparently when they left the bar, a little later than they strictly should have, he and Mr Holdroyd went to buy chips. Mr Watson is quite sure that he had no idea of any danger threatening him."

"So, Mr Watson is the last person we know of to have seen him alive, if we discount young Athlone for the moment. Can he prove that he went straight home, and didn't, for instance make a detour by Holdroyd's flat?"

"I didn't doubt his word on the matter for a moment, Inspector, but I'm sure his movements can be checked without too much difficulty. The other important point I must mention is that Eric Athlone asked to see you as soon as possible. He's adamant that he won't speak to anybody except the man in charge of the investigation. The doctor says that there's absolutely nothing wrong with him that can't be cured by rest, and is quite willing to allow you to see him as long as you don't take too long. Oh, and by the way, may I thank you for getting me more men?"

"Please don't thank me, sergeant. If I kidnap one of your men and permanently place another on duty at a hospital then the least I can do is to keep you operating. Mind you, they may be taken away from you at any time. But cheer up, this call to see young Athlone may be the preamble to a confession, and if so, you won't have to put up with my meddling for much longer. At any rate, I'm sure that's what Constable White's expecting. I hope he realises that confessions aren't always true."

White drove Malone down to the hospital. It was a fairly modest building which had been quite sufficient for the needs of a small population, until that population had begun to grow too fast. Now a large number of local patients were shunted off to the larger units in Kirkcaldy or Dundee. When they entered, they found nobody at the reception, and had to wander along a corridor until they found a nurse who could direct them to the right ward. Fortunately they found one who was willing to lead them to the right place, rather than give the usual directions met with in hospitals, which might perhaps be clear to anyone who was familiar with the building over a number of years, but tend to be incomprehensible to the casual visitor. They were taken upstairs and along a corridor and were then in no further need of guidance. A police officer was sitting on a chair outside one of the small rooms leading off the corridor. The nurse asked them if they would wait a minute until she found out if there were any special instructions about the patient. She returned shortly to say that there were none, but could they be as quick as possible as he was in need of rest. Malone assured her that they would not be long. She then led them into the room, which was identical with thousands of other such hospital rooms up and down the country. It possessed only one bed, which contained Eric Athlone. His appearance was very different from the night before; although the darkness under his eyes betokened tiredness, he looked generally placid and healthy. The nurse spoke to him.

"This is the inspector you wished to see, Eric. Do you want me to stay while you speak to him?"

"No thanks, I'll be perfectly all right." The voice was different too. It was steady, but Malone could not help noticing a slightly effeminate quality to it.

"You wanted to tell me something, Mr Athlone?" he said, rather unnecessarily. "I'm Inspector Malone, and I'm in charge of the investigation into the death of Mr Holdroyd. Constable White is assisting me, and I'd prefer him to stay if you have no objections."

"I don't mind at all if he's here too. I just wanted to make sure I could speak to the man in charge. I know you think I did it, and there's no point in denying that you do. My aunt, that's the nurse who brought you in here, told me that there's been a policeman outside my door ever since the doctor brought me in. I also know that that's why I've been put upstairs in a room on my own. But I didn't do it, and I swear I didn't. You've got to believe me. You see, you'll not understand, but I couldn't have killed him. I loved him."

His voice had risen to a shout, and the nurse came in and ushered them out.

❧ Chapter 4

"WELL, WHITE," SAID MALONE, as they returned to the station, "Do you still think you're right in placing him as the guilty party, or do you think there might be something in what he says?"

"I don't know, sir. But among other things, I've read 'The Ballad of Reading Gaol', and I see no reason for believing his final words.

"You are a surprising chap White. I would normally have expected some remark like 'Bloody poofter, of course he did it'. But, with or without your learned literary references, you're quite right. There is absolutely no reason why we should believe that he's telling the truth. The trouble is that I feel he was being absolutely honest. I know how dangerous it can be to allow personal opinions to enter this sort of affair, but that was very strongly my impression. Sergeant Johnson clearly seemed to think he was a decent enough lad, and it's obvious from his aunt's reactions that she doesn't place him in the role of murderer. Still, we'll have to hang on to him till we find some information to let him out—if such information is forthcoming. The first thing we must do clearly is find out more about Holdroyd. As I said last night, he strikes me as the sort of person who has a lot to hide, or absolutely nothing. By the way, as the young lad suggested, it was very considerate of the hospital to put him upstairs like that, assuming they did it on purpose. He certainly couldn't jump down from there and walk away.

"May I ask if you found anything to work on in Mr Holdroyd's pockets? I noticed that you removed the contents before they took his body away."

"I was hoping for some help there, certainly, but there's nothing definite at the moment. However, there were one or two items which could turn out to be interesting; the trouble is that as we know so little about him, it's difficult to decide what may be important and what may not. Among other things, of course, I have asked for the standard check with his bank manager, to find out if there was anything untoward in his financial position recently. As you know, that can often be a very fruitful area of investigation. In fact, if the bank manager has been co-operative, I'd hope that the information is already in."

They had now reached the Police Station. The car was parked outside and they went in. Sergeant Johnson, accompanied by two respectable-looking citizens, immediately addressed Malone.

"Ah, Inspector. May I introduce you to Mr McCabe and Mr Cormack. You'll remember that they were with Mr Holdroyd on Tuesday evening. Mr Cormack thought they might have some information which could have a bearing on your case, and as you were due back any moment, I asked them to wait."

"Thank you very much, sergeant. Please come into my office, gentlemen, such as it is. I'm sure you won't mind if Constable White joins us. Now, please tell me all about it."

Mr Cormack spoke; "I asked Mr McCabe here along to verify what I've got to say. As you know, we were both in the St. Davids last night. The point is that we both heard someone as good as threaten Jim Holdroyd. It does seem a little theatrical and there was probably nothing in it—which was why I didn't bother to mention it beforehand to the sergeant—but in the circumstances I thought I'd better bring it to your attention now. I must admit that the reason is partly that it's being said that young Eric Athlone is as good as under arrest. No-one who knows the lad thinks for one minute that he could have done anything like that. Well, as I was saying, not long before closing-time—I'm afraid neither of us can remember the exact time—Paul McLeod, a student we all know slightly, accused Jim of being over-friendly with his girlfriend—not to put too fine a point on it, he accused him of having sexual relations with her. We didn't actually hear that part of the conversation, as it took place in the lavatory, but Jim told us afterwards. As this Paul McLeod was leaving, he pointed out some of Jim's more annoying habits, and suggested that someday somebody would kill him for the way he carried on. He then added that he for one wouldn't blame them. As I say it was probably just something said in the heat of the moment, and he was certainly not sober at the time, but in the circumstances..."

"Quite right Mr Cormack, you are undoubtedly doing the correct thing. I shall certainly look into the matter immediately. It is far too much of a coincidence to be neglected. Do you happen to know where this Paul McLeod or his girlfriend live?"

"I don't know the actual address of either of them, but as Paul McLeod's a student, you're bound to find it in the student directory. They're sure to have one here. As for Jean Shaw—that's the girl's name—one of those drop-outs you always find, hanging around University towns—she lives in a flat at the back of a butcher's shop in South Street. As I say, I don't know the number, but it's the only butchers on the left-hand side of the street as you go towards the Cathedral."

"Do you know if they live on their own?"

"I don't know for certain, but I think it's most unlikely with the price of accommodation in the centre of the town nowadays."

"Thank you very much for your information, Mr Cormack, and you too Mr McCabe, for coming along to give corroboration. It always makes the job easier if the public co-operate in this way."

"Not at all, Inspector. Goodbye."

Sergeant Johnson entered the room when they had left. "Inspector," he said, "the hospital has just been on the phone. They say they really can't keep Eric Athlone there any longer. I don't know whether you noticed when you were down there, but they made special provision for him at the end of the women's ward for our benefit. They say they now have need of the bed. The normal procedure, it appears, would be to transfer him to Dundee, if he was in need of further attention. They say it's most unlikely that he is, but they're prepared to recommend a transfer for our benefit, if we would like to keep him under observation. That's their version, at any rate. I think the real reason is that they don't want to see him sent to prison."

Malone thought for a while. "I think it would be preferable if we could keep him in hospital. I don't want to arrest him, for the time being anyway. On the evidence available I probably should, but if he's in hospital under observation I can't see that my superiors can kick up a fuss if I eventually have to charge him. Do you think you could arrange for them to carry out the transfer, and I'll see to the problem of keeping him under surveillance?"

"I think that should be quite straightforward. As you've probably noticed by now, there aren't many people round here who think that the lad could possibly have done it."

After the sergeant had departed and Malone had made the necessary arrangements with Dundee, he turned to White. "Well then, who's to be first? The young lady or the young gentleman?"

After ascertaining that Paul McLeod lived nearer, in Market Street to be precise, they decided to visit him first.

There seemed to be no point in taking the car such a small distance, and they could see no point in advertising their visit, so they elected to walk. They found the flat, which was situated above a draper's shop, and knocked on the door. When it was opened, the first thing they noticed was the smell. It seemed likely to them that neither the flat, nor the inhabitants' clothes, nor their kitchen had received the attention of a cleaner for some considerable time. White was inclined to include their bodies in this list. The individual who eventually opened the door was apparently doing his best to disguise his masculinity, but in the event this was left in no doubt by the pitch of his voice.

"Yeah? What do you want?"

"We're police officers. Does a Mr Paul McLeod live here?"

"I think he's still in his bed. I suppose you'd better come in. I'll go and see if I can wake him up. He was probably on a bit of a binge yesterday, and that's why he's not around yet. But he should be fairly reasonable by now."

Malone and White entered. Neither of them was particularly surprised by the level of general untidiness and near chaos which met their eyes—Malone because he had been quite used to that sort of thing when he had been a student himself, White because he had a firm belief that all students rather liked living in squalor. However, even Malone found the atmosphere rather oppressive. After a short while a fairly tall, weedy looking individual entered the room they had been left in. He too was wearing clothes which made his sex a little difficult to determine at the first glance.

"What do you want?" he said in a rather truculent voice, which betrayed the state of mind of the wakened sleeper, and also seemed to be tinged with apprehension. Yet he apparently was not conscious of any peculiarity in being discovered in bed at this time of the day.

"I'm Inspector Malone, and this is Constable White. We're investigating the death last night of a Mr James Holdroyd of South Street. I have reason to believe that you were in the St. David's Hotel last night, and that you spoke to Mr Holdroyd at some time between ten and eleven o' clock."

"Yeah, that's right."

"Was that the last time you saw, Mr Holdroyd?"

"Yeah."

"May I suggest then, Mr McLeod that you show remarkably little surprise at the news of his death?"

"Very clever. Jock, who let you in, told me about it when he woke me up, in case it was something to do with that. So I'd have time to make up a story if necessary, I suppose. But it isn't necessary."

"According to my information you made a remark to Mr Holdroyd when you left the bar, to the effect that you'd be very pleased to see him dead."

"I could well have. I'd been drinking all day, so I don't remember exactly what I said. But I'm not denying it for a minute. I never could stand the sod."

Malone had no romantic notions as regards the attitude of many people towards the recent dead, so he continued: "Could you please be good enough to tell me exactly why you disliked Mr Holdroyd so much?"

"If you've been speaking to someone who heard what I said to him last night, you'll know already. As I say, I don't know what I said to him, but I do remember what it was about. What annoyed me most about the sod was his attitude towards women, and especially one, as you'll have been told, I suppose. He's one of those bloody middle-aged smoothies who think they can get away with anything—

'thought' I should say in his case. You should see the way he, and his pals for that matter, look at them, as if they're expecting every woman in sight to fall on the floor in front of them. He'd have been laughable if he didn't take it any further. But when he goes and visits Jean—I suppose you'll have nosed out about her—it stops being a joke and becomes bloody immoral. Why can't these guys act their age? He was well over thirty, and looked a lot more, and she's only twenty-one. He was just one of these failures who could never manage with people of his own age. He shouldn't have wanted to muscle in on a young chick like that."

"Wouldn't you like to muscle in yourself?" interrupted Malone, more in sympathy for the deceased Mr Holdroyd, than for any professional reason.

"Obviously. But I can't get anywhere because she's too taken in by his middle-aged smoothie talk. I've sometimes thought she's about to tell me what they do together, but at least she's always drawn the line at that. And when I speak to him to tell him what I think of him all he does is produce that stupid smirk of his and insists that he does nothing to Jean. He only goes there for 'a drink and a chat'. If I believed that I'd believe anything."

"What do you do when you're visiting her?" asked Malone, then like Pilate not waiting for an answer, continued in an official tone: "Mr McLeod, would you please account for your movements between half-past eleven and one last night?"

"Oh, I see, under suspicion. It's like that then. Look, I came back here sometime before eleven last night and crashed out. I didn't wake up until about ten this morning, but as I felt hellish, I turned over and went back to sleep. As I told you, I'd had a lot to drink yesterday, as I have had for several days. I was in need of a long rest. And for God's sake don't produce any moral stuff about wasting public money or students not going to lectures. If you'd only been one yourself you might understand."

Malone passed by this irrelevant, incorrect suggestion. "Can you produce any independent corroboration for your movements, or lack of them, last night?

"No, I don't suppose I can. Perfectly innocent people don't go around making sure that someone knows where they are every minute of the day, you know. And Bill and Jock, who share this place with me, were as far as I know out all night. I suppose you'll disapprove of that too."

Again Malone thought it would be a wasted effort to point out that how Bill and Jock spent their nights was absolutely no concern of his, unless he should come across them in the line of his professional duty. Constable White maintained his silent presence. Malone said "Thank you very much for your co-operation Mr McLeod. I'm afraid I shall have to ask you to remain in this area for the next few days. If you wish to leave St. Andrews at any time, would you please inform us at the Police Station of your destination? You may be required to help us further with our enquiries. We can see ourselves out, thank you."

They took one or two draughts of pure North Sea Air in Market Street, and then Malone said: "Tell me White, do you find it easy to cast Paul McLeod in the role of murderer?"

"I must admit that it would be difficult to imagine on first acquaintance, sir."

"And yet you can see Eric Athlone in that part?"

White, having no reply to give, gave none.

Their next visit was to Miss Jean Shaw. They turned down Bell Street, and as they passed the shops in silence, Malone meditated on the value of the small trader, who was in evidence all around him. Most of the shops still had the same names above them as when he had been a student. He smiled at the sight of the 'Sixty Minute Cleaners', where he used to take his washing. With the altered pronunciation of the word 'Minute' which he and his friends had always used, the visual image which presented itself was suitably bizarre. The tobacconist was still there, who still displayed in the window a wide variety of tobacco products, as opposed to the half-dozen 'popular' brands of cigarettes which are the only things offered in many modern establishments. Aye, he thought, the politicians had a lot to answer for. However could they have swallowed the slogan that small meant worse? He for one had yet to see any convincing evidence to support the theory. As they turned left into South Street at a point not far from where James Holdroyd had lived, Malone found it easy to understand why he had elected to stay in St. Andrews, even if it meant commuting to Dundee every day. Most people, he reflected, would be too frightened of the appellation 'failure', or the accusation of a lack of ambition—he himself certainly would have been when he graduated. They passed by the old University Library, now moved to a hideous modern building. Above its entrance there still stood the Latin inscription from the beginning of St. John's Gospel 'In Principio Erat Verbum', a fine example of the inadequacies of the early translators from the Greek. At the front of this building was the hall where the old Scottish Parliament had sat, and all the while the spectre of the dead Cathedral loomed at the end of the street. Then they were at the butcher's shop, which Malone remembered as the repository of many meat bargains— what had it been? Ox liver 2/6 a pound? —and they turned down the close at the side of it. A door at the end of the passage was decorated with a scrappy piece of cardboard bearing the legend: 'Catriona Duncan and Jean Shaw Straight Through'. Malone pushed open the door, and they found themselves in a small white-washed courtyard leading up to a garden. On the left was a door painted bright purple and attached to it was a knocker, which had been freshly silver-painted, in the shape of an owl.

"It always used to amaze me how many small places of this sort were to be found lurking at the back of shops, White. I suppose they're another casualty when the large stores take over. I must say though, that I was not aware of the existence of this one."

Malone applied himself to the door-knocker. The door presently opened and let out with it the harsh cacophony of some modern music though mercifully not at the level of decibels usually considered appropriate. A female, dressed in a fashion not dissimilar to the inhabitants of Paul McLeod's flat said: "You're the fuzz, I suppose. Jean's been expecting you to appear ever since she heard that her pal Jim had been killed." Malone noted the impossibility of confronting anyone with surprise news or catching them out on something they ought not to have known, amidst such an efficient bush-telegraph system.

They were invited in and directed upstairs. There were two doors off the narrow landing. One of them carried the inscription 'Jean' in peculiar molten letters. Malone knocked on it.

"Yeah, who's that?" said a sleepy voice. A female whose appearance coincided very closely with the one who had opened the door downstairs, presented herself. "Oh, the fuzz?" she said, leaving the door open for them to follow her back into the room. It would have been difficult to say whether she was good-looking or not, as the whole manner of her hairstyle and her dress seemed clearly contrived to confuse the issue. She was certainly a tall girl and had what could possibly have been a very attractive face in different surroundings.

"I'm Inspector Malone, and this is Constable White. I understand from your friend downstairs that you've been expecting us to call. We have indeed come about the death of Mr James Holdroyd last night."

"I didn't expect it would take you long to find out that Jim used to visit me. It's sort of thing you're always onto straight away, especially if it's people like me involved." She walked to the other side of the room in apparent annoyance, displaying several tears as well as the regulation patches on her faded blue jeans.

"I assure you, Miss Shaw, that before I entered this room I had no knowledge of your appearance, and I still have very little knowledge of you personally. We are not always onto people like you straight away, unless you class yourself among the known habitual criminals. But to get to the point. You have a friend called Paul McLeod. We have several witnesses to the fact that he as good as threatened to kill Mr Holdroyd last night"

"Paul kill Jim! Wow, man, the guy can't even get around to making any positive suggestion to me, though he's clearly been dying to for months. It's about as likely as your flying pig, I'd say. Still, I suppose people's minds can suddenly blow; but for all that, it seems a pretty crazy suggestion."

"You don't then think that the threat could have been made with any serious intent?"

"It's your job to know about these things, man, and I don't suppose that my opinion is worth much. I can't imagine it, but if a guy can't make up his mind whether he wants to pull a chick or not, he could maybe do pretty weird things."

"The evidence we have been given, Miss Shaw, is to the effect that you were the reason that Mr McLeod would have liked to see Mr Holdroyd out of the way. It would hardly be the first time that one man has killed another under the influence of what is inappropriately termed 'love', even though their appearance and future actions may have suggested that this would be most unlikely. Now I have just been speaking to Mr McLeod, and he informed me that you used to taunt him with Mr Holdroyd. That could easily have been very dangerous for you, let alone the third party. Could you begin by telling me exactly what you and. Mr Holdroyd had in common?"

"You guys are really crazy. Just because Jim happened to be about ten years older than me, you're convinced that there must be something, pretty lurid lurking about somewhere. You may not have noticed, but there are dozens of people all over the place with much greater age differences who get on pretty well. But your minds are bound to be popping with some weird form of bondage or heavy dope-dealing."

"They are always possibilities, but I don't expect for one minute that you would tell me if either or both of them were true."

"Well you can take it that there was nothing like that."

"You wouldn't deny that you smoke dope yourself?"

"No, why the hell should I? But don't excite yourself, man. You and your flat-footed friend won't find anything here. We're clean. As you know, I was expecting you to call on me."

"I'm glad to hear it, Miss Shaw. But anyway, at the moment we have more important things to consider than your illegal methods of destroying your mind. We're investigating the death and probable murder of Mr James Holdroyd. Could you please tell me why he came to visit you? I'm led to believe it was on a fairly regular basis. And please don't tell me I'm naive."

"Crazy, man. Did it ever occur to your convoluted mind that he might like me?"

Malone surveyed the woman in front of him. A man would have to be both broad-minded and imaginatively perceptive to have considered Jean Shaw sexually attractive in her present state. Perhaps she also had other charms which she kept as effectively concealed; perhaps again he had to admit, he was somewhat old-fashioned in his tastes.

Not unaware of this scrutiny, Miss Shaw continued: "Actually if you really want to know the sordid truth, he normally came round for a drink and a chat. To save you asking, he never smoked dope or took anything else. Don't ask me why he never smoked; he was offered the stuff often though, and he never had any objection to anyone else doing it. When I had gin, he drank that; if not he normally had a cup of tea unless by chance he had brought round a carry-out of wine, which he did once or twice."

"May I ask how close you were to Mr Holdroyd?"

"Wow, this is really delicate stuff. Just what you'd expect from a gentleman. Do you mean did we screw? What do you think?!"

"I have no idea, Miss Shaw, and that is why I ask you. However, I have no desire to press the point. The only thing I know is that according to our information, Mr Holdroyd denied any such relationship when asked."

"That's Paul I suppose. He's always convinced I screw with anyone I speak to. I've no idea why he should think that when you consider his own behaviour, but I suppose that's the old possessive jealousy stuff. Don't get me wrong; I like Paul, but to be fair I preferred Jim. Still, I suppose your mind works just like Paul's."

"Any similarity, or lack of it, between my opinions and those of Mr McLeod are not very relevant at the moment. Will you be good enough to tell me what you were doing between half-past eleven and one last night?"

"Really, man, that's far out. You don't think I'd have done him in do you? Or perhaps I was just the moll hanging around watching for the fuzz while someone else got on with it? Well I neither killed him, nor was I hanging around while someone else did, and that's true, whether you want to believe me or not. In fact, I was sitting on my own here smoking a joint, and I can't prove it, because Catriona was out at the time, and no-one came to visit me."

"In my experience, Miss Shaw, it is not normal practice for people to turn on by themselves. They usually prefer company. Is it average practice with you?"

"So you know all about turning on, do you? I'll bet you guys smoke all the gear you confiscate. You'd call it destroying it. That's really too much. A whole Police Station full of turned-on freaks. She gave an even more pronounced nervous laugh than had accompanied her other statements. "Yeah, you're quite right, though, I don't normally turn on on my own, but there was no-one else around; and I don't intend to give you a list of the people I do normally turn on with. As I said, I was smoking a joint on my own last night."

"Thank you very much for your information, Miss Shaw," said Malone, as he rose to indicate that he was bringing the interview to a close. Will you please inform the Police Station of your destination if you're thinking of leaving St. Andrews during the next few days? It is quite possible that we shall have to call on you again.

"Don't worry, man, there's nowhere special I can think of where I want to go, and I don't suppose I could afford to go there anyway. I've got nothing to hide, so you're welcome whenever you want to call."

Malone and White were soon back in South Street. White was about to turn right to go back to the Police Station, but Malone said: "Before we do anything else, White, I think it would do us no harm to take a stroll round the Cathedral grave-yard. I have always found it a good method of getting things in perspective."

In the circumstances White thought this a rather macabre, as well as wasteful suggestion, but fell in with the wishes of his superior.

🐦 Chapter 5

THEY WALKED TO THE EAST END OF SOUTH STREET IN
SILENCE, passed the Roundel, whose turret always manages
to look a good deal less stable than the Leaning Tower of
Pisa, crossed over the road and went through the iron gate
into the grounds of the Cathedral. Malone led the way
purposefully to the area which contained the graves of
worthies of the town of St. Andrews and stopped in front
of the last remains of the Tom Morrises—Old and Young.
He barely seemed to have noticed those impressive ruins
which still majestically indicate what an immense feat of skill
and engineering the total structure of the defunct Cathedral
must have been.

"You know, White, when I was a student I often used to
come and look at these graves, not just because they
commemorate two of the towns greatest golfers, but
because they happen to be the best examples of the
changeability of fashion that I know. Here's Old Tom lying
under that block of stone. The inscription tells us nothing
except his name, the date of his birth and the date of his
death. To many of us that's a far more eloquent testimony
to his greatness than a vast memorial—a bit like Aeschylus'
epitaph, which mentions his military exploits and not his
plays, although posterity only knows him as one of the first
and greatest dramatists. Then over there we have the
memorial to Young Tommy, with the relief of him playing
golf, and inscribed with the dates and occasions of his
successes. It was doubtless meant as a fitting memorial to a
wonderful golfer who was cut short in his prime, and in
many ways it is. But most of us who look at it nowadays
find, it far less impressive than the bare simplicity of Old
Tom's tomb. It's a question of individual taste and the times

you live in, which always mould that taste to some extent. I find it necessary to think of these graves or other similar indications of fashion when I've been speaking to people like Paul McLeod and Jean Shaw. It puts them in their proper perspective. Their way of life is very different outwardly from mine—and yours I presume—and furthermore different from mine fifteen years or so ago. Their manner towards police officers would have been unthinkable then, but we must try to remember that these things are largely superficial. You may have wondered why I let the matter of Mr Holdroyd's relationship with Miss Shaw drop. Firstly, it's almost certainly a matter of small importance. Secondly, it's not the sort of question you want to persevere with, especially in the case of a woman. With someone like her you may think that's an irrelevant consideration. Had she been an elegantly dressed judge's daughter—she may come from such a family for all I know—I'm sure you wouldn't have been surprised. I see no reason for treating her differently just because she dresses the way she does. It doesn't stop her being a woman. By the way, the reason I think it's probably a matter of small importance, is that if Paul McLeod is our man, it doesn't matter what their relationship in fact was. What is important is what he thought to be the case. I don't think there can be any reasonable doubt as to what his opinion of the matter was. It's unfortunate that she can't produce any corroboration as to her whereabouts last night; as a result we certainly can't eliminate her from suspicion. Different forms of what the French call 'crime passionnel' are after all quite common."

"She was fairly weird, sir, but even without your diversion, I can't say that I picture her bashing his head in."

"Quite so, but that's just the trouble. Unless you're dealing with a clear case of mental derangement, it's always difficult to see someone in the role of murderer. Outside of occasional fantasies we can never seriously see ourselves that way, or almost anyone we know, for that matter. Other people we come across always seem a bit like ourselves or someone of our acquaintance. Therefore, on first impression I quite agree with you. Miss Shaw is most unlike our normal idea of a murderer. We could surmise that she was so blocked after some almighty mixture of drugs that she didn't know what she was doing, but I find that hard to believe as well. She strikes me as being part of the pot-smoking scene, but not really anything else. Incidentally, I tend to believe her denial of any dope-dealing with Holdroyd; she had no earthly reason to state that he never smoked her pot, unless it was true, or perhaps there was something very much deeper involved than we suspect."

"Aye, sir, but just because someone doesn't take the stuff themselves doesn't prevent them from supplying it to other people for their own financial profit."

"You're right of course, and I haven't totally discounted the possibility. We may well have to look into it. We might get some indications of the matter from his bank statement. I suppose Sergeant Johnson will have a good idea of whom we ought to see if we need to pursue the point."

They made their way back to the Police Station. Sergeant Johnson was still there, and as soon as they entered he addressed Malone.

"I've now got the information you wanted from Mr Holdroyd's bank, Inspector, and it may well be helpful. It appears that over the last year or thereabouts, he's been taking remarkably little out of his current account, except to transfer it to deposit. His salary, by the way, was paid directly into his current account. They assumed in the bank that he had another income from some other source and kept an account in another bank to deal with it. I asked the manager if he'd mind ringing round the other banks in the town to see if this could be confirmed. He kindly did so, and discovered that they were right. Just under a year ago he had opened another account. I spoke to his second manager myself, and after consulting his staff, he provided me with the relevant information. Apparently Mr Holdroyd had always paid his deposits in cash. They had apparently been rather suspicious of this and had actually thought of mentioning it to us. But as he said, they have a professional duty towards their clients, and are always reluctant to take such a course. You see, as he said, they're used to occasional cash deposits, especially in the tourist season, from people who give Bed and Breakfast and the like, and also at odd times for a variety of reasons—winnings from gambling being the most obvious example. The peculiarity about Mr Holdroyd's deposits was their regularity throughout the year, and the fact that they represented too much for a lodger. It's not a vast amount of money involved, and it could be explained away on a combination of things. But he certainly didn't make that sort of money on private tuition, and according to my information he never had lodgers."

"Good work, sergeant, and thank you very much. We have to add a fair amount to the sum involved if we take into account that he wasn't withdrawing much of his salary. How much had he deposited in the second bank?".

"A little over seven hundred pounds."

"That means we must be dealing with a sum well in excess of a thousand pounds, however we look at it, and possibly well over two thousand. As they say, it doesn't grow on trees. Ugly thoughts like blackmail are bound to spring to mind in the circumstances. Did you get anywhere with the name and number I found in his pockets? That by the way, White, was one of the possibly interesting items I mentioned to you. There was simply the name 'Harriet' and some figures which I assumed were her telephone number."

"Well, Inspector, if anything that's even more peculiar. As you'll remember, there were only four figures, 6384. We soon found out that it wasn't a St. Andrews number. We then tried other local exchanges in the area, and the only one which possessed a Harriet was rather a shock. It was Lady Harriet Carswell—I'm sure you'll have heard of her husband. It could be purely a coincidence, and the number could refer to something else of course."

"No, Inspector, I'm sure you're right. Lady Carswell recently had a volume of poetry published, and I happened to notice a copy in Holdroyd's bookcase. That would be even more of a coincidence."

"Well, that was certainly the only Harriet we could locate at such a number. I may add that she was not in at the time we rang, and the butler who answered was most uncooperative."

"I'm sorry to hear that; but I suppose that they're trained in that way. Have you anything more for us?"

"Nothing to speak of. Mr Cormack rang and said he had some further information which might be useful. He asked to deal directly with you, and I told him roughly when I expected you back. He should be here soon. Poor chap, he and his family seem to have been the only people who really knew Mr Holdroyd well. There seem to have been no other families he visited on any regular basis. I was questioning Mr McCabe and Mr Watson earlier—purely on a routine basis, as they were not only among the last to see Mr Holdroyd alive, but were also some of the few who knew him at all well. In fact, Mr Watson was at the University at the same time as him. There didn't really seem to be much for them to tell us, but they both mentioned that Mr Cormack and his family seemed rather cut up about the death. In fact, Mr McCabe was saying that their daughter Elizabeth—she's sixteen and very attractive—has had to be given sedatives by the doctor. If it's of any interest, they both stated independently what an extraordinarily honest man Mr Holdroyd was. Mr Watson was of the impression that mild tax evasion was probably quite beyond him."

"With our information from the bank, that is certainly most interesting. I suppose it could be well worth cultivating a reputation for extreme honesty if you're someone of criminal instincts, but it's worth noting that two men who knew him well could make the same observation without prompting."

Constable Smith, who was in charge of the desk, knocked at the door of the office, to which they had adjourned. He entered and informed them that Mr Cormack had arrived. Malone asked him to show their visitor through.

"Ah, Inspector,' said Mr Cormack, "I told the sergeant earlier that we'd noticed something amiss with Jim Holdroyd recently, and as you have doubtless been told, he was very close on the subject, so that none of us really knew the cause. I was speaking to Bill Watson about it again, and between us we tried to fathom out what it might have been. To be quite honest, we still don't know for sure what it was. His impression was that it was something to do with his work, while mine was that it was to do with this Jean Shaw. Be that as it may, we were both agreed that he'd been spending a lot more money in the pub than usual—you know, buying rounds when it wasn't strictly necessary, and that sort of thing. We wondered if he could really afford it and thought that might be at least partly the reason for his obvious depression. You know how people of his age, especially if they haven't got a family, can start searching their souls to try and decide what they're doing in this vale of misery. When they do so they can start acting a bit out of character, that's why I thought it might well be this Jean Shaw that was the reason.

Malone did not totally follow the relevance of this statement and so he said: "I'm given to understand that you and your family were probably much closer to Holdroyd than anyone else in the town, and so I'm always pleased to have your opinions about him. Do you think that while you're here I could ask you one or two things about him? Can you tell me if you think that Mr Holdroyd was an honest man?"

Jim Cormack hesitated for a few moments before he said: "Well, there's no doubt that he always gave that impression, or at least intended to. To a great extent I'm sure that it was a perfectly correct impression. I wouldn't like to suggest for one moment that Jim was a dishonest sort of person, but no-one's quite what he pretended to be. He did rather seem to suggest that George Washington was a bit slow owning up to the cherry tree." He couldn't help smiling at his apt figure.

"I see. You mean that Mr Holdroyd was basically a very honest man, but if you heard that he'd been overstepping the law in some small way you wouldn't have been surprised."

"Exactly so, Inspector. Nothing at all serious, you understand."

"Would you consider selling drugs for profit serious?"

"Good heavens, Inspector, I'm not talking about that sort of thing. I'm quite sure that Jim would never have entertained any such idea, and I'm sure that no other friend of mine would."

"But you wouldn't have been surprised if you'd been told he'd been fiddling his tax returns?"

"That's much more the sort of thing I mean. We'd all do that if we could, wouldn't we? The trouble is that many of us never get the chance. Yes, I'm quite sure he would have had no difficult crisis of conscience over tax evasion, despite the general impression he tried to give to the contrary."

Malone did not think this was either the time or the place to comment on personal views about acceptable and unacceptable dishonesty. Instead he said. "It was very good of you to come to see me, Mr Cormack. If you ever think you have any information, however unimportant it may seem to you, please don't hesitate to contact me. You see, one of our difficulties is that so few people seem to have known Mr Holdroyd at all well. By the way, I understand that your wife and daughter are very upset by his death."

"Yes, I'm afraid they are. He was always very attentive to them you see. It was probably because we were really the only family he had much to do with, and you know how protective women can get about men living on their own. They don't believe for one moment that they can cope without the feminine touch."

"In what sort of ways was he attentive?"

"Oh, you know the sort of thing; he used to bring them flowers or chocolates. A few months ago he was even good enough to take my daughter Elizabeth to the Opera in Glasgow."

"You weren't disturbed about letting her go with him?"

Mr Cormack looked shocked. "I don't know what you're trying to suggest, Inspector, or at least I hope not. Jim Holdroyd was a friend of the family, and I took his kind offer for what it was. Of course I was not disturbed by it, otherwise I would hardly have let her go. Well, if there's nothing else I can do to help you, I think I'll be going. As you were saying, this business has affected my wife and daughter, and I feel that my place is at home."

"Just one thing before you go, Mr Cormack. Do you happen to know if Mr Holdroyd normally wore gloves at this time of the year?"

Mr Cormack seemed somewhat surprised at this question. "No," he said, "he didn't as far as I know; that's to say I don't ever remember seeing him in gloves at all."

"Thank you very much. Goodbye."

After he had left, Malone turned to Constable White. "Tell me White, would you let a daughter of yours go for a night out to Glasgow with a man nearly twice her age?"

"Obviously not normally, sir, or anywhere else for that matter. If you could stop them nowadays, that is. But I can see it's somewhat different with an old friend of the family."

"Yes, I suppose you're right. Well, I must admit that I'm not at all sure where this is all leading to. I think it's probably about time we called it a day. It never does any good if you try to do too much at once. There's just one more thing I want to do this evening, and that's look over Holdroyd's flat again. I could have done with several hours more sleep last night, and I'm sure you're just the sane. Unless something unexpectedly important turns up which won't wait, we'll simply look over the flat and go home. Don't worry, White, there's nothing obvious we should be doing or we'd be doing it. Routine enquiry is far best left to the normal channels. They're very often the quickest, and we can't do everything ourselves. Tomorrow I think we'd better take a trip to Dundee and see the school Holdroyd worked in. We may well pick up something worthwhile over there. Also, while we're over there, we might as well take the opportunity of interviewing young Athlone again. Don't worry, I haven't lost sight of the fact that he's the only person we have a shred of evidence against. I shall also have to make arrangements to see Lady Carswell. That may prove more of a problem and may involve more travelling. Our best policy there is to wait until tomorrow and see how things lie. Come on, let's go to Holdroyd's flat."

Before they left, Malone had a parting word with Sergeant Johnson. "No news of any suspicious departures I suppose, sergeant?"

"No Inspector. The hotels and boarding houses are fairly empty at this time of year, but they've promised to inform us of any suspicious behaviour. We've also had three calls from private individuals to tell us about disappearances. When we checked on them, we found them all to be perfectly innocent. I've kept a note of the names if you should require them. Quite honestly, I think they were nothing more than malicious calls—we always get a few when this sort of thing happens, as you'll know. The University authorities have, of course, offered their full co-operation in the matter."

"It's probably a fairly useless line of enquiry anyway. It's unlikely that the guilty party would want to make himself conspicuous by immediately leaving town. And there's no guarantee that he stayed in the town in the first place; it's just as likely that it was a total outsider who was merely around to do the deed and left immediately afterwards. The trouble is that we just don't have enough to go on yet."

Malone and White took their leave. "There's nothing more to be gained from the forensic reports at the moment sir?" suggested White, as they made their way towards South Street.

"No, I don't think so. The difficulty always is that seemingly irrelevant facts can assume a great level of importance when viewed in the right way, and so I can't be sure. I do feel, however, that the negative evidence of the fingerprints is very suggestive. That's another reason, of course, why I tend to believe that Eric Athlone is innocent. He'd be all kinds of fool to wipe everything clean except for the very weapon used for the assault. I know you saw the state of mind he was in, and I didn't, and I'm prepared to believe that it was pretty extreme, but I can't see how it could have affected him in that way. Surely the first thing he would wipe would be the weapon."

"He might have wiped everything, and then lost his head and, just as he said, picked up the candelabrum and put it where we found it. If he had left the doors open after cleaning the handles he then wouldn't have had to leave any traces on them when leaving."

"That would certainly cover the facts, but I still think it most unlikely. It's just as plausible that he did what he said. Anyway, we certainly have to assume that our assailant either wiped the surfaces he had touched or was wearing gloves. I say he, but of course, given the gloves and the comparatively mild nature of the blow, she is equally a possibility, if not even more likely. If we forget the exact details of the assailant and the time, though, I think we can have a fair shot at reconstructing the sequence of events. Holdroyd came back at some time and expected to find his flat locked. It may have been, but I don't think so. Most people have a habit of putting their front door key away as soon as they have used it. It prevents them mislaying it. If they habitually keep them in the house—something which is most unlikely in his case, as he was out all day—they usually keep them near the door. Now Holdroyd's key was in his hand. This suggests to me that he hadn't followed his normal routine, because he had found his flat unlocked. Somebody was in his sitting room, and it was somebody he knew well. I say that the person was already there for several reasons. The most obvious one is that the key was still in his hand. I feel even more sure that he knew that person well. If it had been a stranger, it is most unlikely that he would not have put up a struggle when attacked. There was no sign of any such struggle, and it is unlikely that the assailant could have erased all traces if such a thing had taken place. If it was a stranger it is unlikely that he would have been taken so much off his guard, unless the attack were particularly sudden. I know that this could easily have happened if the intruder had been a thief caught in the act. But there were no signs of robbery, either actual or attempted, large or small. The fact that the wound was probably inflicted from the front also points to this conclusion. Surely an attack would have occurred to him as a possibility if he had not known the person in his sitting room. Then surely he would have made some attempt to ward off the blow, and that would almost certainly have saved his life. We can add that our killer, after doing the deed showed remarkable coolness in clearing up all traces of himself—or a similar coolness is indicated if he had planned to leave no traces in the first place. I think that we should probably assume that the assault took place immediately on arrival—the key again is the surest indicator of that. That leads us into the difficulty of the time. If the doctor is right, it all fits in except the watch. If the evidence of the watch is decisive, it seems very possible that someone knows something about the movements of Holdroyd between twelve and one, and rather suspiciously is keeping quiet about it."

"I'm not too sure if I can accept all that, sir. It seems to me that there could be other explanations."

"Yes indeed, it could be so. I'm merely trying to consider the most likely sequence, and I think that is it. If we come across any absolute evidence to contradict that theory, we'll have to abandon it, in whole or part. But we must try to find something concrete to build a framework round, and I think that what I have suggested is the best we can do."

"How then did this intruder get in? There was no sign of force on the doors."

"Clearly we would have to assume that Holdroyd inadvertently left the door open. We all do that from time to time, and we've been told that he had not been his normal self for some weeks."

"If you'll forgive me for mentioning it, sir, I would have thought that Eric Athlone fitted the bill pretty well if you are right. He knew how to find Mr Holdroyd's flat; if it was open he would walk in with no difficulty as he was familiar with the place. Mr Holdroyd would not expect to be attacked by him, and the lad clearly has enough intelligence to try to cover up his traces."

"I'm well aware of the fact that he fits the description I've outlined, and we may find at the end of the day that he's our man. But don't forget that it's quite possible for someone else to have been there before him, as he himself maintains."

"The information we have received so far would suggest that any visitor was a rarity; two in the same night seems most unlikely."

"That's so, but it in no way makes it impossible. What I find even more surprising is that no-one has come forward with information about people seen in South Street at that time. I feel that there must have been some people going along there at some similar hour."

Death of a Dundee Teacher

"I think it was the later hour, about half-past twelve to one, that Sergeant Johnson gave out we were interested in, sir. If it were about an hour before that, they probably wouldn't think it worth reporting anything. I might add that you tend to find fewer people at that end of South Street at night. Most of those living over the burn in the New Town would not go by that way."

They reached James Holdroyd's flat. It seemed uncanny to White that the tragedy had taken place less than twenty hours before. He began to feel tired, and now appreciated the wisdom of his superior in suggesting that they should call it a day. A constable had been left on duty at the door of the flat, more to keep away casual sightseers than in expectation of anything more dramatic happening there. Malone asked out of politeness more than in hope of information whether any suspicious people had been hanging about. He was not disappointed, therefore, when he was told that apart from the normal crowd of loiterers who always managed to scent out the scene of a tragedy, there was nothing of any moment to report. He knew that anything else would have been only the vaguest possibility; if anyone had wanted to destroy some damning evidence, they would not be likely to make an attempt in the presence of a uniformed police officer. As the guilty party had obviously shown a degree of intelligence in his actions so far, it could be fairly assumed that he would realise that any attempt of this kind was probably too late anyway. Malone and White went into the flat and entered the sitting room.

"White, did you notice anything peculiar about the bookcase over there last time we were here? I'm not referring to its age or shape."

"Apart from the number of foreign books and the general untidiness of their arrangement, no sir.'

278

"It's exactly the untidiness of the arrangement that I mean. Look at everything else. It's so clean and tidy down to the last detail that our maiden aunts would be proud of it. It seems a strange anomaly. The possibility has occurred to me that somebody was looking for something in there. I don't know if that helps us at all though. If they found it, we have no idea what it was they found, and if they didn't, by the same token we don't know what it was they were looking for; so I don't suppose it would do us much good to have a search."

He looked at the bookcase in silence for a while. It seemed quite likely to White that the untidiness of the books was merely a personal quirk of Mr Holdroyd, and possibly a reflection of the fact that they were in more constant use than many of the other items in the flat. However, he decided to hold his peace.

Malone reached out and pulled a book from a shelf. "Take a look at this, White. 'The Long Road Home, poems by Harriet Carswell'. The most striking thing about her writing, you know, is that she uses exact metrical forms, and usually has rhyme at the end of the line. Schoolchildren seem to be brought up to deny any possible merit in such compositions nowadays, so they are only thought to be appropriate to scurrilous verses. You know, it all has to be a meaningless jumble of sound, preferably with a number of obscure words to indicate the erudition of the writer. You know, something like:

> Where the brown bedrock bays
> At the sands shifting in the sun
> I found at last my erogenous phantasm;
> Not the limping lust of
> Old romantic tales…

Not bad for off the cuff. Anyway, you recognise the sort of rubbish I mean. I must say, for my money Harriet Carswell has the correct approach. Hullo, what's this?" He removed a piece of writing paper from the book and looked at it for a while. "What do you make of that, White?"

White examined the piece of paper he had been handed. There was nothing at all remarkable about the paper; it was from a middle price writing pad. The writing on it, however, could only be one thing. It was clearly the first draft of a poem with corrections. The alterations were few, and it could be deduced that the writer had thought of the original in one piece, as the writing was ill-formed and clearly hurried, as if she had not wanted to forget the words which had occurred to her. It was clearly 'she', as Malone also handed him the book, open at the page where the corrected poem was printed.

"It's the Author's original copy," said White, unnecessarily.

"Exactly, but whatever is it doing in Holdroyd's copy?" Malone took out his wallet and removed the piece of paper inscribed 'Harriet 6384', which he had reclaimed from Sergeant Johnson earlier. "It's not easy to be absolutely certain on such a small sample, but I'd be pretty sure they were written by the same person, wouldn't you?"

White looked at them both and added his agreement. Malone put both pieces of paper carefully back in his wallet.

"Well, White, if she did write name and number, we can be pretty sure of two things; firstly that she was on friendly terms with Holdroyd—or at any rate was recently—and secondly that she saw him, or at least communicated with him not long ago. I think we can discount the possibility that he'd been carrying that piece of paper round with him for a long time; it's too clean. What would seem most likely, is that she called on him, but found he was out and shoved a note through the letter-box containing this slip of paper."

"If they were that friendly, why would she need to leave her telephone number? Wouldn't he have known it?"

"A good point, White, but there could be a number of reasons for it. I should think that the most likely one is that, as she's a married woman, they did not normally communicate by telephone. However innocent their relationship, it is always difficult to explain to a spouse that a call from someone of the opposite sex has no ulterior significance. It could even be simply that Holdroyd was known to her to be forgetful about telephone numbers. At any rate, it should be interesting to see her tomorrow. Let's take a look round the back now. I really should have done so earlier, but as the whole business took place in the dark, it didn't seem a very important step—and it probably isn't."

They went back down the stairs and out into the close. They turned left along it, passed some outhouses which were used as store-rooms by the local shops fronting on South Street—Holdroyd's flat stood above a jeweller's—and found themselves in a small, well-cultivated garden, which was protected from the depredations of the East Wind by six foot stone walls. The bed nearest him, being north-facing, had little growing in it, but it passed quickly into a lawn which had obviously received regular attention. This lawn, with flower beds every side of it, continued to within three feet of the back wall. A narrow concrete path ran around the right-hand side of the lawn, and continued at right-angles along the front of the bed at the back. In the left-hand corner at the bottom of the garden, there was a sizeable compost heap, reaching to about half the height of the wall. Malone walked slowly round to the compost heap, picked up a fork which had been left stuck in the ground nearby, and began to probe the heap carefully. This was taking him some time, and he said to White:

"Wonderful things, compost heaps, you know, White. Almost everything that has ever grown will rot in them given enough time, once they've got a good temperature up. I suppose they're not very useful to anyone who's trying to get rid of anything incriminating, though. Like most natural processes they take far too long."

He carried on his explorations for a little longer, and then said suddenly: "White, take a look at this."

There was a three-inch nail driven into wall slightly to the right of the heap and a little above it. Doubtless it had been used for tying up some climbing plant, like a rambling rose, or string had been attached to it and other similar points to provide a frame for runner beans to climb up. Suspended from this nail was a piece of material. It was not difficult to surmise that it had come from someone's blue denim jeans. "It seems fairly clear to me, sir, that somebody wearing jeans climbed that wall, using the compost heap to give themselves some height, and caught their leg on that nail. They left the piece of material hanging there, either because they couldn't be bothered with it, or because they were in too much of a hurry to care."

"That's exactly as I see it too." Malone stood on the compost heap and looked over the wall. The corresponding garden the other side led into a close similar to that through which they had just come, and Malone assumed correctly that it passed straight into Market Street, which runs parallel with South Street. He remained leaning over the wall for a minute or two, then removed the piece of denim attached to the wall and returned with White to South Street.

"Damn it, that should have occurred to me long before. What's the use of having local knowledge if you make no attempt to employ it? I should have known quite well that somebody could have left over the back wall. The trouble is that there's a concrete path leading right up to the compost heap, and then another similar path the other side down through the close. No hope of finding any traces there, I'm afraid. With the brightness of the moon last night it would have been easily done. What a simple way to leave without being seen in South Street!"

"You think that we should be looking for someone with torn blue jeans, and possibly female?"

"Don't jump to conclusions yet. First of all, we have no way of knowing how long that piece of material has been lying there—it could easily have been weeks. Secondly, there are hundreds of students in St. Andrews, let alone others, who wear torn blue jeans. I believe that as soon as they buy them, they rip bits out of them to fit in with the fashion. Thirdly, the image of the gloved female recedes a bit, if she was clambering over walls in her jeans in the middle of the night. But for all that, I think we should certainly try to match up that piece of material tomorrow. No, the main thing that troubles me at the moment is being responsible for the foolish assumption that our killer must have left by South Street. We'll have to let Sergeant Johnson know that we're interested in people seen in Market Street as well, especially if they happened to be wearing tatty jeans. I'm sure it won't take him long to put the word around."

They therefore returned to the Police Station to inform the sergeant of this new consideration, and when they had ascertained that there was no new information which needed prompt attention, the Inspector offered to drive White home.

"I think we'd better make a fairly early start tomorrow. Would eight o' clock at the Police Station be too early for you?"

It did not seem at all early to White, who was one of those people who felt like leaping out of bed as soon as he had woken, and so he readily agreed.

Before White left the car, Malone said: "Thank you for all your help. It's extremely helpful to have someone around who doesn't make unnecessary fatuous remarks. I assure you that many in your position would have. All that you have said today has been both brief and to the point. But please don't hold back from saying anything merely because of my rank, if you think your contribution could be of importance. The worst I can say is that I think you're wrong."

"That's very kind of you, sir. A number of obvious points did of course occur to me, but as they would be just as obvious to you as well, I didn't bother to mention them. If I may say so, I feel you were making too much of the state of the bookcase, but there may be something there I don't understand. Apart from that, all I can say is that if Eric Athlone isn't the guilty party, I've no idea who it was. If I do have any helpful suggestions to make in the morning, I'll make them then."

"Good man. As you heard, I've left instructions only to be called in an emergency, and I'll only call you if I really have to. You'll learn soon, if you don't know already, that it's no use being tired when you have a large number of disparate facts to juggle with. The mind just won't cope. Well if there's nothing more, I'll see you at eight in the morning."

Malone left White at his house, but he himself did not go straight home. His mind was indeed baffled with the information it had so far received. He knew that he could not reflect usefully on the facts until he had had a rest or was presented with more information. He decided that his best course was to have a few pints of beer to help him relax. Therefore, after parking his car outside his house, he went along to his local, and consumed five pints of heavy, before depositing himself in the bosom of his family.

🙤 Chapter 6

MUCH TO HIS WIFE'S RELIEF, there was apparently no emergency, and Malone was not contacted during the night. Malone himself had every intention of reaching St. Andrews before the time agreed upon with White, as he wished to be absolutely up to date with any further developments which might have occurred, before he went to Dundee. As it happened to be fairly obviously a one-off murder— assuming that it was indeed murder, and Malone could see no way it could be otherwise—he could hope that his superiors would not be demanding concrete results for a day or so yet or so he hoped.

He had decided that if the worst came to the worst, he would have to make a formal arrest of Eric Athlone. There was certainly enough circumstantial evidence to merit it, and no certain evidence as yet to connect anyone else with the crime, unless the piece of denim should lead to something. If, however, he failed to find the guilty party in the next day or two, he shuddered to think of all the formalities and paperwork he would have to go through to justify his actions. At least, he thought rather uncharitably, he could shove a lot of that off onto White. What disturbed him most about this case so far, was if his assumption that Holdroyd knew his assailant well should turn out to be false. If that proved to be so, it would be very difficult to know where else to start. For the sake of economy of effort, he found himself hoping that the school in Dundee and Lady Carswell would turn out to be total red herrings.

It was another fine day, and the towns grey groped its way out of the sea into the blue sky, as Malone swung round the bend into St. Andrews. The same old feeling of warmth the town always brought to him entered his being as he passed the old Petherham Bridge, dismantled now, a broken relic of the old railway. As he drove up North Street, the tower of St. Salvator's stood up to accuse heaven on his left, a striking reminder of the religious strife which once bedevilled Scotland; now, it was to be hoped, long dead.

He entered the Police Station shortly before half-past seven. Uncharacteristically, but hardly surprisingly, Sergeant Johnson was not there. However, Malone was welcomed into his office by the constable in charge with an offer of tea and biscuits. He gladly accepted. The sergeant, who had gone off duty at midnight, had left a note to say that nothing of importance had turned up, and this had been confirmed again at six in the morning. The only piece of information was that Lady Carswell had telephoned shortly after he had left for home, but on hearing of his absence had not been prepared to give the reason for her call. There were one or two reports which he had asked for lying on his desk, but after a short perusal of them he decided that nothing of great moment was to be gleaned from them. There was also a letter, presumably just delivered, addressed to him. First, he looked at the postmark; Glenrothes. He could not for the life of him think who could be communicating with him personally from there. To save idle speculation he immediately opened it and looked at the signature. It was from Lady Carswell. He wondered what she could have to say for herself. He read the following:

Dear Inspector Malone,

I understand that a policeman was enquiring for me. I read that you are investigating the death of James Holdroyd and assume the two matters to be connected. I prefer not to be visited by policemen at home and shall therefore present myself at St. Andrews Police Station at half-past two on Thursday afternoon.

Yours faithfully,

Harriet Carswell.

Malone looked at the letter, and couldn't help feeling that there was something wrong, but at the moment was unable to put his finger on it. It certainly wasn't the attitude which she displayed so clearly: he was perfectly familiar with affectations of superiority to humble policemen. He began to wonder why she had telephoned the evening before and decided that it was probably to confirm the appointment in case the letter did not arrive on time. Why then had she not mentioned it to the sergeant? Could it be simply that she did not like dealing with humble sergeants? He looked at the note again, and a thought suddenly struck him. He took out his wallet, and carefully removed the note saying 'Harriet 6384' and the draft poem. The enormity of the implications suddenly stuck him.

He was still feeling rather pleased with himself when White arrived, early, as seemed his wont. "White," he said, as soon as the constable entered his office, "what do you make of that?"

White took Lady Carswell's letter and read it over a few times. "Well sir, I'm not at all certain what I'm supposed to notice. I'd say that it indicates that she doesn't want her husband or family to know that she was mixed up with Mr Holdroyd. Apart from that, I'd say that the general tone seems rather offensive."

"Right on both points. But doesn't anything else strike you about it? I must admit it didn't occur to me immediately."

White examined the letter again, with even greater care. He shook his head. "I'm sorry sir, I can't really see what you're getting at."

Malone was on the point of enlightening him and then suddenly changed his mind. He carried on in a somewhat less excited tone. "Never mind. It's quite possible that I've been jumping to too many conclusions. On reflection it might be better if you were present at the interview with Lady Carswell without having come to them yourself, or being prejudiced by my views. But for all that, some of them seem to be inescapable. I had better not go out of my way to try to be mysterious. Tell me, have you had any further thoughts on the matter since last night?"

"Nothing worthwhile. I'm afraid that the more I considered it, the more unlikely possibilities came to me. I ended up having watertight cases against Miss Duncan, Mr Cormack and Mr McCabe. I thought I'd better give up theorising at that juncture."

"Aye, you'd better leave the wilier shores of theorising to me. I'm used to finding myself stranded. But I sympathise; we just don't have enough incontrovertible facts to go on at the moment. Have you noticed the surprising fact that no-one seems to have mentioned anything about Holdroyd's life in Dundee? And yet he has spent around half his waking life there for a number of years now. That seems to give us all the more reason for calling on his school as soon as possible. We won't leave immediately, or we'll just get jammed up in the commuter traffic. Did you know that the queue at the tolls on the Tay Bridge can sometimes be nearly a mile long at about quarter to nine? I think we should also be polite enough to give the rector of the school some warning before descending on the place."

They left St. Andrews at about ten minutes to nine. The road was clear, and they made good time past Guardbridge and Leuchars, with its fighter squadrons, Norman Church and exposed railway station, where the East wind could make you feel you had been transported to Siberia. They reached the Tay Bridge in not much more than a quarter of an hour. The gun-metal grey of the New Railway Bridge over the silvery Tay celebrated by William McGonagall in his immortal, if not beautiful verses, strode over the river to their left. The Tay as normal did not conjure up the epithet 'silvery' in Malone's imagination, and he wondered what had driven McGonagall to use that description. In front of them the stark multi-storey blocks of the Hilltown of Dundee reached skywards, dwarfing the kindly grey of the decrepit tenements which still survived the onslaught of progress. As Malone had hoped, there was no queue to bar their progress at the tolls at the end of the bridge, and as a result they found themselves with no difficulty in the centre of Dundee.

"As I told you, White, I don't know the middle of Dundee well, but I think the rector's instructions will be good enough for me to find the school, despite the one-way system." Malone had been driving, as he knew the geography of Dundee better than White, and all of a sudden he laughed. "Never mind, if we get lost, we can always ask a policeman." White failed to find quite as much humour in the suggestion, but managed to force a polite smile.

They did not get lost, and found the school, Wellgate Academy, with little difficulty. It was one of the new concrete and glass structures, standing far from the area in which it had originally stood, and from which it had derived its name. Malone commented to White on the immense amount of public money it always cost to repair broken windows in such establishments but conceded to him that the temptations of large panes of glass to unruly boys were too great to be overcome. They parked the car in the front of the school and entered by the main door. As it was not immediately clear where they should go to find the rector, Malone decided not to waste time in a possibly fruitless search. He therefore hailed a scruffy looking boy and asked him where the rector's office was to be found. The boy looked at them as if he thought they had just escaped from the local lunatic asylum and pointed to their left. There was a door which carried the legend 'A.S. Dalkeith, Rector' in small insignificant letters. Without thanking the boy for his information, Malone went straight up to the door and knocked on it.

"Come In." said a severe voice.

As they entered, the stony look of disapproval which he clearly reserved for pupils and possibly his junior colleagues, disappeared from Mr Dalkeith's face. He beamed at them and came over with outstretched hand.

"I'm terribly sorry, gentlemen. You must be the detectives. I was expecting you to call at the office, but I see you've found me first." It seemed worthless to point out that, although they had entered through the front door, it was not immediately obvious where the office was. "Please sit down. I must admit that I've been expecting a call from you ever since I heard of Mr Holdroyd's death."

From the tone of voice employed for the last sentence, Malone was surprised that Holdroyd had not received the traditional epithet 'poor'. He said: "Thank you very much, Mr Dalkeith. As I'm sure you'll have guessed, I'm Inspector Malone, and this is Constable White." Mr Dalkeith gave White a patronising smile. Malone continued: "We've really come here to find out something about Mr Holdroyd's professional life. As he lived on his own, we're not very far on with his private life either, if the truth be told. Now, I feel that the more I can get to know about Mr Holdroyd, the nearer I shall be able to get to finding out who was responsible for his death. Oh yes, I'm afraid there can be no doubt about it. Mr Holdroyd was killed deliberately by somebody."

"Well Inspector, if you're sure that that is the case," said the rector in a serious voice, which betrayed a feeling of his own importance in the matter, "please tell me exactly what you wish to know."

"To begin with, I'm surprised that no-one in St. Andrews I've spoken to so far has volunteered any information about Mr Holdroyd's job here. I suppose it's quite possible that he never talked about it to his friends. If that is so, I have to assume that there was some reason. Was he happy in his work?"

Mr Dalkeith adopted his didactic tone: "First of all, Inspector, I must say that I'm not at all surprised that Mr Holdroyd did not communicate much about his job. You must understand that unlike any other professional occupation, which is respected for the great knowledge and experience its practitioners bring to bear on it, teaching is considered to be any man or society's football. You may occasionally suffer from the same problem in your own line. As a result, it becomes tiresome after a bit to listen to any fool's theories about how it should be done. Teachers, on hearing such views expressed, tend to react in one of two ways. Either they become very rude to those who produce such views, or they resolve never to discuss their profession with members of the general public. It is quite likely that Mr Holdroyd was in the latter category. As to your question about whether he was happy here, my answer would be that I think so. It is however very difficult to be sure about teacher's attitudes towards their work nowadays. All the various strains they are required to undergo every day of their professional life can affect them in so many different ways. But all the evidence I can point to would suggest that Mr Holdroyd was quite content. He had remained in the same school for over five years, his relations with colleagues and pupils were excellent, if a trifle distant, and, possibly the most telling point of all, he was never off sick. Teachers are of course liable to any small infection brought into the school by the pupils, and there are those who are inclined to take advantage of the small ailments they are continually subjected to. They are usually the ones who are not very satisfied in their work. But back to Mr Holdroyd. He took a sufficient interest in extra-curricular activities, if not an outstanding one. For instance, whenever the school orchestra was playing, he was always willing to stiffen the violin section. Not a particularly brilliant player, I believe, but quite competent enough to shine at our level. To sum up, I would say that he was a fine example of a good, competent, professional teacher.

"I believe that he taught Russian?"

"Yes indeed, but by no means all the time. There aren't enough pupils doing Russian to provide a full time-table in that subject, and so he in fact spent the majority of his time teaching English."

"When he was teaching Russian, he would normally have very small classes I suppose?"

"Yes, that is so. In fact, we've never had more than three in any one school year doing Russian. It's quite a hard subject, as doubtless you know, and when you take into account the relatively small time-allocation we can give to the subject, and the small number of good pupils in any given school under the comprehensive system, you can understand why."

"Have you ever had any reason to suspect Mr Holdroyd's relationship with either boys or girls in these classes? He could clearly have had the opportunity to get to know them fairly closely. Please don't pretend to be shocked that I can make such a suggestion about this school. You know as well as I do that it has happened elsewhere and could happen here."

"I'll be totally honest with you, Inspector. About four years ago, I think it was, I received an anonymous letter—you people get the same sort of thing from time to time, I'm sure—suggesting in no uncertain terms that Mr Holdroyd was rather too fond of both boys and girls, I don't have to go into the exact wording of the letter, as you'll have seen them before. Whenever I receive such a letter, I immediately destroy it, of course. But the evil thing about such communications is that the damage is already done—you have to read them before you can consign them to their proper place. I have a duty towards the parents of pupils at this school, and I am as well aware as you are of the theoretical risks to children in a small class. Teachers are as variable in their attitudes as people in any other walk of life. As a result I snooped on Mr Holdroyd a little—you know, finding an excuse to go and see him in his classroom when I knew he would have only one pupil there—but in a very snort while I was completely satisfied that he could be left alone with any daughter of mine in absolute safety."

"Thank you for being so forthcoming. I suppose that you have no idea where this letter could have come from?"

"No. I don't remember anything peculiar about the postmark, so I assume that it was posted in Dundee. As I say, I immediately consigned it to the bucket where it belonged."

"Could you please tell me if Mr Holdroyd had any particular friends among the other teachers in the school?"

"As I was suggesting before, he always seemed a little distant with his colleagues. He was never rude or anything like that, but he acted as if they all came to work in the same place, but there was no reason to carry on their relationship beyond that sort of formal level. If you want to pursue the point, I suggest that you go and see Miss Gillespie—she's the Assistant Rector directly in charge of girls. I think the women on the staff tend to gossip a bit about their male colleagues, and I rather think that Miss Gillespie might know if Mr Holdroyd had formed any strong friendship with another member, whether male or female. You could also pursue your point about the girls with her, if you wish, but I rather suspect that her answer will be the same as mine."

"I shall certainly see her if I may, Mr Dalkeith. But just one other small point before I do. Do you happen to know if Mr Holdroyd wrote poetry?"

"If he did, I never heard of it. Speaking personally, I would have thought he was too well-balanced for that sort of thing."

The rector took them to Miss Gillespie's room, which was just down the corridor to the left. He knocked gently on the door and walked straight in; "Ah, Miss Gillespie, two detectives to see you for a change. This is Inspector Malone, and Constable White. I'll leave you with them if you think you'll be safe." Mr Dalkeith giggled at his outrageous suggestion, and Miss Gillespie attempted a weak smile as he left the room.

Death of a Dundee Teacher

White had visions of a tweedy, bespectacled, long-faced sixty-year old, just like the Lady Superintendent, as they had formerly been called, at the school which he had attended. Wherefore he was surprised at what he saw before him. Miss Gillespie was certainly not young, probably in her late forties or early fifties, but she was dressed in an elegant manner, which owed nothing to the caricature of the schoolmistress which he had conjured up.

Malone addressed Miss Gillespie; "I presume you've been expecting us too, so I'll get straight to the point. First of all, could you please tell me if Mr Holdroyd had anyone he was especially close to on the staff?"

"I don't think he did, Inspector. It's not as if he was unpopular, in fact I would say that he was very much liked; but I never heard of him being very friendly with any of his colleagues—of either sex."

"Could you now tell me if you have ever entertained any suspicions about his relationship with the girls—or the boys for that matter."

"As you get straight to the point, Inspector, so shall I. I'm as certain as anyone can be that no such relationship, however slight, ever existed, with either girls or boys. It may well seem to you that as he was dealing with small classes, occasionally with only one pupil in them, he would have had ample opportunity for irregular behaviour. But in some ways the conditions make it less likely. If he had been that way inclined, he would probably have started acting that way years ago, and no longer be in the profession. In some cases in the past I would have said that he was in more moral danger than the girls involved. As to boys, I think it extremely unlikely. If you'd like, I'll get a girl who was in his sixth-year Russian class—or rather who was his sixth-year Russian class. I think she would be prepared to be straightforward with you on any matter you care to ask her about."

"Thank you, Miss Gillespie, that would be very kind." Miss Gillespie left them to go and search for the girl.

"Why did you ask that question about poetry?" said White. "was it simply to establish a connection with Lady Carswell?"

"Aye. I shall of course ask the same question of his friends in St. Andrews at the earliest opportunity. One of the difficulties with people who write poetry is that they're almost ashamed of it, as if it were some unpleasant skin disease. They're worried about the sort of condemnation we've just heard from Mr Dalkeith. As a result, they won't even let their closest friends know. I came across no evidence of a collection in Mr Holdroyd's flat, though, and unless he's hidden them particularly well, I have no idea where he could have kept his verses—if he wrote them at all, that is."

Miss Gillespie re-entered bringing with her a tall attractive girl, aged about seventeen or eighteen. "This is Rosemary Crighton, Inspector. I've asked her if she minds being questioned by you on her own, and as she raises no objection, I'll leave her with you." She left the room and shut the door.

"Well, Miss Crighton, do please sit down," began Malone. Miss Crighton complied in a manner which left no doubt that she expected to be observed in this delicate operation by members of the opposite sex. Her expectations were not defeated. Malone and White sat down also.

"You will have been told, if you had not already guessed, that we're here in connection with the death on Tuesday night of Mr Holdroyd. I'd like to ask you one or two questions which might seem rather personal." Miss

Death of a Dundee Teacher

Crighton did not appear to be too daunted at the prospect. "I'd be very grateful if you could answer with absolute honesty. I believe you have often been in a classroom on your own with Mr Holdroyd?"

"Certainly," said Miss Crighton with a slight smile. "you see I've always been the only one in my year doing Russian. More often I'm stuck at the back of another class, but there has always been at least one period a week when I'm on my own."

"Did Mr Holdroyd ever make advances to you, even of the most rudimentary kind?"

"No. Not that I believe no other teacher would have for a minute. But Mr Holdroyd certainly never did to me, and I've never heard anyone suggest that he did to anyone else, either boy or girl. We talk about that sort of thing, sometimes, you know, and I'm sure some of the things said about the staff aren't in fact true. But no-one has ever suggested such a thing of Mr Holdroyd that I've heard."

"Thank you for the honest answer. It saves everyone a lot of time. There's really only one other small point I want to ask you about. Do you by chance know if Mr Holdroyd wrote poetry?"

She smiled. "Well I must say I don't know for sure. I used to think so and make him into a romantic poet figure. I remember about a year or so ago, I think it was, he was explaining about epitaphs, and gave an example which he said he had made up himself. Whether he really had or not, I don't know. I can even remember how it went:

> Bury me by the water's edge
> Where flies attract the trout,
> And round me plant a holly hedge
> To keep the righteous out.

For some reason or another it's easy to remember. It must be the rhythm and the sound, I think, as well as the rhyme. He never mentioned making up poetry to me again, so I don't know if he was serious or not."

"Is there anything else you can tell us about Mr Holdroyd which might be of interest to us? For instance, did he have any marked peculiarities as far as you are concerned?"

"Not really, except that he always insisted on keeping his watch at British Summer Time. He said it was a form of patriotism."

"That is an extremely useful piece of information, Miss Crighton. In fact, it has solved one of our major problems so far. If you can think of anything else which might be of use, please contact me at St. Andrews Police Station. If I'm not there, they'll take a message for me. Thank you very much for your help."

Malone and White rose. Miss Crighton rose with the same consciousness with which she had sat down, smiled at them, and left the room.

"I don't think they made them that way when I was at school, White, or perhaps I was just too young to notice." Before White could make a suitable reply, Miss Gillespie knocked on the door and entered.

"I'm never too sure about girls like that, Inspector, but I thought she would probably be admirable for your purpose. I feel quite confident that she would not have come over shy and coy at the wrong time. I hope I was right.

"You were quite right; Miss Crighton was very helpful and to the point. If all the people we interviewed acted in that way, our job would be a lot easier. I hope you'll tell her I said so. However, I don't think we need trespass any longer on your time and space. I'm sure you have plenty to do."

Malone and White said goodbye and began to make their way out. Mr Dalkeith was waiting in ambush for them by the main door. "Is there anything else I can do for you, Inspector?"

"Yes, there is one thing. Could you please find out from the other members of staff whether they had any idea if Mr Holdroyd wrote poetry? If you get any information to that effect, could you please contact St. Andrews Police Station and leave details? It would be very helpful if you could find out before this afternoon. If there is no positive information, don't trouble yourself to let us know. Thank you very much, Mr Dalkeith."

As they left the school it occurred to White that the Inspector was rather overdoing the poetry line, and so he was even more amazed when Malone said: "Would you mind driving, White? I'll direct you if it's needed. I want to stop off in town and buy a volume of poetry. As there may be some difficulty in parking near the bookshop, you can drop me there and then drive round the nearest circle until I've finished."

ᔕ Chapter 7

"WELL, WHITE," SAID MALONE, as they drove in the direction of the centre of Dundee again, "in many ways that was quite a relief. I was half afraid we might uncover some dark secrets in Holdroyd's life over here. Unless all three we've spoken to are totally wrong, we can probably put the Dundee connection to the back of our minds, if not dismiss it altogether. I was especially pleased that Miss Crighton cleared up the matter of the watch by remembering that remarkable point. Who'd have thought it. If that clears young Athlone once and for all from suspicion, I must tell him to write and thank her. He might well improve his views towards women—if there's anything wrong with them now. If you turn right here you'll find a bookshop. Here we are."

White stopped the car, but as Malone had predicted there was nowhere for him to park it. Malone said to him as he climbed out: "Take your first right, keep going round and pick me up when you see me. I hope it'll be the first time round."

Malone managed to effect his purchase swiftly, and it was indeed on the first complete circle that he was ready to be picked up. Malone eased himself deftly into the car. "I was lucky, White. The assistant told me that they had been selling so well there was only one left after this."

"Excuse my ignorance in the matter, sir, but could you tell me firstly why you're so insistent on poetry this morning, and secondly what book of poetry you've just bought?"

"The answer lies in Lady Carswell's letter. For the reasons I gave before, I'm afraid I shall have to keep you in the dark about the significance of it. The volume I've just bought is, of course, 'The Long Road Home' by Harriet Carswell."

Death of a Dundee Teacher

White had nothing to add on this point, as he had clearly received all the answer he was going to on his first question. He continued: "I assumed you wanted to go to the hospital next. I think this is the right road. If not, could you please direct me?"

"You're quite right. Just keep going along here for another two miles or thereabouts, and then turn right. I'll tell you when if you want, but you can in fact see the hospital from this road."

Malone then sat back to consider exactly what information he wanted from Eric Athlone. The fact of the watch made his involvement even less likely than before, but he had to admit that he was prepared to explain it away before he had this new information, and therefore he had to consider the possibility of doing the same in reverse. He was well aware that evidence, or apparent evidence, could be forged. Unlikely, he felt in this case, but it was one of the variables he would have to keep in his mind. He also had to bear in mind the likelihood that the hospital would not oblige them for much longer, by keeping an individual who, by now, must be perfectly fit, in a much-needed bed. He came to the conclusion that he would be justified in letting the lad go free now. Clearly if he made a bolt for it, that would be as good as an admission of guilt. He decided simply to wait and see what would become of the interview. They arrived at the hospital, a vast new edifice, supposed to be one of the most advanced of its type. They entered the building through glass doors which opened automatically, always an uncanny experience to Malone; but he supposed very useful in a hospital. The area they then found themselves in was more reminiscent of an airport lounge than a hospital entrance hall, but they had little difficulty in locating the reception desk. Malone identified himself and

White, and asked for precise directions to the ward containing Eric Athlone. They passed further along the entrance hall, which contained Kiosks selling, among other things, flowers, sweets and books. As they passed the bookstall, Malone could not help pointing out that here too the poems of Harriet Carswell were on sale. He offered to buy another copy for the improvement of White's literary education, but the offer was politely refused. They next turned right down a long corridor, and half-way along mounted some stairs, then down another corridor, and up some more stairs, opposite the end of which was the ward containing Eric Athlone. Malone identified himself to the sister in charge, who asked to have a word with him in private before he visited the patient. He rejoined White after a minute or two, and they went together to see the patient. He was again in a room on his own with a uniformed policeman at the door. They entered the room. Young Athlone no longer gave the impression of being a patient in the normal sense of the word; He was sitting in a chair fully dressed, reading a magazine. He got up when they came in.

"I suppose you've come to arrest me," he said, still betraying a slight lisp in his voice. I've been expecting that to happen all day—it starts early in hospitals, you know. I suppose I can't really expect the police to believe a word I say. I'm lucky I haven't been beaten up, some would say, but I swear to you again that I had nothing whatever to do with Mr Holdroyd's death, and I wish to god I had never seen him like that."

There was no sign of any of the earlier hysterics, merely an aggrieved resignation. Physically he looked the picture of health. Doctor Cathcart's diagnosis had evidently been correct, and there was clearly nothing wrong with him now.

His tiredness and shock had completely disappeared after the relaxation of a day in medical care.

"Don't get so persecuted, Mr Athlone. I have never had any intention of using physical violence on you, and at the moment have absolutely no desire to arrest you, although you must realise yourself that the circumstantial evidence against you is pretty damning. It is quite clear from your last remark that I cannot expect a convenient confession out of you. Now, to indicate my good intentions towards you, I'll give you a piece of information. In return I would like you to be absolutely honest with me about your relationship with Mr Holdroyd. I assure you that such facts as you give me can probably be used in your favourassuming you're innocent. Now for my part of the bargain. One of the strongest pieces of evidence which we had against you was the time on Mr Holdroyd's watch. You may well not have noticed, but it was broken, presumably when he fell, and the hands stood at ten minutes to one. As you appeared at the Police Station not long after that time, in a state which can only be described as extreme, suspicion was bound to fall on you first. Were you aware that Mr Holdroyd kept his watch at British Summer Time all the year round?"

"No sir, and I can't say I really understand what that has to do with me."

"It simply means that his watch was probably an hour fast, and that's a very strong point in your favour. To be fair, it by no means clears you, but it does fit in neatly with your version of your actions. If I add that the doctor thought that the most likely time of death was shortly before midnight, it makes your position even brighter. Therefore, if you are innocent, the more you tell me about your visit and the reasons for it, the more likely I shall be able to eliminate you from any enquiries, and get on the track of the person who did actually perpetrate the crime."

"I'm very glad that you have some belief in me, even if it's only because of what someone else has told you." He still looked somewhat doubtfully at White, who, however, remained impassive.

"I suppose I might as well tell you everything I can. I let you know enough last time I saw you. My father works at Leuchars Air Station, and he thinks working for the government is by far the best way anyone can spend their life. I suppose it's something to do with the mass unemployment and poverty he can remember when he was a child. I was always good at languages at school—in fact I was top in Latin all the way and the teacher tried to persuade me to do Greek. I wish I had now, but I was misled by the narrow-minded talk you get about preparing yourself for a job. My father wanted me to learn Russian, as with the science I'm doing he thought it would help me to get a good job in the Ministry of Defence. I didn't think for a minute it would and I had no intention of working there, but as I knew that I had always been a bit of a disappointment to him, I decided I'd better do what he wanted. I couldn't get Russian at school, so I thought he'd drop the idea anyway. But he immediately started asking about private lessons, and was eventually put onto Mr Holdroyd. He was apparently told that if he explained the reasons and his financial circumstances, Mr Holdroyd would be very understanding about the fee. He was, and agreed on a very low price. My father was very grateful, and even more insistent that I should take advantage of the offer. As I said, I was always good at languages, and so didn't really mind. I was a little frightened that he might be one of these dreadfully jolly people I can't stand, but as it turned out he was totally different. I enjoyed doing the Russian, and after a short while found myself doing extra work just to please him. After a month or two I realised that I was in love with him. It became a sort of agony going along, as he never showed any personal interest in me, but just my progress in the subject. Last week I couldn't stand it any longer, and told him honestly what I felt about him. He just became very embarrassed and said he was very sorry it had come to that. In the circumstances he said that he could no longer go on teaching me. He promised to write a letter to my father giving some other reason for having to stop and added that he would recommend a woman he knew who would probably accept the same terms. I broke down into tears and said that I wouldn't mention it again if he'd only let me still come. He was very kind but absolutely unshakeable. Eventually, feeling utterly miserable, I left. You wouldn't know how it feels, and it's not worth explaining to you. I didn't know how I could possibly tell my father, but eventually I managed to. As I had expected he was very angry, accusing me of bringing shame on the family and wasting his money too. Remember that that was without knowing the reason. When I told him that it was nothing to do with me, and that Mr Holdroyd was going to write to him explaining the cause and suggesting another teacher, he began to calm down a bit. Then of course I started wondering what would happen if he told the whole story. I was out of my mind with worry, and hardly slept for the next two nights. It was last Saturday I had managed to tell my father and expected him to get the letter on Monday. It was probably something to do with the post, but it didn't come then. By the time Tuesday morning came, I felt an absolute wreck, but of course still had to go through the motions as if nothing was wrong. My father read the letter and to my immense relief told me he was sorry for what he'd said to me, as from Mr Holdroyd's letter it was quite clear that I'd been working very hard and was doing well. He was also very pleased about the suggestion of another teacher and said he would see about fixing me up with her as soon as possible. I don't know what was said in the letter, but you can imagine how grateful I felt towards Mr Holdroyd after seeing the effect it had on my father. Perhaps it was because of my tiredness as well as my relief, but I began to think he might have changed his mind about me. I decided to go and see him, to thank him for what he had done if nothing else. I was still rather frightened in case he got angry with me, and decided I'd wait till he got home from the pub. I'd found out quite a lot about his habits by this time and knew that he usually stayed in the St. Davids until closing time. I went to see a friend who I knew would give me a few drinks—for confidence, you know—and kept putting off going. I should think it was well after half-past twelve when I was along South Street. There was still a light on in his sitting room, so I decided to go up. The doors were open and I walked straight in. When I saw him lying there, I assumed he must be drunk. I tried to rouse him for a short while, and then I noticed the wound in the side of his head. I felt for his pulse and could find nothing. Then I got into a dreadful panic, which only those who're forced to carry a burden of guilt around with them all the time could understand. The only thing I remember doing is picking up the candelabrum and thinking that Mr Holdroyd would think it was untidy to leave it lying there, I don't know exactly how long I was there, or how long it took me to get to the Police Station. That's the honest truth."

"Thank you for giving us the whole story, Mr Athlone. If you needed to, could you prove where you were about midnight?"

"I'm not at all sure about exact times, but I expect someone else was. That's to say, I'm pretty sure I was still in my friend's house at that time. I suppose I'd better tell you where I was. I don't suppose he'd mind. The friend I was visiting was Joe Stewart—Dr Stewart in the Chemistry department of the University, that is. He likes people like me, you understand. He lives on the new estate; I did wander around a bit before going to South Street—still trying to pluck up the courage—but I don't think I left his house before midnight. I'd rather not have him brought into this if it can be avoided."

"Don't worry, I understand your attitude perfectly well, and I'll only contact him if I have to. Even if you were going directly, it would take you at least a quarter of an hour to walk from there to South Street. Did anyone who can identify you see you going between the two places?"

"Not as far as I know. There were one or two people going home in the estate, but they were all in cars. I don't remember seeing anyone else along the pavements."

"That's a pity. I might as well tell you that I have always been doubtful about your involvement with Mr Holdroyd's death, but one or two things still look a little black against you. For instance, as you're probably aware, Mr Holdroyd did not as far as we can establish, have many visitors, and we also have reason to believe that he was acquainted with his attacker. Your presence in his flat, therefore, must still look rather suspicious, despite your version of events. However, as I said earlier, I have no intention of arresting you at the moment, so don't fret about that. You're free to leave here whenever you want. The hospital have need of your bed, and I've just been asked by the sister to make a decision about you. They say that there's absolutely nothing the matter with you, and the presence of a uniformed policeman disturbs the other patients. Shall I tell them you'll be leaving immediately?"

"Yes, please. And thank you very much, sir. You've been very sympathetic."

Malone and White maneuvered their way out of the hospital and regained the car. Malone elected to drive, and they began the journey back to St. Andrews.

"Well White, perhaps you think I'm a prize idiot for letting young Athlone go like that?"

"Not in the least, sir. With the new evidence about the watch, and presuming he's telling the truth about his visit to Dr Stewart's house, I don't see that you could have followed any other course. I'm sure we could easily lay hands on him if he tried to disappear, and if he did, he would be as good as confessing his guilt. That would save us a lot of trouble, if he is guilty."

"Very well put, White. I must say, that although I don't in fact think he's our man, it was exactly those considerations which brought me to the decision to release him. Although I said that I'd only test his alibi if I had to, I'm very much tempted to do so as soon as we get back. In fact I think it would be unforgiveable not to. Well the next thing on the agenda is Lady Carswell. One of the reasons that I'm driving is to give you the opportunity of widening your literary education. You'll find her volume of poems in the back seat. Please read some of it."

White, a little sheepishly, leant over into the back and picked up the slim volume. "Any particular ones you'd recommend, sir?"

Death of a Dundee Teacher

Malone shook his head, and so White followed the simple course of beginning at the beginning. He was by no means averse to reading poetry, and he was very much impressed, by the clear language and metrical form of the pieces. He was beginning to think that he should have taken up the Inspector's offer of a free copy.

A smile was beginning to play around Malone's lips, when, as they were nearing Guardbridge, White emitted a quiet blasphemy.

"What is it? Some immortal gem, or something quite shocking? Please read it aloud to me."

From the tone of voice, it was clear to White that he had found what he was supposed to have found, and the apparent concern for his literary education was merely a secondary consideration. He therefore obeyed, and read rhythmically:

> Bury me by the water's edge
> Where flies attract the trout,
> And round me plant a holly hedge
> To keep the righteous out.

6♦ Chapter 8

THEY ARRIVED BACK AT THE POLICE STATION shortly after mid-day. Reluctantly, but as was clear to him necessarily, Malone decided to ring Dr Stewart immediately. He reflected that if young Athlone were telling the truth, he need never know about this slight breach of his word, and, if not—well, he would clearly have done the right thing. He tried Dr Stewart's home address first, but as he got no answer there, he rang the Chemistry Department of the University. He spoke to a secretary, gave his name, and was put almost immediately through to Dr Stewart.

"Inspector Malone? I believe you're investigating the death of Mr James Holdroyd. I have also heard that Eric Athlone is under suspicion, so please don't think it suspicious that I immediately assume you're about to ask me about Eric's visit to my house on Tuesday night. Whether it will implicate him or not, I don't know, but he arrived at my house at about ten o' clock, had a couple of gins, no more, and left, as far as I can recall, about midnight. I'm afraid I can't be any more exact, as I had more than a couple of glasses. Yes, it could have been a quarter of an hour either way, but I shouldn't think any more. I also have to admit, before you ask me, that he intended to visit Holdroyd's flat after he left me. Whether he got there or not, and at what time, I have no way of telling. I can say, however, that when he left, his attitude towards Holdroyd was one of gratitude and excessive meekness. Violence seemed to be the last thing in his mind. If there is anything more that you want to know, could it please wait until later? I've got a rather delicate experiment on the go, and it needs my close attention."

"Not at the moment, thank you. Could I ask you to make out a statement in writing of what you have just said, and deposit it at the Station as soon as convenient? There's no terrible hurry, but I would like it today. I'm very sorry to have interrupted you." Malone rang off.

"If you heard that, White, it's not absolutely conclusive, because he can't remember the exact time that the lad left. But if the doctor is right about the death occurring before midnight, and the watch was generally an hour out, it should put young Athlone in the clear."

"It does seem to me, sir, that he would have just had time to commit the crime. For a start he could have run to South Street from Dr Stewart's. On his own admission he was seen by no-one on his way there. Dr Stewart was after all rather vague about the times, and he could be more than quarter of an hour out. And I can't forget that the hands of a watch can be turned."

Malone admitted the justice of these observations but decided to leave matters as they stood for the time being. He then turned his attention to some more reports which had arrived in their absence. One of them seemed to engage his interest for some time. White asked him what it was as soon as he had finished with it.

"It's the one I asked for about the connection of the Russian and Leuchars. The authorities there are certain that there's nothing in it. It appears that David Athlone made no secret of his ambitions for his son with Russian and the Ministry of Defence. Any such matter which comes to their notice is investigated as a matter of policy. They even appear to have been aware that Holdroyd was the tutor involved as well. Any connection with subversive activities of any sort seems to be highly improbable. If that's not conclusive, it certainly allows us to put that aspect into the background.

Death of a Dundee Teacher

Let's hope that a skulking Boris and his habitual fur-hat can disappear back into the Siberian wastes where they belong, Well, we have Lady Carswell to contend with this afternoon. I think it's about time for a lunch break. I won't need you again until around quarter-past two, so do what you want until then. Please borrow Lady Carswell's works if you wish to."

White decided that poetry had already taken up enough time, and declined the offer, as he went off for his lunch. Malone then made his preparations for the break—not a total one as far as he was concerned. He intended to have a chat with Bill Watson. Another of his reports had informed him that Lady Carswell—or Harriet Wilson as she had been then—was an exact contemporary with James Holdroyd at St. Andrews University. He himself could not remember her, but that was hardly surprising, as she would have been a Bejantine in his last year. She would have had to be highly outstanding in some way before he would have known her. However. Bill Watson had been another contemporary of James Holdroyd, and it would be reasonable to assume that he could provide some information about her. Not that he was worried about dealing with her; he was a bit of an intellectual snob and tended to reckon that women from expensive schools who managed to get an ordinary degree after four years had little to recommend about their intellects other than tenacity. He had not been far from sneering when he had seen the subjects which contributed to Lady Carswell's degree. They had all been of the type which had been invented or expanded to meet the needs of an ever less capable student population.

He managed to get hold of Bill Watson at the school before he went off for his lunch, and arranged to meet him in the Arklay hotel, where, he was informed, they served tolerable bar lunches. Malone arrived first and ordered a light lunch and a pint of heavy. A few minutes later Bill Watson came in. Malone offered to stand him his refreshment, and he accepted with thanks; however, he refused to take more than a half-pint of shandy and a bowl of soup. The reason he gave was that he found he could not teach so effectively in the afternoon if he had anything more than the lightest of lunches. Malone was quite happy to see this, as he did not like putting in expensive claims—or any claims at all, for that matter—for entertainment. He felt that he could perfectly well stand this out of his own pocket.

They found a table in the far corner of the bar, which was as yet fairly isolated, and Malone immediately ate his lunch, as he was genuinely hungry after his efforts that morning. As soon as he had finished eating, he came straight to the point of the meeting.

"Mr Watson, I understand that you were at the University here at exactly the same time as both Mr Holdroyd and a young lady called Harriet Wilson, now styled Lady Carswell. Could you be good enough to tell me how well they knew one another?"

"Certainly, Inspector, but before I do, may I draw your attention to that man at the bar? The one with long black hair and the rather loud sports jacket, talking to the small blonde woman. He's a reporter on the local newspaper. He's probably here purely by accident but he may have followed you in."

"You may be right about the last point, Mr Watson. He certainly wasn't here when I first came in; in my job you have a disquieting way of noticing that sort of thing. But as long as he stays over there it's of no concern to me; he's entitled to a drink as much as anyone else. I don't suppose he has some devilish electronic device hidden in his tie to enable him to home in on our conversation. If you think he's a lip-reader, all you need to do is turn around a little." Bill Watson immediately did so, not because he had any startling information to impart to Malone, but because he had a healthy and understandable fear of misrepresentation in the press.

"In answer to your question, Inspector, Jim did know Harriet—Lady Carswell very well, especially during our last two years at the University. Even if I wanted to go into exactly what I meant by very well, I couldn't. Jim was always very discreet about his relationships with women; he had somewhat old-fashioned views about the sanctity of the weaker sex. Perhaps that's why he never got married. I'd say that there was no doubt that he was extremely fond of her, if not in love with her. Exactly how she felt about him I couldn't say; at the time I would have thought it was mutual, but she married the man who is now Lord Carswell less than a year after graduating."

"So there is no doubt that Mr Holdroyd and Lady Carswell were close friends for at least two years?

"Exactly so."

"Could you tell me a little more about Lady Carswell? To put you in the picture, we had reasons to make enquiries about her yesterday, and the upshot is that she's asked to come and see us here this afternoon. As I know nothing to speak of about her, I would like to correct that position before I actually see her."

"There's not all that much I can tell you. I haven't seen her myself for ten years. She was always very elegantly dressed and could clearly afford to be, although not particularly good-looking. As I remember she had to struggle somewhat with her university work, but to her credit she did end up with a degree. I remember her being a little unpleasant to Jim from time to time for no obvious reason, but that sort of thing is inclined to happen in any relationship between a man and a woman."

"In what ways was she unpleasant?"

"Nothing terribly significant. She used to ridicule his lack of ambition. I don't think it disturbed him much; he just used to ask what the point of reading the poet Horace was, if you learnt nothing from him, or sentiments to that effect. She also used to laugh at his honesty, as I remember."

"Do you happen to know if she had seen Mr Holdroyd recently?"

"Not that I'd heard of; but that by no means proves they hadn't met. It's just the sort of thing that Jim wouldn't have mentioned, what with her being a married woman. The only news I have heard about her recently was the publication of a volume of poems by her. Not too bad, I thought, compared with most of the trash that goes out in the name of poetry nowadays. I know that Jim Holdroyd liked them, but he wasn't keen on talking about them. I assumed that was because of some hangover from their old friendship"

"Do you know if Mr Holdroyd wrote poetry himself?"

"If he did, he never let on about it."

"I think that's all I want to know for the moment, Mr Watson. Thank you very much for your co-operation." He then turned the conversation into more casual channels until they had finished their drinks.

"Well, back to the grindstone for both of us, I suppose," he said as they rose. While they were making their way out of the bar, the reporter disengaged himself from his blonde friend and cut them off.

"Any juicy tit-bits for a poor reporter, Inspector Malone?"

"I'm very sorry, not at the moment. All I can produce at this juncture is: 'The Police are investigating a number of leads and hope to make an arrest soon.' You know as well as I do the value of such statements. By the way, I'm not to be quoted on that last sentence."

They left the Arklay Hotel. Bill Watson returned to the school, and Malone made his way slowly towards the Police Station, wondering what line of attack he should adopt with Lady Carswell. Eventually, he decided it would have to depend on her attitude towards him. There was no point in being antagonistic merely for the sake of being so, but from the tone of her letter he rather suspected that that would be how it would end. When he was back in his office, he began to fill in his time by reading over some of Harriet Carswell's poems again. They were certainly very different from the norm of modern female poetry. He had not come across a single one which displayed an obvious sexual hang-up.

While he was engrossed in the book, there was a knock on the door and Sergeant Johnson entered. "I'm sure you'll forgive the interruption, Inspector. We have someone here who claims to have been in Market Street at about half-past twelve on Tuesday night. He says that he also saw a woman there."

"A woman, eh? That's very interesting. Could you please ask him to come in here now—and stay yourself, if you'd be good enough. In the majority of cases a solid official front leads to greater veracity, and anyway, if there are two of us he'll find it difficult to change his story on a later occasion if he should so desire."

The sergeant went out and returned with a thin pale-faced individual, in his late 'teens or early twenties. "This is Mr Sean Murphy, employed as a barman in the Lochnagar Hotel, Inspector."

"Good afternoon Mr Murphy. Please sit down, and you too sergeant. Well, Mr Murphy, it's very good of you to come and see us. I believe you were at the West End of Market Street at around half-past twelve on Tuesday night?"

"Yes sir." Mr Murphy spoke in a pronounced Irish accent. "The only trouble is I'm not at all certain of the exact time. I'd say it was about twelve-thirty, but it could easily have been at least ten minutes either way."

"I quite understand, Mr Murphy. Unless someone by chance has good reasons for noting the time, it's rare that they can be any more accurate than that. In fact, had you been more certain of the exact time, I would have wanted to know why. But let us take things in order. Could you tell us exactly how you happened to be in Market Street at that time?"

"I was on my way back to the digs. The bar shuts at eleven, as you'll know, but then we've got to get the customers out, unless they happen to be hotel residents. Only after that do we get a chance to clear up. I suppose we'd finished washing the glasses shortly before midnight. I then had a couple of drinks with the head barman before leaving. That's why I think it was about twelve-thirty, but as I said, I can't be absolutely sure when I left."

"And you saw someone at the West end of Market street?"

"Yes, sir. The reason I remember that so clearly was that it was a woman. She came out of a close when I was just behind her on the other side of the road. I was thinking of going across and trying my luck with her, but she immediately hurried off. I supposed she was trying to get away from me. I wasn't that worried, so I didn't bother to try and catch her up."

"You couldn't by any chance give me a description of her, could you, Mr Murphy?"

"When I say I remember very clearly that it was a woman, I don't mean that I saw her at all clearly. For the start it was dark, and although there was a bright moon you'll remember it was behind us, in the West. I didn't really even see her face. She was quite tall and wearing the sort of tatty jeans that the student lassies usually have on nowadays, but I can't tell you much more about her. You see apart from anything else, some of the residents had been very generous with buying us drinks earlier in the evening, and I'd had one or two, if you know what I mean."

"Quite understandable, Mr Murphy. Very few people can describe others at all accurately if the truth be told, and it's no help to invent features which you're not sure about. Your information, such as it is, could be very valuable to us. Could you please leave your address with the sergeant here in case we need to contact you again? I presume you can be found either at the hotel or your digs?"

"I'm never away from one or the other for too long. I'm very sorry I'm not able to be of more help."

"Don't worry yourself at all about that, Mr Murphy. If by chance you do remember anything else worthwhile, don't hesitate to contact us."

The sergeant and Mr Murphy left. Malone considered the implications of this new piece of information. They had only come across one woman in connection with the case so far who knew Holdroyd well, wore tatty jeans and was tall; the fact that Mr Murphy had mentioned nothing about hair colour was also sufficient for Malone to deduce that her hair was almost certainly dark. People usually notice fair hair on women, especially at night, and if they are amorously inclined. Jean Shaw also had dark hair, and he only had her uncorroborated word that she was in her room at the time in question. But why? Drugs was always a possibility, and if Holdroyd had been a dealer in a small way, that would explain the peculiarity of his bank accounts. Yes, they would have to look a bit more closely at Miss Shaw.

Malone was jerked out of his deliberations by the arrival of Constable White. "Ah, White. I think you had better be acquainted with our latest piece of news immediately." He told him the evidence of Sean Murphy, and the possible deductions that could be drawn from it. White's reaction was that they should go straightaway to South Street and arrest Jean Shaw, but Malone restrained his enthusiasm.

"Your zeal is highly commendable, White, but do please remember how thin our evidence against her is. At present we only have a doubtful description from a man who on his own admission had had a drink or two, against her insistence that she never left her room. We'll need a bit more than that of course, if we could show that the piece of material suspended from the nail actually came from her jeans, we'd be on much stronger ground. But even then, we'd have no way of proving beyond doubt when and how the piece of material got there. If Miss Shaw is the guilty party, it knocks some of my theories about Lady Carswell right on the head, too. She'll be here any minute now. I want you to look carefully at her reactions when I pull a few surprises on her, as I assure you I shall. It could well help if you are a little surprised too."

He refused to say anything more until the arrival of Lady Carswell.

Punctually at half-past two, a constable announced the arrival of their visitor. Malone and White both rose to greet her. She was a woman of some presence and reasonably good looks, though by no means a beauty, just as Bill Watson had said. She was tall with dark hair, and a little on the thin side, for Malone's taste at any rate. Her whole attitude however, made it quite clear that as far as she was concerned, she was doing them an immense favour by appearing in these unaccustomed surroundings.

"Please sit down, Lady Carswell. It was very good of you to come. I hope you had a pleasant journey." She did not bother to reply to this pleasantry, but sat down with more studied elegance, if less natural charm, than Rosemary Crighton had done earlier.

"There is no need to thank me, Inspector Malone. As I'm sure you are aware, I am a woman of some social standing. As a result, it would be exceedingly inconvenient to have policeman swarming round my house. It would almost certainly attract the press, and for obvious reasons I would prefer to avoid that. As it seems likely that I would have to see you at some time, I chose to come here, and may I add that, as my own family—and of course my husband's—have always been staunch upholders of the law, I wish to help in as many ways as I can. I presume I was correct in assuming that the interest in me was connected with the death of Mr James Holdroyd?"

She had been speaking in what, as far as she was concerned was the grand manner. It certainly had the intended effect on White, who wondered how Malone would be able to deal with her. Malone himself, however, was totally unperturbed by her approach, and was contriving to look a trifle bored.

"May I ask, Lady Carswell, why you assumed you were being contacted because of the death of Mr Holdroyd? I believe that it was not mentioned specifically by the officer who telephoned your house."

"I could not imagine any other reason for a call from the St. Andrews Police, although that seemed unlikely enough. It's true that Mr Holdroyd and I were quite friendly ten years or so ago—we were students together, as doubtless you have discovered—but we had not kept it up. After all, I have myself been married most of that time. I have come here to make a statement to that effect, and as I have many calls on my time, the sooner I do so formally, the happier I shall be."

"Lady Carswell, if you wish to co-operate as fully as possible, I would find it most convenient if you would answer a few questions for me. A formal statement might then be unnecessary."

"Very well, if you prefer it that way. But there is very little that I can tell you, so please confine your questions to the absolute minimum."

"As you have already admitted, you knew Mr Holdroyd well when you were both at University here. In fact, would it be too much to say that you were good friends over your last two years here?"

"I do not know Inspector, what connotation the mind of a policeman puts on the words 'good friends'. If you mean was I often in the company of Mr Holdroyd, the answer is yes."

"And you say that you have not seen him since you both left the University?"

"That is so."

"Did he ever communicate with you in any way? Congratulations on your marriage, or anything like that?"

Lady Carswell permitted herself a smile. "No, nothing like that. But I did get a letter from him about six months ago, shortly after the publication of my volume of poems."

"I see. Did you reply to his communication?"

"Oh yes, I think so. I got quite a spate of letters at that time which could loosely be termed 'fan mail'. I did my best to answer every one of them personally. But there was certainly nothing I can think of to distinguish his letter from the rest—or for that matter, my reply."

Malone looked at her for a few seconds. He slowly took out his wallet and carefully extracted a piece of paper from it, which he then handed to Lady Carswell. "Perhaps you'll be good enough to explain this. I found it when searching Mr Holdroyd's pockets the night he died."

It was the slip of paper giving her Christian name and telephone number.

She immediately appeared to lose some of her composure. "I don't know what the precise significance of this piece of paper is, but you force me, against my will and better feelings, to reveal what was in Mr Holdroyd's private correspondence to me. I suppose you'll claim that that sort of thing is your job. When I told you that I did not particularly remember what was in his letter to me, that was not strictly true. However, I saw no point in volunteering the information, as it could do no possible good to either the living or the dead. In his letter he protested his continuing love towards me, which he claimed he had always felt since the first time we had met, and said that in my honour he had never looked seriously at another woman since. I, though of course flattered, replied that as he knew only too well, I had been happily married for nearly ten years. I added some slightly cutting comment to the effect that most people grow out of their adolescent infatuations. I hope that satisfies your inquisitiveness, Inspector." She rose as if to leave.

"Please sit down, Lady Carswell. I'm afraid that I am by no means satisfied. Now, to begin with let me read you something.

My mind's a broken army
Of grey men bored of flight,
They've run for thirty years or more

And hope the end's in sight.

"Very good, Inspector, but I think you have four words wrong. Your memory does not appear to be faultless."

"Perhaps, Lady Carswell. Would you care to tell me how you composed that stanza?"

"It is undoubtedly very flattering to be asked about my poetic inspiration in a Police Station, of all the unlikely places. However, I did not come here for a literary discussion. If you have nothing germane to the death of Mr Holdroyd to ask me, I shall leave."

"I assure you, whatever you may think, this is absolutely germane to the issue. Would you therefore be good enough to answer my question?"

"If you feel it is absolutely necessary, I suppose I shall have to comply. Most of the stanzas I compose occur to me fully formed. That is why most of my poems are short, and also why I can only compose when the correct mood is upon me. I am certain that the stanza you have just quoted, in the correct version, came to me in that way."

"The words 'Bored', 'flight', 'mind' and 'run' never occurred to you then?"

"Flight might have, but I can't remember it doing so. A bit of reflection should even convince you that my version is superior to yours. Why you should be driven to make those changes in the first place totally escapes me."

"Lady Carswell, I made no changes. I was reading the original draft of the poem. Incidentally, the author, you and I are all agreed about the superiority of the published version." He handed her the piece of paper he had removed from James Holdroyd's copy of 'The Long Road Home'.

She looked at it, fidgeted a bit, made as if to say something, stopped herself, and looked at it again. Malone pressed home his advantage. "There can of course be no doubt whatsoever that the version you are holding is the author's original copy. If the changes had been made the other way, or the author was known as a literary imbecile, some defence might have been concocted. But even you, if I may say so, have no hesitation in recognising the superiority of the corrected version. He read it, slowly and rhythmically, to bring out the alliteration:

> My brain's a broken army
> Of grey men feared to fight.
> They've fled for thirty years or more
> And hope the end's in sight.

I suppose South of the border they might find the word feared a little peculiar, but we can't help that. However that may be, as I said the point is not merely of literary interest, but germane to the case I am engaged on. Before you try to concoct some explanation for this small piece of manuscript, I had better let you know that I can produce a Dundee schoolgirl who first heard 'Bury me by the water's edge' over a year ago. The author must have forgotten that it had already had a public airing. It was quoted to her once in a Russian lesson by the self-confessed author, and by chance she remembered it. Her Russian teacher was, of course, none other than Mr Holdroyd."

Lady Carswell looked uncertainly around her, but the only face she saw was the immovable visage of Constable White. Malone continued; "Will you now admit that James Holdroyd wrote most, if not all of the poems published under your name?"

She opened her bag, took out a cigarette, and, without removing her gloves, lit it. She did not speak immediately.

When she did so, her voice had lost its former confidence, but for all that she by no means gave the impression of being cowed.

"There would seem to be little point in denying it. I'm sure I could explain the two cases you have produced if I had a desire to deceive you, but anyway, for all I know you have more evidence of a similar kind. However, as far as I know there is nothing illegal about paying for someone's literary services and publishing their efforts under your own name. In fact, there are people called ghost writers you know, who make a living out of selling their literary talents.'

"Lady Carswell, you seem to misunderstand the point I am trying to make. If you wish to buy a dubious literary reputation, that is of no concern to me. I am also well aware that there is nothing criminal in such a course of action, assuming there has been no conspiracy to defraud or anything of that type. However, it is illegal to try to obstruct the ends of justice, and that is undoubtedly what you have been trying to do since you entered this room. You told me that you wished to leave a statement to the effect that you had not seen Mr Holdroyd for the last ten years, and that you had only communicated in writing on one occasion since. That statement would patently have been a pack of lies. Perhaps now you would be good enough to tell me the truth. Remember that every question I ask has a bearing on the investigation and must therefore be answered with absolute veracity. You say that you paid Mr Holdroyd for the poems?"

"Yes, in cash, bank notes. I paid him well, too. Something well in excess of a thousand pounds. He would never have got a penny for them on his own. I paid cash for two reasons; firstly so that there should be no record of the transaction, in case it should be an embarrassment to me later, and secondly because Jim was himself worried about a large cheque."

"Why should that have worried him?"

"He became all honest about avoiding income tax. I told him not to be so foolish, but he always had this thing about scrupulous honesty. For some reason connected with that he found it easier to accept cash in instalments. I think it made him think of it as a genuine gift."

"Will you now try to tell me the truth about when you last saw Mr Holdroyd? And please do not waste my time and yours again."

"Let me think. It's difficult to remember these things exactly. It must have been about two or three weeks..."

"Lady Carswell, how much more of this bad amateur acting have I got to take from you? As you are doubtless more than necessarily aware, you are a figure not unknown in the social world. St. Andrews, being the sort of town it is, has more than its fair share of people who regularly read the sort of magazines in which photographs of you are likely to appear. There are therefore those who can recognise your face. You were seen, not two or three weeks ago, but..."

"For God's sake Inspector, if you're aware that I saw him last Tuesday afternoon, why the hell can't you say so?"

"I was not aware of the fact until you mentioned it, or I can assure you that I would not have wasted my time with the possibility of having to disprove another lie. To be frank with you, I doubt whether there are more than half a dozen folk in St. Andrews who could recognise you anyway. But thank you for the information. I shall have to make myself clear again. You have been telling me a lot of lies, Lady Carswell, if the simple word does not offend your sensibilities. You have only admitted the truth when forced to. This puts anything further you say on a very suspicious footing. You appear to be aware that I might have information about you or your movements which may conflict with any statements you choose to make. Please stick to the truth. Will you now tell me at what time you saw Mr Holdroyd on Tuesday, and what your reason was for seeing him?"

She stubbed out her cigarette clumsily in an ashtray Malone had offered her and lit another one.

"My publisher had asked me to prepare another volume if possible, as against their normal experience with poetry my book has sold well. How much of that is the result of any intrinsic merit, and how much the result of my name, I don't know. It could be that the public have become tired of the obscure ravings or obvious juvenilities which pass for poetry now. But that's beside the point. I had asked Jim if he could supply more contributions, and he sent me a few. Then on Monday night he rang to say that he could no longer carry on the deceit. I presume that was the occasion of writing down my name and number. For obvious reasons I did not encourage him to contact me by telephone. It was then that he declared his lasting love for me and gave that as the reason for his former moral backsliding. After I'd heard that, I thought I would probably get somewhere if I called to see him. It appeared to me that it would be fairly easy for me to make him change his mind. I went to see him at six o' clock—I am always punctual—but he was quite adamant, saying that there was nothing which would make him change his mind. When I offered to return his love, he was visibly shocked, and asked me to leave. I could see no future in our conversation, as I was beginning to get extremely angry. To have both your femininity and your reputation treated in such a way by a miserable failure of a schoolmaster is no pleasant experience. I therefore left and went to visit some friends in the neighbourhood. I returned home shortly before one o' clock."

"Had your husband nothing to say about your late arrival home?"

"My husband is a man of great social standing but is either a fool or does not care what I do. I had told him that I was visiting an old school friend in Edinburgh."

"Can you prove where you were at around midnight that day?"

"Good God, do you never leave off? When I said I was visiting friends to suit your devastatingly accurate mind, I should have said that I was visiting a friend. As I told you, I was by no means flattered by the reception I received in South Street. Have you absolutely no decency or sense of discretion? Can you take my word or nothing?"

"In the circumstances, Lady Carswell, I see no reason at all why I should believe any statement that you make, unless there is external corroboration for it."

"Well, you'll have to take my word on this point."

Malone looked her straight in the eyes, without a trace of emotion on his face. "On Tuesday night, probably around midnight, James Holdroyd was done to death by a blow to the side of his head. It was not a particularly violent blow. Its lethal effect was caused by the exact positioning. Any woman of normal physique could have struck that blow, and it's quite possible that his assailant had no real desire to kill him. I also know a few facts about the circumstances of that blow. It was struck by somebody who James Holdroyd knew well, and from whom he expected no violence. As the blow was struck by an object picked up in the room, it is also possible that the person who struck it had no expectation of violence either. This unknown person was almost certainly wearing gloves. Again, it is likely that this was habitual, as apparently no surprise was occasioned by the sight of the gloves. It has not escaped my notice that you even keep your gloves on to smoke. Mr Holdroyd was not a man to receive many visitors; yet you have admitted, albeit reluctantly, that you at any rate visited him earlier in the evening the day he died. You have also given me two personal reasons why you may have wished to use violence against him. Perhaps therefore you can realise why I feel that I must demand a proper alibi from you?"

Lady Carswell hesitated for a moment, then opened her bag, tore a page out of her diary and wrote briefly on it. She then handed the piece of paper to Malone and said: "That is the name and address of the man who will, if necessary, provide an alibi for me. But I trust that you will not think it necessary to contact him."

Malone continued in the same tone, apparently unimpressed by the name and address with which he had been provided: "I cannot see what possible justification I could have for believing your uncorroborated word." He folded the piece of paper and handed it to White. "Constable White, at the end of this interview would you be good enough to check Lady Carswell's alibi?" She began to look violent, but Malone continued: "I may also remind you, Lady Carswell, that leaving aside the pack of lies which you tried to mislead me with, and which I was fortunately able to expose for what they were, you have as good as admitted to an extra-marital . . ."

"How dare you," hissed Lady Carswell. White tensed himself to restrain her from the violence which she clearly intended against the Inspector, but she managed to restrain herself with a great effort. Malone therefore continued: "an extra-marital relationship with the gentleman you wish me to contact to support your alibi. Now, even if he were to support it, I am not at all sure that we could consider it sufficient corroboration. I must ask you therefore to surrender your passport at your local Police Station within the next two hours. If you fail to do so, I shall have no alternative but to issue a warrant for your arrest. Good afternoon, Lady Carswell."

Malone rose, followed by Lady Carswell. She had a look of thunder on her face, and said in a low voice, trembling with emotion: "Inspector Malone, I'm sure you think that you have been tremendously clever. But however this affair turns out, I shall make it up to you with interest. Oh yes, I can, and I will. Whenever you fail to get the credit or the promotion you feel you deserve, remember how you treated me this afternoon." She turned, walked out of the room and left the Police Station.

"Hand me back that piece of paper, White. I shall see to my own dirty work. You doubtless would not have failed to notice that she did her best to pretend that you did not exist. It made Mr Dalkeith look quite a democrat. It was merely to force her to take notice of you that I handed it to you; I find that sort of attitude rather trying. I hope it won't cause her to include you among her items of revenge. I must say, I can't imagine for a moment what Holdroyd saw in her."

Malone went off to the telephone.

❦ Chapter 9

WHITE, LEFT ALONE IN THE ROOM, reflected on the astute performance of the Inspector. He now, of course, realised what he had missed earlier about the letter. The handwriting had not been the same as that on the manuscript of the poem. Perhaps Malone had been right to keep him in the dark about this fact. As it had turned out, his opinion on Lady Carswell's reactions had not been needed; but what if she had managed to explain away the apparent evidence against her? His more open mind—Malone would understandably be convinced that his view was correct— might possibly have gauged the reliability of her answers with more accuracy. However, with great skill, Malone had forced her into admitting all he had apparently wanted. White thought of his original certainty about the guilt of Eric Athlone, followed by his equal certainty less than an hour previously about Jean Shaw. He decided to stop coming to premature conclusions.

Malone came back into the room, and White gave him a questioning look. "Oh yes, White, he confirms the alibi all right. First of all, I received a good deal of abuse, until I was able to get across to him the seriousness of the evidence against the good Lady. He then reluctantly admitted that she had been in his company from half-past seven until half-past twelve. I then informed him that we would require a signed statement to that effect. I was immediately greeted with threats similar to those we have just heard in this room, but eventually he agreed to deposit such a statement within the hour."

"It seems to me that it's just as well there's no way they can carry out these threats."

"Don't be naive, White. They can, and quite possibly they will. If you don't believe me, I shall attempt to convince you by telling you something about myself. When I was not much older than you, I was very much an up-and-coming young man in the Glasgow force. In fact, not without good reason, I was very pleased with my progress. As a result, neither I nor my friends were too surprised when I was handed rather a complex and delicate case, which clearly was going to involve some of the more important public figures on the West Coast. I myself actually thought that here was an indication at last that my considerable talents were receiving recognition. Foolish ass that I was; I did not realise that I had merely been chosen as the sacrifice. Anyway, I brought the case to a very swift, and to the best of my ability, discreet conclusion. Of course, one or two rather surprising resignations followed, but because of my efforts to prevent it, the true reasons for them were not disclosed. I therefore expected double gratitude. All I was given, though, were a number of verbal threats similar to those we have just witnessed. I gave them as little credence as you apparently do. After a bit, however, despite some successful work in a number of fields, my lack of promotion became glaringly obvious. To be quite honest, I think I was rather fortunate to get my present job here with Fife. You see, once they've blocked you for long enough, they don't have to bother themselves about it anymore. The damage is already done, because everyone assumes there must be something unmentionable wrong with you to keep you in the same position so long, especially when your identifiable record gives no hint of a reason. At any rate there are always others in line for the same job about whom they don't have to entertain any doubts."

"I'm sorry sir, I had no idea."

Death of a Dundee Teacher

"Please don't be sorry, White. I'm not. If I had been particularly disturbed, I would have left the force long since. I'm simply trying to give you an example of what can and does happen. It makes me think that the more I hear about James Holdroyd, the more I understand why he chose his way of life. You must have noticed how everyone mentions his honesty, even if one or two of them are a bit dubious about the extent of it. It's very easy for me at any rate to see why he wanted to keep the righteous out. There aren't many genuinely honest or righteous people around, and they may get rather tired of hearing those terms used of people they know to be trimmers and time-servers. Aye, live on your own in St. Andrews and teach children in Dundee, having as little as is practically possible to do with your colleagues; that's the holly hedge planted."

Neither spoke for a while, until White volunteered: "May I say how much I admired your handling of Lady Carswell, sir?"

"Thank you White. I know that is said with the best of intentions. It was not however that difficult. Remember for a start that I had a lot more information about her than you, as a result of obvious deductions from her letter. You will by now, I presume, have understood the point that I did not reveal to you. I hope it does not seem now that I did it from vulgar showmanship. I assure you that was not at least the conscious reason. People like Lady Carswell think they have a monopoly on pride. Well, they haven't; my pride lies in my intellectual ability, which I knew from her record at University was vastly superior to hers, although she would probably not recognise the fact. It is a common fault with those who have not had to deal with the ancient languages or mathematics to a considerable depth. I was also fairly sure that my knowledge and appreciation of literature was somewhat more profound than hers; therefore I was confident that I could be her superior in the two areas of verbal combat and literary criticism. As I knew a lot more about her than she could possibly have guessed, I couldn't really go wrong. It was very fortunate, though, that before she came, we had confirmation of a female figure in Market Street, coming out of a Close in the area we're interested in, but not very clearly identifiable with her. Otherwise I might easily have gone too far for the present evidence and had her under lock and key by now.

"Could you tell me how you came to the conclusion that Mr Holdroyd had written all the poems?"

"It didn't actually occur to me that this was a possibility until she had been speaking for some time. I had spent some time at lunchtime trying to work out if there were more by him and could find absolutely no criterion for deciding. Such is the danger of preconception: you have in your hands a volume purporting to be by Harriet Carswell; there is little or no difficulty in accepting the proposition that she was helped. But the enormity of a total fraud is for some reason too much for the intellect to assume as a probability. It's like the proposition that a person can be totally evil. It's not at all hard to believe that our fellow man is guilty of more moral backslidings than we ourselves are, but to accept that their whole life is lived on what we would term wicked principles, is really beyond our comprehension."

"For all you say it was easy, I for one would not know how to begin to deal with someone like that."

"Sadly, I know you're speaking for quite a large number of people. People like Lady Carswell are usually fine upstanding members of the community. But if by chance they're not, they can get away with murder—I use the term advisedly—because of a certain attitude of mind that's trained into them. They speak and act in a way that makes most people worried about challenging them, and many of Holdroyd's 'righteous' are to be found in their ranks. I suppose that the main reason that I don't share your attitude is that I knew a large number of people like Lady Carswell at University, and after a time you tend to disregard a facade you are familiar with. Dare I mention that you would probably put my wife in the same company? And I tend to find their outward manner just the same as everyone else's, something they were brought up with. A fraud is a fraud, however you wrap it up, and Lady Carswell as far as I am concerned is a fraud—not just because of her doubtful dealings in poetry. The way she turned to threats when her first line was shown to be insufficient, is also indicative of a rather unpleasant character—it's really no different from the Glasgow thug saying: 'Just wait, pal, I'll get you later.' Now I must stop ranting on about the personal characteristics of our fellow men; we've still got a lot of work to get through today. We mustn't forget that less than an hour ago you were all for dragging Miss Shaw kicking and screaming to the cells."

"I'm sorry about that, sir, but I don't think I'll jump to conclusions quite so quickly again. I'm afraid I'm not used to dealing with anything as complicated as this. On any normal murder I've come across you wouldn't find so many suspects hanging around. I've started wondering if we'll get more than the three we have already."

"By the three, I presume that you mean Eric Athlone, Jean Shaw and Lady Carswell. Don't forget Paul McLeod and the possibility of a Russian angle. And there may as you say, be more. I think I remember you saying that you had made a case out against Mr McCabe, Mr Cormack, and Miss Duncan."

"I wasn't very serious about the last three, sir, and I thought we had near enough disposed of the Russian angle."

"I hope you're right on the last point, just as I hope the school connection is a dead letter. But I'm afraid we can't totally disregard them as possibilities, however unlikely they may seem. But for all that, as far as our practical investigations are concerned, as long as we have something worthwhile to follow up, Russia and Dundee can stay in the background. If we find ourselves with nothing else, we'll have to go back to them. It's only when the rest of the field fall that the hundred-to-one outsider wins. Let's hope our favourites don't fall; there are always a large number of outsiders. Come on, though, it's time we stopped speculating, and got on with the real job. First, we'll go and see Miss Shaw, and if nothing comes of that, we'll go and see Paul McLeod again. He's probably a total red herring but we'd better make sure. If he can be consigned to the hundred-to-one group, we'll have a better idea of where we stand."

They left the office and went through the front of the station.

Before they left, Malone asked Sergeant Johnson if he had anything more of interest for them, not expecting anything of any importance, as he was sure the sergeant would have informed him already if there had been any such information.

"Nothing with any direct bearing on your case, Inspector, but there is one thing you probably ought to know, if you're likely to be seeing Mr Cormack again. I've heard through certain channels that his daughter's pregnant. He'll be taking it hard, as I'm sure he was very ambitious for her. Even with these abortions you can get with no difficulty nowadays, things will not be quite the same again, He's always been very keen on respectability; you know, it's the sort of thing that happens to other people's daughters, and usually as a sign of their parents' neglect—I'm sure you'll have come across the attitude. I must say, though, that it does appear a little hard on him."

"I quite understand, sergeant. I'll certainly bear it in mind if I need to see Mr Cormack again, although I can think of no obvious reason for having to do so at the moment."

Malone and White made their way on foot to South Street. As it was early closing day the streets were almost empty, and it occurred to Malone what a pleasant stroll it would make if he had no such business on hand to dampen his appreciation.

As they neared the residence of Miss Shaw and Miss Duncan, Malone said: "I have of course brought the fragment of material from the wall with me. I hope it won't be too embarrassing if I have to ask to match it up. I probably shall have to."

They passed down the close next to the butcher's shop, through the door labelled 'Jean Shaw and Catriona Duncan straight through' and knocked on the purple door. It was opened as before by Miss Duncan.

"Oh, the fuzz again." She spoke with a certain degree of studied casualness, but not unpleasantly. "I suppose you're wanting Jean again. You're out of luck, I'm afraid; she's gone to the laundry."

Malone realised how lucky they had been to find everyone they had gone to see already just when they wanted them, and so he was not too perturbed by her absence. He decided to take advantage of it. He asked in a matter of fact way: "I don't suppose you know what she's taken to the laundry? I mean, if you'll forgive me for suggesting it, you don't look like the sort of people who patronise such places often."

If there was an implied insult, Miss Duncan did not appear to notice it. She merely giggled.

"Wow, you fuzz really are a kinky bunch. What do you think she took to the laundry? Dirty clothes of course."

"To be specific, I was wondering if she took the pair of jeans she was wearing yesterday. To tell the truth, they certainly looked as if they needed it."

"How am I supposed to know what she decides to wash? I'm afraid. I'm not really into women's dirty clothes.'

Malone had a well-developed sense of humour, and great deal of tolerance towards the young, especially if they were of the female of the species. He now realised that it was just as well. On their last visit they had been accused of purloining confiscated drugs for their own use, this time of having an excessive interest in women's unwashed clothes. He had to admit that there appeared to be little if any malice in the accusations, and so there seemed no point in over-reacting to them. Whether they thought there could be any substance in such allegations, he was unable to say. He continued his line of questioning.

"Could you tell me how often Miss Shaw takes clothes to the laundry?'

"I've no idea; as I said, it's not the sort of thing I tend to notice. She'll be back soon, I expect, and you can ask her yourself. Perhaps you could even work out some kind of deal with her. Come into the living-room if you like. Don't be frightened, I'm not going to offer you a joint." This apparently amusing statement caused her to produce more giggling.

Malone accepted the offer, and they were shown into the living room. Although it would have been found wanting to those with the strictest views on hygiene, it was quite comfortable. Malone noted the absence of a television, and then he and White selected suitable armchairs and sat down, Miss Duncan left them on their own, shutting the door behind them.

"I hope I'm not making a big mistake, White. It's Thursday afternoon and most of the shops are shut, and therefore I find the laundry story a trifle suspect, although to be fair it's quite possible that there is some laundry open. Do you happen to know yourself?"

"I'm afraid I'm not at all sure, but it does seem that nowadays fewer and fewer shops are taking their half-day on Thursday, so it wouldn't surprise me at all. I'd also think it possible that Miss Shaw was not too sure which day of the week it was."

"Let's hope you're right. I just have this fear at the back of my mind that she may have gone out either to alter her jeans beyond recognition or destroy them altogether. I suppose the only advantage is that if she has, we'll want to know why, and be in a very strong position for questioning her. We'll just have to wait and see."

About ten minutes later Jean Shaw returned. She was hailed by her friend as soon as she came in, presumably so that she could be informed of her visitors. Malone realised that she might be told of his questions, but he thought that this might even be an advantage, if she had anything to hide. He and White stood up in expectation of her entrance, and almost immediately she came into the room. The first thing they both noticed about her was that, although she was dressed over-all in a similar fashion to before, this time she was wearing different jeans.

She addressed them first of all, in a pleasant voice with a touch of amusement in it: "Catriona tells me you've been asking about my dirty underwear. I'm afraid neither she nor I wear much of that sort of stuff. I'm sure you'd have much better luck in one of the women's residences."

Malone felt that in view of the possible serious consequences of their visit, this was hardly a way to approach them, but for his part at any rate he was unable to take offence. "Miss Shaw, you're very fortunate that I'm broad-minded about abuse of officers of the law. To give you fair warning, though, it would not always be the most sensible approach to employ with some of my colleagues. For instance, I don't get the impression that Constable White here finds it the most amusing routine since the Marx Brothers. You'll have to be careful he doesn't come snooping around here looking for illicit substances to get his own back at some future date. However, I'm here on rather serious business at the moment, but to put the record straight, it was Miss Duncan who brought up the subject of underwear and not either of us. What I did ask about, though, were the jeans you were wearing when we visited yesterday. Would you please allow me to see them?"

She seemed totally unperturbed by the request. "They're hanging in the garden to dry. I washed them in the sink this morning, so I don't suppose they'll be much good for your purposes."

Malone took this remark to be an extension of the underwear insinuation, and not some guilty slip. "Would you be good enough to bring them here?

She went outside and returned still a few moments later with the jeans, still apparently totally unworried. As she handed them to Malone, she said: "I'm surprised you haven't yet made one of those exceedingly unfunny remarks about people like me never washing our clothes and registering the standard amount of surprise to find that I do.

Well you have my secret now, I just don't make a big song and dance about it like some apparently need to."

Malone was examining some of the tears. "Do you find that some of these tears get bigger when you wash your jeans?"

"I've no idea what you're on about. Of course, if you catch a hole on something it'll get bigger, but I don't know of any magical washing powder that'll have that effect. Anyway, it doesn't bother me. I like tears in my jeans. They don't come from the shops like that, you know. You have to do it yourself and it can take quite a long time."

"I don't doubt your word on the matter, Miss Shaw. Did they happen to tear more while you were washing them this morning?"

"You're a pretty strange guy. I never expected to be questioned closely by the fuzz on the subject of the after-care of jeans. Yeah, as a matter of fact one of the tears caught on the tap and ripped so badly that I had to take the whole bit of material that was hanging loose off. It takes a bit of time afterwards to make the hole the shape you want, but I haven t got round to that yet."

"Would you please tell me what you did with the piece of material you removed totally?"

"Wow man, you're pretty screwy. Still, I haven't had any guy take such an interest in my clothes for many a dark year, so let's carry on. I don't really know. I suppose I just threw it away."

"Where?"

"Don't ask me. Just look around if you want it. I don't expect it could have walked off. It was getting pretty clean." She giggled appreciatively at her joke.

Malone detached White to look around for the piece of material, suggesting that he might call in the aid of Miss

Duncan, just in case the two young ladies were concerned about the disappearance of certain articles of their clothing. Jean Shaw raised no objection at all to the planned search, and for the first time Malone began seriously to doubt the provenance of the material he had found in Holdroyd's garden. He took it out of his pocket and tried to match it up with the holes in the jeans he was holding. There was one tear near the right knee, which was a tolerably good fit, but by no means exact. Obviously, deliberate alteration could have caused the slight discrepancy, but equally possibly the cause of the tear was something completely different. He wondered what approach he should use. She had admitted that she altered the shape of holes to suit her own artistic ideas on the matter, and he would have said that this hole had recently been altered. He decided on a frontal attack.

"Miss Shaw, I have reason to believe that you were in Mr Holdroyd's flat at about the time he met his death." He watched her carefully for her reaction and was not disappointed. The accusation had clearly given her a nasty shock.

"But I told you, I was here. I know I can't prove it as I was on my own, but you've got to believe me. Most people who live on their own or with friends who are out a lot can't prove where they were at many times of the day. Aren't I allowed to be on my own?"

To Malone's immense surprise, tears began to well up in her eyes. "You can't really believe that I had anything to do with Jim's death, can you? No, no, I couldn't have. You see, I was in love with him." She began to weep unashamedly.

Malone was taken aback by this sudden exhibition of traditional emotion, but he decided he had better carry on. "I'm very sorry, Miss Shaw, but this piece of material I brought with me, was taken from a nail in the wall at the bottom of Mr Holdroyd's garden. You, or someone answering your description, was seen coming from the close in Market street which leads directly to that wall. The time, as far as we can judge, was just after the time of death. The material, as you can see, is clearly of the same sort of cloth and age as your jeans. Moreover, it's a pretty good fit for this hole here. The right knee would be just where we would have expected to find the hole, after considering the position of the nail in the wall."

She seemed to look a little relieved rather than more disturbed by these last revelations. "It's not true, Inspector, I was here all the time. Goodness knows I'd have loved to have been in Jim's place; I'd have loved to live there. But he never invited me round there, and I was sort of frightened of him. I know I tried to give you a different impression last time you were here, but he never appeared to take any interest in my body. God, he wouldn't have had to mention it twice. But I respected him as well, and he told me once that he had given up being serious with women about ten years ago. He told me that the only woman he had ever loved had eventually told him that he was a failure with no ambition and had gone off and got married to some rich man. If I got hold of that woman, I don't know what I wouldn't do to her—yes, even now. But you must believe me; I wouldn't have hurt Jim in any way."

"Miss Shaw, quite honestly, I would love to be able to believe you. But the evidence pointing to your presence in Mr Holdroyd's flat on Tuesday night is still rather strong. As I feared, Constable White and Miss Duncan are finding some difficulty in locating your supposed piece of material. Can you tell me if it came from the hole I have mentioned, or some other part of the jeans?"

"I think it's that hole, and I hope so even more now. Do you want me to help look for it? It can't be far off."

"Certainly, if it is not found in the near future."

"By the way, when you say that somebody saw a chick looking like me coming out of that close in Market Street, did you ask him how he knew for sure that it was a chick? A lot of guys do their best to look like that nowadays, if that's the right way round. Anyway, it's called the unisex look." Malone pointed out that he was aware of this approach to sartorial elegance but was also forced to admit that that sort of confusion was not impossible. Privately, however, he thought that such a mistake was less likely in someone as young as Sean Murphy than it would be for him. She continued: "Anyway, there must be dozens of people answering my description around. I can't see how your informant could possibly have given an accurate description in the dark, especially with the moon behind the person, unless he was close enough to be absolutely positive about the identity. No, don't ask me how I know the moon was behind the person. Obviously, if you're coming here from the end of Market Street—if you think it was me, I suppose he or she was coming in this direction—and there was a bright moon in the west, the moon will be behind you. I know the moon was in the west, because I was watching it out of this window here, which, if you hadn't noticed, faces west. As I say, I was here; you say I was in South Street and then Market Street. You say that piece of material comes from my jeans; I say it doesn't. You say I killed Jim: I say I didn't. If the best bits of evidence you can produce are an old piece of denim and a doubtful figure in the dark—if it wasn't doubtful you'd have said so by now—I think I should probably be all right."

Death of a Dundee Teacher

"There is always the question of motive. Now if you and Mr Holdroyd had fallen out over the distribution or sale of some drugs..."

"For Christ's sake, I keep telling you, Jim never touched dope or drugs of any sort. The idea of him dealing in it is totally loopy. I suppose he's got vast amounts of unexplained money, and you're trying to find some way of accounting for it?"

Malone was temporarily stunned. First, she had got the direction of the moon and the pedestrian correct, and now she seemed to know about the extra money. "I must ask you what reason you have for suggesting that Mr Holdroyd had sums of unexplained money."

"I didn't know. But you keep on about this dope, and I know you'll find nobody who knows anything about Jim who would possibly suggest that he had any dealings with it. So, I presumed you must have some reason for going on about it, and the obvious one is that he's got more money than you expected him to have. Exactly why anyone should want to kill a small-time dope-dealer in the first place escapes me. If he gave bad deals, all his customers would need to do is go elsewhere. It's not a government monopoly yet, you know."

Malone tried once more: "I think there's one thing I should make quite clear, Miss Shaw. We are in no way convinced that Mr Holdroyd's death was necessarily an act of murder, in the strict definition of the word. There was of course an assault, but we feel that it was quite possible that it was an unpremeditated attack, and that death was caused unintentionally. That would be a far less serious charge than murder."

If he was expecting this statement to precipitate a confession, he was sadly disappointed. The effect on Jean

Shaw was that she began to look tearful again, and said in a quiet voice: "Look, it doesn't really matter a damn to me at the moment how Jim died. He's dead and you ought to appreciate how I feel about it. And I'll tell you for the last time, I didn't kill him, either by accident or on purpose."

Malone fully expected the tears to begin again, but the re-entry of White altered the situation. "With the assistance of Miss Duncan, I've managed to find the piece of material Miss Shaw referred to, sir. It was lying at the back of the dustbins in the coalshed. Clearly through carelessness she missed her target, and hence the long search. He held out a fragment of blue denim. Malone took it and tried to match it with the hole near the right knee. It was nowhere near the right size. He tried another couple of holes, and eventually located the one from which it had come. He then turned to Miss Shaw.

"I was hoping that this might be of some assistance to your case, but as it does not explain the hole in the right knee, all I can say is that it makes your position no worse than it was when we came in. Is there no little fact you can think of which would establish that you were here around midnight on Tuesday night?"

"I don't think there's anything. I didn't even have the light on, as the moon was shining quite brightly enough through that window for my purposes. No, there's absolutely nothing."

Malone looked at her for a few moments with a certain amount of compassion. "Miss Shaw, I shall have to ask you to stay in St. Andrews and report at the Police Station every morning and evening until further notice. If you should fail to do so, I shall have no alternative but to place you under arrest. May I assure you that if you feel like telling us anything else, you will be listened to with the greatest sympathy."

"For Christ's sake, fuck off," shouted Miss Shaw.

🙰 Chapter 10

"INSPECTOR MALONE." SAID SERGEANT JOHNSON URGENTLY. He had clearly been awaiting their return to the Police Station with some impatience. "I'm afraid it looks as if young Eric Athlone has skipped."

"What?" said Malone, in genuine amazement.

"It seems to be so. About half an hour ago a lad called Jimmy Robertson, who's a friend of his, came in with a letter for you. I asked him why young Athlone had not brought it himself, and he replied that he didn't know, and he was just doing a favour for a pal. I then asked him where Athlone was, and he smiled and said that he'd gone to Edinburgh. Thinking that we could have him picked up as soon as the train reached Edinburgh, I of course tried to find out which train he was getting. Young Jimmy continued to smile at me in an insolent manner—the way these young lads do now— and said that he'd been asked not to deliver the letter until after the train reached Edinburgh; as he had said, he was just doing a favour for a pal. I next asked him if he knew whereabouts in Edinburgh Athlone was going, but he said that he had no idea, and I must admit that I believed him. I can of course get young Jimmy in again if you'd like to question him yourself."

"I don't think it'll be necessary, sergeant. If this letter contains what I think it does, we'll just need to get the Edinburgh men in right away. That is, if he really is in Edinburgh; if he is, I'm sure they'll be able to pick him up quite easily. Well, it looks as if I've been all sorts of fool. I've only just restrained myself from arresting two separate women already this afternoon.

He opened the letter and after a few lines a smile appeared on his face. By the time he had finished it he was chuckling audibly. He put the letter down and said: "I'm very sorry. Actually, there's nothing particularly amusing in it at all. You'll understand from my reaction that it does not contain a confession. I suppose theoretically I should be sorry, as that would almost certainly have brought the case to an end. However, I'm not sorry, and I hope that's not just because of personal pride in being right. I'm sure you'll feel the same way, sergeant. It's been pretty clear all along that you didn't think the lad was capable of doing any such deed."

"If I may say so, sir," interrupted White, "just because he hasn't confessed in no way means that he can't be guilty."

"You are of course quite correct to point that out, but a few moments ago, when I first heard of his disappearance, I had to assume he was guilty. But the letter gives a very good reason for his departure. I'd better tell you what it says. It seems that when the poor chap got home, he expected a warm welcome. After all he's just a youngster, and he'd suffered rather a nasty shock. On top of that he'd been as near as you can get to being accused of murdering a man, whom, on his own confession he loved. What actually met him at home was somewhat different. His father—he doesn't explain why he was at home in the first place—immediately started beating him up, maintaining that he wouldn't have any bloody poofter in his house. Young Eric's understandable reaction was to relieve his father of that dreadful burden. He says he'll let me know where he's staying as soon as he can, and ring me at seven o'clock anyway to inform me of where he is then. He adds some complimentary remarks about how sympathetic policemen are. If I'd known he was going to Edinburgh, I would probably have pointed out that some of the force there are by no means as broad-minded about such matters as we are."

"Inspector, you are of course quite right in suggesting that I did not believe Eric Athlone was the guilty party. But for all that, I think that Constable White is right. It looks very much to me as if he's made a bolt for it. That letter with the offer of telephoning at seven may simply be a way of gaining more time to get himself hidden. Don't you think it would be sensible to get him picked up as soon as possible?"

"If he really has made a bolt for it, sergeant, I credit him with more sense than to tell us his true destination. We'd probably be just as well looking for him in Bolton or Kingsbarns if that is the case. If he hasn't rung up by half-past seven, I'll certainly have to do something about it; but rightly or wrongly I believe him. I suppose we can do one thing immediately, though. We can find out if his story about his father's actions on his return is correct. Is he on the telephone?" Sergeant Johnson nodded his assent. "Well, as you know him, do you think you could ring him up and find out if that part at any rate is true?"

The sergeant went off to the main telephone, leaving Malone looking a little worried. "It can't be him." he said at last to White. "Can you really imagine a young chap like that in the state of exhaustion he was in, subjected to a day and a half in isolation with a policeman at his door in addition, not breaking down if he was in fact guilty? Some would do so even if they were innocent. Could Dr Crenshaw be so far out in his timing of the death? Can it be purely by chance that an unsolicited statement from a Dundee schoolgirl appears to confirm his timing of the death? I know that Dr Stewart could not be absolutely exact about the time that he left his house, but could he really have run to South Street with no-one noticing, then have committed the crime, and after that spend an hour covering up his traces, but forgetting to wipe the weapon he actually used? I know some sort of explanation could be produced, but not one which is normally credible. The alibi at Dr Stewart's would have to have been set up, and then some remarkable acting put on. If he was as cool about it as that, why didn't he turn the watch back, to cover himself completely?"

"He could have been unaware that the watch was broken, and I don't suppose anyone, however cool they might appear, really likes tampering with things on a dead man's person."

"That's undoubtedly possible, but the broken watch was one of the first things you yourself noticed. Any such explanation presupposes a degree of premeditation, but the weapon hardly seems premeditated. It's the sort of thing you get in Edwardian parlour games, but not very likely in fact, unless it was the first thing that came to hand. I don't find any such version likely at all."

"If it's any help, I quite agree with you sir. The original point I wanted to make was that even if we found that there was a good reason for his departure for Edinburgh, it made him no less and no more guilty than we had thought him before. It was just that I didn't think we could forget about him totally, merely because we felt sorry for him"

"You produce the correct note of caution, White. I suppose it really does get down to a question of simple personal pride; like everyone else, I hate to be proved wrong. Well, let's hope to goodness he rings at seven."

Sergeant Johnson reappeared. "I've rung up Davie Athlone. It's his day off, and that's why he was in when his son got back from the hospital. He said that of course he had hammered the boy. He'd brought a lot of trouble on his mother by this business, I was told. To have to be told by several people on top that his son was a fruit was too much for anyone to stand, he said. His view is that Eric won't have gone far, and he'll be back soon. He thinks he's taught him a valuable lesson which he won't forget in a hurry."

"Strange beliefs some people have. By the way, sergeant, what would you do? Would you hammer a son of yours if you were told that he was a 'fruit', apparently without any attempt to establish whether it was true or not in the first place?"

White could not restrain a smile at the thought of his sergeant being forced to answer such a question. He was, however, surprised by the moderation of the answer.

"I don't really know, but I hope I wouldn't hit the boy for something which after all would hardly be his fault. I suppose it's a bit like finding your daughter's pregnant; it's bound to be a big shock at first, but most people learn to live with it. One thing I can say is that I wouldn't believe I could suddenly change his attitude by beating him up. It's more likely to strengthen it, I'd have thought. I certainly hope that before I took any action, if I did take any, I'd make sure that the information was correct."

"I think your view is more representative than most people realise, sergeant. I think I shall stick to my former faith in the lad, until he fails to ring up, if he fails to. Now I'd better put you in the picture about Miss Shaw, in case she happens to come in while I'm not here. We really have as good evidence against her as anyone else at the present moment."

He explained the position. "What she really seems to lack is any good motive, unless we fall back onto traditional views such as Hell having no fury like a woman scorned. That is indeed a possibility. The rather doubtful suspicion of some sort of irregularity with drugs has rather been overshadowed by the discovery of where Holdroyd got his extra funds. I'm inclined to accept that Miss Shaw's repeated denials finally screw the lid down on that theory. I think our best course would be to have another chat with Paul McLeod. He, if anyone, will supply information about any possible cause of a rift between Holdroyd and Miss Shaw, out of spite if no other reason. Incidentally, he and Mr Cormack, and possibly Lady Carswell, seem to be the only people who doubt the exceptional honesty of Holdroyd that we keep hearing of. I wonder if we shouldn't try to speak to Mrs Cormack sometime? After all, she does seem to be one of the few people who knew the dead man well, and women often notice things which we just take for granted. Don't worry, sergeant if I do see her, I'll remember about the daughter. Well, White, do you feel like braving the atmosphere of Paul McLeod's abode? I thought we both stood up to it remarkably well last time. I'd like you to come with me if you would. It has so far been an exceedingly unrewarding day. As the poet said:

"Solamen miseris socios habuisse doloris."

No translation was offered, and White decided not to give Malone the satisfaction of being asked for one. He simply followed him out of the Police Station. They again walked to their destination, as it was only a few hundred yards.

"We've almost certainly pushed our luck too far this time," said Malone. "We've been extraordinarily lucky in finding everyone so easily. If this is different, we shouldn't be too surprised."

White was fully expecting some such difficulty to arise. So far, they had only once had to wait a few minutes, and if Paul McLeod was a little more elusive second time around, he was not going to let it put him out. He wondered why the Inspector had bothered to mention it, and came to the conclusion that, however well he might be trying to conceal it, Malone must be feeling the strain imposed by the uncertainty of the case.

The prediction was in fact correct. The door was opened as before by the individual called Jock, he informed them that, as was his habit between about five and seven o' clock, Paul McLeod was in the Carleton Bar. They'd be sure to find him there if they wanted him. Malone pointed out that they were reluctant to embarrass him more than was absolutely necessary, and people had a way of recognising stray policemen fetching customers out of bars. At this, Jock offered to fetch him for them and told them to make themselves comfortable till he should return.

White had assumed that this was some stratagem for getting the flat to themselves, and was surprised when Malone merely sat down in one of the armchairs in the room they had been left in. He therefore sat down too, in a chair which felt as though many a can of beer, having failed to find the throat of its intended recipient, had instead in vain attempted to feed the sparse material which covered it. To White's question as to the purpose of getting Jock out of the way Malone replied:

"No, White, there was no ulterior motive. If you hadn't noticed, I've gone through quite a lot today, and honestly an embarrassing scene in the pub would be more than I could put up with; and as I said, I see no future in putting Paul McLeod against us by not exercising simple tact."

They had nearly a quarter of an hour to wait before Paul McLeod returned. He was on his own. Presumably Jock had stayed in the pub to keep out of the way. It was clear from his attitude that their visitor was not pleased at being dragged away from his second womb; his appearance still gave Malone the impression of ambiguous sex, but his features also displayed a somewhat truculent expression. Malone reflected that Jean Shaw had had a strong point when she had suggested that their informant, Sean Murphy, could easily have been mistaken about the sex of the person he had seen so indistinctly.

"Have you come to arrest me on some trumped-up charge, then?" he said in a voice echoing the expression on his face.

"That was certainly not our original intention, Mr McLeod, unless of course you are about to provide us with information to indicate that course. No, actually I've come to ask for your help. We are rather lacking in personal information about Mr Holdroyd. Although it was clear from our last meeting that your opinion of him was, to put it mildly, rather low, you still seem to know more about him than most people we've come across."

"As far as I'm concerned, the less I know about the sod the better."

"I appreciate that that's the way you feel but do remember he's dead and isn't going to affect your life anymore. But I very much got the impression that, because of the relationship you suspected..."

"Suspected! She was absolutely nuts about him. Anyone with half a brain could see that. And women don't get that way about a man from talking to him. Oh yeah, I'm sure it's all very easy for these middle-aged smoothies, putting on that act of immense experience behind them. They know all the chicks fall for that line. It's just the flattery scene all over again. Isn't it exciting when a man like that takes an interest in me, they think. Bloody fools; why can't they see that the only reason they go after young chicks like them is that they can't fool people of their own age? They're just a bunch of failures who are frightened of growing up. Why the hell he had to pick on Jean for his nasty games I don't know. There must have been dozens of others for him to play his smoothie game with. I'm sure it would have made no difference to him who it was, as long as she fell for his smoothie line. And what the hell she saw in him, I don't know."

"Is there any other reason apart from this suspected relationship why you should have taken so strong a dislike to Mr Holdroyd?"

"Look, I can't stand that type of smoothie anyway, as I've already made quite clear. The way he and his pals hang around a bar where everyone except themselves is quite young is literally obscene. I've told you why they did it. Anyway, you can be sure it wasn't to stare at guys like me. He was a bloody hypocrite, too. You should have heard Jean going on about his wonderful honesty, and how rare it was, especially in men. I thought she'd have grown out of that sort of rubbish when she stopped reading her Prince Charming stories. Made him sound just like the handsome king's son out of every little girl's dreams."

"Have you any specific reasons to disbelieve in this supposed honesty of his?"

"I told you before, didn't I? He actually stood there on several occasions and told me in his smoothie way that all he did with Jean was have a drink and chat with her. Is that the talk of an honest man? I nearly punched his head in a number of times."

Malone considered Paul McLeod's physique. Perhaps there was some well-disguised power somewhere, but in general he decided that it would be most unwise for him to attempt to punch anyone's head in, unless their arms were firmly anchored behind their backs first.

"You say that Miss Shaw was 'nuts' about Mr Holdroyd. Do you happen to know if she ever visited him in his own flat?"

"I must admit that that was a funny thing. I don't think that she ever did. To me though, that just indicates again the sod's attitude. It was all right for him to go and see her whenever it happened to suit him, but he was too mighty or respectable, or some such crap, to have her coming to see him. I suppose he thought that his place with its fancy books and violin was too good for her."

"You know his flat then?"

He was clearly very much taken aback by this sudden question. However, he recovered himself quickly and said:

"No, I don't mean to give that impression at all. I've never been there myself. But I've been told he plays the violin—that shows his age for the start—and guys like that always have a lot of books, usually fancy ones too. I don't suppose for a minute they ever read them, but they keep them there to impress their visitors, especially when it's young chicks they're trying to knock off."

"They wouldn't be much use for the purpose you suggest, Mr McLeod, if he never invited the young chicks round in the first place."

"Just because he never invited Jean round doesn't mean that he didn't do it to others. Maybe that was why he didn't encourage her to come. She might have seen what else he got up to. If I was her, I wouldn't have put up with it for one bloody minute. I offered to knock his head in for her on several occasions, but all she said was that I wouldn't dare. Well, I can tell you I would have dared. I'm only sorry it's too late now to prove it. When she said that I got really angry. Whenever I asked her why she allowed him to treat her the way he did, I always got a lot of nonsense off her.

She'd tell me how I didn't understand, and after all, she was a woman, and quite liked being treated like one from time to time. She wouldn't have dared say that in front of most of her friends. She always went on with that romantic fairytale rubbish, like I say, as if she was some innocent little girl. It made me want to puke, I can tell you."

Malone began to wonder how much of these ravings was the result of the drink he had been taking—he had clearly begun long before five o' clock—and how much was caused by his undoubted love for Jean Shaw. Despite the rather unpleasant way that he was carrying on and the unnecessary repetition they were being subjected to, Malone had to admit that he felt a certain amount of compassion for the young man. It is hard at the best of times to feel you have failed with the woman you love, but when your apparent opponent is of a type which you have habitually despised, it becomes almost impossible to bear. He supposed that Paul McLeod, like almost everyone else in this world to a greater or lesser degree, would have to accept this cruel aspect of life sooner or later. He continued his questions.

"Do you think it possible that Miss Shaw herself could have done any harm to Mr Holdroyd?"

"What are you trying to suggest now? Do you think she bumped him off? If so, you're right up the creek. Even if I had hoped she might feel like that towards him, I now know better. Before you think I'm making some sort of admission, I'd better tell you why. I went to see her not long after you'd left her yesterday. All I got from her was how difficult it was trying to keep up a front in the presence of you guys, when all she wanted to do was lie down and be cuddled by her Jim. You can imagine how I felt about that. Then I was subjected to a great outflow of tears. If she expected me to be sympathetic in the circumstances, she was wrong. God knows how he brought her down to that sate—she was like one of those nineteenth-century weeping heroines you read about. Anyway, I'm damned sure she wouldn't have reacted in that way if he'd just been drinking tea with her. In some ways I felt quite sorry the bastard was dead. I felt like going off there and then and smashing his face in. And don't get moral about attitudes to the dead. I hated him, and I see no reason to deny it now."

"If you'll forgive me, Mr McLeod, I am here on business. Now if I may make a summary of what you've been saying, will you tell me if it's correct? Can I take it that you do not believe in Mr Holdroyd's honesty, you don't think that Miss Shaw would have done him actual bodily harm, but you yourself would have done so if you had had the chance?"

"Right on all three. But don't try putting anything on me just because I'm pleased he's dead. As I told you, I was asleep in here from the time I got back from the pub on Tuesday night."

"Yes, I know that you have told us that, Mr McLeod, but so far we have only got your word for it. Have you considered any way in which you could corroborate your claim?"

"How do you expect me to have any witnesses for what I was doing when I was asleep? Plenty of people saw me leaving the pub, as clearly you know, and I could find plenty of others who'd tell you how much I'd been drinking all day. There wasn't much else I could have done except crash out afterwards. Nobody saw me any later, because I was asleep here."

White, who as usual had held his peace while the Inspector was asking questions, now saw fit to enter the conversation. "If I may interrupt, sir, I have been fascinated for some time by that new patch on the right knee of Mr McLeod's jeans."

Malone stared. Good heavens, was he becoming that obtuse? He knew that he was very tired, but after Miss Shaw's remarks about unisex dress, and his recalling of them when they had seen Paul McLeod again, he should have been looking for exactly that sort of thing. And yet he had not noticed it. With the unreasonable attitude of those who are genuinely over-tired, he said:

"Thank you, Constable White, I was about to question Mr McLeod on that very point." He was sorry as soon as he had said it, but concluded that in the circumstances there was no point in apologising at this juncture.

"Mr McLeod, would you be good enough to tell us how long you have had that patch Constable White has just mentioned on your jeans? If I may say so, it looks like a fairly recent addition."

Paul McLeod was visibly disturbed, far more so than when the suggestion that he knew Holdroyd's flat had been made. He spoke in the same sort of truculent voice with which he had begun the interview.

"What the hell has the state of my jeans got to do with you fuzz? They gave up national service quite a long time ago, you know."

"Mr McLeod, I asked a simple question, and if it's not too much effort, I would like a simple answer. Would you be good enough to give me one? I repeat, how long have you had that patch on the right knee of your jeans?"

He eventually decided to answer, and said in an evasive manner: "How do you expect me to remember exactly? I don't keep a diary of everything I do. As far as I remember it was pretty recently. I think it was probably the day before yesterday, but I'm not at all sure."

Death of a Dundee Teacher

"I think I can expect you to remember, especially if it was done in the last couple of days. May I suggest that you did not put it on the day before yesterday, but that you put it on either yesterday or today?"

"As I told you, I can't be expected to remember these things. And I can't see what the hell repairs to my jeans have got to do with you anyway. Also, you may not have noticed, but it's a fashion we have nowadays. I'm not the only person who likes to patch my jeans, and I've also done it before." He stood up, turned around, and exhibited further patches for their inspection. "See, I've got them on the back as well. Has that become illegal since the last time I heard?"

Malone, because of his tiredness, was finding it increasingly difficult to keep an even temper. "It is indeed very considerate of you to show us your artistic efforts. However, at the moment I am not interested in fashions or your particular interpretation of them. I am interested in the patch you sewed onto your jeans at the right knee either today or yesterday. Would you be good enough to remove that patch?"

Paul McLeod now began to look very worried indeed, but for all that persisted in his defensive line. "I thought you people were paid to notice things. You saw me yesterday, didn't you? You should know whether I had this patch on then or not."

"May I point out that yesterday did not conclude with our visit here? The actual time that you put the patch on is however of secondary interest to me. Primarily I want to know what it's concealing."

"What the hell's all this about? I can do what I want with my own clothes, can't I? That patch took me a long time to put on, and I see no earthly reason why I should take it off just to suit you fuzz. Why don't you take your old-fashioned fascist stuff elsewhere? I've no intention of removing it."

Malone was relieved that he had taken up this line in the end. He was far too used to it to be perturbed by the approach, and it was also a sure indication that he was on the right track. "Mr McLeod, if you will not take off that patch voluntarily, I shall have to ask you to accompany me to the Police Station. I would not make any such request if I was not sure that it was necessary to the performance of my duty. If you continue to refuse, I shall be forced to use all the means at my disposal to encourage you to co-operate, not excluding what you call 'fascist stuff.'"

Paul McLeod looked at Malone, who looked back at him in a calm manner. He also looked at White, but there was no sign of weakness there either. There was silence for a while. He appeared to be about to say something, then began fidgeting, and eventually got up and went over to a drawer. He took out a pair of scissors and began to pick out the stitches around the patch. It did not take him long, for despite his protestations, the number of threads he had to deal with indicated necessary haste rather than painstaking tailoring. When he had finally removed the patch, he tossed it over to Malone and said: "There you are; it may come in handy sometime. you can keep it."

Malone was far too interested in what lay beneath the patch to be troubled by this gratuitous insult. He took the piece of material he had removed from Holdroyd's wall from his pocket. While doing so he watched for the reaction. It was immediate and obvious. A look of near horror passed over his face. Malone said: "Constable White, may I ask you to ascertain if this piece of material came from the right knee of Mr McLeod's jeans?

White walked over to Paul McLeod, having taken the piece of material from Malone. No attempt at a protest was made as he matched it up with the hole. "It's an almost exact fit, I'd say, sir."

Malone continued in a quiet, almost fatherly voice: "Mr McLeod, I think it would really be a lot easier for all of us if you now told us exactly what you were doing on Tuesday night. Before you try some tangential line, I think it would be fair to tell you exactly where I found that piece of material. It was attached to a nail in the wall at the bottom of Mr Holdroyd's garden. No, please don't interrupt me. I am well aware of the fact that there are hundreds of pairs of jeans in St. Andrews of similar age and material. However, I don't think it very likely that we would find quite such a good fit for our fragment in any of the others, especially on the right knee, the very place we expected to find damaged. Nor, incidentally, am I likely to believe that it was planted there by someone who wished to get you into trouble. If we add to this undoubted piece of evidence against you the fact that on your own repeated admission you held a strong dislike of Mr Holdroyd for personal reasons, we have quite enough to connect you with events in South Street on Tuesday night. But in fact, we have something else as well. We have a witness who saw you emerge from the close in Market Street which corresponds to the rear of Mr Holdroyd's house. The time was shortly after half-past twelve on Tuesday night. Yes, before you ask, he would almost certainly be able to make a positive identification of you. That is to say, you would need to have positive proof that you were elsewhere, and your present story does not provide that sort of proof. Our witness was even aware of your attempt to be mistaken for a woman. He got just close enough to you to disabuse himself of the impression."

This final exaggeration had its desired effect, and Paul McLeod gave a gesture of resignation.

🔊 Chapter 11

PAUL MCLEOD WAS CLEARLY VERY SHAKEN. He took tobacco and cigarette papers out of his pocket. With unsteady hands he tried to roll himself a cigarette. The tobacco kept falling off, but eventually he managed to produce some sort of smoke and light it. When he spoke, his earlier truculent manner had totally disappeared, and was replaced by a peculiar jittery, jerky style of delivery.

"I promise you I had absolutely nothing to do with his death. When I got there he was dead already. You must believe me. At first, I intended to go to the Police Station and report it, but as I was leaving the close door, I heard somebody in South Street. I panicked and imagined getting arrested for murdering him. You'll know how loudly footfalls echo in the town at that time of night. I immediately thought it must be policeman. I..."

"Mr McLeod, you're not being very clear. I suggest it would be better if you told us exactly what you did from the time you left the St. David's Hotel."

"All right, if you want me to do it that way. I'd had a lot to drink by that time—I'm like that most days, but I was even more so on Tuesday night. That's probably one of the reasons that I was even more annoyed than usual with Holdroyd. As you've heard, I told him exactly what I thought of him, and then left. I was meaning to come straight back here to bed, but you know the feeling of finality that can give you, especially when it's not even closing time. So I didn't come here straightaway. I dropped in to the Carleton for a couple, with a sort of vague hope that something a bit more exciting than going to bed would turn up. You could easily have found that out if you'd asked in the Carleton, but as you haven't mentioned it, I suppose you haven't been there. As nothing did turn up, as usually happens, I went home at closing time. Then I started thinking about that Jim Holdroyd, and what he might be doing to Jean. I don't suppose you've got any idea what it's like to be in love with someone and know that she might be with some other man who doesn't care tuppence about her. What I decided was that I'd go and hammer him when he got home. I don't know if I'd have been capable, but that wasn't a consideration that bothered me at the time. Anyway, in spite of all the drink I'd already had, I decided to have a couple more drams before I went. I don't know the exact time, but it must have been well after twelve when I reached his flat. I saw the light on in his front room, and I started wondering if he had Jean in there. I was almost going to go away—you'll appreciate that I preferred not to know if my guess was correct—but then it struck me that the best time to hammer him was when she was looking on. The close door was open and I went straight up. I was very surprised to find his inside front door open too. There was no noise from inside, so I walked in. It struck me that he must be drunk, and I was glad because I thought it would make it easier for me. I'm quite honestly a bit of a physical coward, but I really wanted to batter him. Then I saw him lying on the floor. I was a bit sorry about that, because I didn't think I'd get much pleasure out of kicking him when he was too much in a stupor to know about it. I kicked him gently a few times to try and get him to come round. Then I suddenly realised that if he was that drunk he should be making a lot of noise breathing. I looked at him and noticed the bash in the side of his head and realised that someone else had been there before me. It still hadn't really registered with me that he might be dead. I suppose I just thought that someone had robbed him and hit him over the head. As I said before,

Death of a Dundee Teacher

I had decided to go round to the Police Station to report it, but as I went into the close I heard those footsteps and it suddenly occurred to me that I might well be accused of something. After all I had no good reason for being there. It was then that the possibility of his being dead flashed across my mind. I was at a loss as to what to do, and quickly went down the close to the back. I was just intending to hide down there at first, because I had no idea how easy it would be to get out that way. These was a bright moon that night as you'll remember, and when I saw the wall at the back, it suddenly struck me that I could probably make my way out over it. So I went down the path to the bottom and stood on what I think was a compost heap. I could see a path clearly the other side which appeared to lead into a passageway which would go out into Market Street. I started climbing over the wall, but got my jeans caught on that nail. That really worried me, as it felt as if somebody was trying to prevent me getting away. I pulled as hard as I could, and a bit of material ripped off. I didn't give it much consideration at the time. I was too pleased at getting over. I then hurried down the path, and soon found myself in Market Street. I saw a fellow who looked a bit drunk on the other side of the road—by that time the shock of what had happened had made me feel quite sober. Guys like you are always saying that I look like a woman, and I decided to take advantage of it. He was obviously hoping I was, as he started crossing the road as soon as he saw me. I hurried off trying to imitate the style of a coy woman. After a bit I looked round and couldn't see him any longer, so I assumed he either lived in Market Street or had taken a turning off it. To tell you the truth, I was quite certain that he hadn't got a good look at me. I wondered what to do next. I knew no-one had seen me leaving Holdroyd's flat, and when I thought about it, I couldn't remember touching anything there—even the doors had been wide open. I also thought I had fooled the person in Market Street. The best thing seemed to be to disappear for a bit. I decided to go to Jean's and pretend that I was too tired or drunk to go home. I knew she'd let me kip on the floor, even if that was all. But then I knew I wouldn't be able to stop myself telling her what I considered to be the good news about Jim Holdroyd. There was no telling how she'd react, and although I was nearly at her place by then, I doubled back and went home."

"Thank you, Mr McLeod, I'd say your story hangs together quite well. It certainly does not contradict any of the information we already have. Now will you tell me if you saw anyone while you were on your way to Mr Holdroyd's flat?"

"I don't think so. I don't really remember. That's to say, I wasn't really watching out."

"Mr McLeod I would have thought that anyone on their way to commit a criminal assault would be rather careful about not being seen."

"Criminal assault? I suppose it would have been, according to your way of looking at things. It seemed to me as if I was about to do the most honest deed of my life."

"You are entitled to your private opinion, but sadly I am not allowed mine in this sort of matter. The law decides the thing for me. The point I am trying to establish is whether you can prove that you did not arrive in South street until well after twelve."

"I certainly don't remember seeing anyone, and there was nobody here to see me leave."

"May I ask how you know that it was well after twelve when you arrived there?"

"I can't be absolutely sure, but as I never wear a watch my ideas about the time are usually pretty accurate."

Malone was not at all sure that this was a very convincing argument. "In fact, there is no way you can prove you were not there shortly before twelve, or considerably after half-past."

"No, I suppose there isn't."

"Therefore, as far as I know, you could have gone there any time after you left the Carleton. As you have already gone to considerable lengths to deceive me, I see no reason for taking your word for anything. Now will you tell me if you saw anything of the weapon which killed. Mr Holdroyd?"

"I didn't notice anything like that. I wasn't there for very long and all I was interested in was him."

"So it could have been lying by the body, and you wouldn't have noticed?"

"I suppose so. As I say, I wasn't looking for that sort of thing."

"And you saw nothing of the person you heard in South Street?"

"No. As I told you, I assumed it was one of you people, and I went round the back as quickly as I could. I don't know if the person, whoever it was, was just walking past. I didn't stop to see."

"The only person who can corroborate any of your story is our witness from Market Street. I may as well admit to having practised a slight deception on you. In fact, he could not have identified you, and is quite convinced that the person he saw was a woman. As he can make no positive identification, I see no reason for believing any of your story at this juncture. Did you see anyone else on your way to Miss Shaw's, or from there back to here?"

"I'm not absolutely positive, but I think I saw that Jim Cormack—he's one of those middle-aged guys who used to hang around with Jim Holdroyd—coming out of the public lavatory. I think I made sure that he didn't see me though. What I thought at the time was that he must have been up to something like that Holdroyd was with Jean. I didn't want him to see me, and even if things had been different, I'd have done my best to avoid speaking to him. I've told you already what I think of that type of person."

"You are not certain that it was Mr Cormack you saw?"

"Not absolutely certain, but I think it was. I didn't get close enough to be able to swear to it. I've no idea how their wives put up with it.'

"And you don't think Mr Cormack, or whoever it was, saw you?"

Paul McLeod's unpleasant conversational style was returning. "I did all I could to make sure that he didn't, but you can never tell with that sort of person. They could notice something and not let on, hoping to use it against you later."

"As far as I can see, then, there is absolutely nobody who can confirm your version of what you were doing and when you were doing it. Tell me, Mr McLeod, do you wear gloves?"

"What?"

"I said: do you wear gloves?"

"No, never, not since I was a schoolboy cycling to school. Why do you want to know?"

"Never mind, it's probably a point of no importance. But now let me tell you what would occur to the mind of the average man about your actions on Tuesday night. You admit with readiness that you disliked Mr Holdroyd, and further had a specific reason for doing so. In addition, there are plenty of witnesses to the fact that you threatened Mr

Holdroyd earlier that very evening. You admit that you went to his flat with the intention of assaulting him. You say that you found him in an unconscious state when you reached his flat, which you entered without permission; and yet you made no attempt to contact the police or medical services, though you were under the impression that there was an officer of the law just outside in the street. You left by a route designed to conceal the fact of your presence in the flat. Given the circumstances, I'm sure that no juryman will accept your reasons for your rather peculiar method of trying to hide your identity from a casual passer-by in Market street, and later on from someone of your acquaintance. The fact that the first version you gave of your movements on Tuesday night was a total fabrication would also be taken into account. Now I shall tell you the probable time of Mr Holdroyd's death. It occurred shortly before twelve o'clock. You say that you did not arrive at the flat until about half-past, but you produce no evidence for this except that you thought it was about that time. The average juryman, in case you are unaware of the fact, has at some time during his life experienced the effect of excessive drink, and the result it can have on personal ideas of the time. Many will also know that it is possible to be unaware of what one is doing when in such a state. In short, Mr McLeod, can you think of any good reason why I should not arrest you for the murder of Mr James Holdroyd?"

"I tell you, it's not true!"

"Yes, Mr McLeod, but I have already pointed out, you told me a number of things which you were later forced to admit were lies. Why should I believe your present story in preference to the last one?" He was not expecting any answer, and he did not receive one. After a few moments, he continued: "The only reason that I am not arresting you now, is because there are one or two points I would like to clarify before taking such a step. You will report at the Police Station at nine o'clock tomorrow morning, at three in the afternoon, and again at nine o'clock tomorrow evening. I may add that if you fail to do so, it will be taken as a strong presumption of guilt. You should also be aware that the police are very efficient at tracing people who try to disappear, especially if they are wanted in connection with a case of murder."

Malone rose, and White followed suit. As they were taking their leave, Malone said: "If you feel like coming to the Police Station at any time to make a statement, please do so. Don't worry, we'll see ourselves out."

When they had regained the street and the pure air, Malone said: "Thank you very much for pointing out that patch. I suppose I must have noticed it, but the significance totally escaped me, despite my remarks at the time. I think you'll understand why I didn't place him under arrest. Although he seems a more likely candidate than Lady Carswell or Eric Athlone, not forgetting Jean Shaw as well, the possible involvement of any or all of these three makes the case against him far from certain. Things are getting very bizarre, though. We establish that it was very rare for anyone ever to visit Holdroyd's flat, and then, lo and behold, we find at least three people there within a matter of hours on Tuesday. They all deny they were there at the time of the death, but I suppose that if any of them is guilty, he or she would know what time it occurred, and make sure that they don't admit to that time. Exactly how to work out if any or all of them are lying, I have no idea. Their presence there reminds me of the lines of Mr Shakespeare:

When these prodigies

373

Do so conjointly meet, let no man say
"These are their reasons; they are natural"
For I believe they are portentous things
Unto the climate that they point upon."

If Malone was trying to impress White with the depth of
his learning, he did so but slightly. White had been to school
where they were old-fashioned enough still to believe in
Shakespeare, and almost everyone was forced to do 'Julius
Caesar', and do it well. He therefore said: "Yes, sir, Act One,
Scene Three, if I remember correctly. But if we're really
looking for amazing coincidences, it's quite possible that
more than these three visited Mr Holdroyd that night."

"You grasp the point immediately, White. But if there
was someone else there, where do we start looking for him
or her? If Paul McLeod is telling the truth in the main, by
the way, we can probably exclude young Athlone again. He
would almost certainly be the person heard in South Street.
I suppose it's always possible that he was returning to
obliterate any traces he might have left, but that's a rather
cool way to act, and his state after he reached the Police
Station does not suggest that sort of character. But since his
disappearance we may have to revise our ideas on the lad.
There is of course another possibility, which I at any rate
have not taken very seriously until now, and that is that two
or more of them could have been working together."

"Aye, sir, but it's very difficult to imagine what pairing
you could make out of them. It's possible that McLeod and
Athlone were acquainted, but their points of view seem to
be totally opposed. It could be put on for our benefit, but
that's not the impression I've had. And I can't see at all how
Lady Carswell would fit in with either them. We haven't any
proof of any sort that Jean Shaw was anywhere near

Holdroyd's flat that night, and I can't see who to connect her with, unless she's been doing a very good acting job. You tend to get the feeling about all of them that they'd either have done it on the spur of the moment or not at all."

"A very sensible statement of the problem, White. It is indeed very difficult to see any coincidence of interest, except perhaps between Paul McLeod and Lady Carswell. But then you have to consider how and where they conspired, or even met in the first place. I suppose any chance meeting is possible, and perhaps we ought to find out if they attended the same poetry recitals, or something of that nature. Yet it seems totally unlikely, and almost absurd. Your last point about none of them seeming to be that type is very important too, especially when taken in conjunction with the fact that all the circumstances of Holdroyd's death bear the hallmarks of a sudden unpremeditated action. No, I keep thinking we'll have to wait for someone to make a false move—that is, if young Athlone hasn't already made it. If the killer is in St. Andrews, he's very likely to know that we have several people under suspicion. If he, or she, is not one of those already suspected, we might get somewhere. People have an amazing need to advertise their misdeeds, and in a place as small as St. Andrews, we're in with a good chance of hearing about it if he does. There's a strong possibility that he'll think he's been terribly clever at clearing up his traces, and that would make the possibility of his boasting about it even more strong. If, however, he's one of those already under suspicion, we'll have to hope he breaks down under the strain. But for all that, I hate to sit around waiting for a move. I would hate to have to try and break Lady Carswell's alibi, but I shall make the attempt if necessary. She at least strikes me as being far more capable of the deed than any of the others. I must say though, that as far as I can judge the situation at the moment, there ought to be another late-night visitor. The rare conjunction would be just the sort of thing that made the ancients, and many moderns too, for that matter, believe in astrology."

"You believed Paul McLeod when he said that he never wore gloves?"

"I see no reason not to. It's something we could so easily check up on, so I think after being proved a liar, he'd be unlikely to try to deceive us on that. That doesn't mean that he couldn't have worn them for the occasion, but his reaction to the question seemed to be one of genuine surprise. Add to that his circumstantial statement that he was pleased he had touched nothing. But we must remember that the assailant was not necessarily gloved: that would merely have made his task easier."

They reached the Police station well before seven o' clock, but Malone, tired though he was, decided to await the expected telephone call from Eric Athlone. He was anxious to receive it, not only because he had reposed his trust in him, but also because he did not want to have to instigate a search for him. In the circumstances he would be morally bound to head that search himself, and all he wanted was a good rest. On their way to the office they were stopped by Sergeant Johnson, who said: "Mr Cormack rang up to say he had a piece of information which might be of some slight use, Inspector. I told him you'd be here at seven o' clock, and he said he'd call round then. I hope that meets with your approval?"

It occurred to Malone that the sergeant might well be a hard taskmaster to work under, but he said: "Fine, sergeant. I've just been saying that we'd need to wait for some development to come to us. Let's hope this is it."

𝕤 Chapter 12

MR JAMES CORMACK ARRIVED PROMPTLY AT SEVEN and was ushered into the room that had become Malone's office. Malone himself was feeling rather impatient, as the telephone call had not come through yet. He knew quite well that there can be considerable difficulties in the way of someone using a telephone kiosk in a large town— vandalised machinery, missing directories, or simply queues—but he still had the unreasonable expectation of having the matter of Athlone's disappearance cleared up one way or the other by seven. He asked Mr Cormack to sit down but did not shake hands with him. This did not go unnoticed by Mr Cormack.

"I'm sorry about the gloves, Inspector, but I suffer from a skin disease on my hands, and when it's bad, it seems more sociable all round to cover them up. Don't worry, I share the same objection to shaking gloved hands, and I have no intention of taking offence."

Malone was glad of his open, pleasant manner. "Thank you for coming again, Mr Cormack. In what way do you think you can help us now?"

"First of all, I take it that you haven't found the culprit yet? I mean, if you have, there's no point in my wasting your time."

"No, I'm afraid we haven't. We're working on several angles and hope to come up with something soon."

"I see. I presume you've been to see Paul McLeod?" Malone nodded. "Well, it's really about him. I told you before about his threats to Jim Holdroyd in the St. David's and that I thought that they were not made with any serious intent. I withheld another piece of information from you for purely selfish reasons, and to be fair, because I didn't think it of any great importance. You see, I did not in fact go straight home after leaving the St. David's. I'm not too keen on admitting it to anyone—you know how if you tell someone something in confidence in the morning, the whole town can be talking about it in the evening—but I have a lady-friend in the centre of town. But I'm sure I can trust your discretion in the matter."

Malone was indeed surprised at this side of Jim Cormack's character. It was the last thing he would have expected, but he knew as well as anyone else that affairs of sex were so complex in their reasons that only a fool would try to put them in categories. He therefore assured him that his judgement about his powers of discretion was well-founded. Mr Cormack therefore continued.

"Well I was leaving to go home at about a quarter to one. When I got as far as the Public Lavatories I realised that my bladder was unlikely to last me all the way home. It's one of these slight infirmities which strike you as you get older, and I stopped to relieve myself. When I left, I saw someone hanging about in the shadows, as if he was trying to avoid being seen. It didn't disturb me as such, as there must be a lot of people hanging around at that time of the night who have a strong interest in not being seen—myself included, I suppose. Well, anyway I have absolutely no doubt that the person I saw was Paul McLeod. I'm not trying to suggest for a minute that he could have had anything to do with Jim's death himself, but he might well have seen somebody who was out on the streets at that time. I understand, you're interested in contacting people who were out at that sort of time. If you can get him to admit that he was, he might be able to help you."

"Can you suggest any reason yourself for his presence on the street at that time of night?"

"I'm sure I could think of dozens of reasons. After all, I had one, and I'm sure you'll appreciate that I always had one or two more up my sleeve for my wife's benefit. The only surprising thing, I suppose, is that a young chap like that should go to such lengths as to try to conceal himself. That's the real reason I decided to come and tell you, even though it meant admitting to a certain irregularity in my own behaviour."

The conversation was interrupted by the arrival of Sergeant Johnson. "Excuse me for breaking in, Inspector, but that's the telephone call you were waiting for."

"Thank you very much, sergeant. I'll come almost immediately. Could you tell him to give you his number, and ring him back so that he won't have to fiddle with coins? I expect he's in a 'phone box. If he's in someone's house, he won't need to get worked up about the cost."

The sergeant departed to carry out these instructions. Malone turned to Jim Cormack again and said: "It's rather an important call, I'm afraid, and won't wait. May I ask you to stay here until I come back? I certainly shouldn't be more than five minutes."

This suggestion was readily agreed to, and Malone went off to the telephone feeling somewhat relieved. It would indeed have looked bad if a prima facie suspect had disappeared, even if he should be proved innocent in the event.

"Hallo, Inspector Malone speaking."

"I'm sorry I left like that, Inspector. I knew that as I was under suspicion I should stay, but after the way my father treated me I really couldn't. You do understand, don't you? You strike me as one of the few who might. I'm staying with friends at thirteen Woodborough Terrace. You'll be able to get hold of me there if you want to. The only trouble is that they've got no telephone. I'm in a 'phone box just down the road at the moment. You do believe me all right, don't you?"

"I've trusted you up to now and see no immediate reason for discontinuing to do so. Now, would you be good enough to answer a couple of questions for me? I hope you'll tell me the exact truth. Firstly, do you know any of the following people: Lady Harriet Carswell, Paul McLeod, Jean Shaw."

"I certainly don't know your Lady, even by reputation. The only Paul McLeod I know is in fourth year at the school. Is that the one you mean? There must be quite a lot of people called that. I've heard of a hippy student called Jean Shaw who lives along South Street somewhere, but I don't know her. I've just heard her talked about at school. That's the absolute truth."

"Thank you. I have no reason not to believe you, at least at the moment. Now the second question. You must have given it some thought already, if I've been right in trusting you. Do you know of anyone who could have wished to harm Mr Holdroyd? Remember that it's quite possible that there was no intention of killing him. It's very likely that it was only meant to be an assault."

There was no answer for a few seconds. Malone was about to ask him if he was still there when, he said: "After the way that my father treated me earlier I'm prepared to believe that he'd do almost anything. That is, if he thought there was anything between Mr Holdroyd and me, I mean. I know I shouldn't say this sort of thing about my own father, and anyway he said that he hadn't heard about me until after Mr Holdroyd's death. I suppose what I'm trying to say is that there are a lot of people around like my father, who feel justified in doing almost anything, as long as they're convinced they're in the right. Even if they turn out to be wrong, if you understand me."

Malone understood very well what he meant. He told him to keep in regular touch with the St. Andrews Police Station—morning and evening until further notice—and then rang off. He was now feeling extremely weary but had one or two things more to ask Jim Cormack before he could go home. He took a deep breath and went back into the office.

White and Jim Cormack were having a conversation about the state of the Old Course—a subject which would normally be of some interest to Malone—but he interrupted them unceremoniously. He especially hoped that Jim Cormack would not waste more time glorying in his sordid little affair, although he understood quite well that if people of his age could manage a regular bit on the side, they might well feel proud of it. But that depended on the bit, he decided.

"I'm very sorry to keep you waiting, Mr Cormack. I'm very grateful for your information, but in fact Paul McLeod did eventually admit to us that he was where you say he was, and that he was trying to conceal the fact from you. I may add that he did not have a very satisfactory explanation for his presence there. But please don't let that put you off telling us this sort of thing. I take it that you saw absolutely nobody else in the town on your way home?"

Jim Cormack seemed somewhat disappointed that his news was no longer news, and replied: "No, absolutely nobody apart from Paul McLeod. I was merely trying to be of assistance in your enquiries. You really should have told me that you knew about him, before I needed to mention the reason for my presence in town at that time of the night."

"I'm sorry, Mr Cormack, but I wanted to know if you had anything to add which might have thrown suspicion on McLeod's version of his movements. Now could you be good enough to give me the name and address of your lady-friend, in case we should want to interview her?"

This suggestion produced an immediate shock reaction in Jim Cormack, and he actually went red in the face: "That's exactly why I was unwilling to give you this information in the first place. There are one or two of us left, if it had escaped your notice, who believe in the honour of women. I have no intention whatsoever of answering that question, and, I may say, I think a lot less of you for daring to ask it."

"I'm sorry you see it that way, Mr Cormack. I can assure you that it is of no possible interest to us to enquire into your relationship with this lady. It merely occurred to me that if someone were awake in the middle of town at that time of night, they might have seen or heard somebody on the street. We're in desperate need of such information."

"I'm prepared to accept your explanation as genuine, Inspector, but I still have no intention of giving you the name or address of the young lady, unless I am required to do so in a court of law. That is my final word on the matter."

Malone did not pursue the point, as he was reasonably certain that it would not be too difficult for the local police to ascertain these straightforward pieces of information. No-one's secrets are quite so hidden as they believe. "Don't worry, Mr Cormack. I'm sure the matter would turn out to be of no consequence. Just one more thing, if you'd be kind enough. Have you had any more thoughts about the cause of Mr Holdroyd's recent depression? It doesn't matter if the explanation you offer seems inconsequential; I assure you it would be most helpful to have your opinion."

"Well, it does seem a bit silly, but you know Jim was always a little vain about his age. We had a dreadful time with him when he was just coming up to thirty. Anyone would have thought it was sixty. In general, we found it fairly amusing; any of the others in the pub will tell you. Well, anyway, it struck me that had he lasted a few minutes longer he would have been thirty-two. I mean it would have been his birthday yesterday. It may not seem terribly likely, but that could have been the reason."

"It's very good of you to mention this; that's just the sort of thing which is likely to escape us completely. As you say, unlikely though it may seem, it is quite possible that such a thing could upset him. Bachelors in their thirties often start getting peculiar ideas about the justification of their existence. Thank you again for coming, and despite what you may think about the propriety of my questions, I hope you won't hesitate to call any time you think you can help us."

Jim Cormack, who seemed mollified, said his goodbyes and left.

"Well White, as you've had good reason to notice, I'm tired. It's time I called it a day. If it hadn't been for you, there is a very good chance that I would have completely missed the significance of the patch on Paul McLeod's jeans. You've seen what's been done today, and so I hope you're not surprised by my weakness. I'm immensely relieved that young Athlone rang, but in many ways that adds to my weariness. The trouble is that he raised a possibility that hadn't seriously occurred to me before. He suggested that his father, or somebody like him, could easily have assaulted Holdroyd for alleged interference with their sons. Now, as I said earlier, it doesn't really matter whether there are any solid grounds for believing such a thing or not. It's a question of whether the would-be assailant is certain that it is the case. We have a perfect example of that sort of attitude in the case of Paul McLeod. If we take the evidence of the school—assuming we relegate that anonymous letter to its proper position of malice without foundation—and add to this the statements of Eric Athlone, Lady Carswell and Jean Shaw, it seems most unlikely that there could be any real grounds for such a belief. But Davie Athlone, or any other self-appointed upholder of public morals, does not always need proof in the accepted sense of the word. They act on the assumption that the righteousness of their motive is sufficient justification, so that even if they turn out to be mistaken, they are in no way themselves culpable. We come back to Holdroyd's epitaph. He clearly understood that type of person well. And we find ourselves back with the most common motive for killing our fellow man—self-involvement of some sort; and our difficulty partially lies in the fact that the dead man apparently went out of his way to avoid personal involvements.

I then have to ask myself what Mr James Cormack was hoping to achieve. Does he perhaps know something we don't, and is trying to protect somebody? Being, it appears, one of the 'righteous', he may wish to indicate that he is such a person by presenting himself in front of us with information, on every possible occasion. His other motives I can think of would be less praiseworthy. It's quite possible that he wants to tell someone about his extra-marital sins, and finds us convenient listeners, knowing full well that his admissions are unlikely to go any further than us. Many people find little satisfaction in such affairs unless they can let others know about them. The other possibility of course is that for some reason, legitimate or illegitimate, he has his knife into Paul McLeod. After all, it was Jim Cormack who told us about the drunken threats on Tuesday night, as well as providing further possible incriminating evidence this evening. There is an outside chance that he could suspect Paul McLeod as the author of his daughter's pregnancy. From what we know of the chap it seems a rather unlikely proposition, but to repeat myself, whether the suspicion is well-founded or not need be of no consequence to the suspicious person. If he believes his suspicions are correct, that is sufficient for him. No, White, the whole business is too complex for me in my present state of mind. Is there anything you can suggest that we need to do before packing up for the day?"

"Not really, sir, unless there's any possibility of involvement of the dead man's family."

"I'm not at all sure that there's anything positive we could do about that at the moment anyway, but the report I have on them gives no such hint; that's why I've let that consideration lie. The report's here if you want to have a look at it. Both his parents are dead. He has one brother, married and living in Birmingham, and as far as I know, although they were not particularly close, they were on perfectly good terms. No-one can suggest any reason of family finance to cause him, or his wife for that matter, to wish Holdroyd dead. On top of that, neither his brother, or his brother's wife, left Birmingham at the time we're interested in. I very much doubt there would be any future in pursuing that line, although you're quite right to bring it up. No, I'm more and more convinced that the answer must lie in St. Andrews, and even more specifically amongst the people we have already dealt with. We, or at least Sergeant Johnson should have heard of anyone else who was closely involved with Holdroyd by now, if there is any other such person. No, it's no good; I'm too tired. I'll see you in the morning."

Malone got into his car and began the drive home. He was wondering how his wife would feel about another tired, late arrival, as he went down the hill towards the Guardbridge-Leuchars junction, when the probable truth belatedly struck him.

ᏁᏴ Chapter 13

CONSTABLE WHITE, TRUE TO FORM, arrived at five to eight the next morning, five minutes before the time they had agreed upon. He found Malone already firmly installed in his office, looking bright and very cheerful. White assumed that he must have received some good news.

"Well, White," he said, "there's absolutely nothing to help us in these new reports here except in a negative way. I have one here from the Ministry of Defence, which is apparently so classified that only I am allowed to read it. If there were any lingering doubts about Russian agents, or British counter-espionage for that matter, they must disappear now. Here's one from Mr Dalkeith, who has clearly gone to town on the matter, and any last possibility of a Dundee involvement seems to be almost as remote as Comrade Boris. That leaves us, as I suspected last night, with St. Andrews and St. Andrews only. And as I said last night, as we have still not been informed of anyone else who knew Holdroyd well enough to be in his flat when he arrived home, and attack him off his guard, we must already have seen or at least heard of the true assailant. What is more, I'm almost certain I know which one it is. There are one or two uncertainties left lying about, but I hope to dispose of them this morning."

"Who was it then?"

"A natural question, White, and if I thought I had sufficient proof at this stage I'd tell you. But I may yet be wrong, and from the point of view of personal pride, I'd prefer not to stick my neck out until I'm absolutely certain. You've been with me almost all along, and you know that we have absolutely no proof that anyone was in Holdroyd's flat shortly before midnight on Tuesday. Ah, thank you, Constable."

Two more envelopes were delivered. One was clearly an official document, and the other a private letter. Malone opened the official communication first. All it did was help to confirm his former statements. There had always been the unlikely chance that some known dangerous lunatic had been at large in the area. Not only did this appear to be inapplicable to the area, but also there were no known abscondments from any asylum in the country. Again, from a purely negative point of view, Malone was pleased to have received this information. He then turned his attention to the other letter. He had no difficulty this time in recognising either the post-mark or the handwriting. It was from Lady Carswell. He opened it and read it.

"White, we have another communication here from the good Lady Carswell. She has returned to her magisterial manner, at least as far as her literary style is concerned, and all but demands to see me at half-past nine. I shall be quite happy to keep her waiting this morning. For the start, I feel in that sort of mood, and secondly, I had already planned out my movements for the earlier part of the day. I don't mind accommodating pushy people generally merely because it tends to produce an easier existence—but when it is at the expense of my own convenience, I never treat such people any differently from anyone else. Sometimes, as now, I think it would do them good to be treated in the same way, or possibly worse, than others. I feel that might even make her more co-operative. There are in fact two people I haven't seen yet whom I want to see this morning and doing so might well take me past nine-thirty."

"I remember you saying that you would like to see Mrs Cormack, but who's the other?"

Death of a Dundee Teacher

"You're quite right about Mrs Cormack; I've not been keen on seeing her before, as I've felt that she had enough trouble already. The other is of course Davie Athlone. I was hoping to persuade him to come in on his way to work. In fact, I'd better ring him now."

After a short conversation, Davie Athlone was persuaded to come to the Police Station, although his tone was somewhat belligerent. He told Malone in no uncertain terms that some people had an honest day's work to do, and that the work of others depended on their turning up for it. Perhaps, he suggested, that was a little difficult for people in part-time jobs to understand. Malone offered to explain personally what the reasons were if he happened to be detained from his work, to his immediate superiors. This calmed his attitude a little, but he still wanted to know what his boss would make of the fact that the police wanted to see him in the first place. Malone assured him that he would see that no unnecessary inconvenience would be caused him from that direction, and Davie Athlone reluctantly agreed to come.

When Malone met him, he was not surprised that young Eric had elected to depart for Edinburgh. He was a powerful man, though not particularly tall, and his first words were not obviously reminiscent of an indulgent father.

"I don't know why you wanted me to come here, but if that son of mine has been claiming that I assaulted him, I have no intention of denying it. Some parents still want to bring their children up decently and give them a proper sense of right and wrong, even if you lot have given up believing in that sort of thing. While I'm at it, I'd better tell you that I'd have no hesitation at all in doing the same thing again. Don't you worry, I'll knock it out of him somehow. After all his mother and me have done for him, I'm not having him turn out to be a poofter. And if you know where he is, I think you'd better tell me. You mark my words, I know exactly how to deal with him."

"Firstly, Mr Athlone, your son has not asked for any charges to be preferred against you. I have not seen him, and therefore have no idea how serious your assault on him was; it is probably my duty, however, to remind you that assault is a criminal offence. Secondly, I do know where he is, but I have no intention of telling you, unless he gives me express permission to do so."

"What do you mean? I thought we paid you people to keep law and order in this country. When you fail to do so, and one or two of us are forced to do your job for you, all you do is interfere. It's a bloody disgrace."

"Before you carry on in this way, Mr Athlone, the only person I know to have committed a criminal offence between the two of you is not your son. Secondly, may I remind you that it is our job to protect people from assault, as well as apprehend those guilty of it. Neither category excludes assaults within the family. However, that is not what I wanted to see you about. As I am sure you will be aware, I am investigating the death of Mr James Holdroyd of South Street. Would you now be good enough to confine yourself to answering the questions I put to you? Am I right in assuming that you employed Mr Holdroyd to teach your son Russian?"

"Aye, but if I'd had the slightest suspicion that he was a poofter..."

"Mr Athlone, you have already made your views on that subject abundantly clear. Did you have any grounds for suspecting that Mr Holdroyd had any homosexual relationship with your son?"

"Of course I didn't, otherwise I wouldn't have let him anywhere near him, would I? It was only after he was dead and people told me about Eric that I put two and two together. I suppose that was why he charged such a small amount. Absolutely disgusting. The world's a much better place without that sort of person around."

"Could you please explain exactly how you put two and two together, Mr Athlone?"

"It's obvious, isn't it, I don't need to explain it to you, do I? He was no longer young, he wasn't married, he lived on his own, and he had boys round to teach Russian to. And just in case he found difficulty in getting them, he was prepared to take a ridiculously low rate. I wondered at first why Eric was so keen on his Russian, as I knew he hadn't been too keen on the idea originally. Now I know."

"The only evidence which has so far come into our hands, part of which you possess yourself, would suggest that Mr Holdroyd was not a homosexual. But to return to the point. Had you come to these same conclusions before Holdroyd's death, what would you have done?"

"Sergeant Johnson will tell you any time that I'm an honest, law-abiding man. But if I'd had good reason to believe that he'd been interfering with my son, I'd have given him a hiding he wouldn't forget in a hurry. Aye, and I'd have no trouble in getting other people to help me, if I'd thought I might need it. But I don't think I would have."

"Mr Athlone, I hope you realise what you're saying. We have a man who died as a result of an assault, and you sit there saying that you would have happily assaulted him. We know of only one other person in St. Andrews who entertained the same attitude towards Mr Holdroyd, and we cannot with any certainty connect him with the crime."

Death of a Dundee Teacher

"Look here, what are you trying to say? I only said I'd knock him about a bit, not kill him. There's a big difference you know. As I was telling you, Sergeant Johnson will confirm that I'm an honest law-abiding citizen."

"I also recall you saying, that the world is a better place without the likes of James Holdroyd, and anyway, people quite often die as a result of assaults, you know. And I have no intention of denying that you are in general an honest citizen. However, your attitude makes it clear that you consider an assault such as I suggest would be above the law. Therefore, I suppose if death resulted from the assault it would still be no crime in your eyes. Now we only have your word for it that you began to have suspicions about Mr Holdroyd's behaviour towards your son after his death, and not before. Could you please therefore account for your movements on Tuesday night between, say, half-past eleven and half-past twelve?"

"Here, what's all this? I just came round to help you, or so I thought, and I find myself as good as being accused of murder!"

"I have not yet accused you of any such thing, nor have I even used the word murder. Will you be good enough to answer my question?"

Davie Athlone was not a man with the off-the-cuff ability to produce long speeches. There were many things he would like to have said, but as he could not find the words to put them in, he decided to answer the question, though in a not especially co-operative manner.

"I've no idea why I should tell you, but I went to bed just after eleven, like any normal working man with a job to go to in the morning, I know there are plenty of people in the town who seem to live in a different way, but I'm not one of them."

"Can you prove it?"

"Prove it! Do you have to prove when you go to bed now? Anyone can tell you that it's a habit of mine to go to bed at eleven or shortly afterwards every night. I've got my work to do in the morning and get up sharp at six. I think a routine like that would be good for everyone, and I've often said so. That's why you'll find a lot of people who'll tell you I always do that."

"Your son was still out at that time, and you must have been aware of the fact. Did that not delay your bed-time?"

"I've never seen any reason to destroy my routine just because of his bad behaviour. I've always tried to bring him up to keep the same sort of hours as me and was going to give him a piece of my mind in the morning. His mother insisted on waiting up for him, though. Some nonsense about him not having looked well recently."

"I can then assume that not even your wife can substantiate that you were in bed at the time in question?"

"She knows if I'm in bed or not, doesn't she? She doesn't have to stand over me watching every movement I make to know that, does she? She saw me going off to bed and she woke me up—when was it? Half-past one or two, I don't remember—when the doctor rang to tell us that Eric was in hospital. Isn't that enough proof for you?"

"You have produced no proof at all, I'm afraid, Mr Athlone. I asked you to account for your movements between half-past eleven and half-past twelve. You can find corroboration for your version of the facts for before eleven and after half-past one. May I suggest further that it would be extremely useful to somebody who wished to commit a crime at about midnight, to have a public reputation for going to bed every night at eleven. If his son happened to be late out unexpectedly that night in addition, it would be a very good reason to give to anyone who by chance noticed him out on his way to or from the crime. Understandable, and even creditable fatherly concern would be the verdict. What have you to say to that, Mr Athlone?"

"It's monstrous. It's a lot of lies. I'll not say another thing until I've consulted a lawyer."

"May I ask you to remain in the area until this business is cleared up? That's just in case we need to interview you again. But before you go, let me give you a bit of friendly advice. I wouldn't waste your money on a lawyer yet, unless you're sure you've got something to hide. I'm inclined to believe your story. However, I will say that I find it easier to believe that you were responsible for the death of Mr Holdroyd, than that he and your son had any homosexual relationship."

"All I can say is that it's a pity there aren't more people like Sergeant Johnson in the Police. I'd never have got all this rubbish off him. He knows a decent man when he sees one, and he wouldn't go around protecting poofters from their just deserts."

"I assure you, Mr Athlone, that Sergeant Johnson, being the excellent officer you imagine him, would consider an assault an assault, regardless of who perpetrated it, or their imagined just reasons. Good morning. I'm sorry to have kept you from your work."

"Have you any opinions on that conversation, White?" said Malone after their visitor had left.

"I would never have considered him as a real possibility, but the way you put it, it sounded quite convincing."

"Och, I should put it right out of your mind. I don't for one second think he had anything whatever to do with events on Tuesday night. I only hope I haven't turned him off the police in general, rather than just me. He was always an outside possibility, so I had to make absolutely sure about him. I really pushed the matter for the sake of young Eric and the late James Holdroyd. If he is the reflective type, which I doubt, the truth of my remark about greater evidence against him as a murderer than against Holdroyd as a homosexual may strike him. His last remark seemed to indicate that he was more concerned about the legal position of queer-bashing, and his own status in society, than a possible murder charge. That does not really smack of a guilty conscience. I must say that the sudden mention of a lawyer took me by surprise, and I wondered if I was onto something after all, but I suspect that's something he just picked up off the telly. The last thing people like him normally do is run to a lawyer, if only to save the exorbitant fee."

Malone was silent for a bit, and then he consulted his watch. "The next thing we have to consider is whether to see Mrs Cormack before Lady Carswell or wait until the good Lady has gone before dealing with Mrs Cormack. I think I shall stick to my original plan of keeping our poetess waiting. You never know, the experience of waiting in a Police Station might inspire her to produce some immortal verses of her own. I want Mrs Cormack here without her husband, and so I don't want to get in touch with her until he's out at his work. Another couple of minutes, and I think we should be safe."

Accordingly, he rang Mrs Cormack after a minute or two had elapsed, and, as he had hoped, found her alone in the house. She said that she would be happy to co-operate with the police in any way she could but was unable to present herself at the Police Station until a quarter to ten at the earliest. Malone thanked her and said that he would expect her then. He was a little disappointed, as that removed any good reason for keeping Lady Carswell waiting. Never mind, he thought, perhaps he had already brought personality in quite enough in his dealings with Davie Athlone. He next began to consider what Lady Carswell could be asking to see him for but could come to no satisfactory answer. He asked White's opinion, but he too could offer no constructive suggestion. Neither of them thought it likely that she had come to make a confession. They fell into silence, as Malone clearly wished to consider some points of the case. White began to read through some of the reports again. They were interrupted briefly by an announcement that Paul McLeod had come in to report. Malone said that there was no need to detain him, as clearly he was still easily obtainable.

Exactly at half-past nine, as they had expected, Lady Carswell appeared. She was dressed in the same, or at any rate a similar, manner to the day before. She looked possibly even more elegant.

"Must this Constable stay in the room, Inspector?" were her first words on entering the office. Malone wished more than ever that he had found some excuse for making her wait. It was all very well to allow such people their whims, he thought, but then all they did was take advantage of your consideration. She offered no reason for her demand for, despite the interrogative form, that was clearly what it was. Malone realised that he was supposed to understand that she was entitled to less formal and more personal treatment. He immediately adopted an official line.

"Lady Carswell, it is customary wherever possible to have two police officers present at an interview. The intention, whether you wish to believe it or not, is to make sure that you will not be misrepresented as a result of personal animosity, or even simple misunderstanding. As Constable White has been with me on this investigation from the start—he was in fact one of the officers who discovered the body of Mr Holdroyd—I think it most suitable for him to be present in a discussion of any matters concerned with the case. Now would you please be good enough to tell me why you requested this interview?"

Lady Carswell had, as intended, visibly winced at the term 'officer' being used twice to describe a mere Constable. However, she made no comment to that effect. She said: "Firstly, I would like to know how far you have reached with your investigation."

"I would normally consider that an improper, if not highly suspicious question. But as it is you, I shall tell you. We have been following up a number of leads and expect to bring the matter to a successful conclusion in the near future."

She was of course, well aware of the implications, or more properly lack of implications in such a statement. She was also aware that Malone must have produced it to provoke her. She refused to rise to the provocation.

"Inspector Malone, would you at least be good enough to tell me if you intend to produce the information I asked for or not?"

"Before I answer that, I shall need to know exactly why you wish to know what position our investigation has reached."

"Why I want to know? My dear man, have you any idea what it is like for a woman in my position to be under police suspicion? I hate to have to admit it, but I hardly slept last night in my fear that my husband or some of our friends might find out about it. It's totally unthinkable that any connection between myself and Jim Holdroyd should be thought to exist."

Death of a Dundee Teacher

Her slight show of humility mollified Malone somewhat.
"I do appreciate your difficulty, and although you have
apparently failed to notice the fact, I have done my best to
keep your place in my enquiries discreet. If I was absolutely
sure that I could eliminate you from these enquiries, rest
assured that I would. But I must remind you that you began
by telling me a number of straightforward lies. When I had
exposed these for what they were, you had to admit to
certain practises, which, whatever their legal status, are not
far divorced morally from fraud. You have given me no
grounds at all for trusting you. For instance, you say your
lack of sleep was the result of a fear of your husband finding
out some facets of this matter. I might just as well say that
it was the workings of your guilty conscience. Was it, Lady
Carswell?"

She was somewhat taken aback at the suddenness of this
question. "You're doing a very democratic job, I'm sure, in
treating me no differently from a shop-girl you might think
had some sordid little relationship with Jim. It's high time
you realised that I should be treated otherwise. I'm clearly
wasting my time in trying to approach you as I would a
gentleman, as you obviously have no idea whatever of the
meaning of the term. Secondly, I want my passport back."

"In the circumstances, Lady Carswell, I find that a very
suspicious request, and I am afraid that I cannot grant it."

"There is, I suppose, little advantage to be gained in
pointing out that your attitude is offensive. My last request
is this. I would like permission to go to the late James
Holdroyd's flat and remove any poems which might be
there. After all, I did pay him well for his efforts."

"Again, I'm afraid, you ask me something impossible.
The rightful ownership of anything in Mr Holdroyd's
possession when he died is not for me to decide. If you wish

398

to pursue the matter, the correct people to see are his executors. You must be well aware of that fact, Lady Carswell."

"Of course I am aware of it. You also are aware that I have no record of ever having bought them off him. You also know quite well why it is vitally important for me to get hold of any manuscripts which may be lying around. If by any chance, in a fit of duty towards the dead, or whatever, the executors should decide to get them published, even in some local rag, I could easily find myself in a very embarrassing situation."

Malone remembered the state of the bookcase, and his first thought that somebody might have been searching there. What more likely than that it was Lady Carswell searching for manuscripts of poems? He kicked himself for not having established, if such a matter could be established in the case of a man with so few visitors, whether Holdroyd's bookcase was always kept in that untidy state. It would certainly be strange if the only untidy thing in the room, the bookcase, was kept in that state permanently by someone who was clearly such a house-proud man.

"Have you already made such a search on any previous occasion? Be sure you answer me truthfully."

"Are you now accusing me of breaking and entering? No, I most certainly have not. If I had done so, I would hardly be asking you for permission to do so now."

"It occurs to me that you could have attempted a search beforehand but were interrupted in your attempt. I think that even you would be more circumspect than to go and search the house of a man who had died in suspicious circumstances shortly after that death. Do you know whether Mr Holdroyd was an orderly man?

"That is a strange question from one who has supposedly spent several days investigating his death. You will know as well as I do that his flat was always kept in immaculate condition—that is, all except his bookcase. I could never understand the state that it was kept in, especially as most of the contents of it clearly cost rather more than his furniture."

"You are now willing to admit to knowing his flat well?"

"I thought I had made it quite clear during our last conversation that I had visited it on more than one occasion recently."

"I suppose you did. As regards manuscripts of poems, Lady Carswell, I think that I can put your mind at rest. I myself found absolutely no trace of a collection. It was only by chance that I found his original version of 'My Brain's A Broken Army', which was lying in his copy of the poems put out under your name. I don't suppose there'll be others lying around in his Russian books or any such place. I think you can be pretty certain that there is nothing else there, unless you know of some special place to look?"

"No, I do not. But you do not appear to grasp how serious the consequences could be, if someone tried to publicise any such writings. If you are quite sure there is nothing there, I can see no earthly reason why you should not allow me to go and see for my own satisfaction."

"I do not think there is any advantage to be gained from pursuing this point. I have no intention of conniving at stealing for the benefit of your personal pride, and no desire to waste public resources by providing a couple of police officers to observe your movements. Is there anything else I can do for you?"

"No, but I should advise you to remember the remarks with which I ended our last conversation."

When she had left the room, Malone said: "White, would you mind going and keeping an eye on Mr Holdroyd's flat? The time of day being what it is, you should be able to mingle somewhat with the shoppers in South Street, I'd prefer it if you could be as unobtrusive as possible. If Lady Carswell attempts to enter the flat, bring her round here immediately. If she refuses to come, threaten to arrest her, and if necessary do so. I'll take any responsibility for your actions, and I mean it."

"If I see her attempting an entrance, should I stop her immediately or wait until she has made a proper attempt? I mean, if I see her going up the close, I'll know quite well what it's for, but she could quite easily claim another reason."

"Aye, I think you'd better wait until it's clear she's at least trying to enter the front door—that is, of course, if she makes such a move in the first place. I rather suspect she will, however, so could you get a move on, White?"

White left and made as quick time as he could to the vicinity of the dead man's flat. Malone was glad to have had this legitimate reason to send him away, as he wished to carry out his interview of Mrs Cormack on his own. As White had hardly left his side for the past two days or more, it would have seemed very rude at this stage of the operation to ask him to make himself scarce; and in fact, Malone did not like being rude. He began to consider how exactly he was going to order his questioning of Mrs Cormack to achieve the result he desired. He was sure it would be easier without her husband, but he would have to bear in mind the condition of their daughter.

❦ Chapter 14

MRS CORMACK ARRIVED ABOUT TEN MINUTES LATER than she had suggested. She looked extremely tired and worn, and apologized profusely for her lateness. Malone assured her that it was of no great consequence and added that he was grateful for her presence at all. This approach apparently did nothing to reassure her, but Malone thought it pointless to repeat himself in a different way. He therefore began gently to ask her for the information he desired.

"You will be aware, Mrs Cormack, that your family was really the only one in St. Andrews which knew Mr Holdroyd at all well. He was, it appears, a man of fairly wide acquaintance, but very few real friends. For this reason, I feel sure you can give me information about him which no-one else possesses. Now, could I ask you first of all if you have ever been in Mr Holdroyd's flat?"

Mrs Cormack blushed a little. "I don't know what you mean, Inspector."

"Please don't misunderstand me, Mrs Cormack. I'm not using euphemisms, and I'm certainly not trying to hint at a suspicion of any untoward relationship between yourself and Mr Holdroyd. The question was meant to mean exactly what it said."

"Oh, I'm sorry. I just never know nowadays what innuendo I'm supposed to read into what people say. As you probably know by now, Jim wasn't really much of a man for entertaining in his own flat, but I have been there a couple of times. It always made me wonder why he didn't ask people more often. You know how you expect men living on their own to be a bit—well, messy. His flat was spotless, and I'm quite sure it wasn't a show put on specially for my benefit. I found it rather surprising."

"Could you tell me about his bookcase, Mrs Cormack?"

"I'm not at all sure what you want to know about it. As far as I remember, it was fairly large and fairly old, but I don't think there was anything terribly special about it, though I must say, seeing all the higgledy-piggledy books was a strong contrast to the tidiness everywhere else."

"It was exactly the state of the books which I wished to establish, Mrs Cormack. I also was struck by the strange contrast and wondered if anyone could have rummaged through them recently. But from what you say it was probably not so. Can you tell me about Mr Holdroyd's interests—outside his job, that is to say?"

"He never seemed to me to have enough to do. At the right time of year, of course, he was very keen on his garden. He often used to bring vegetables and flowers that he had grown himself. Apart from that, I don't really know what he did. I suppose he must have spent a fair amount of time reading, and he used to like going around the pubs, Not that he ever drank very much—I don't suppose he could have afforded to—and it was normally only beer he drank, so I'm told. I only once saw him at all the worse for drink, and that was at New Year, when you rather expect that sort of thing. There must have been a lot of hours to fill in, though, living on his own."

"He didn't play golf?"

"No, never, as far as I know."

Malone always found it difficult to believe that anyone who chose to live in St. Andrews did not play golf. He was convinced that he would never have allowed his game to deteriorate to its present abysmal level had he lived here. It flashed across his mind that the average Muscovite would probably find it rather difficult to give exact directions to the Kremlin, and that most inhabitants of Venice thought of canals as nothing but smelly, damp nuisances.

He spoke again. "Now may I ask you if you were fond of Mr Holdroyd?"

She blushed a little again. "At least you put it in straightforward words. Well, as you're the only other person in this room, I don't mind telling you. Yes, I was extremely fond of Jim. I don't think I ever let him realise it, and certainly he never acted towards me as if he felt anything other than friendship for me. Had he done so, I can't tell for certain what my reaction would have been, but I think he would have found me responsive."

"Did your husband have any suspicion of these feelings of yours?"

"No, I'm sure he didn't. As he wouldn't dream of anything like that himself—dream is probably the wrong word; that's exactly what he might do, but no more—he wouldn't have imagined it of me. If you hadn't noticed, he is very sure of his own importance. And please don't misunderstand me on that. I'm extremely fond of my husband but I think after twenty years I should know him pretty well.

"Do you know if Mr Holdroyd had any regular girl-friends?"

"I don't really know. My husband told me that he used to visit some girl who was apparently on the dole, and according to my husband quite possibly took drugs. His view was that Jim should have known better. I never offered an opinion, because I think that any man of his age ought to have close female friends of some sort. But she's the only one I've ever heard of."

"Now I'm afraid. I must be even more personal. Do you think it's possible that your husband's concern about Mr

Holdroyd's relationship with this young lady, could be a reflection of his concern about your daughter? I'm told that she is very good-looking."

"How dare you make such a suggestion. You're as bad as he is!"

"As bad as who, Mrs Cormack?"

Mrs Cormack wrung her hands and screwed up her weary eyes. "Oh, I suppose I may as well tell you, though I don't know what the point of this conversation is at all. My daughter's pregnant. Yes, Inspector Malone, it can happen to our daughter just like anyone else's. I'm beginning to find it a little easier to accept as time goes on. The only thing that still keeps bothering me is that I imagine everyone is staring at me and blaming me for it. I'm well aware that the only reason the majority of girls were not pregnant when they got married when I was young was sheer luck. The same would be true now, except possibly more so, I suppose, if it weren't for the spread of contraception. But for all that it's just like road accidents, they always happen to somebody else. Well, when my daughter told me she was pregnant, of course I had to tell my husband, although I knew it would be a greater shock to him than to me. He tries to compensate for his immense conformity and desire to be respectable, by going to the pub most nights for a couple of pints of beer, but somehow that makes him even more conventional. For instance, he would never get drunk in the pub or attempt to pick up a woman on the way home. Anyway, as I expected, he was very disturbed when I told him, and demanded to know who the father was. Elizabeth, my daughter, refused to tell us. He thought there was something suspicious in this and started threatening her. When she still wouldn't tell us, it suddenly struck him that the time just about coincided with her visit to the opera in Glasgow with Jim Holdroyd.

He started making wild accusations, but all Elizabeth could do was burst into laughter at such an absurd suggestion. I think it must have been a relief to her to know that a responsible adult could be suspected of such a thing. It took me a long time to calm my husband down, but I eventually managed it. He apologised to both of us for the silly things he had said and added that we would have to understand what a dreadful shock the whole business was to him. He told Elizabeth that, whatever he had said as a result of anger or worry, he still loved her very much, and would look after her just the same as ever. He didn't speak about it the next day, which was last Sunday, and by the Monday he seemed to have calmed down totally, and like me began to accept it. I knew it must still hurt him a lot, but I was very pleased he could put such a face on it. I'm sorry if I answered you rudely just now, but perhaps you can understand why."

"Perfectly, Mrs Cormack. I'm afraid that a good deal of my working life is spent in asking people unpleasant questions, and I hope you'll forgive me if I go a little further. You are quite certain that Mr Holdroyd could have had nothing to do with your daughter's pregnancy?"

"I am absolutely certain that he was not the man. Unless you had known him, you wouldn't have had any idea how incredibly honest he was. I'm not suggesting he was a saint, or any nonsense like that, just honest. Although I in fact think it most improbable, I wouldn't maintain for a minute that he would never have considered the possibility of seducing Elizabeth. But if he had done so, I am absolutely certain that he would have made his attitude quite clear to me at any rate. If he had had any inkling that he might have caused a pregnancy he would undoubtedly have admitted to it immediately, of that I am quite certain. As he said nothing to me, either about his intentions towards Elizabeth, or the possible results of them, I'm convinced he had nothing to do with it. I'm sure my husband would have come to a similar conclusion."

"I believe your husband has a skin infection on his hands, which causes him sometimes to wear gloves?"

"Yes, that's so. It's one of those psychological things. It hadn't actually been bothering him for some time, until I think it was Tuesday or Wednesday. I suppose a mixture of Elizabeth's pregnancy and Jim's death caused it."

A constable knocked on the door and entered. "Excuse my interruption, sir, but there are two individuals out here demanding to see you, and we're finding it difficult to deal with them satisfactorily."

"All right, I'll come immediately. If you'll excuse me, Mrs Cormack, I'll be back in just a minute."

He went through to the front of the Police Station. Two people stood there, gesticulating with their gloved hands, and speaking in unnecessarily loud voices to Sergeant Johnson and Constable White, who preserved the solid stance and impassive faces found only on British policemen and statues of severe old Romans. Malone, without any apparent account of the visitors, addressed Sergeant Johnson.

"I believe there are some people who wish to see me, sergeant. Can you tell me what it's all about?" Both visitors again spoke simultaneously, but the sergeant ignored them as completely as the Inspector had done.

"I've been trying to find out for the last few minutes, Inspector, but it's very difficult when they refuse to tell me anything I ask, and in addition insist on saying whatever they do want to say at the same time. I'm very sorry to interrupt you, but I don't think I can manage the situation myself."

"Thank you for trying, sergeant. Now, Mr Cormack, I have been speaking to your wife, and I presume that is why you have come yourself. She is still in my office. You may go in and join her, and I shall be through as soon as I possibly can." Mr Cormack was led through to the back of the Station. "Lady Carswell, I suppose I don't have to ask you what you are doing here again. Presumably Constable White was forced to ask you to accompany him here. Why did you disobey my instructions?"

"Disobey your instructions! Who the hell do you think you are to try to prevent me from regaining what is virtually my own private property? I have rarely been so grossly insulted as when this side-kick constable of yours threatened to arrest me. Him arrest me!" The monstrosity of the proposition seemed to rob her of more words, as well as an appreciation of the proper place of the accusative case in the English language.

"Constable White was merely carrying out my instructions. I am bound to inform you that this attempt at breaking and entering with intent to steal—serious enough charge in itself—must be looked upon with the gravest suspicion in the circumstances. I am in the middle of an interview at the moment, but I shall have to ask you to wait until I have finished, as I shall wish to speak to you then. If you attempt to leave, you will be placed under arrest."

"Oh, yes, and on what charge?"

"Attempted larceny to begin with. I shall then decide if graver charges should follow."

"How dare you." She was shouting now and looking extremely dangerous. Malone walked right up to her.

"It is not I who dare, but the law. Because of my presence these officers have shown commendable restraint. Unless you wish to be treated as you have acted, like a common criminal, I advise you to sit down and shut up." He turned and went through to the office at the back.

He was immediately addressed by Mr Cormack. "Inspector Malone, you are a bloody disgrace to the police force. All the time you have been engaged in this case I have done my duty as a citizen, and tried to help in every way I can, even to my own detriment. My reward last time was a piece of unnecessary rudeness. Now you have dragged out my wife when, as you have forced her to confess, she has quite enough to trouble her without being molested by you. You may think it's impressive to look busy, but as a member of the public, who do after all pay your salary, I would prefer to see some results."

"May I ask how you knew your wife was here?"

"We're not all incapable of finding out simple facts, Inspector. I have of course been worried about my wife's health recently and telephoned this morning to see how she was. When I got no answer, I tried our next-door neighbour, who had been informed by my wife where she was going in case of emergency. It is not especially difficult to find out simple things, if you go about the matter in a simple way."

"I assume that you are suggesting that if I adopted that excellent method, I would have no difficulty in establishing who was responsible for the death of Mr Holdroyd."

"I would have thought it was fairly obvious who the guilty party was. Look, I don't like telling other people how to go about their jobs, any more than I expect others to tell me how to do mine. But you have upset me, and, even more importantly, my wife, I don't know how many others you have treated in a similar way, although one other at least seemed to be outside with me. I have tried to give you information on two occasions to lead you to arrest Paul McLeod, though I made excuses for him on both occasions, in case I should seem to influence your judgement too much. It was undoubtedly he, although I would not suggest for a moment that he intended to kill Jim. He probably went round to give him a piece of his mind, and in a drunken fury—you heard how drunk he was on Tuesday night— picked up the nearest weapon and struck out with it. He might not even have realised that he had killed him until he heard the next day that he was dead. You have the evidence that he uttered threats, and that he was seen in the town around the time in question, acting in a most suspicious manner. From what Sergeant Johnson told me earlier, there was no-one else reported seen in the middle of town at the time in question. All you need to do is establish that he was in Jim's flat. Even if with all your modern expensive equipment you can find no traces of his presence, I'm sure you can manufacture something. After all, it's quite clear that he's guilty."

"Before you continue to advocate such an approach to police work, Mr Cormack, I had better inform you that I have established by regular means that Paul McLeod was in Mr Holdroyd's flat on Tuesday night. I have even forced him to admit it."

"Why on earth haven't you arrested him then? Everyone knows that Jim almost never had visitors. It's hardly likely that anyone else would have been there too. I don't know what we pay you for if you can't arrest him on all that evidence."

"I suspect you are aware, if you think about it, that Eric Athlone was also there on Tuesday night. I shall tell you further that his finger-prints were on the weapon that caused Holdroyd's death."

"That seems to me to make it even more obvious. I presume you must have very good reasons for believing Eric

Athlone innocent if you have not arrested him with such damning evidence before you. It would clearly be unthinkable that more than two people visited Jim on the same night."

"I may then add, Mr Cormack, that the woman who was doing her best to cause a disturbance with you outside, was, by her own admission, present in his flat that very evening. The reason that she was brought in here was that she was trying to gain entry again into the flat, in order to remove some documents. On top of that, there are at least two other people who could have been involved in Mr Holdroyd's death who cannot account adequately for their movements on Tuesday night."

"I'm sorry if I've been a bit hasty, Inspector. I see that you have indeed been very busy, and this case is somewhat more complex than I had imagined. I suppose you're trying to gather more evidence, so that you can decide which of these people it was, and understandably you hope to get it from those who knew Jim best. But as you know of our personal circumstances, I trust that you'll appreciate my attitude."

"I think you misunderstand the state of my case, Mr Cormack. I am reasonably satisfied that none of the people I have mentioned struck the blow which killed Mr Holdroyd. I am looking for yet another person who was there and did strike the blow. Before we continue this conversation, would you like your wife to leave?"

"Whatever for? As you have brought her here, and thereby forced my presence also, I think we'd be as well to leave together, in case she should be worried about what you are saying to me. Wouldn't that be best, dear?" Mrs Cormack nodded her agreement.

"As you wish, but remember that I gave you fair warning. As I was saying, unlikely as it may seem, there must have been yet another person in Mr Holdroyd's flat that night."

Mr Cormack broke in before, he could continue. "But that seems to be a totally unreasonable line to take. As you know well, it was sufficiently rare for Jim to have one visitor, therefore to suggest that he had more than—how many was it you were suggesting? Four or five, I think, well to suggest that he had more than that is clearly absurd. Surely even you can see that."

"It is not absurd, and you know that it is not. You were the other visitor."

"Hey what's going on now? I presume you're having a little joke at my expense. But it's not the time for that sort of joke."

"Mr Cormack, perhaps you would like to tell me again what you were doing between half-past eleven and half-past twelve on Tuesday night. And please tell me the truth this time."

"This is absolutely monstrous. My dear, perhaps you had better go after all. The only reason I can imagine for this peculiar carry-on is that the Inspector here is trying to drive a wedge between us. What motive he could possibly have I cannot guess. But I'll make it clear to him that after twenty years of marriage it's not quite so easy as he seems to think."

"May I suggest that you take your husband's advice, Mrs Cormack? I had no desire to have you here with him at this juncture. That is why I asked you on your own."

"As far as I can see, my proper place is by my husband. I have no intention of going."

Malone did not press the matter. It seemed pointless at this stage.

"Would you please answer my question, Mr Cormack?"

"I told you yesterday evening, and for obvious reasons I have no intention of repeating that statement in front of my wife."

Mrs Cormack suddenly burst into laughter. "I see it all now. Jim's been trying to convince you that he was with some other woman on Tuesday night, and you'll have found out that it wasn't true. Oh Jim, who are you trying to fool and whatever for?"

"I'm afraid it's not as simple as that, Mrs Cormack. I wish for your sake that it was. I'm sure you're quite right about that story being a fabrication. Had I not suspected it anyway, your certainty of the impossibility of the thing would have convinced me. The point is, that if he wasn't with this hypothetical other woman, where was your husband?"

"Oh, he told me that. He took a walk along the East Sands. He sometimes does that sort of thing. He told me about the moon over the sea. It must have been lovely. I wish I'd been with him."

"The trouble is, I'm afraid, Mrs Cormack, the moon was in the west, not the east at that time."

Mrs Cormack suddenly began to look frightened. Jim Cormack broke in: "All right, I'll admit that I lied to you both. You'll obviously have to listen to this my dear, but it's nothing very terrible. I normally never have more than three pints in an evening. For some reason—I think Jim Holdroyd was forcing the pace—I had about five on Tuesday night. That's enough to get me a bit drunk. Well, I fancied my chances of finding another woman, and I hung around the town hoping that some likely one would come along. I've done it before occasionally, but I've never found one, or at any rate been too shy to try my luck. I hate to have to admit it dear, but I'm afraid that's true."

His wife did not look at all convinced; nor did Malone. "I don't believe you, Mr Cormack. I say again that you went to the flat in South Street occupied by Mr James Holdroyd, and assaulted him, causing his death. I suspect that you have told us the general circumstances of how it came about in your accusation of Paul McLeod.

"Inspector, you do not have a shred of proof that this was so, I think we have wasted quite enough time here, and before you upset my wife further, I think we had better go." He rose and put his hand out to his wife.

"Sit down, Mr Cormack. I had obviously better tell you how I know it was you. To begin with, the general points. The blow in question was struck from the front, and yet Mr Holdroyd did little or nothing to defend himself. Why not? Because his assailant was well known to him, and the last thing he expected was violence. It is almost certain that his attacker was in the flat before he arrived home—of that I cannot be absolutely sure, but I am reasonably certain of it—yet, although Mr Holdroyd was a man of few visitors, he made no apparent attempt to raise an alarm. Why? Because again, his assailant was well known to him, and someone from whom he expected friendly treatment. It is a clear indication, also that the person was well aware of where he lived. Given the sort of person Mr Holdroyd was, that narrows down our field to a surprisingly small number of people. Now the evidence which points more specifically to you, Mr Cormack. The assailant almost certainly wore gloves, and this again occasioned no surprise. Why? Because Mr Holdroyd was not unaccustomed to seeing him in gloves. This, incidentally, was one of the points which at first made me think it might be a woman that I was searching for, and therefore why it has taken me so long to arrive at the truth. If you reply that you were not wearing your gloves on

Tuesday night, I shall merely reply that I do not believe you, and furthermore that it is not vital to the case. Now we must move to the reason for the attack. Nothing appeared to have been stolen, and despite suspicions I entertained at the time of first searching the flat that his books may have been rummaged through, now I know this to be most unlikely. If robbery was not the reason, then, short of some maniacal attack, there must have been some personal motive. The more you look into any man's private life, the more reasons for personal animosity can be found; and indeed there were several possibilities. Suspicions about the cause of your daughter's pregnancy—about which, by the way, I heard yesterday—would clearly be sufficient reason for you to contemplate an assault, if not more than an assault. The fact that you volunteered the information about your daughter's trip to Glasgow with Mr Holdroyd was doubtless to make it seem of no significance. The perfect opportunity came your way when you, and several other witnesses, heard Paul McLeod issue drunken threats against Mr Holdroyd. Since his death occurred, under the guise of being helpful, you have, as you yourself say, consistently tried to implicate him. I presume that the occasion you told me that Mr Holdroyd's age might be the cause of his recent concern, you were worried in case I should look too deeply into the possibility of a relationship between him and your daughter. I must admit that I had never really considered you as a serious suspect until you unnecessarily mentioned that had Mr Holdroyd lived a few minutes longer, he would have been thirty-two. The significance of that statement escaped me at the time, as I was very tired. But later the obvious fact occurred to me that, as not even I was absolutely certain about the time of death, anyone who could be so precise must have knowledge that I did not possess. There was really only one way that this piece of information could have been acquired, as I rejected the possibility of a conspiracy. You must have been there. There are a few other indications, but that is basically how I know that you are the guilty party."

"This is of course preposterous. Although I didn't like doing so for one moment, I have told you what I was doing at the time in question. As to the statement about when he died, either you or Sergeant Johnson gave me that piece of information."

"As you know well, there is absolutely nothing preposterous in what I have been saying. It is also grossly unlikely that Sergeant Johnson or myself would tell you as fact something we could not be sure of ourselves. I certainly did not. May I add that I do not find it very difficult to think of you as a liar. You, Lady Carswell and Paul McLeod are the only people I have come across in the investigation who have doubted Mr Holdroyd's honesty. I have already had to force the other two to admit that they were lying to me. It is a common human failing to be unable to admit that others are capable of a greater moral depth than oneself."

"As I am not telling you lies, you will not be able to prove a word of this idiotic accusation."

"The first part of your statement is false, but sadly the second part is correct. I have as yet no absolute proof that you killed Mr Holdroyd, but the proof will come, and we shall wait until it does. After I had seen your wife, I had intended to ask you to come along here and say to you what I have just said. I shall now outline to you what your best course of action is. As I said before, I am quite prepared to believe that the actual death was an accident and happened very much in the way you suggested when describing the hypothetical actions of Paul McLeod. You would be well advised to make a full statement to that effect. If you do, I shall not indicate that I forced you to. A voluntary statement including your personal reasons for the attack would, I am sure, be looked upon favourably by the courts. It is most unlikely, but in view of your undoubtedly honest way of life, there is the outside possibility that you would get away with a suspended sentence. I tell you this for your own good."

"You won't trick me into getting you out of a difficult hole like this, Inspector. I had always disbelieved stories I read in the papers about dubious police methods, but now I know better. Don't you worry, your superiors will hear of this."

Before he could continue in this vein, there was a knock on the door and Sergeant Johnson appeared. Malone was by no means sorry for the interruption, as it had stopped Mr Cormack in the midst of this routine flow, which he had suffered several times before.

"There's a young lady who's very insistent on seeing you, Inspector. From the little she has been prepared to tell me; I think you would be advised to see her immediately. It's a Miss Jean Shaw."

"Thank you very much, sergeant, I'll be straight through. I must ask you to stay here until I return, Mr Cormack. Your wife is free to leave whenever it suits her. I hope I shall not be long."

"Don't worry my dear," said Mr Cormack to his wife. "I don't know what his game is, but he's got no proof against me, as you heard him admit. He seems to be serious, so we'll have to treat it like a bad dream, I'm sure it won't be long before we wake up from it. These things can happen to anybody.

Mrs Cormack's reaction was to burst into tears, whether of relief or desperation it would have been hard to say. She was still in this state when Malone returned a few minutes later. He immediately addressed Mr Cormack.

"I am not going to repeat what I have been saying. I hope in my absence you have decided to make a voluntary statement. It doesn't matter too much what you think of me, but you may have noticed that I have been on my own with you this morning. That was for your benefit. Whatever unnecessary or foolish things you have said so far will not therefore be any part of an official report. In this way, no-one can deny that a confession from you is entirely voluntary. I give you the chance to make it again, though now I have positive proof of your guilt."

"You won't extract a phoney confession out of me in this rather patent fashion. Any fool could see that this departure of yours was prearranged to take place at what you thought was a psychological moment. Jean Shaw with important information indeed! You'll have to do better than that. What do you think I am? A raving idiot?"

"To be quite frank, yes. I have no idea why I am taking so much trouble with you. I shall convince you with a few words. What about: 'I have many qualities, but my mother was not Gipsy Rose Lee'?"

The words had their desired effect. Mr Cormack looked as if he had been stuck staring dumb. Malone felt a little sorry for him, and even more so for his wife, and so he said in a kindly voice: "You will find pen and paper on the desk. When you've finished, present the document to Sergeant Johnson. I think you'll find him the easiest man to deal with. Please do what I say. You will not leave here a free man anyway."

Malone walked out of the office, and into the front of the Station. Lady Carswell was still there, sitting down quietly, but as soon as she saw the Inspector appear, she got up quickly and made as if to address him. He turned to her wearily and said: "Before I have to listen to your personal opinion of my social position and level of intelligence, may I thank you for all the co-operation you have given us in this case. You may go now, and please reclaim your passport as soon as you find it convenient. I need hardly add that I have no desire to press charges against you. As for the reasons for your actions this morning, remember that James Holdroyd was genuinely an honest man. I suspect he has been burning other things as well as coal in his grate recently."

He did not wait for a reply from Lady Carswell, but turned to the sergeant: "Sergeant Johnson, I wonder if you could please do me a favour. I hope that Mr Cormack will provide you with a statement in a few minutes. Read it, and you'll know exactly what to do. If by any chance he should try to leave the Police Station without doing so, arrest him."

"Arrest Mr Cormack? On what charge?"

Malone stared at him blankly. "The murder of Mr James Holdroyd of 235 South Street." He turned to White, who was talking to Miss Shaw. "White, come along and I'll stand you a drink. You too, Miss Shaw, if you'd care to come. We need something after all that. We'll have to spend all afternoon writing about it anyway."

White and Miss Shaw joined him, and they left the Police Station.

❦ Chapter 15

WHITE DECIDED THAT, DESPITE THE EARLINESS OF THE HOUR, they would run into too many people who knew him and his profession if they went into one of the more popular bars in the centre of town, he did not want to be questioned closely by well-intentioned inquisitive gossips at this stage. He therefore recommended that they go to one of the hotel lounge bars near the golf course.

"Miss Shaw," said Malone, as they set off in a westerly direction down North Street, "I know how you must feel about what you have just done. You'll feel like the worst sort of clipe and informer. The fact that you were under suspicion yourself and had reason to fear further revelations won't make it any easier for you. By the way, did you actually see Mr Cormack?"

"No. As I told you, I don't know what got into me, but I decided to go round to Jim's. I even dressed for the occasion, thinking that would have to impress him. I think you're one of the few people who seem to have noticed, that whatever my appearance might usually be, I'm still a woman. Whether it's the way we're conditioned, when we're brought up, or simply natural as they used to say, we don't find it easy to get away from the fact. And so in some ways I can be just as vain as any other woman. I reckoned that if I got hold of him when he had nothing but a cold night to look forward to, I couldn't go wrong. When I got to his place and found the doors unlocked, I thought, I'd give him a surprise. When I found he wasn't there, I looked round the flat for a bit— I'd never actually been inside before, but you'll understand that I knew where it was—and I was in his bedroom when I heard footsteps coming up the stairs. I thought it would really turn him on if he found me in his bedroom, so I stayed there. I had of course assumed that the footsteps were those of Jim. I was just about to give up waiting in the bedroom and surprise him in the sitting room, where the person who'd come in was, when I was startled to hear someone else coming up the stairs. My first thought of course was that it was another woman, and that really put me in a confused state. I wanted to disappear, but there was no way in which it could be done. Then I heard Jim speak and I realised that the first person hadn't been him after all. I didn't have time to start wondering who the first person might be before he spoke. I immediately recognised the voice but couldn't place it. Then I heard this blow, and no more words. I was really terrified then, imagining all the most amazing things you've ever heard about guys flipping. I was petrified of what he might do to me if he found me, so I hid behind the bed. I heard him moving around for quite a time—I don't know how long—and then I heard him go out. I was still frightened to leave the bedroom, but eventually I did. I saw Jim lying on the floor there and was about to rush up to him when the reality of my position suddenly hit me. In sheer terror I left the flat, without so much as a look at Jim. I still don't know how I came to do it. The doors were open, so I rushed straight out. There was no-one in South Street when I got there so I hurried off home. Two cars passed me, but I saw no-one on the street. When I got home, I actually had a couple of hefty glasses of gin, to try to make me go to sleep. I eventually managed to, and by the time you saw me on Wednesday, I was able to exhibit my casual don't-care attitude again. I don't suppose you thought there was anything wrong with me. That's the advantage of artificial types of talk, they can cover up anything. Guys with English public-school accents have been getting away with things for years because of that.

"Why did you finally decide to come and tell us?"

"I didn't have time to tell you earlier, but the Cormack's daughter Elizabeth came round to my flat this morning. I don't know if you've heard, but she's pregnant. Some friends of hers brought her round to see Catriona and me, because they thought we could gather some advice without putting on the heavy moral thing. She told me that although her father was pretending to be bothered about her, all he was really concerned about was his social reputation. That sort of thing always annoys me, and I thought of coming straight round to see you then, but then I realised that I might only be incriminating myself. I was pretty sure it had been his voice that I had heard, but I don't know him well, and if he'd denied it—well he's the man who authorises Social Security hand-outs to me. It was only when Elizabeth told us that he suspected Jim of being the father that I realized that it must have been him, and that he had a solid motive. Then, as much for my own benefit as anyone else's, I came round to see you. I don't know why, but perhaps because you had treated me as an ordinary individual rather than a freak, I thought you'd probably believe me; and you did."

"Do you think you could swear in a court of law that it was Mr Cormack you heard?"

"I think so, but I'd rather not have to. I suppose it'll be necessary though."

"I hope not. You see, I had come to the conclusion that Mr Cormack must be the guilty party last night. Just before you came in, I was trying to persuade him to make a voluntary statement. I think it's most unlikely that he intended to kill Mr Holdroyd when he went round, and he might not even have intended to strike him. As he's clearly normally a quiet law-abiding person, and decent enough—

despite what you may feel about his attitude towards his daughter—there seems little point in being vindictive. I understand that your feelings may be different."

"Strangely enough, I don't feel like going and tearing him apart, if that's what you mean, although I have to say that's how I would have expected to feel."

"I'm pleased to hear it. He was not in any mood to admit to it at first, but before I left him, I quoted some of the words you overheard. His reaction appeared to be speechlessness, and I think either he will decide himself, or his wife will persuade him to make a confession. If that happens, your evidence should not be needed. By the way, how was it that you managed to leave no traces in the flat? Surely you must have touched something?"

"I'm sure I touched several things, though I don't really remember. As I told you, I dressed for the occasion, and that included wearing gloves. I hadn't thought to take them off. And anyway. I spent most of my time in there cowering in the bedroom."

"Miss Shaw, do you follow the stars?"

"You mean astrology? Well, like everyone else, I suppose, If I'm reading a paper or a magazine that has them in. I usually glance at my sign. I don't know anything about it, though. But that's a funny question; why do you ask?"

"I feel there should have been a strong conjunction of planets in Mr Holdroyd's sign. At least Venus and Mars, and probably Mercury as well. And of course, Pluto. It is absolutely amazing when you think about it. A man normally has no visitors, and suddenly within the space of a few hours he has five, and maybe more for all I know."

"I'm afraid I don't follow about the planets."

"Ah, I keep forgetting that young people nowadays are being deprived of a Classical education. Venus fairly

obviously would cause your visit, and that of Eric Athlone,
I suppose. Mars, the god of war would drive on Paul
McLeod and Jim Cormack. Lady Carswell's visit was of a
rather shady business nature, and so Mercury, the god of
trade and trickery would inspire her. Pluto the god of the
Underworld made his presence felt too."

They had progressed down North Street and were now
turning into Golf Place. In the front to the left was the solid
grey clubhouse of the Royal and Ancient Golf Club,
standing ready for its members who had just finished a
round on the Old Course. Beyond was the blue of the sea.
It was one of those clear days when the range of vision
seems only to be limited by the human eye. A dozen miles
away Sidlaw Hills rose green above the city of Dundee,
which was itself hidden by a rise in the ground between.
Beyond that, the Grampians could be observed greying into
the distance, as White selected a suitable place for their
refreshment. As he had hoped, they were the only
customers in the bar they entered. Malone bought drinks
and they sat in a window seat with the expansive view in
front of them.

"Do you play golf, Miss Shaw?" asked Malone.

"No, I never have."

"It's strange that so many people living here don't. When
I was a student here, I used to play at least two games a week,
and more whenever possible. Mr Holdroyd never played
golf either. I wonder how he filled in his time? You may not
know, Miss Shaw, but he was quite a competent poet. But
that still doesn't explain all his leisure hours."

"He used to learn a lot of things you know. He always
said that was what stopped you getting old before your time.
He'd been learning Ancient Greek over the last couple of
years, and he told me that if he ever had enough money,

he'd go back to University to do a course in it. He never will now."

The tears were beginning to well up in her eyes, and so Malone thought he had better change the subject. "You know, if you don't mind me boasting, I used to be a pretty good golfer. I used to play to five in my best days. I even ended up as captain of the University Golf team. I bet you didn't know that, White."

"As a matter of fact, I did. Would you now permit me to make a couple of deductions about your golfing career? Firstly, I would deduce that you gave up serious golf shortly after you left University, probably through pressure of work."

"Quite right. Getting married soon afterwards didn't help much either."

"Your interest kept waning over the years, to such an extent that by a couple of years ago you no longer even gave newspaper articles on golf any great attention, and you hardly even read them at all nowadays."

"Quite right again. I'm sure you'll go far in the force. Assuming this isn't pure guesswork, how do you know?"

White produced a rather sheepish grin. "Well sir, otherwise you might have known that I was second in the Scottish Amateur last year."

Lightning Source UK Ltd.
Milton Keynes UK
UKHW052138281022
411251UK00020B/899